With best wishes —
June Koblich Chick

SCI-FI
WOMANTHOLOGY

compiled and edited by

Forrest J Ackerman

and

Pam Keesey

WOMANTHOLOGY SCI-FI

compiled and edited by
Forrest J Ackerman and
Pam Keesey

Sense of Wonder Press
JAMES A. ROCK & COMPANY, PUBLISHERS
ROCKVILLE • MARYLAND

Sci-Fi Womanthology
Compiled and edited by Forrest J Ackerman and Pam Keesey
Introduction by Terri Merritt-Pinckard

is an imprint of *JAMES A. ROCK & CO., PUBLISHERS*
This compilation Copyright © 2003 by Forrest J Ackerman
Copyright © 2003 by James A. Rock &. Co., Publishers. All applicable copyrights and other rights reserved worldwide. No part of this publication may be reproduced, in any form or by any means, for any purpose, without the express, written permission of the publisher.

Address comments and inquiries to: SENSE OF WONDER PRESS
James A. Rock & Company, Publishers
9710 Traville Gateway Drive, #305, Rockville, MD 20850
E-mail:
jrock@rockpublishing.com   lrock@senseofwonderpress.com
Internet URL: www.SenseOfWonderPress.com
Paperbound ISBN: 0-918736-33-1
Hardbound ISBN: 0-918736-50-1
Printed in the United States of America
First Edition: July 2003

Front cover art by Margaret Brundage. Back cover art by Virgil Finlay.
Both pieces are from the personal library of Forrest J Ackerman.

Many thanks, once again, to Anne Hardin for her unflagging assistance on this and other Sense of Wonder Press projects.

"All Cats Are Gray" by Andre Norton (as Andrew North), *Fantastic Universe Science Fiction*, Sept. 1953
"Creatures of the Light" by Sophie Wenzel Ellis, *ASF*, February 1930
"Earthlight" by Lilith Lorraine, *Stirring Science Fiction*, June 1941
"Extra-Curricular" by Garen Drussaï, *F&SF*, February 1947
"Eye to the Future" by Ree Dragonette, *ASF*, February 1947
"The Feminine Metamorphosis" by David Keller (as Amy Worth), *Science Wonder Stories*, August 1929
"The Final Victory" by Jill Taggert, 1976, Ace Books
"Flood" by L. Major Reynolds, *F&SF*, February 1952
"Heartache" by Helen M. Urban, *Authentic Science Fiction*, January 1956
"Kiki" by Laurajean Ermayne, *Vice Versa*, 1947 (© 1975 Forrest J Ackerman)
"The Last Gentleman" by Dorothea Faulkner, *If*, January 1953
"A Leak in the Fountain of Youth," by Amelia Reynolds Long, *ASF*, August 1936
"A Letter of the 24th Century" by Leslie F. Stone, *Amazing Stories*, December 1929
"The Man from Space" by Louise Taylor Hanson, *Amazing Stories*, February 1930
"The Man Who Fought A Fly" by Leslie F. Stone, *Amazing Stories*, October 1932
"Miracle in Three Dimensions" by Catherine L. Moore, *Strange Stories*, April 1939
"The Miracle of the Lily" by Clare Winger Harris, *Amazing Stories*, April 1928
"Nyusa, Nymph of Darkness" by Catherine L. Moore and FJA, *Fantasy Magazine*, April 1935
"A Peculiar People" by Betsy Curtis, *F&SF*, August 1951
"Servant Problem" by Thelma D. Hamm, *Authentic Science Fiction Monthly*, August 1954
"A Small Planet of Our Own" by T. E. Merritt-Pinckard, *Womanthology*, 2002
"The Statue" by Mari Wolf, *If*, January 1953
"The Three Marked Pennies" by Mary E. Counselman, *Weird Tales*, August 1934
"Time Enough at Last" by Lyn Venable, *If*, January 1953
"The Tunnel Ahead" by Alice Glaser, *F&SF*, November 1961
"To Live and Die in the World of Sci-Fi" by Jana Wells, *Womanthology*, 2003
"Yvala" by Catherine L. Moore and Amaryllis Ackerman, *Weird Tales*, February 1936
"Let There Be Silence" by June Koblick, *Womanthology*, 2003

DEDICATIONS

Katalin Urszulm
Siegi Menningen
Helena Binns
Samanda Bjeude
Edythe Eyde
Inge Glass
Morgan Fox
Ildiko
Thai Annie
Thai May
Ethel Johnson
Lupe Amador
Lois Ellison
Gina Main
Lisa Pierovich
Liz Gilbert
Linda Conrad
Anne Hardin
Winky Cervon
Veronica Carlson
Cynthia Goldstone
Zita Szalontay
Kristina Hallind
Vanessa Koman
Gwenae Meadows
Angela Orofino
Debbie Painter
Bjo Trimble
Shana Malanowski
Mary Ellen Daugherty
Alta McGovern-Hamm
Misty
Trina Robbins
Celeste DePinto
Chantelle Covington
Irene Thrupp
Amy Jewett
Christine Lyons
Oulde Soul
R. Laurraine Tutihasi
Mary Trelawney
Ingrid Pitt
Chinchinella Anthony
Coco Kiyonaga
Jean Marie Stine
Eva Ford

Contents

All Cats Are Gray, *Andre Norton* 1

A Letter of the Twenty-Fourth Century, *Leslie F. Stone* 9

The Feminine Metamorphosis, *Amy Worth* 15

A Small Planet of Our Own, *T.E. Merritt-Pinckard* 53

Kiki, *Laurajean Ermayne* 65

Nyusa, Nymph of Darkness,
Catherine L. Moore & Forrest J Ackerman 69

The Miracle of the Lily, *Clare Winger Harris* 83

The Three Marked Pennies, *Mary Elizabeth Counselman* 99

The Man from Space, *L. Taylor Hanson* 107

The Tunnel Ahead, *Alice Glaser* 129

Time Enough At Last, *Lyn Venable* 137

Yvala, *Catherine L. Moore & Amaryllis Ackerman* 143

Creatures of the Light, *Sophie Wenzel Ellis* 169

The Man Who Fought A Fly, *Leslie F. Stone* 203

Earthlight on the Moon, *Lilith Lorraine* 229

A Peculiar People, *Betsy Curtis* 231

The Last Gentleman, *Dorothea Faulkner* 245

Servant Problem, *Thelma D. Hamm* 253

The Statue, *Mari Wolf* 257

Heartache, *Helen M. Urban* 273

Miracle in Three Dimensions, *Catherine L. Moore* 277

Eye To The Future, *Ree Dragonette* 291

Flood, *L. Major Reynolds* 305

Extra-Curricular, *Garen Drussaï* 311

Contents

A Leak in the Fountain of Youth, *Amelia Reynolds Long* 319

To Live and Die in the World of Sci-Fi, *Jana Wells* 335

Let There Be Silence, *June Koblick* 337

Final Victory, *Jill Taggart* 349

Other SF & Fantasy Oriented Female Works 351

Illustrations:

Title Page, detail from cover by Brundage; page 14, unknown; page 68, Hannes Bok; page 98, unknown; page 115, H. Wesso; page 127, H. Wesso; page 209, Morey; page 303, Paul.

Introduction
From Female Pioneers to Present-Day Writers

My husband and I were co-creators and Host and Hostess of the Pinckard Science Fiction Writers' Salon for over 25 years. And Forrest J Ackerman was and still is my agent, selling every science fiction and fantasy story I wrote, including "The Hate" which was in both the British-European and the U.S. editions of *The Year's Best Horror Stories* (1971, ed. Richard Davis).

"Creatures of the Light" (*Astounding Science Fiction*, 1930) stretches back some 70 years. Clare Winger Harris's "Miracle of the Lily" is considered a classic and was featured in *Amazing Stories* before I was born.

Rod Serling was a master of imaginative twists in his "*Twilight Zone*" and was contemplating having "The Tunnel" as one of the episodes when the authoress unexpectedly died. (Ray Cummings might have considered this episode as a Tale of Unwrought Things.) One story in this anthology that did make it into the *Twilight Zone* was Lyn Venable's "Time Enough at Last," a top favorite of many fans.

Shambleau's creator Catherine L. Moore's virtually forgotten story "Miracle in Three Dimensions" is rescued here. L. Major Reynolds' name suggests a male writer, but was the pseudonym of Louise Leipar. Contributor Mari Wolf, Forry tells me, hasn't been heard from in a long time and he requests if anyone knows of her present whereabouts he hopes they will have her contact him.

And, famous for their open-mindedness on sexuality, FJA and his collaborator, Pam Keesey, have included the first Lesbian science fiction story.

My husband Tom and I do look forward to spending hours in our beautiful four-level gardens reading and re-reading all the following stories. We hope you will share this book with some friends, with the promise of a unique treat in the enjoyment of these pioneering and modern women's contributions.

Terri Merritt-Pinckard

All Cats Are Gray
by Andre Norton

This story by a modern master storyteller has been lost in the black hole of time because not every anthologist realizes "Andrew North", the pen name under which it was originally published, is today's popular science fiction & fantasy novelist and creator of the High Hallack retreat for burgeoning sf authors. The blurb that accompanied its publication read: "Here is another story about cooperation, this time between a woman and her cat. While humans and dogs have a long history of teamwork, cats have not always been our most cooperative friends. They have been worshiped as gods and cursed as devils. But it is a rare cat, indeed, that has deigned to be a partner with a human. Here is a story about one such, written by an exceptional writer."
—PK

(In England in 1938, the late William F. "Four-Sided Triangle" Temple had a remarkable cat story published in *Tales of Wonder* called "Smile of the Sphinx" and some years later the late Anna Louise Germeshausen had a collection of feline fantasies published—I regret, if you're a cat lover, I can't remember the name. Cat-astrophe! And then there's van Vogt's "The Cataaaa" . . .)
—FJA

Steena of the Spaceways—that sounds just like a corny title for one of the Stellar-Vedo spreads. I ought to know, I've tried my hand at writing enough of them. Only this Steena was no glamorous babe. She was as colorless as a lunar planet—even the hair netted down to her skull had a sort of grayish cast, and I never saw her but once draped in anything but a shapeless and baggy gray spaceall.

Steena was strictly background stuff, and that is where she mostly spent her free hours—in the smelly, smoky, background corners of any stellar-port dive frequented by free spacers. If you really looked for her you could spot her—just sitting there listening to the talk—listening and remembering. She didn't open her own mouth often. But when she did, spacers had learned to listen. And the lucky few who heard her rare spoken words—these will never forget Steena.

She drifted from port to port. Being an expert operator on the big calculators, she found jobs wherever she cared to stay for a time. And she came to be something like the masterminded machines she tended—smooth, gray, without much personality of their own.

But it was Steena who told Bub Nelson about the Jovan moon rites— and her warning saved Bub's life six month's later. It was Steena who identified the piece of stone Keene Clark was passing around a table one night, rightly calling it unworked Slitite. That started a rush which made ten fortunes overnight for men who were down to their last jets. And, last of all, she cracked the case of the *Empress of Mars*.

All the boys who had profited by her queer store of knowledge and her photographic memory tried at one time or another to balance the scales. But she wouldn't take so much as a cup of canal water at their expense, let alone the credits they tried to push on her. Bub Nelson was the only one who got around her refusal. It was he who brought her Bat.

About a year after the Jovan affair, he walked into the Free Fall one night and dumped Bat down on her table. Bat looked at Steena and growled. She looked calmly back at him and nodded once. From then on they traveled together—the thin gray woman and the big gray tomcat. Bat learned to know the inside of more stellar bars than even most spacers visit in their lifetimes. He developed a liking for Vernal juice, drank it neat and quick, right out of the glass. And he was always at home on any table where Steena elected to drop him.

This is really the story of Steena, Bat, Cliff Moran, and the *Empress of Mars*, a story which is already a legend of the spaceways. And it's a damn good story, too. I ought to know, having framed the first version of it myself.

For I was there, right in the Rigel Royal, when it all began on the night that Cliff Moran blew in, looking lower than an antman's belly and twice as nasty. He'd had a spell of luck foul enough to twist a man into a slug snake, and we all knew that there was an attachment out for his ship. Cliff had fought his way up from the back courts of Venaport. Lose his ship and he'd slip back there—to rot. He was at the snarling stage that night when he picked out a table for himself and set out to drink away his troubles.

However, just as the first bottle arrived, so did a visitor. Steena came out of her corner, Bat curled around her shoulders stolewise, his favorite mode of travel. She crossed over and dropped down, without invitation, at Cliff's side. That shook him out of his sulks. Because Steena never chose company when she could be alone. If one of the man-stones on Ganymede had come stumping in, it wouldn't have made more of us look out of the corners of our eyes.

She stretched out one long-fingered hand, set aside the bottle he had ordered, and said only one thing. "It's about time for the *Empress of Mars* to appear."

Cliff scowled and bit his lip. He was tough, tough as jet lining—you have to be granite inside and out to struggle up from Venaport to a ship command. But we could guess what was running through his mind at that moment. The *Empress of Mars* was just about the biggest prize a spacer could aim for. But in the fifty years she had been following her queer derelict orbit through space, many men had tried to bring her in—and none had succeeded.

A pleasure ship carrying untold wealth, she had been mysteriously abandoned in space by passengers and crew, none of whom had ever been seen or heard of again. At intervals thereafter she had been sighted, even boarded. Those who ventured into her either vanished or returned swiftly without any believable explanation of what they had seen—wanting only to get away from her as quickly as possible. But the man who could bring her in—or even strip her clean in space—that man would win the jackpot.

"All right!" Cliff slammed his fist on the table. "I'll try even that!"

Steena looked at him, much as she must have looked at Bat that day Bub Nelson brought him to her, and nodded. That was all I saw. The rest of the story came to me in pieces, months later and in another port half the system away.

Cliff took off that night. He was afraid to risk waiting—with a writ out that could pull the ship from under him. And it wasn't until he was in space that he discovered his passengers—Steena and Bat. We'll never know what happened then. I'm betting Steena made no explanation at all. She wouldn't.

It was the first time she had decided to cash in on her own tip and she was there—that was all. Maybe that point weighed with Cliff, maybe he just didn't care. Anyway, the three were together when they sighted the *Empress* riding, her deadlights gleaming, a ghost ship in night space.

She must have been an eerie sight because her other lights were on too, in addition to the red warnings at her nose. She seemed alive, a Flying Dutchman of space. Cliff worked his ship skillfully alongside and had no trouble in snapping magnetic lines to her lock. Some minutes later the three of them passed into her. There was still air in her cabins and corridors, air that bore a faint corrupt taint which set Bat to sniffing greedily and could be picked up even by the less sensitive human nostrils.

Cliff headed straight for the control cabin, but Steena and Bat went prowling. Closed doors were a challenge to both of them and Steena opened each as she passed, taking a quick look at what lay within. The fifth door opened on a room which no woman could leave without further investigation.

I don't know what had been housed there when the *Empress* left port on her last lengthy cruise. Anyone really curious can check back on the old photo-reg cards. But there was a lavish display of silk trailing out of two travel kits on the floor, a dressing table crowded with crystal and jeweled containers, along with other lures for the female which drew Steena in. She was standing in front of the dressing table when she glanced into the mirror—glanced into it and froze.

Over her right shoulder she could see the spider-silk cover on the bed. Right in the middle of that sheer, gossamer expanse was a sparkling heap of gems, the dumped contents of some jewel case. Bat had jumped to the foot of the bed and flattened out as cats will, watching those gems, watching them and—something else!

Steena put out her hand blindly and caught up the nearest bottle. As she unstoppered it, she watched the mirrored bed. A gemmed bracelet rose from the pile, rose in the air and tinkled its siren song. It was as if an idle hand played . . . Bat spat almost noiselessly. But he did not retreat. Bat had not yet decided his course.

She put down the bottle. Then she did something which perhaps few of the men she had listened to through the years could have done. She moved without hurry or sign of disturbance on a tour about the room. And, although she approached the bed, she did not touch the jewels. She could not force herself to do that. It took her five minutes to play out her innocence and unconcern. Then it was Bat who decided the issue.

He leaped from the bed and escorted something to the door, remaining a careful distance behind. Then he mewed loudly twice. Steena followed him and opened the door wider.

Bat went straight on down the corridor, as intent as a hound on the warmest of scents. Steena strolled behind him, holding her pace to the unhurried gait of an explorer. What sped before them was invisible to her, but Bat was never baffled by it.

They must have gone into the control cabin almost on the heels of the unseen—if the unseen had heels, which there was good reason to doubt—for Bat crouched just within the doorway and refused to move on. Steena looked down the length of the instrument panels and officers' station seats to where Cliff Moran worked. Her boots made no sound on the heavy carpet, and he did not glance up but sat humming through set teeth, as he tested the tardy and reluctant responses to buttons which had not been pushed in years.

To human eyes they were alone in the cabin. But Bat still followed a moving something, which he had at last made up his mind to distrust and dislike. For now he took a step or two forward and spat—his loathing made plain by every raised hair along his spine. And in that same moment Steena saw a flicker—a flicker of vague outline against Cliff's hunched shoulders, as if the invisible one had crossed the space between them.

But why had it been revealed against Cliff and not against the back of one of the seat or against the panels, the walls of the corridor or the cover of the bed where it had reclined and played with its loot? What could Bat see?

The storehouse memory that had served Steena so well through the years clicked open a half-forgotten door. With one swift motion, she tore loose her spaceall and flung the baggy garment across the back of the nearest seat.

Bat was snarling now, emitting the throaty rising cry that was his hunting song. But he was edging back, back towards Steena's feet, shrinking from something he could not fight but which he faced defiantly. If he could draw it after him, past that dangling spaceall . . . He had to—it was their only chance!

"What the . . ." Cliff had come out of his seat and was staring at them.

What he saw must have been weird enough: Steena, bare-armed and bare-shouldered, her usually stiffly-netted hair falling wildly down her back; Steena watching empty space with narrowed eyes and set mouth, calculating a single wild chance. Bat, crouched on his belly, was retreated from thin air step by step and wailing like a demon.

Toss me your blaster." Steena gave the order calmly—as if they were still at their table in the Rigel Royal.

And as quietly, Cliff obeyed. She caught the small weapon out of the air with a steady hand—caught and leveled it.

"Stay where you are!" she warned. "Back, Bat, bring it back."

With a last throat-splitting screech of rage and hate, Bat twisted to safety between her boots. She pressed with thumb and forefinger, firing at the spaceall. The material turned to powdery flakes of ash—except for certain bits which still flapped from the scorched seat—as if something had protected them from the force of the blast. Bat sprang straight up in the air with a screech that tore their ears.

"What . . . ?" began Cliff again.

Steena made a warning motion with her left hand. *"Wait!"*

She was still tense, still watching Bat. The cat dashed madly around the cabin twice, running crazily with white-ringed eyes and flecks of foam on his muzzle. Then he stopped abruptly in the doorway, stopped and looked back over his shoulder for a long, silent moment. He sniffed delicately.

Steena and Cliff could smell it too now, a thick oily stench which was not the usual odor left by an exploding blaster shell.

Bat came back, treading daintily across the carpet, almost on the tips of his paws. He raised his head as he passed Steena, and then he went confidently beyond to sniff, to sniff and spit twice at the unburned strips of the spaceall. Having thus paid his respects to the late enemy, he sat down calmly and set to washing his fur with deliberation. Steena sighed once and dropped into the navigator's seat.

"Maybe now you'll tell me what in the hell's happened?" Cliff exploded as he took the blaster out of her hand.

"Gray," she said dazedly, "it must have been gray—or I couldn't have seen it like that. I'm color-blind, you see. I can see only shades of gray—my whole world is gray. Like Bat's—his world is gray, too—all gray. But he's been compensated, for he can see above and below our range of color vibrations, and apparently so can I!"

Her voice quavered, and she raised her chin with a new air Cliff had never seen before—a sort of proud acceptance. She pushed back her wandering hair, but she made no move to imprison it under the heavy net again.

"That is why I saw the thing when it crossed between us. Against your spaceall it was another shade of gray—an outline. So I put out mine and waited for it to show against that—it was our only chance, Cliff.

"It was curious at first, I think, and it knew we couldn't see it—which is why it waited to attack. But when Bat's actions gave it away, it moved. So I waited to see that flicker against the spaceall, and then I let him have it. It's really very simple . . ."

Cliff laughed a bit shakily. "But what *was* this gray thing. I don't get it."

"I think it was what made the *Empress* a derelict. Something out of space, maybe, or from another world somewhere." She waved her hands. "It's invisible because it's a color beyond our range of sight. It must have stayed in here all these years. And it kills—it must—when its curiosity is satisfied." Swiftly she described the scene, the scene in the cabin, and the strange behaviour of the gem pile which had betrayed the creature to her.

Cliff did not return his blaster to its holder. "Any more of them aboard, d'you think?" He didn't look pleased at the prospect.

Steena turned to Bat. He was paying particular attention to the space between the two front toes in the process of a complete bath. "I don't think so. But Bat will tell us if there are. He can see them clearly, I believe."

But there weren't any more and two weeks later, Cliff, Steena and Bat brought the *Empress* into the lunar quarantine station. And that is the end of Steena's story because, as we have been told, happy marriages need no chronicles. Steena had found someone who knew of her gray world and did not find it too hard to share with her—someone besides Bat. It turned out to be a real love match.

The last time I saw her, she was wrapped in a flame-red cloak from the looms of Rigel and wore a fortune in Jovan rubies blazing on her wrists. Cliff was flipping a three-figured credit bill to a waiter. And Bat had a row of Vernal juice glasses set up before him. Just a little family party out on the town.

A Letter of the Twenty-Fourth Century
by Leslie F. Stone

Leslie Frances made her mark in the 30s with "Men with Wings" and its sequel "Women with Wings", "The Man Who Fought A Fly" and "Rape of the Solar System" (I believe my name appeared as a character in the latter; we were good correspondence friends).

This story was published 73 years ago and there is no mention of television in the 24th century, only radio, but unnamed television keeps alive great musicians, there's a common language (Esperanto?), use of atomic power, "childbirth a safe and beautiful function", well, I'll let Leslie give you a guided tour of 2300 A.D. Incidentally, one line stands out in commenting on the 20th century, as timely as the recent school tragedies: "Demented creatures who murdered for nothing at all"!

I hope the name Kay Francis means something to some of you; Leslie Stone was the auctorial equivalent of that filmstar who was the epitome of liberated ladies. I met them both.

—FJA

My dear Joe:

It is a long time since we have seen each other and I am aching to have a quiet little chat with you. Do not be surprised if I drop in on you some bright afternoon. I have long been threatening my wife that I shall take off a day to have a little jaunt down your way if you do not hurry and visit us before long.

There is not much news for me to write you. What new news could we discuss when you are aware of every little thing that happens here, immediately, in your little out-of-the-way place of the globe.

However, I did come across something that would interest you, I believe, quite as intensely as it has interested me. You know that old grotto in which we used to play that was once presumably the cellar of some old house, and which proved such a source of interest to us kids?

Well, a month since, for want of something else to do, I went down to it with the intention of learning if there was anything there that should be preserved in the way of a curio, for if you recall the fact, the ruin is at least several centuries old. I found that it was very well preserved, and that rot and decay had not as yet set in. I did find some articles of interest back in the shadows, where we as children feared to creep, picturing it filled with snakes and rats which we knew once had hidden in such out of the way places. I found an old shot-gun of the twentieth century, some utensils I took for cooking pots, some odds and ends whose uses I did not recognize, but what proved more interesting to me than anything else was a pile of magazines together with some old books in a box. Though yellowed by age they still appeared readable, so I brought them home.

And how interesting they have been! I was glad that as a child I had studied the language that they were written in, the English of our forefathers. They dated for the most part from the year of 1920 to about 1935, and proved to be stories of predictions, prophecies of the future, jaunts into interplanetary space, of strange finds and of stranger discoveries. What a wealth of imagination was disclosed!

And what our ancestors thought of us, Joe; what creatures they suggested we should turn into, what catastrophes they planned for us, what wars, what unholy terrors! In one tale we were to become mechanical geniuses; in another it was prophesied that we would become the mere pawns of people from another planet, again we were torn by wars; the white race to be subjected to the black, or the alternative of all being submerged into one great race!

Another tale had to do with the supremacy of woman and the deterioration of man; of children bred and reared by machines; a third told about machines that controlled mankind; still another told of peoples of the underworld conquering us; another told of creatures who had lost the use of their legs because of the continued use of motive power. Of ... oh, I could go on and on indefinitely with the details of the stories I found, but I leave the rest to your imagination.

Now what would these ingenious writers, these prophetic ancestors of ours, say today if they could come among us? Would they be disappointed to find that the world is still moving along in its usual every-day grooves; to find us still the same people with two legs and two arms, two eyes and one chin; the same people of habit that they were; would they marvel to see us still enjoying family life and simple amusements?

Of course they would find changes, the world does not stand still for a single night. They would find airplanes as common as the automobiles of their day; they would find that we moved around this little globe as rapidly as

A LETTER OF THE 24TH CENTURY

they made a day's trip through one country; they would find us using radio in the same manner as they used the telephone.

They would find us enjoying home life far more than they ever dreamed it would be enjoyed. We have no need of leaving the house now, no need of pushing through crowded traffic to get to a show. Instead we can sit in our own living room and watch and listen in complete enjoyment; we have no need to go to churches for our religion; nor of sending our children to schools for their education.

HOW MUCH OF an improvement are our ways over their ways? Now a man can sit at his home and conduct his business as safely and as successfully as they once did in their offices, merely by having installed his own private mirror and radio receiving and sending sets. His children can sit in their own playroom and see their teacher many miles away and recite to her their lessons, learned without leaving the house, learn their geography and chemistry as well as and better than our ancestors did. We can sit in our comfortable chairs and watch and hear the greatest actors and actresses of all time perform before us. We can see and hear the greatest of musicians fill our lives with the beauty of their art. We can hear lectures, art discussions, economic treatises from across the world. We can "tune in" on the World Court and know their decisions as quickly as they are made.

Of course we have progressed. We have done away with the barriers of the old-world boundaries of nations; we have evolved for ourselves a common language by which we can all understand our fellow-men; we have done away with kings and presidents and each of us has his little say in carrying out new policies, of deciding what is best for our old planet. If we consider it necessary to build a new observatory to discover new worlds in space, to appropriate new money for the enlargement of our educational centers, to decide whether Yokohomo deserves a new air-port, if new farmlands should be opened up in New Zealand, we can speak!

We certainly have progressed. Our chemists have found new worlds to conquer. They have given us a new process of generating power from the atom instead of using oil and coal which are less efficient. They have discovered that certain chemicals in various foods are needful to the human body, and know how to separate the chaff, so that we no longer need eat the whole vegetable to obtain its small source of energy. They have learned how to turn ore into metal by one process as it is mined by machinery. They have learned to make glass that is unbreakable, materials that know no wear!

Of course we have progressed. Our medical men have discovered that we no longer need suffer from disease, from death-dealing scourges, from the ravages of old age so that we die as we have lived. They have discovered how to keep us healthy; how to make our children strong, virile and wholesome; how to keep our mind and bodies alert; how to operate upon us without pain and without drawing blood. They have discovered how to make child-birth a safe and beautiful function!

YES, IT IS easy to go on and on, and if only our poor misled ancestors could see us now! They predicted that we would all be living in great cities; spending our lives within four walls of tremendous skyscrapers; eating only synthetic food that had no flavor whatsoever of the sky and the earth and the sunlight. They predicted us as being no more than automatons, being born, living our lives and dying in the manner prescribed for us by scientists!

They could not see this beautiful world that is ours, this world that no longer knows the black, hideous smoke of factories, of the squalor of ghettos, of tenements, of a poor half-starved population struggling to earn a few cents for a loaf of bread, of thugs that killed for money, and demented creatures who murdered for nothing all.

They could not see that one day civilization was to sicken of its cities, was to demolish them one by one as they moved away to dwell in peace and beauty with the birds singing in the trees and flowers nodding their heads at us! They could not realize that even the deserts might be made to bloom again and the swamps to be lifted into the sun. They could not see a sweet, simple home life where men and women could grow in natural surroundings; where workers earned their daily bread in glass-roofed buildings with the sunlight filling their veins as they toil, and the assurance that their loved ones have their gardens, their flowers, their health.

They could not know that the world's knowledge would be freely given to all, worker or idler alike; that radio would make the whole world kin and the poorest of the poor would have their little airplanes in which they could, with their children and wives, climb to the heights of heaven or circle the world in a day.

No, they saw none of this, but it was they who made it possible, just as their ancestors of a few hundred years earlier made it possible for them to realize their dreams!

SHALL WE now conjecture about the future, Joe? Will someone years hence read these words and smile to think of all we have missed, and of all that they have got? The earliest of men progressed, whether from the dank hole of his ancestral cave, or from the dust of the centuries, and Man will continue to progress, progress each century to a better and greater life.

A LETTER OF THE 24TH CENTURY

Perhaps one day our descendants will fly from planet to planet as we do from island to island; perhaps they will find food in sunlight; perhaps they will discover cloth in fire. Well, whatever the future may be, I am sure it will be far happier and better than even that which we claim today. At all odds, life is good and it is good to be living.

And you, my friend, down there on the edge of nowhere puttering around the ruins of what used-to-be, try to remember and pay me a little visit. If you desire, I will send you by next mail a bundle of the stories I have mentioned, I assure you that you will gather as much enjoyment in reading them as I have. I extend my thanks to the long-dead friend who so kindly cached them away for my perusal.

As ever, your devoted friend,
HARRY

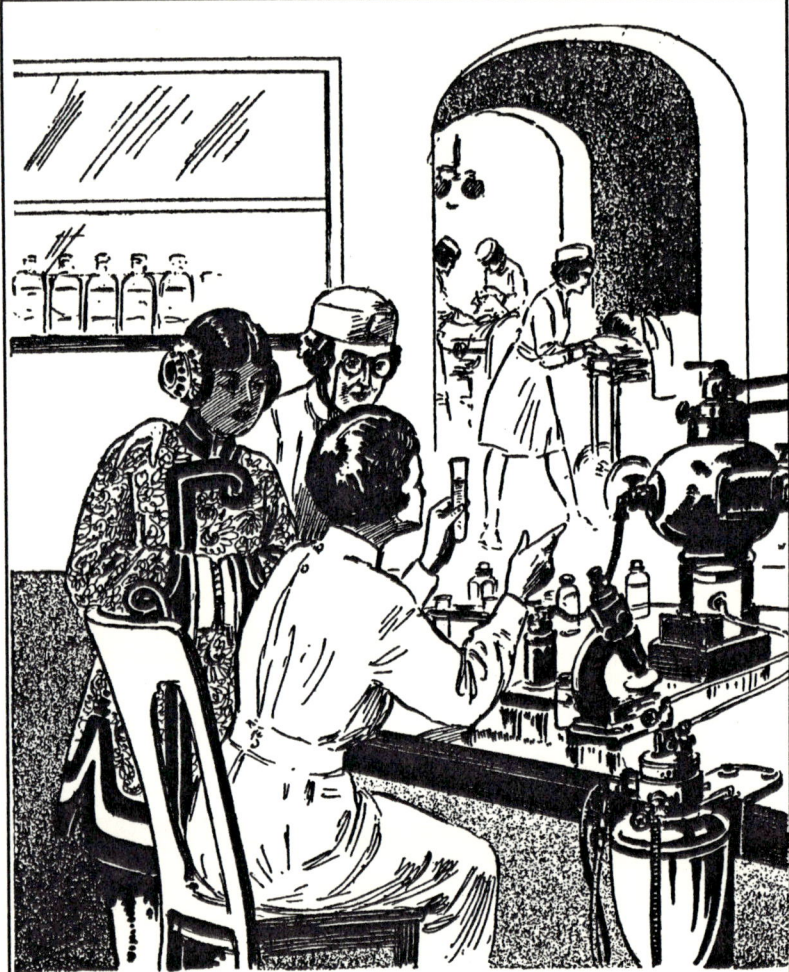

"There was one of those girls, she was a chemist of some kind. I suppose she might be called a biological chemist. Anyway, she did not have anything to do with the operating, but she would take the glands into her laboratory and work with them. I used to go in and see her work—she liked me—I taught her to say some words in Chinese—and when she finished with her work, she would have a little clear liquid that she called ampules which she put into glass tubes."

The Feminine Metamorphosis
by Amy Worth

I first read this story 73 years ago! I have never forgotten it. I had forgotten that Chinese were called Chinks in the story, but I don't believe it was a derogatory term 14 lustrums ago when I was 12 and in any event I don't think that an extraordinary story should be prohibited from being reprinted even if one term's propriety is problematical. I suppose all references to Chinks could simply have been changed in the republication to Chinese but I thought it historically interesting unedited. A couple of years ago I spent a marvelous time among one billion 200 million Chinese in Beijing and Chengdu.

The story obviously takes place at some indefinite time in the future but individuals were still traveling on a slow boat to China rather than flying—not too prophetic.

The author injects a bit of anti-nicotine advice.

The editor stated, "The author has given us a most clever O. Henry ending—a climax as surprising as it is unique." See if you can intuit it.

In this day & age of increasingly commonplace sex changes I think it fascinating to read the first known science fiction story employing the theme. I will be watching reviews of this anthology to see if "The Feminine Metamorphosis" raises eyebrows or temperatures.

Incidentally, "Amy Worth" is a pseudonym for an individual now dead, a pen name that will probably not be known to more than a handful of the readers of this book. If you're really curious, just send me a stamped, self-addressed envelope with a blank sheet of paper in it and I'll tell you.

—*FJA*

From the original introduction:
When a physician-author writes a story on a biological subject, you may be sure that it will be more than interesting. Only during recent years have the functions of the various glands in the human body assumed a tremendous importance. It seems that the glands are responsible for almost everything imaginable in our mental and physical makeup. It is also true, very frequently, that these functions can be interfered with by altering or otherwise influencing the glands.

It has been known for some time, that extracts from various glands can be used as a stimulant to the live glands of human beings, although the extract has been secured from animals or human beings.

It may be safely said that the wonderful field of gland surgery and medicine is as yet practically untouched. Some of the most surprising and far-reaching discoveries will come when we know more about them.

CHAPTER I
A Woman Protests

"I cannot understand why I was not promoted!" protested the speaker. "I am more competent than the man you appointed to that position, and you ought to know that I have been in full charge of the department during the illness of the late occupant."

"You were not promoted because you were a woman," replied the man on the opposite side of the table. "I am willing to admit that you are capable and also that you have been filling the position for over a year. But there are certain places in this company that have always been filled by men and always will be filled by men. It is the policy of the company. We feel that we cannot compete with our opponents in business unless these places of trust are filled by men. So, you will have to be satisfied with an increase in salary, and your usual place in the office."

The protesting woman flushed angrily as she cried:

"It is not fair to discriminate against me because I am a woman!"

"The question of fairness does not enter into it. We are in a business to make money. I have been elected by the Directors as the President of this company. We expect to make a profit. The Directors believe that certain offices have to be filled by men. You have gone up in this company rather quickly, but you have reached the limit. If you want to stay, we shall be glad to have you, but you will have to be content with your present position."

There was no doubt about the fact that both the president of the company and the most brilliant woman who had ever worked for it were thoroughly mad. They were so mad that the interview came to an abrupt ending by the woman's leaving the room.

A few minutes later, when the man realized the necessity of keeping her, he wrote her a nice letter to the effect that from that time on her salary would be $15,000 a year instead of $12,000, and he sent it to her by special messenger. He thought that the increase would end all the hard feelings.

The next day Miss Martha Belzer seemed to be in her usual good humor. She was as capable as ever, in fact, the letters and reports that she dictated fairly sparkled with intelligent and shrewd conclusions. John Buchanon, the

President of Aviation Consolidated, reading over some of her reports, perceived their value, and smilingly told himself that a few thousand extra dollars was worth more to a woman than her pride, and at once forgot the incident.

That afternoon, after office hours, Martha Belzer took her portable Corona into her private office and locked the door. Several times during the night she sent the watchman out to get her a bite to eat. When she finally emerged it was one in the morning. During those long hours she had written nine letters to nine of her intimate friends—business women all over the United States—and these letters she personally mailed from a sub-station, sending them registered, receipt required.

The next morning she was at her desk as usual, opening and answering the mail and tending to the thousand and one details of the department, many of which should have been looked after by the new head of the department. However, he had been in a poker game that night with other heads of departments; so he was not able to begin work till after his luncheon. When he did arrive at the office, he made a great pretense of business and efficient direction, but as all the work had been done by that time, he soon relaxed, and made arrangements for a golf game. Life, at $30,000 a year, looked rather pleasant to him. He had worked hard to secure the position that he now held, and, with such a capable assistant as Miss Belzer, he did not see any reason for killing himself with too great attention to little details that she could attend to just as well as he. The fact that she had taught him all that he knew about the business of that department and that the business of the company would suffer without her services, irritated him, but he felt that he could forget such unpleasant matters.

The humiliation of Martha Belzer was not an isolated one, by any means. Similar occurrences were happening every day in the large concerns of the United States. During the World War the feminine sex had tasted the sweetness of responsibility with increasing incomes, so that at the close of the war they were reluctant to return to their former humble positions. Well educated, capable, and hard working women were striving to occupy positions on a par with men, and the situation had become so acute that many corporations had passed regulations, strictly limiting the advancement of women in their employ. The stand that Aviation Consolidated had taken was by no means unique in the industrial life of the nation.

The result had not been a happy one. More and more women were preparing themselves for positions of trust and large salaries. Every phase of business activity, especially those requiring brain power, was being handled by the members of the fair sex, who, by their constant application to work, their ability to look after the smallest details, and their one-track minds, were far more capable of holding positions of trust than was the average business man.

There were women in the House of Representatives. It was rumored that a western state was preparing to place a female Senator in Washington. Several states had elected women as Governors. The legal and medical professions were gradually surrendering to the demand of the feminine portion of society for a change to compete on equal terms. Entire banks were officered by women. Only in the priesthood had men dared to entirely exclude the opposite sex.

More and more women were refusing to stay in the home. It was a common thing for a well-paid woman to have bachelor apartments down town where her comfort was well cared for by capable servants.

A Rich Man Dies

Women in positions of responsibility easily made from twenty-five to fifty thousand dollars a year. A large number were in business for themselves. Naturally, they could not handicap themselves with husbands or cripple their earning capacity by child-bearing. They had their social life. Some married, but retained their maiden names, lived on in their own apartments and breakfasted or dined with their husbands three times a week.

But, up to the present time, they had only been able to nibble at the crusts of finance. No woman had been elected to the Presidency of a large concern. Not a single one was drawing the large salaries, as high as several million a year, paid to the big men of industrial America. While the brainy women knew that they were as capable as men of doing the great things of life, the men, so far, had been very careful to see that they did not have a chance to show this ability.

And, so far, there had never been a really rich self-made woman in the United States. The few wealthy ones had inherited their property and were content to leave the directing of it to their husbands. A few women, mainly those who owned their own business, reached the millionaire class, but the great wealth of the nation still rested in the control of the male sex. And there seemed to be no way that it could be taken from them.

The fact of the matter was that the men of the United States who owned the greatest part of the wealth of the nation were afraid. They did not fear the election of a Democratic president, or a change in the tariff, or even a lowering of the immigration bars. What they were afraid of was the possibility of feminine control of the great corporations of the nation. And they were endeavoring to prevent this in the most logical manner that occurred to them. They believed that the best thing was not to allow the women to start securing that power. Unless they did start, they would never succeed. So, the word passed from the President of one great concern to the chief executive of the next that under no circumstances should a woman be promoted to certain positions in these companies, and it was the following of this rule that had prevented Miss Martha Belzer from securing the promotion which she and everyone else knew that she was entitled to.

Miss Belzer nourished her indignation.

But she was not the only woman who was resentful.

In the hearts of the business women of America seethed revolt.

It was an interesting coincidence that in the week following the date of Martha Belzer's great disappointment, Patrick Powers, the richest man in America, died. He was not responsible for this occurrence, or for the fact that his only child was a daughter. He had lived as long as he could and had tried his best to change the destinies of his family. But, eventually, the end came, and at his bedside was neither kith nor kin save the fifty year old daughter, who was single and, to say the least, peculiar.

For some years the rich man had been growing more and more obstinate. It had finally become an impossibility to do business with him. Efforts to influence him, to aid him in arriving at decisions only served to make him more hard-headed and more stubborn than ever before. As he grew older he kept his own council and thanked others to do the same. The truth of the matter was that he was basically a miser and in his old age developed paranoiac ideas that others were trying to rob him of his hard-earned wealth. Consequently, he resisted all efforts made to influence him in drawing up a will and left every cent of his enormous estate to his daughter.

For some weeks she gave no indication as to what disposition she intended to make of this property. Finally, it was learned by several magnates that the only thing that she was really acquainted with was cash and Government bonds and that she intended to sell all of the stocks, bonds and interests that her father had owned and that she was going to sell them to the highest bidder for cash.

Patrick Powers had held the controlling interests in a dozen of the largest corporations in America. The purchaser of these stocks would acquire this power. Half a dozen interests had been waiting for just this opportunity and were more than willing to bid against each other.

As a commercial event, it was not nearly as spectacular as it might have been. Miss Patricia Powers held it in her home. She invited a dozen financiers to attend. The certificates, stock and bonds were actually there, in great brass bound boxes, neatly arranged on the parlor floor, and securely guarded by a silent group of well-armed private detectives. The stock was put up, block after block, and auctioned off. When a sale was made, the fortunate man was asked to come up to the central table and deposit a certified check. He carried the package of stock back with him for deposit in his own brass bound box, to be guarded there by his own private detectives.

The sale lasted several days. The prices secured were high. In some instances the shares sold for well over the value Powers had set. The auction was conducted in a quiet, dignified manner, but when it was over, Miss Patricia Powers was the owner of over three billion dollars worth of certified checks, good for gold when presented to the proper banks.

There was one interesting feature about this sale. No one commented on it, even if he did happen to notice it. The auctioneer, the clerks, the bookkeepers who conducted this sale were all women.

After it was over, Miss Powers went into conference—with women.

CHAPTER II
Taine Gets a Commission

Taine, of the Secret Service, was spending a few days at home. He had just returned to San Francisco from a rather trying trip to New York, where he had rendered great service to that city. Always shy, he had refused to set any specific value on this service, but the check given him was enough to keep him comfortable for the rest of his life. As soon as he could do so, he had given ten percent to his wife, who was in the habit of giving this extra cash to the Woman's Missionary Society of her church. However, the ten percent in this instance was so large that she held back a part of it to buy a year's supply of clothes for herself and her two daughters. She also bought a scarf pin for her husband. She was rather proud of his appearance, and his refusal to buy himself an appropriate scarf pin was a source of much sorrow to her. The one that she selected, a large question mark of platinum, with an equally large diamond at the bottom, seemed singularly appropriate, as she remarked to the pastor's wife, who had accompanied her on this special shopping trip.

"My husband makes a very fine living, solving unusual questions for other people who are too stupid to solve those questions for themselves. So, this question mark will not only represent his profession, but will also serve as an advertisement. You know, Dearie, that he draws a regular salary from the government, but this is so small that we should really suffer were it not for his extras. So I think that I could not do better than to buy this special pin for him."

"But do you think he will wear it? Has he ties that will go with it?"

"Certainly, he will wear it. That reminds me. I must buy some new ties for him. He thinks my selections in such things remarkable. Don't you think red ties with a black polka dot would go well with this pin?"

So, that evening Mrs. Taine presented the pin and the six new ties, and her husband kissed her and thanked her and put every one of the new ties in a special drawer and the pin with the rest of his jewelry. He was really a very remarkable man. The next morning his daughters observed that he wore the black bow tie as usual, and commented on it, but he simply said that he was going down to the city headquarters and he did not want the Chief to think that he had grafted too much in New York. His wife was busy cooking waffles on the new electric waffle iron, that had a red signal to tell when to put the batter in and blue signal to indicate when the waffle was done, so she did not notice what kind of tie he had on. So, blithely calling his little black puppy to follow him, Taine walked slowly down to Headquarters.

The day before, the Chief had told him to take a week's vacation. Taine had replied that he would do this with pleasure, as the *Arbor Vitae* hedge around his house needed trimming badly. Yet, the Chief had sent for him today by special messenger, and Taine knew by past experience what that meant. Reaching the building that housed the Secret Service of the Queen City of the West, Taine put the puppy to sleep in one of his overcoat pockets and walked in to see what all the trouble was.

The Chief welcomed him, at the same time apologizing for breaking into his vacation.

"Sorry, Taine, but the Government wants to send a man to China, and I made up my mind that you were the one to go."

"But I do not want to go." The little man was almost indignant as he said it. "The very idea of me going to China, when you said I could go off duty for a week—the very idea—and my wife just giving me a fine scarf pin with a diamond in it and six new red neckties with large black polka dots in them—the very idea! You know as well as I do that a real detective could not wear such ties—in China. She will feel disappointed if I do not wear them. China? Why, naturally, you had to send for me to go. I am about the only man on the force that can go to the Orient as a Chinaman and get back alive—when is the next boat?"

"I thought you refused to go."

"I ought to. But, if it is something special, I guess I had better leave my vacation go for a while. I suppose there will be a special bonus of some kind—that will make my wife more kindly towards the idea of my leaving right away. You see, she gets ten percent and that goes to the Missionary Society. So, give me the details, and I will go home and pack up."

"That's the way to talk. I knew you would go. I really do not know what the work is. All I can tell you is that I received a wireless from the Department in Washington, asking me to have my best operator report at once to Washington Headquarters for instructions. The wireless specified a man who was well acquainted with China. Of course, I thought of you at once, and I thought you would have objection to going. That New York trip gave you some publicity among our profession and I am sure that you will get a promotion if you keep on."

Taine stood up and stuck his hand in his overcoat pocket.

"I can tell you what I will get if I have another trip like that New York one. I'll get killed. That is what I'll get. This here little dog I have sleeping in my pocket, he and I almost got killed in New York. I hate to go to China, Chief. You remember that last time I was there I made Ming Foo awfully mad at me. Still, my wife won't like it if I continue to ignore her presents, and—did you ever see a red tie with big, black polka dots all over it? Honest, Chief, I would rather drink tea with Ming Foo than wear that kind of a tie downtown—might look all right when I was just out clipping the hedge, in the back yard. Guess I had better go to China. Send a good man up to clean the yard and cut the hedge for me, will you? Do I get transportation to Washington from you? Suppose I have the wife send you a few of those ties? Well, the little dog is restless, so, off we go to China—if anything happens, see that the Mrs. and the girls get the pension and anything else that is due them."

So, he put the little black dog on the floor, and the man and the dog trotted off.

Taine Goes to China

As soon as possible Taine reported to the Chief of the Secret Service at Washington. That official greeted the San Francisco man as a long lost friend. He remembered only too well that danger that had threatened New York and the part that Taine had played practically single handed in destroying that danger. In fact, he had urged Taine to sever his connection to the Secret Service of the western city and come to Washington. Taine had refused to do this, pleading a long residence in the city of the Golden Gate and the fact that his wife enjoyed her position as President of the Missionary Society. Come right in," he said to Taine, "we will shut the door and start right in to business. Have a segar?"

"No, thank you. I used to smoke, but I found that the tobacco was bad for the delicate enamel of my teeth, and once that is destroyed, it is never replaced."

The Washington Chief laughed.

"I remember hearing about that delicate enamel when you were in New

York. You had a narrow escape there, Taine, but that is nothing new for you. I understand you had a good deal of service in China. You ought to go into private work. If I only had the nerve, we would go into business together, but, after a man becomes accustomed to office work, it is hard to go on the road again. Do you want to go out to China for me?"

"Not very much. There is a man over there, Ming Foo, who is not very friendly to me."

"Never heard of him. But you will go?"

"Guess I shall have to. You see, my wife gave me some neckties—"

"Let's talk about the ties later on. There is a peculiar situation over there. About two years ago some doctors went over there and started a charity hospital. For a while, there was nothing very extraordinary about it. Then things began to break loose, and at the present time, affairs are all sixes and sevens in that part of China, and no one seems to be able to tell what the trouble really is. All the doctors in this hospital are women, and the State Department, not wanting them killed, asked them to come down to the coast and bring their hospital with them, and these young fools at once refused. It is a singular fact that the Chinese Government in power in that part of China wants the hospital to stay there, and we cannot understand why. To complicate matters, a revolutionary part is trying to capture the city—and swears that it will control the hospital. Everybody seems to want the hospital to stay there, yet, they all are fighting among themselves in regard to it. Meantime, the young fools are operating day and night and seem to have all the work to do that they can handle."

Taine looked annoyed.

"I can see it all now," he sighed. "You want me to dress up like a Chink and go over there and be operated on so you can find what those girls are really up to."

"That is it exactly."

"And if I take my black dog over with me, I get operated on and he gets into the stew. You better send a real Chink over, Chief. I can give you the names of a few good ones out home. They would not mind being operated on by a white girl. Personally, I object. I have too great an imagination."

"But they would not operate on your imagination."

"I know but I just don't want to go. Every time I mix up with women I get into trouble."

The Chief paid no attention to him.

"You can get your letters of credit and other credentials fixed up today. You have unlimited funds at your control. The only thing you are not strong in is our support. Of course, we will help you all you will let us—up to a certain point—but that is a wild country—lot of bandits. If anything goes wrong, we will take care of your family. I have a lot of recommendations in this envelope. This evening we will put you on board the *Mayflower* and transfer you later on to one of our cruisers that we are sending to China for just one purpose—and that is to carry you. Only a few know who you are and just two of us know why you are going on that cruiser. The Captain will see that you are royally entertained. Can you arrange to leave tonight?"

Taine thought of those six red neckties with the black polka dots—he thought of Ming Foo, waiting to kill him in a very honorable way—he remembered that he always became seasick, never really liked the ocean—and, after thinking of all these things, he sighed as he replied.

"Guess I might as well go. Send a Chink from the department over with me so I can practice talking the language on the voyage. I used to do rather well at it, but since my teeth went bad, I may have trouble. You look after my family, Chief, if I don't come back—tell my wife that my last request was to have those neckties distributed among my friends—and you can have the diamond scarf pin. You would like it, Chief."

Under the friendly nonsense and banter was a strange air of constraint, for both men realized that there was danger on the other side of the world, danger, and perhaps death for the little operator from San Francisco.

CHAPTER III
Taine Returns with a Tale

Exactly six months and three days later Taine silently re-entered the private office of the Chief of Government Secret Service. He looked about as healthy as when he left, though, perhaps, he was underweight. During those six months and three days he had not sent a single word of a report. He had simply gone to China, disappeared, and reappeared in Washington in due course of time. The Chief was delighted to see him, for more reasons than one. He was also almost bursting with curiosity as to what had actually happened. Enthusiastically greeting Taine, he demanded an immediate report.

Before answering, Taine took a little black dog out of his pocket and put him down on the floor. The Washington man looked at the dog in astonishment.

"You don't mean to tell me that you still have that dog?"

Taine shook his head in a peculiar gesture of sorrow and amusement.

"No. This is the same breed of dog, only this is a she dog. That little dog I took to China looked just like this dog, but that dog was a he dog. I got into a place where the men were not very popular; so, I had to change dogs."

"If you were anyone else, I would say you had gone insane!"

THE FEMININE METAMORPHOSIS

"I know, but facts are facts. Part of the trip was dull and then parts were lively. All my life the women have kept me busy and they did not miss it this time. However, I settled with Ming Foo. He will not bother me anymore. That was one of the satisfactory parts of the trip. In fact, I helped operate on him."

The Washington Chief forced Taine down into an easy chair. He pulled an automatic out of a drawer and pointed it at Taine.

"You tell me what happened, and if you leave out anything of interest, I am going to shoot you."

"Don't shoot, Chief. You might hurt the delicate enamel of my teeth. Well, I arrived in Shanghai, and wandered around the country and finally came to the city where these girls were operating. I was disguised as a Priest for a while, and then later on I dressed up as a flower girl—I suppose you know what they are in China. Well, when I came near the hospital, I put a lot of my cash into real jewelry and hired a lot of Chinks to chase me into the compound of the hospital. It looked just like a scene from the movies. There was the poor girl running as fast as she could from the Chinamen who wanted to capture her and ruin her life in an opium den, and just in time the Marines dashed out through the opening gate and the girl just managed to get inside in time. They led me to the Captain of the Marines, and I told him my story, how I was really a rich man's daughter but ran away from home because my father wanted me to marry an old man that had three wives already. Then this Marine, filled with pity, took me in to see the Chief Surgeon, and I told her the same story, only I proved it to her by showing her my jewels, and I told her that I learned to speak English in London, have had ideas of becoming a doctor, but my father brought me home before I could complete my education. Naturally, she and the other lady doctors were very sympathetic and they promised to keep me, and perhaps after a while I could work in the operating room as an orderly. That looked like a hard life, because, it meant shaving three times a day, but the only way I saw to get in there and find out what was going on was to go in as a woman. They were all females except the Marines.

"It was a peculiar situation. The Marines were guarding the hospital and the Government was guarding the hospital, and outside the city the bandits were guarding the hospital, and everybody was trying to capture the hospital so he could run it better and protect it more efficiently. It looked like a peculiar state of affairs, and I was there over a month before I could make anything out of it.

"We were just as busy as could be. They had five doctors there, and they just kept a regular line of patients going into that operating room. I never saw a lot of Chinamen that were so anxious to be operated on. Finally, I tumbled to it. Those girls were paying the Chinks for the operations. Every Chinaman got a hundred dollars in gold when he left the hospital, and all his hospital expenses thrown in. But just as soon as he left the hospital, the High Mogul of the city picked fifty dollars of that gold and the Little Mogul took another twenty-five; so, all the poor devil who was operated on got out of it was a little twenty-five. But that was a fortune to most of them, and there was always a long line waiting for a chance to get in. As far as the Government was concerned and also the lesser officials, it was a sweet piece of graft, and there is no telling how many of them divided that gold. That was the reason why they wanted the hospital to stay there. And that was the reason the bandits wanted to capture the city. There was just a steady stream of gold going out of that operating room, and whoever held the city could grab a big piece of it. The Marines were there to see that nothing stopped those girls from operating; so, they did not care who was in power, so long as the supply of Chinamen held out.

"Of course, I am acquainted with women, being a married man with two daughters, to say nothing of the third one who is married and whose clothes are bought by another man—so, you might say I know a little about females. But I never in all my life saw women like these Doctors. They just did two things besides eating and sleeping. They operated on those Chinamen and talked about equal rights for women. To listen to them talk, you would think that man was just a worm and that their chief delight was to step on him. They even seemed to take a great pleasure in their operating—brag about it—the different doctors would boast as to the number of Chinks they had operated on.

Strange Happenings

"I became a great favorite with them. In fact, some of those lady doctors became quite fond of me. Of course, you must not let on to my wife about that—she would not understand—but those women doctors sure did like me, and thinking all the time I was a little Chinese girl; they thought I was cute—and I let them think so—and I studied hard and, by and by, they let me sort of help with the operations.

"There was one of those girls, she was a chemist of some kind. I suppose she might be called a biological chemist. Anyway, she did not have anything to do with the operating, but she would take the glands into her laboratory and work with them. I used to go in and see her work—she liked me—I taught her to say some words in Chinese—and when she finished with her work, she would have a little clear liquid that she called ampules which she

THE FEMININE METAMORPHOSIS

put into glass tubes. It must have been delicate work, because there were whole parts of it that she said could not be trusted to anyone else. Every week or so a special agent of the Express Company came out from Shanghai with an army of Chinese soldiers to guard him, and he would take a box of these little ampules for shipment to some place in Paris. Of course, all this cost a lot of money, but those girls seemed to have enough and to spare. Someone is putting up a world of gold on this proposition.

"I did not have any textbooks and, to be sure, the Doctors were close-mouthed about it all, and the chemist, she was even worse than the Doctors. But the way I figured it out, those girls were cutting something out of those Chinks and making some kind of a medicine out of it and shipping it to Paris, and it must have been awfully valuable, judging from the cash they were getting and spending. Every operation cost a hundred, to say nothing of the cost of running the hospital and taking care of the patients until they were able to leave, and besides that, there must have been over a million spent to soothe the really big people in China—perhaps several million more.

"Of course, they got the money from somewhere—gold in that amount does not grow on bushes—but where they got it from is not as interesting to me as what they were doing it for, and why there were only women in it. Perhaps it was some kind of beauty culture treatment—you know women in Paris and New York will pay anything to be made good-looking.

"But I do not believe it was beauty they were after. I helped, at the last of my stay there, with a few of the operations, and I do not think they were after beauty. It must be something different from that—anyway, I finally got the best of Ming Foo. I do not think he will bother me anymore. You know you gave me unlimited credit; well, I spent some of it in bribery, and the first thing Ming Foo knew he had been drugged by some of his men and brought to the hospital. He was a big, handsome brute, and the doctors thought he was one of the finest specimens they had found. They liked his heavy beard; most of the Chinks did not have so much hair on their faces; so, they did a bilateral operation on him—most of them they just operated on one side, and when Ming Foo came out of the ether and finally recovered from his dope to realize what had happened to him, he was real provoked—we had to keep him tied down for a while, and even the fact that they gave him two hundred dollars instead of one hundred did not seem to relieve his feelings. Finally, he became so raw in his actions that the Marines had to kick him out of the hospital. He had his men attack the city the next week, and it looked for a while as though he was going to get us, Marines or no Marines, but they finally drove him off. I think he recognized me as he was dragged out of the hospital by the Marines; at least, he said some horrible language to me—but I think the operation took away a lot of his pep.

"It was soon after that that the hospital broke up. The last night I was there I managed to see the records. They must have done a lot of those operations. It seems that they had been working night and day for months. Anyway, they quit. The hospital was turned over to the Government as a present, and the girls all went to Shanghai. I gave some of the doctors presents of my jewelry. They were sort of keen about jewelry, even if they were ranting all the time about the equality of the sexes. Then I left the country by the quickest route and came back by way of Europe. I spent a little time in Paris; in fact, I grew a little beard on my way back—I was so tired of shaving three times a day that it was a relief not to have to shave at all. But I suppose I will have to cut it off before I go west; my wife likes a smooth-shaven husband, and, of course, you know, I am a married man, very much of a married man, though I feel that I have almost forgotten the fact for a minute or two during the last half year."

The Chief of the Secret Service of the United States slowly replaced his revolver in the desk, as he sighed.

"You are a remarkable operator, Taine. I do not know of anyone just like you. You are so peculiarly matter of fact. You either have no nerves or you are too dumb to know what danger is. You go over to China and lead that life for half a year—you impersonate a rich Chinese girl; you even go right into the hospital and finally help them operate on your most dangerous enemy in that heluva land, and then you come back and tell about it all just as the average man would tell about a trip to Coney Island. You tell me all about it—about those girls, as you call them, and you do not even intimate that your curiosity was aroused. Personally, I am a rather self-possessed man, but I had all I could do to keep from interrupting you. What were they doing it for? Where did they get all that money? Who was in back of it? And, by the Seven Sacred Beasts! what did they cut out of those poor Chinks? You calmly sit there and tell all about it, and you have not told me a single thing I want to know except that the girls are gone and the hospital is being run by men and that they sent some kind of dope to Paris in bottles. 'Pon my word, man, have you no imagination? No curiosity? What did you come back for before you learned the whole story. Something big there. You might become famous! And you sit there and tell me about giving jewelry to women. Bah! You ought to be kicked off the force."

"I wish I were," sighed Taine. "This little female dog looks like my old buddy, but she is not half as bright as he was. That's the way with all the women. You ought to have heard the doctors talk in the hospital. Do you know something? I believe there is a secret society of women, something like the Masons. I could sort of feel it, but I have not a single fact to prove it. Now, *if there was such a society*, that might account for part of it. I believe that I just nibbled at one corner of a Brazil nut—like a blooming mouse. It is bigger than we think, Chief; something is going on, and that hospital was just a little piece of it. Now, in regard to the operation: I learned a little about that in Paris. What those girls did was to perform an operation called *gonadectomy*."

The Chief turned red.

"You think you're smart, don't you. Springing a new word like that on a man, just to show how smart you are. What did they do to those little men? You tell me or I will have a stroke of apoplexy."

"Don't get excited, Chief," replied Taine, as he put the little black dog back in his pocket. "You would not believe me if I told you—you would not believe half of it, not even a little bit of it. If I told you all that I really think about this, you would accuse me of having become an opium smoker. I had that happen to me once. Remember when the *Circle Internationale* exploded? Well, I started in one night to tell my Chief out in San Francisco about it, and before I got half way through he called me a liar. I don't want you to do that. Here is a written report and the vouchers for my expenses. Of course, I had to spend some money, but I think it will be worth it to somebody. In fact, I think that you are going to call me back to Washington before long, and perhaps when you do I will nibble a little more at that same nut; maybe we shall find it rather rotten. Some of my imaginations about that affair are certainly peculiar. Oh! I forgot to tell you. There is a new College for Women in the suburbs of Paris. Very exclusive, and all that sort of thing. They tell me a lot of American women have been going there for the last two years. Some kind of a finishing school. Women come and go, and there is a high wall around the whole property. No men admitted. Convent. Now, just one thing more, Chief. Those girls in China were shipping all that dope in the little glass bottles to that address in Paris. That is why I looked it up. That is about the only reason I had for going to Paris. Does that mean anything to you? You think about it for a while. Use your imagination."

CHAPTER IV
A Silent Revolution

Perhaps something might have come out of Taine's trip to China at once had it not been predestined otherwise. The Washington Chief read the lengthy report that night and made up his mind that something ought to be done about it. But then that very night trouble broke loose from the I. W. W., and for the next six weeks every government operator was busy, and, as a result, the report that Taine made was lost sight of. When it was remembered, its importance was underestimated, and many valuable months passed.

Slowly the masculine minds of America, the great Captains of Industry, became worried over a peculiar state of affairs. The control of many of the leading companies of the nation was passing over into the hands of a new financial group. Many of the banks were being directed by members of the same group. Already they had charge of a great Trans-Continental railroad. Aviation Consolidated was slowly coming under their power, and even Radio and Television Associated Companies, one of the wealthiest of all the new financial giants, was being undermined by their active efforts to secure fifty per cent of the Directorate.

It had just been a few years when the entire charge of these basic industries had been securely in the hands of men between forty-five and seventy, big, two-fisted, go-getters, who knew what they wanted, were willing to pay the price, and who never ceased fighting till they won their objective. Most of them were college graduates, many of them had been in their undergraduate days, great athletes. Every one of them, even the old men, still loved the open air, gold, and some of them still hoped to live in Paris when they died.

It took them a long time to realize that anything out of the usual was taking place. Even after they realized it and began to resent it, they were uncertain as to the proper action to take. They were big men, but, after all, it took big men to look at a great sociological movement, from a national standpoint; and this thing that was happening was affecting the entire nation.

It was something that was slowly, insidiously, pervading the business life of every State. For some reason, it was hard to analyze, difficult to comprehend; but there was no problem in realizing that the economic supremacy of the giant group of go-getters was being directly challenged.

After all, it was not the fact that their rule was being contested by a new group that bothered them. Had it been just that, they would have been willing to effect some kind of a working compromise and divide the spoils. It was the personality of their opponents that aroused their ire and constant resentment.

In the first place, the new leaders were young men who were hard workers and did not seem to know the value of recreation. They simply seemed determined to drive themselves and all the subordinates under them till the day's work was done and good part of the next day's work done in addition. They were not only hard workers, but they were efficient, and when they started in to accomplish a task, they usually stayed at it till they won out. Of course, the go-getters, the old timers, had the same determination, but the old men used clubs and bludgeons to accomplish their purpose, and all these young men were smooth; and when they won a financial victory, they did so before their opponents realized what was happening to them. They were smooth, suave, and remarkably clever.

Another irritating quality was their ability to dress well. The old timers spent a lot of money on their clothes, but, for some reason, they never looked well dressed, while these younger men had the peculiar ability of always being just a little ahead of the prevailing masculine fashion. It was not long before the tailors had to admit that they were being dictated to and that these youthful financiers were really telling the tailors what the styles of the next six months would be. Their clothing was masculine, but, at the same time, it had a dash of color to it, a peculiar something that was different. When one of this group walked down Fifth Avenue, his general appearance was such as to make passing women, and men also, turn to look again at him.

Without exception, they were well groomed, took wonderful care of themselves, shaved twice daily, and avoided, in every way, the breath of scandal. In a quiet way, they participated in all forms of civic improvements, and it seemed that everything that they had a hand in succeeded. They seemed to carry around them an atmosphere of success. They seemed to have resources to begin with, and, without exception, they all appeared able to make money.

Socially, they did not fraternize with the old timers. They made no effort to join the ancient clubs that had always been considered the heights of fame. Instead, they established, in every large city, clubs of their own, which, for exclusiveness and fashionableness, seemed in every way to completely eclipse the established social centers of the rich men of the land. It was this very exclusiveness, this tendency to act as though they considered themselves better in some way, that worried the older men. Why the young upstarts would not even accept their invitations to play golf with them!

And, finally, affairs reached such a point that something had to be done, politicians became upset. The Millionaires' Club in the Senate at Washington was invaded. And, eventually, one of those sleek young men actually had the nerve to suggest that he run for President, and advanced many excellent reasons why he should be permitted to do so. With that the battle was on!

Yet, even then, no one seemed to have a clear idea of what all the stifled excitement was about. It was all very well to whisper, but what was the use of either whispering or shouting, when there was really nothing to say? Besides, there were just a lot of people who were not backward in stating that the country might be better off in the control of these younger men, and it was all the more credit to them if they were a little particular in their dress and reserved in their manner. At least they were hard workers and could almost always be found in their offices instead of being "in conference" or out on the golf links.

More Mysteries for Taine

The old business group became uneasy; then they became more uneasy. They finally reached the point at which they actually grew nervous. There had been several raids on Wall Street, gigantic, underground attacks on the multi-millionaires, that increased their anxiety. And finally, they decided that something must be done about it. They had conferences and special investigations, and nothing happened; they were just as ignorant, just as much at sea as they ever had been. Then one day, in utter desperation, one of the big men of the group (a man so big that he sat with a few others in a back room in a hotel and sent word to a Republican Convention whom they should nominate for president) went to Washington, saw the President, and secured from him a written and signed order to the effect that the Secret Service Department should render such aid as was in their power.

Naturally, the rich man saw the Chief of the Secret Service.

After listening to the story of the man from New York, the chief secretly thought that he was listening to a paranoiac chaser of moon-beams.

"I really do not know what you want my department to do, Mr. Johnson," he finally answered. "It seems that you are afraid of something and yet cannot give me any definite idea of what it is. Certainly you do not fear these men in a business sense. Our department cannot protect you against superior brains of financial opponents. This is a free country. And, with the past success of the group that you represent, you certainly ought to feel competent to deal with them on the stock exchange."

That kind of answer made Johnson mad. He was not accustomed to it. Yet, at the same time, he realized that it was a well-deserved criticism. He started to answer it, stuttered, stopped, started again, and finally blurted out,

"One of the things that makes us so tarnation mad is the fact that those upstarts are playing bridge all the time, and when we ask them to join us in a real he-man's game, like golf, they always cut us cold—say they are too busy. Yet, they have the crust to put up a twenty-five million dollar clubhouse, the finest in New York, and call it the Bridge Club, and, so far, not one of the men that I know has been invited to join."

"Now that," replied the Chief, "is real news. If you only had a dozen more facts like that, we might have some idea of what the trouble was."

"Well, I am no detective. I thought that was your business."

"It is; but, at the same time, we have to have something to start with. We cannot raid the biggest private club in New York just because some of you gentlemen are sore because you are not invited to join."

"We don't want to join them, but, all the same, they way they act makes us sore. Pretending they are so much better than we are. Won't join us in any of our deals—just won't have anything to do with us—and all the time trying to knife us, secure control of our corporations—why, they even think they should have a voice in who is to be President."

The more Johnson talked, the more positive the Secret Service Chief was that the New Yorker was simply sore and trying to secure revenge for fancied slights or actual financial losses. The Chief was a busy man, and had all he could do with the counterfeiters and patriotic citizens who were trying to smuggle jewelry into the country. At the same time, he was a politician. He knew that this man could not be handled brusquely. So, he shut his eyes, leaned back in his chair, and passed into an attitude of deep thought. Meantime, the money-king savagely chewed his pipe stem.

"I think that the best thing to do," finally announced the Chief, "is for you to go out to San Francisco and see Taine, a detective connected with the Department out there. I will give you a letter to his Chief that will help you. He is a wonderful man, a real detective, and he has imagination."

"Why not have him come to New York and see me?"

"I do not think he would do that. He won't work for you at all unless he really wants to. He is temperamental. Yes! That is the thing for you to do. If Taine wants to, he will get to the bottom of this mystery."

Johnson slowly shook himself out of the chair.

"Guess I will go. Some one has to get to the bottom of it, or those upstart, bridge-playing fools will take our clothes away from us. Write your letter, and I will get the next train west. Wish I could travel in a plane, but I am too old for it.

CHAPTER V
A Ring Turns Up

For a few years Taine had been having the time of his life. That meant hunting a few murderers of the common variety, running down some opium importations, and even doing a little political work on the side. His monthly salary was not large, but he had some extra cash in the bank, and his living expenses were not great. Three years had passed since his trip to China. Life had become very ordinary, almost commonplace. He was nearly on the point of believing that not much could happen. Then, within a week, a number of unusual circumstances called his attention to the fact that there were several lines of investigation that needed a real detective to work on them. Secretly,

Taine thought that he was a great man; in fact, he believed that he was as good a detective as there was in America; at times he even went beyond that and included England and the Continent.

What happened was this: A little fire destroyed the Presbyterian Church and parsonage that was the delight and religious consolation of his wife. Immediate plans were made for their rebuilding, but the heavy part of this financial burden would fall on the Missionary Society, of which Mrs. Taine had been president for many years. She felt that she should lead in raising the money. She always gave the ten percent of her husband's income, but for the last few years this had not amounted to very much. So, after spending an afternoon with the building committee, she calmly told her husband that she would just have to give the Society one hundred thousand dollars or resign from the presidency. She even cried a little, and the little black female dog howled, and the daughters were sure that papa had done something horrible. Taine told his wife to go ahead with her plans, for, after all, one hundred thousand was ten percent of only one million and he could earn that in no time. Then he took an old envelope out of his pocket and a stub of a pencil and figured out that he was worth, including real estate and insurance, exactly eleven thousand dollars. The next day he wore a troubled look.

That look was deepened by the news that his wife had fainted while washing the dishes. She was nearing the thirty-ninth year, but on the three previous times that she had fainted, washing dishes, she had later on presented her adoring husband with a girl baby. Taine had three daughters and was not sure that he wanted any more. So, he rushed home (his wife was all right when he arrived) and insisted that she go at once and see a doctor.

That night all she could talk about was the New Doctor that she had called on. He was such a perfect gentleman, so kind and sympathetic, and had such a sympathetic understanding of her difficulties. There was no addition to the family in sight, but the Doctor had told her that for a few years she would be in a nervous state and should be careful not to be disappointed in any way. He had said that if her husband really loved her, he would see that every desire of her life was granted. Taine promised her that he would see to it that this was the case, and silently he promised himself that he would see this wonderful physician and give him a pointer or two as to how to handle women.

He called on the physician that evening, and gave, as his excuse, a troublesome cough. He found Dr. Williamson all that Mrs. Taine had pictured him— and he found something else. As the Doctor took his history, and later on, as he percussed Taine's chest, the detective saw a rather old Chinese ring on the left hand little finger. He thought that he knew that ring. He was sure that he had seen it somewhere; in an odd way he was also sure that he had seen Dr.

Williamson before. All that night he tried to connect the ring and the man and the past, and, when morning came, the solution came with it. That ring was one of the pieces of jewelry that he had carried with him into the Chinese hospital. He had given it to one of the Doctors, and, now, that he concentrated on it, he realized that the lady Doctor in China and Dr. Williamson were very much alike—

Only the one was a woman and the other was a man.

They looked enough alike to be brother and sister.

Perhaps that was the solution.

Or perhaps it was not the same ring after all!

The next day one of the operators started to joke with him in the office.

"Nothing singular about all your children being girls, Taine. You were just a little ahead of the fashion. Did you see the report from the National Department of Vital Statistics? Last year there were three times as many girls as boys born in the United States. They are not shouting about it, but they are doing all they can to find the reason. If that keeps up for a few years, this will be a sure-enough female country."

"Well," replied Taine. "There must be some reason for it. Everything has to have a reason. Now, we had these three girls because my wife is partial to girls, and I guess they are easier to raise than boys are. Of course, three girls to one boy is all wrong. If that keeps on—well, I guess I will go out and find some more opium!"

And that very evening Taine read in the papers about another raid on Wall Street. It seems that Johnson had been away from the Stock Exchange for a few days and his enemies had taken advantage of his absence. Taine read that item out loud to his wife, and even when he was reading it, one of the daughters answered the doorbell and in walked Johnson of New York. He introduced himself, he shook hands with the detective and with Mrs. Taine and with the Misses Taine. He acted like a god, condescending to visit a human habitation, and determined to make the humans like him.

"Have a cigar, Mr. Taine? I presume your wife will excuse us if we smoke?"

"Thanks, but I do not smoke," the detective replied. "Long ago I found that the nicotine was bad for the delicate enamel of the teeth, and once that is destroyed, the teeth soon follow. Now, you go ahead and smoke all you want to, because Mrs. Taine has no objections to it. Girls, you had better go to the nursery and study your lessons. Mr. Johnson may have something to say to us privately."

"I want to talk to you privately, Mr. Taine, if your wife will excuse you?"

"Oh! You can talk in front of my wife. Especially if it is professional business. She is really very wonderful in offering suggestions. In fact, she is my chief inspiration. More than once I have left home and gone to the far off places of the earth for more than a year at a time, and she was my only inspiration to do so. So, go ahead with your problem."

Johnson looked at the little man sitting on the worn haircloth sofa. He shook his head doubtfully.

"The Chief in Washington said you were the only man that would be able to help me. I guess he made a mistake. I am afraid that the problem is too enormous for you."

Mrs. Taine looked up from her sewing.

"You say that because you do not know my husband's ability."

"As a matter of fact," added Taine, "in my best moments I feel that no one fully understands what I am capable of. I am small, weigh about one hundred pounds, and, yet, you can believe me or not, there are times when I seem to be inspired, endowed with superhuman power. I had a medium tell me once that I was a duel personality, and, of course, if that is true, it is a very wonderful asset. I think, if I might be bold enough to advise you, Mr. Johnson, that you can accept me as being just as capable as the Washington Chief says I am. Now tell me your troubles?"

Taine Gets A Commission

Johnson surrendered. For over an hour he poured out his story, which grew more and more bitter as he recited it. Taine acted most of the time as though he were asleep, but Mrs. Taine listened with the most intent expression. Finally, she could not contain herself any longer.

"Why, those mean men!" she exclaimed. "They act just like a lot of catty women."

Taine stiffened in his chair, and began to breathe a little fast. Finally, Johnson finished. The little detective sighed deeply.

"I can help you, sir, but it is going to be a rather dangerous affair. There is all the evidence of big things happening, and when big things happen, human life does not count for much, especially not the life of a human such as I am. They would kill me just as they would squash a potato bug. But I will go into it and give you a report when I finish, and I won't stop till I am either through or dead."

"You don't mean to say that you have a clue?" demanded Johnson.

"There are a lot of scattered threads. If I told you what each one was, you would not believe me. I believe I see something. Enough to make me want to investigate. I will begin at once, just as soon as you show your good faith by paying me one-half of my fee; the other half can be paid when I make my final report."

Johnson smiled. He saw the threadbare furniture, the "GOD BLESS OUR HOME" and "A GOOD WIFE IS THE NOBLEST WORK OF GOD" signs on the wall, and without hesitancy, he pulled out his checkbook and fountain pen and said smilingly, "How much?"

"One million dollars for the first payment," and Taine said it without blinking an eyelash. His wife sank back in her chair and closed her eyes. Johnson looked at the man in front of him. Suddenly the New Yorker smiled.

"I will write it at once. Any man that can do that to Johnson can get away with murder—Here is the check. If you ever make your mind up to go into business in New York, you come and see me. I would rather have you as a partner than an enemy. Now, get busy. I must get back to New York. They are raising Cain with the stock market in my absence. Good-night, Taine! Good-night, Mrs. Taine! I congratulate you on your having such a husband," and he was out of the house before they could realize it.

"You are wonderful, dear," whispered Mrs. Taine. "Now, I can stay on as president of the Missionary Society. Won't we be proud to see the new church that was built so largely through your efforts?"

Taine refused to smile, as he replied, "You save enough out of that hundred thousand to put in a Memorial Tablet for your departed husband, because I have an uneasy feeling that when I finish this, it will finish me. I am sure enough scared of those people."

"But you always have been able to take care of yourself?"

"Yes—so far—but then I always had men to work against."

"But I thought Mr. Johnson said these were men?"

"Yes—that is what he said—"

The next day Taine left San Francisco. He did not even take the little black dog with him.

CHAPTER VI
Taine Goes to Work

There was no doubt as to the exclusiveness of the Bridge Club of New York city. It was rumored to have cost twenty-five million but that, no doubt, was an exaggeration. It was said to be very elegant in all of its furnishings, and that also was open to question, for no one except the members ever entered its doors, and they were rather shy about whom they invited to go with them as guests. Rumor said that it was really the headquarters of the new business group, that the name was just a cover for other more formidable activities, but no one could either prove or disprove this.

It had been built rapidly but soundly. Its walls were thick and soundproof; even the best of inventors would have encountered the greatest difficulties in detecting the sounds originating in some of these rooms. The problem of finding out what was happening in that building was thoroughly discussed in Washington between Taine and some other interested gentlemen, and it was finally decided that the only way to secure this information was to go in and secure it; and this was more easily said than done.

Taine had all kinds of ideas. Some he talked about freely with anyone that would listen to him. Others he whispered to himself at the dead of midnight in his bed, and some of them he did not even dare whisper. After the conference in Washington, he decided that the only way to do a thing was to do it; so, he started in to do it in the only way that seemed practical to him. A thousand wild, foolish plans occurred to him, but always he came back to the same idea—the only way to find out what was going on in the Bridge Club was to go inside and find out. He was confident that the solution to the entire problem was inside that building—in combination with what was inside of his brain.

Careful investigation in New York disclosed one thing. Every servant working in the Bridge Club was a carefully selected, highly intelligent person. The next interesting thing was that all of the employees were women. That was so very opposite to the rule that, in itself, it constituted a very interesting fact. Here was a club of men, highly moral, very rich and sedate business men, many of whom lived at the Club, and all of the servants were women!

Taine had been a woman in China. He did not like it very much—this idea of masquerading as one of the opposite sex—but he had done it and he could do it again. For a few days he just watched the women come and go through the back entrance of the Club. Finally, he selected one who looked just a little like Taine, about the same height and age, and this little woman had red hair. The detective studied her on the street, in the subway and finally in her boarding house. By the end of a week he had a very accurate idea of her habits. Then he secured a room in a boarding house near-by; an introduction was effected in a neighboring church, and in no time at all Taine was courting the red-haired lady, who turned out to be a telephone operator at the Club.

She was rather flattered to have such a distinguished looking man pay attention to her. Of course, Taine was really rather commonplace, but his manners were elegant, and he had lots of money to spend, and he was so sympathetic, and kind. At the end of another week the red-haired girl was beginning to dream, and even talk a little about her ambitions. Then one night she left in a drawing room for the West, heavily guarded by several determined women. Her room in the boarding house was occupied as usual by a red-haired woman, who spent some hours of the early morning in preparing an elaborate make-up. That morning at eight, Minnie Smith, the telephone operator for the eight hour day shift, passed with other female employees into the rear entrance of the Bridge Club. Once again Taine had accomplished the apparently impossible.

For a week the little detective, in a red wig and a rather gay dress, worked eight hours a day as a telephone operator. He found out a great many things about the Bridge Club. To be exact, he found out about one-millionth part of what he wanted to discover. To say that he was discouraged was a rather mild way of expressing his disappointment. The mystery that he was trying to solve was all around him, in fact, he was able to feel part of it, but nothing happened to make it possible for him to come closer to it. He watched the members of the Club pass in and out, he heard their voices over the telephone, very occasionally one spoke to him as the opportunity presented—otherwise, his time was wasted.

He worked at the switchboard in a rather automatic manner, his past work having enabled him to have eyes in the back of his head and ears all over. Between calls he thought, and, finally, he was satisfied that he was thinking in a circle, ending where he began and producing no results. In reality, his subconscious mind was working far faster and to better effect than his conscious mind, but, of course, he was not aware of that comforting fact.

In final despair, he decided to leave and start all over again, but the night before he did this he had a dream—not much of a dream, but interesting. A number of cats were tormenting a man, attacking and biting him in every possible way, and just as he awoke he heard his wife say, "They just act like a lot of catty women!"

He remembered the dream when he awoke. In fact, he wrote it on a piece of paper. Then he began to put some of the threads together—the hospital in China, the Doctor in San Francisco who wore a ring that he had given to a woman in China, the fact that all these people played bridge, the clothing that they wore, the resentment which they aroused in the golf-playing money-men of America.

For a week Taine worked hard. As a red-headed telephone operator he put in his eight hours a day. During the rest of the sixteen hours he received strange callers in his small boarding house room. Scientists, psychiatrists, college professors came from all parts of the East to see him, and from each of them he gathered the special little piece of information that they possessed and that he needed. They were well paid for their trouble by orders on the multi-millionaire Johnson. They thought that they were dealing with some mild form of insane crank, but Taine simply kept his colorless personality and found out what he wanted to know; and at the end of an exhausting week the little man had more threads gathered together.

Then, to his delight, he was promoted to attend to the telephone in the Manager's office. He had an idea that there he might have an opportunity to learn something about the real meaning of the Club. He found, to his great pleasure, that from that office ran private lines to all parts of the United States, and that the so called Manager often spent hours in conversation with men of importance all over the country. These calls were all handled by the red-haired operator, and he lost no time in making a list of those who had possession of the other ends of these long-distance wires. He even listened in on some of the conversations, and gathered what he felt was partial evidence, which proved that some of his surmises were correct.

He was sure that in a short time he would have all of the threads gathered together into a real rope of evidence.

Then one day he was kept busy for several hours, connecting the Manager with a dozen of the big men. It seemed that they had been called to New York for a conference. That meeting was to be held at 9 P.M. that evening in the Manager's office. Taine made up his mind that he would be there. No matter what happened, he just had to be there. He knew that in that conference there would be disclosures of the greatest importance. The telephone conversations had indicated that something great, gigantic, stupendous was brewing in the steaming pot of destiny, stirred by these financial giants. All that afternoon as he worked he cast glances around the office. Where could he hide?

The Big Meeting

The meeting was held that evening as he arranged. It was a peculiar gathering. Probably never, in the history of the world, had there been one like it. At the head of the table, as was her due, sat Miss Patricia Powers, now nearly sixty years old. When her father died, she had been the richest woman in America. Now, she was probably the richest woman in the world. During those years, following her father's death, her financial life had been interesting on account of the fact that every investment that she had made had been directed by another woman. Not a single dollar had been under the control of the masculine sex.

The greatly increased financial ability of the feminine world was shown by the fact that during all those years not a dollar had been lost; every investment had been wisely planned and had brought a rich reward, and the women who had worked thus for Miss Patricia Powers had received, as their reward, the hearty and generous support of this rich woman in all their plans. Thus, she was entitled to a place at the head of the table. She was a rather ugly woman, and her elaborate costume, her garish display of jewelry, her peculiar taste in regard to cosmetics but accentuated this ugliness. Gossip stated that no man had ever offered to marry her. It may easily be seen that this neglect had been a large factor in her conduct during the past ten years.

At the other end sat Miss Martha Belzer, not the one who became so incensed years before because Aviation Consolidated had refused her a promotion which she knew that her ability merited. That Martha Belzer had gone to Europe on a vacation, news had come of her death in the Alps, her body had never been located; this person was a capable looking, well dressed, carefully shaved, financial giant, by the name of Mark Bonds. He had come over from France some years ago, well recommended, and by sheer ability had become a leader in the financial circles of America.

Years before, Miss Martha Belzer had spent a night writing to nine of her friends. Like her, those friends had all met tragic deaths, by fire or water, but always in some out of the way part of the world where their bodies could not be found. Those nine business women had also undergone a metamorphosis.

The twelfth place was occupied by a physician. She was, without question, the greatest biologist of hers, or any age of history. She and Miss Patricia Powers were women, dressed as women. The other ten persons at the table were the leaders in the new financial movement that was threatening the economic life of the group of old-timers.

Miss Powers started to open the meeting.

The telephone rang, and Mark Bonds answered it from his seat.

After listening intently, he curtly replied in a deep, masculine voice: "Bring her up."

And looking around, he remarked:

"You know that little red-headed telephone operator? Well, she is raising Hell downstairs and says she has to see us right away. Says she has news that is vital to our interests."

"Do you mean Dorris Bahnes, the one just promoted to be our private operator?" asked Miss Powers.

"That's the one," answered the Manager, smiling as he spoke. Then he went to the door and opened it. In rushed the red-haired girl, breathless, her dress torn, her shoes muddy. Gasping, she almost fell to the floor. The great physician personally helped her to a seat and saw that she was given a stimulant. At last she was calm enough to tell her story.

"I know that you are going to punish me," she faltered, "I know I done wrong, but how was I to know? About three or four weeks ago I met a man in our church. He treated me swell, and made love to me and then one night when I was on my way home from the Club I was caught by three big women and put in a taxi, and before I could say a word we were on our way to California. They would not tell me a word, would not even talk to me. Every time I tried to escape, they beat me. Out there I was chained to a bed in a shack in the desert. I thought I would die there. Finally, I got away. The Salvation Army helped me, and I finally reached New York. When I went to the boarding house, the landlady abused me. She said I was a liar, that I had been in New York all the time, and had paid my board regular, and even while we were talking a red-haired girl came out of my room with some of my clothes on and tried to catch me, and I ran as fast as I could to the Club for help, and when I heard that you were all here, I was bound to tell you, because something is wrong about it. Has there been a red-haired girl here? In my place?

The Manager nodded, yes. Then he said kindly:

"You have had a terrible experience, my dear girl. No doubt about some rascal trying to harm you in some way. You sit near me till we get through this meeting and then we will take up your case. In the meantime, I will have our private detectives go to your boarding house and try to find this other woman or whoever it is that is masquerading in your clothing. Your conduct shows how loyal you are to our movement, so, we will have no hesitance in discussing matters freely with you. Tomorrow I want you to dictate the exact details to one of our private stenographers. It was certainly a most unusual experience. Now, Miss Powers, suppose we start with our meeting. Miss Bahnes, you just rest. No one is going to harm you now since you have reached us.

"I am so glad," murmured the little girl.

Miss Powers began to speak.

"As President of our Association, I have called this meeting to make a careful survey of what has been done so far, and decide on a course of action in the future. I believe that the time has arrived for our more ambitious plans to start. Dr. Hamilton, will you give us a brief account of your invaluable work for us?"

A Revelation

The wonderful biologist smiled as she replied: "My work has really been interesting. When, years ago, you asked me for suggestions that would enable you to finally assume control of all America and perhaps the entire world, I had already done some very beautiful work, but, of course, I was handicapped by lack of funds and material. Your organization supplied both. You felt that it was necessary, for a few years at least, to place your financial campaign in the hands of five thousand brilliant, well trained, financiers and business executives. These had to be men on account of the inability of women to even secure a finger-hold on the important positions. You asked me to solve that problem. I did. I asked you for a list of five thousand brilliant young unmarried women, well versed in the business management of great enterprises, who were willing to sacrifice their lives to the accomplishment of our great idea. You furnished me with that list, headed with the names of ten of the most remarkable feminine minds that the world had ever produced. At the top of that list was the name of the brains and originator of the movement, Miss Martha Belzer.

"We built up an organization and went to China. There we secured material for twenty-five thousand ampules of male gonadal solution, highly concentrated and of uniform strength. We purchased our so-called College in France and there, after all forms of imaginary deaths, our five thousand heroines came. First, they were thoroughly treated with radium and the X-ray to produce bodies that were natural, as far as sexual characteristics were concerned, and, after that, each one was given five doses of the substance that I was able to isolate and which, for convenience, I called MALE-FINE XXX. In a remarkably short time, these heroines experienced the desired physical changes, their voices deepened, became wonderfully masculine; they developed such growths of hair on the face that they had to begin shaving once a day. There was also a rather typical change in certain deposits of subcutaneous fat. But why go into all these details? It is sufficient to say that five thousand well educated, rather beautiful women entered our French laboratory and five thousand persons who looked like well-bred cultured men left it. What those five thousand did in the financial world can best be told by some one else.

"That was our first great task. Of course, this had to be done only once, because we felt that by the time that our new men grew old the women would be in complete control, without the necessity of such substitutes. In fact, it may be possible to reverse the process and change some of these heroines back into their original bodies.

"Our next important point of attack was to begin turning the human race into a feminine one. As you know, the relation between the number of male and female babies is very close. For centuries scientists have been trying to influence the sex of the unborn child. The problem was attacked from every possible angle. I was fortunate enough to arrive at what seems to be the correct solution. As you know, we patented a Modified Maternity Food for Expectant Mothers. It was a good food, and, as we sold it at cost and extensively advertised it, it was used by millions of mothers. As a result, last year there were three times as many girl babies as boy babies born in the United States. If we can continue this rate or increase it, we will soon have a feminine nation.

"That brings me to my final dream of a manless world. I feel that our organization can easily be spread over the entire globe. We do not want two sexes in this fair world of ours, not as long as one sex can run it so efficiently. But, of course, that sex has to continue on in its existence; we do not plan to destroy humanity. What I have in mind is the perfecting of *parthenogenesis*. By that I mean the reproduction by virgin females of eggs which develop without being fertilized by the male principle, or sperm cell. This is an actual fact at the present time in certain insects, worms and crustaceans, the most familiar example being that of the aphid, in which a number of parthenogenetically produced generations occur entirely composed of females.

"If worms and crabs can do that, the human female can; and the time is near at hand when we will. Later on, we will consider the production of females from *ovamaters* in the laboratory and thus save our mature females the time and suffering of bearing their young. The growth of the young female, from the egg up to the second or third year of life, will be provided for in our Government laboratories and nurseries. I am at work on these problems now, and, just as soon as we feel strong enough to take over the government, I shall be able to present a perfect plan for the development of future feminine generations that will in no way have the curse of masculine associations.

"As you know you are well aware of our plans, it is useless for me to go into details. Enough for me to say that when the time comes you will not find my department lagging behind in our effort to make this world perfect by the complete extermination of the hated male element of our population. In all this I have had your hearty support and cooperation.

CHAPTER VI
Mistaken Identity

The eleven persons around the table heartily applauded the great biologist. Even the awe-struck, red-headed, telephone girl timidly clapped her hands.

"Now, Martha, how about your end of it?" asked the wealthy woman, whose enthusiasm and wealth had made all this possible. The person at the other end of the table, Mark Bond, elegantly attired in the height of fashionable clothing, stood up and smiled.

"We financiers have done well. At this moment we are planning an attack, which, if it succeeds, will put the entire wealth of the States in our hands. There were only five thousand of us who willingly sacrificed our sex to conquer womanhood for the purpose of climbing to success. Five thousand, but what a wonderful group that was! Their names will be engraved in letters of gold in the memorial that we are thinking of building for them in

THE FEMININE METAMORPHOSIS 45

Washington. The men of the financial world have been but toys in our hands. We have played with them, as a child with his teddy bear, a cat with his mouse. All we have to do is to go onward toward the final glory. For a generation men can stay as messenger boys. Then we hope for a wonderful manless America."

And again the eager listeners applauded one of their greatest heroines. Miss Patricia Powers smiled. That only made her uglier.

"It seems to me," she said, "that we are going ahead nicely with our plans. I have carefully gone over your reports with the Manager of the Bridge Club. Everything is working out as we want it to come out, but I am sorry to report that quite a few of our brave five thousand are in private hospitals, suffering from a form of nervous exhaustion. Fortunately, we are in complete charge of these hospitals, and, so far, have been able to keep this news from becoming public. I am having a special investigation made of this unfortunate break in our health. We are unfortunate not to have a well-trained psychiatrist in our organization, and we do not feel that it is safe to refer these cases to a man. Otherwise, all is going well. Tomorrow we will start our final attack on Wall Street. Juliette, as Manager of our organization, have you any remarks to make?"

Juliette, known as James Jones, Manager of the Bridge Club, stood up, as he started to answer the inquiry.

"I am sure that anything I can say will be of interest to you. We are certainly fortunate in finding our little red-haired stenographer. Her conduct proves the loyalty of our organization, the high ideals of even the smallest member of the movement. I think that this brave girl should be rewarded. A thousand dollars would not be too much—"

"Oh! Please do not give me anything," murmured Dorris Bahnes. "I only did my duty, and I am sorry it happened, because that bad man might have found out some of your secrets. If you think it safe, I would like to go back to the boarding house and go to bed. I am so tired."

"We will see that you are well guarded," the Manager assured her, and he pressed the button at his desk. A messenger girl answered the summons.

"Any news?" the Manager asked.

"Yes, Sir, your private detectives have a red-haired woman down stairs, and they want to bring her up as soon as you let them."

"Send them up. That was quick work! It did not take them long to catch that female impersonator, did it?"

In a few minutes, three determined women walked in. There was something in their manner that conveyed the impression that they could be rather hard boiled if they came in conflict with a criminal. With them was a red-haired girl. They were not holding her, but anyone could see that they were not going to let her get away. Except for the fact that she was a little better dressed, more carefully rouged, she was the exact duplicate of the red-haired girl, who sat at the table with the Directors of the Bridge Club.

"Now, this is very interesting," began the Manager. "Here by my side is Dorris Bahnes, who has just arrived in town, having escaped from her kidnappers, and there in front of us is a person who looks like Dorris, who has been staying in her room and doing her work at the telephone exchange, and, in reality, all the time she was a detective. Our private detectives tell us that this person is none other than Taine, the great operator from San Francisco, paid by Johnson and his crowd to find out what we are doing in this Club."

She walked over to the girl who was now held on either side by one of the detectives.

"What did you do it for, Taine? How much were you going to get out of it?"

The red-haired girl did not answer.

"How do you like to wear a red wig, Taine?"

No answer.

"Suppose I take it off?"

Silence.

The Manager took off the girl's cap, and then grabbed the mass of red hair. It stuck. The girl cried out in pain.

"Bless me!" exclaimed the Manager. "It's real hair. I am sorry that I hurt you Dorris, if you are Dorris. But if you are, how did you get here and where have you been?"

"What do you want me to tell? Everything?" asked the girl whose hair had just been pulled.

"Yes, come over to the table and tell us all about it."

"You see," said the girl, rather nervously, "this man was good to me and so I reported it to you as our instructions were, and so when he had me kidnapped, why, of course, you knew it all the time. His women took me out to a shack somewhere in the California desert and it was not long before a dozen of our women came out there and over-powered his women and some of them stayed there to guard the three women and rest brought me back to New York. I have been in New York for about a week, all of that time I have been in one of the private rooms in the Club. Of course, as soon as I arrived I told the Manager all about what had happened; I had to in order to keep my vows to the Organization. That is all I have to say. I am sure that I have done nothing wrong."

"No. You have acted in a wonderful way, Dorris. We are proud of you."

He turned to his fellow members of the Directorate.

"Some of you have been in my confidence during these last few weeks, others know of this for the first time. Johnson, with the group of men he represents, was determined to learn our secrets. They engaged one of the most brilliant detectives in American, a man by the name of Taine. We knew when this enemy of ours went to Washington and when he went to San Francisco. We were informed when Taine arrived in New York. Every time he turned around we had a report of it. We played with him—like a cat plays with a mouse. He had one of our girls kidnapped and she has just told you what happened. Then we made it possible for him to attend this meeting—and he did. He is here now. Of course, we wanted him to know all that he had taken such pains to learn; so, we went right on with the meeting, and I hope you have enjoyed it Mr. Taine." Here the Manager looked at the red-headed girl by his side.

Confusion!

The red-haired girl whom he had called Mr. Taine looked at him and smiled.

"I guess I might as well own up, Mr. Manager. I am not Mr. Taine. I am Flossie Ruffles from the Lyric. My specialty is impersonations. For a week I have been trying to duplicate a red-haired girl and, for some reason, she gave me five thousand to come here tonight and put on this act. I am sorry if I worried you, but I really needed the money and I thought you would not care. I believe from what you have said that it must have been Mr. Taine, the detective, who gave me the five thousand, though why he should have wanted me to do it, I cannot say."

The Manager looked first at one of the red-haired girls and then at the other. Both seemed genuine. They were as much alike as though they were identical twins. She even went and examined the hair of the girl who had first entered the room. It was as genuine as the other girl's was.

The Manager sat down. For what seemed hours she sat there, her eyes covered with her right hand. Suddenly she jumped up and leaned excitedly over the table.

"That man Taine is in this room!" she cried. "There are twelve of us here at the table, these two girls and the three detectives. One of us is Taine. I know that I am not, and I can vouch for Miss Powers, and I am also sure of Dr. Hamilton and Mark Bond. But how about the others? Dr. Hamilton, I am going to ask you to examine these Directors. Everyone one of them, you know, should be a woman. But I am sure that one of them is a man, and that man is Taine."

The men seated around the table looked at each other. One drummed on the polished surface with his finger tips. Tap-tap-rappity-tap-tap. On his hand glowed a wonderful Chinese ring. It was the San Francisco physician. He suddenly stood up.

"Suppose I say that I am Taine, Juliette? If I say that, will you spare these friends of ours the humiliation of your proposal—of showing their real sex by your inspection of their bodies?"

The Manager looked across the table at the Doctor—she looked long and piercingly. Then she shook her head—

"No. Lucy, old girl. You are not Taine. I could swear that you are Lucy, the girl that went to China and helped Dr. Hamilton with her work there. Why, I have seen that ring a hundred times."

"But I insist that I am Taine. Let's put an end to the melodrama. These women here may be insane in their ideas, but they are, at least, women. I do not want them undressed—not here. I would rather tell you right now that we have come to the end of the play."

Miss Powers started to laugh, a high pitched, hysterical laugh.

"But suppose he is telling the truth, my dears. For God's sake! Stop the act and get down to business. If he is Taine, let's be sure of it. If it is Lucy, it just means that one more of the poor girls has gone mad. Can't one of you tell? Please find out in some way. If something is not done soon, I shall scream!"

Several went to quiet her. One by one the Directors seemed to draw away from the San Francisco man, the physician whom they called in such a familiar fashion, "Lucy." He seemed undisturbed, and yet, at the same time, he glanced in an uneasy manner from one side to another, and both of his hands were now in his Tuxedo pockets.

Finally, the room became quiet. Dr. Hamilton looked at Lucy.

"Where did you get that ring?" he asked.

"Oh! That was my ring one time in China. Do you remember that little Chinese girl whom you saved and thought so much of in the hospital? She gave you all a piece of expensive jewelry. She gave you a piece of jade, Dr. Hamilton, and she gave the doctor whom you call Lucy this ring. Lucy thought the little China girl rather nice. Well, to make a long story short, I was that little girl. I lived in the hospital with you for some months. The Government sent me over to find out what you girls were doing there. I had some ideas then and during all these years those ideas have been slowly working into definite form. I suspected some of the things you spoke of tonight, yet, at the same time, you went a lot further than I thought sensible people would go. I know a lot about women, but I cannot understand what's the matter with you—unless you really are insane."

THE FEMININE METAMORPHOSIS 49

Dr. Hamilton shook her head gravely.

"I guess he is right, girls. I remember that little Chinese girl, and she did give me the jade. He would not have known about that unless he had been there. I have heard about him, but I had no idea that he was so damn clever. But is he clever? To get the best of Lucy and come here dressed to impersonate her? And then this chorus girl. Well, he says he is Taine, and I really do not think he has harmed Lucy—just locked her up somewhere. So, the best thing we can do with him is to kill him right away. He knows too much—we can handle this chorus girl, but this man—the only way to keep him quiet is to kill him. I hate to commit murder, but I have been working on this plan for years and I am not going to have it go to pieces just on account of a man."

Miss Patricia Powers agreed with the Doctor.

"You are right, Hamilton," she said. "He knows too much. If he is dead, we will put through our financial coup, and in a week it will not make any difference if they do find out he died here at the Club."

Suddenly the San Francisco doctor, Lucy, who was really Taine, seemed to change. His face grew hard, and his hands, within his coat pockets, twitched.

"Now, you sit down, ladies, and listen to me talk. You are not going to kill me or anybody tonight. There are about five hundred policemen around this building. If I am not out safely by midnight, they are going to find out why. No one is going to leave. You women have played a great game, but it was a selfish, inhuman sort of a game, and you are going to lose out and it's not your fault or my fault, but just one of those happenings that make me believe in predestination. You want to run this world, and have all the men die off and make it a female Paradise, and you forgot there was a God and that He made man just the same as He made woman. I admit that some men are rather bad sort of fools, but some of us are really rather good sorts—take me, for example. My wife thinks I am wonderful—of course, all my boys are girls, but, at the same time, she would have been tickled had the last one been a boy. You go and change your bodies, and try and make men out of yourselves, and all the rest of what you call your programme, and now you think that you are going to win out by killing me. If it were not for the Missus and the kids, I would not mind much if you did, but even if you were able to, what good would it do you?

"I think your Dr. Hamilton is a rather bright expert. I always shall be indebted to her for operating on Ming Foo. She had a wonderful plan and she has worked it our in a wonderful way—but she did not know the Chinese people—not the way I do. I have lived with them and slept with them and I know a little more about them than you would think, just by looking at me. During these last two weeks I have been having long talks with scientists from all over the East. Perhaps your detectives know who they were, though they could not tell what we talked about. But I wanted to learn all I could about the medicine Dr. Hamilton prepared in that hospital, and these men told me. I said so and so and they agreed with me that my idea might be right. What you have said tonight convinces me that I was right."

Taine Explains

"You went on with your plans, but you forgot God. He had certain plans for the human race, and it was not part of His plan that women should live on, century after century, without men, as you were preparing them to do. So this is what happened. For thousands of years, over in China, they have had a deadly disease. They have had it so long that by this time practically the entire nation has it without knowing it or without having many signs of it. They have just become accustomed to it, so that it is a very mild disease—but, at the same time, it is all through their bodies. Once in a while a white man contracts that disease, and then he dies a rather unpleasant death in a few years. Most of them become insane before they die. Now, when you girls operated on those poor Chinks for so many pieces of gold, you were operating on men who had that disease. Every ampule of medicine you prepared from their glands had the germs of that disease in it. You took five thousand of your smartest women, the ones you were counting on to lead in this feminine revolt, and you injected this disease into their blood. You gave them what you called male characteristics, but you gave them something else. You infected every one of them with this disease. Dr. Hamilton flirted with this idea—she even went so far as to test each Chink with a Wasserman test, but she did not know that the disease was so mild in the yellow people that it does not show a Wasserman. So, she lost sight of the danger. Of course, she realizes it now. She is not a specialist in mental diseases, but she sees now that your comrades who are going insane have *paresis*. I suspected all this—I have talked about all this to the specialists—and tonight I find, by your own statements, that I am right. Ladies, the harvest you planted ten years ago is just beginning. Inside of another year every one of your brilliant five thousand financial leaders will be insane. Your movement will fail because there will be no brains left to carry the gospel of what you call feminine supremacy to the nation.

"One of the great men I talked to a few nights ago said that you had performed a feminine metamorphosis. He told me that meant changing a woman into a man. You did better than that. You took five thousand of our best women, girls who would have made loving wives and wonderful mothers if they had been well advised—you took the best that we have bred, and, through your desires to rule, you have changed them into five thousand insane women.

"There is no need of Johnson's trying to fight you. There is no need of his ever knowing what happened. I am ashamed to tell him—ashamed to tell anyone, because you belong to the same sex that my mother and wife and daughters belong to. I did not really think women could be so—peculiar. I really thought women like us men—my women folks are wild about me—you ought to see the neckties my wife selects for me and the scarf-pin. I am not going to say a word about this to anyone. I will just tell Johnson that he need not worry—and my advice is to give those poor girls some of the new arsenic preparations that sometimes works so well in these mental cases. Now, I am going to take my chorus girl and leave, and please be sensible and do not try to stop us, because, if you do, there are going to be a lot of us get hurt, and you, poor fools, are hurt bad enough as it is, if you believe what I tell you, and I guess you do—you look as if you did. You need not worry about Lucy. I will send her back just as soon as I am safe."

So, Taine and Flossie Ruffles walked out of the room and out of the Club, and out into the realities of little old New York.

That same night Taine called on Johnson.

"You owe me," he said to that worthy, "twenty-seven thousand dollars expense money. That is in addition to the money you had to pay those college professors. Me—you don't owe me anything except this expense money. I have your million and that is enough. The work is done. It was being done before I started. You need not worry about those people at the Bridge Club. In another year there won't be one of them that will know the minimum requirements for the dealer to bid club. You can just take my word for it that they are through. But, at the same time, don't gamble on the stock exchange for a week or two, because they may try to get you."

Johnson looked at the little man in amazement.

"I suppose," he said, "that you will give me a full report?"

"No," replied Taine. "No use. You would not believe me if I did."

A Small Planet of Our Own
by T.E. Merritt-Pinckard

A brand new story by the author of Ackermanthology's popular "For the Good of Society". Mrs. Pinckard is a Grand Dame of the Count Dracula Society and as co-hostess with her husband, of the famous quarter century Pinckard Science Fiction Authors Salon has intermingled her mind with Catherine Moore, Philip José Farmer, Ray Bradbury, Arthur C. Clarke, Edna Mayne Hull, Robert Bloch, A. E. van Vogt, H. L. Gold, Helen Urban, Wendayne & Forry Ackerman, Larry Niven, Jerry Pournelle, Geo. Pal, Poul & Karen Anderson, Jerry Bixby, Anaïs Nin, Spring Byington, Anthony Boucher, Laura & Kelly Freas, Bea & Aubrey MacDermott, Georges Gallet, Kris & Lil Neville, James Gunn, Bebe Barron, Jacque Fresco, Brother Theodore, Jean Cox, James Warren, Walt & Mary Ellen Daugherty, John Brunner, Bill & Peggy Crawford, Gene and Majel Roddenberry, E. Everett Evans & Thelma Hamm, Curt & Henrietta Siodmak, Ion Hobana, Sir Alvin & Louise Germeshausen, Colin Wilson and many others whose unique brains have been bound to stimulate hers.

If I don't watch out this introduction will be longer than the story! But I thought it pertinent.

Terri is currently returning to writing in the sci-fi field with a passion. Lucky genre fans!

—PK

Note: This story was conceived and written a number of years prior to the "Ewe" story of Daisy's cloning. The explanation and the figure of six days division of the cells also predated the new release of the Scottish experiment.

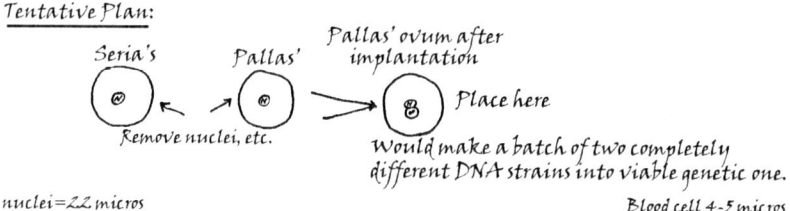

When space travel became a common occurrence, expedition after expedition took off from Earth. For thousands of years Civilization had fought and worked toward Universal unity, a sharing of the hopes and dreams of the peoples of Earth. Still, when the opportunity to begin on new planets was at hand, it was separate entities that licensed the expeditions. Private entities! The Blacks, Muslims, Jews, Feminists, Chauvinists, Democracies, Monarchies—all wanted their own planet! Only one group, whose dreams included those of all colors, creeds, religions and political realms, had but one criteria. The inhabitants would all be women; moreover, they would be all Lesbian women. Now, at last, Lesbians could be a people in their own right.

They found a planet and named it Mytilene, which had been the true name of the Isle of Lesbos in ancient Earth history. It was a very small planet. The surface was generally mountainous, with large areas of fertile coast and valley lands. Building materials were provided by the plentiful supply of fibrous wood stumps and fungi-like masses that grew at the base of the tall reeds and grasses spread along the banks of rivers. Fruit and vegetable substances grew in abundance and the odd little creatures that roamed the stumplands provided meat.

The colonists came from every background, level and profession and with trade commencing with other planets and Earth soon made great inroads on a political and sociological framework. Of course, it had cracks in its very fabric. There had been folly and blindness to the misfits, the malcontents as they appeared in the society, but they were few, and when in History did civilizations not contain such problems? Yet, there was much wisdom demonstrated, too, for all the colonists had a common dream. A planet of their very own. Mediation solved most of the problems. Today, the young planet had reached a degree of civilization technically and scientifically astounding.

***

The institutes squatted on the banks of a river in the part of Sappho City that grew up first, as settlements do because of the convenience in transportation and the easy availability of water.

Dr. Seria Donner was one of the 10-member Directorate and also Head of Medical and Scientific Research and Progress at the Institute. With her at its head, Mytilene was assured that Science and a moral imperative to impel its research had integrity in its use. Although Seria Donner had returned to Earth for her medical training, Mytilene was her home, as it had been her two mothers, Omi and Momi and her foremothers before them. Seria was completely dedicated to Mytilene in all its affirmation to better mankind, especially that of Lesbians.

Now, Dr. Seria Donner wished to make a change that might cause great problems. It involved her position as Head of the Scientific Branch of the Legislature. Donner's specialty was biogenesis and a decade ago she had begun a study to put into effect the agenda hidden deep within the corridors of her heart for so many years. The only one whom she'd allowed to share her hopes and dreams was her love, Pallas Carter.

Seria was older than Pallas. She had remained abstinent for a long time, waiting for someone to share her soul rather than just her body. Then she met Pallas. Pallas Carter had but recently arrived on Mytilene. She walked into Seria's laboratory and proudly asserted she had just completed her Master's degree in Biogenesis at one of Earth's more prestigious Universities. As she grew to know her better, Seria depended more and more on Pallas. Whereas Seria saw the world in terms of facts, blacks and whites, rights and wrongs, Pallas always concerned herself with the emotional implications of her research, and what effect whatever she did might have on the community. Seria found this to be a boon rather than a debit, for Pallas was the redeeming balance to Seria's constant logistical approach, and as the months passed they became more than scientific partners.

"Pallas, have you seen the latest virtual reality cell slides? They were here by my microscan but now I can't find them. I've got cells in nutrient all over the lab and can't continue until I compare their progress to the ones I did yesterday!"

Dr. Seria Donner was frustratedly searching her desk.

The lovely dusky-skinned girl sat on the high stool at the lab counter and pushed the shade visor back as she looked up. "Seria, I think they are in the Scanfile where they should be. I filed everything last night before we left."

Seria banged her fist onto the desk, and scattered papers on it, shaking her head in dismay. "No wonder I couldn't find them. I don't like things filed away! They belong in one of the piles on my desk!"

Pallas laughed. "I know! You know exactly what pile they should be in and under exactly how many pages of notes on top of them. But the pile was getting too high!"

Seria grinned. "You just know me too well!"

A blush rose on Pallas's face and Seria put her arm around the girl's shoulder. "C'mon, sweetheart. We'll find it tomorrow. Let's go home now!"

A deep and lasting love had grown between them since they were Committed to each other. Because of Seria's high position in the Directorate, their bonding was celebrated more publicly than they would have wished. Representatives from other planets attended as well as many of the offspring of colonists who had attended Seria's classes when they were children and she was still teaching at the university.

One night Seria and Pallas were curled together on the divan in front of the fireplace. Remnants of dinner were still on the table and Pallas held a glass of wine in her hand, holding it high so that the firelight played on the rich color infusing it with varied hues and shades. Seria stroked Pallas's long, shining golden hair and rocked her gently to the lilting sound of her own humming.

"Pallas, I've succeeded in the beginning stages of my life's dream. I have perfected a method of parthenogenesis!"

Parthenogenesis was a means of reproduction in which only the female was involved. Throughout History there had been only eight recorded cases of it, each time the child, a female, was born being a perfect duplicate of the mother, with no father being involved and most times the mother was a virgin. Up to now, this had always been considered a "miracle birth," yet different than Christianity's story of the birth of Jesus. Donner wanted to take Parthenogenesis out of the realm of the supernatural, making it a true scientific achievement, occurring each time it was attempted.

Introducing this into the society would be an easy task. The Lesbian population would no longer be dependent on the male sperm or the adoption of a bloodline not their own, nor the implantation of closed seed into the uterus. Seria had spent many frustrating months not only on the scientific project but in trying to answer Pallas's concerns about other effects.

"I've been wanting to talk to you about something, Pall. How would you feel about starting our family now? I'm ready for the actual test run."

"Seria, are you sure about this? There are so many consequences and implications to what you plan!"

"You know I've searched every corner of my thoughts about it. Pall, are you worried about this politically and socially or is it something more personal that's concerning you? The tests I have done show there are absolutely no unexpected problems to concern yourself about. Genetically, you are an ideal subject. You'd have a wonderful baby!"

"I don't know, Seria. I really don't know! To think of us being a family is wonderful. I've ached for that for a long time. And, especially, to think this will truly be our very own baby! Yet, now when the moment is here I am filled with all sorts of feelings. Will our babies be the only ones born by parthenogenesis? Will they be considered freaks? What do we do if they choose our way of life? What do we do if they don't choose our way of life?"

"I can't answer *all* your questions. There are many couples who feel the way we do about having their own babies born out of their love for each other. Up to now, the closest thing to this has been the cloning of one of their genes still using the DNA from a male's sperm. My hope will be the first instance of a true bonding of two souls becoming a third with no outside donor. I would imagine every couple on Mytilene would choose that way if they are able to bear children at all. And the babies certainly wouldn't be considered freaks . . . they would be a more natural product of the love relationship than any other. A child born of our cells and DNAs alone. Tonight, I want to hold you, to love you and tell you that I want to be one with you. I want to start a family!"

Pall set the now empty glass of wine down. She raised her eyes to Seria and held them in a long, loving look. Then, with a smile that was like a breaking dawn, she raised her arms to Seria. "First, the love!" she laughed. "Then you can take a sample of my blood, or ova or whatever!"

***

The two scientists had performed many tests over the past months. The ones that failed sadly went down the drain, literally as well as figuratively. Now, today, they were through with testing. Neither had genetic recessive genes or anomalies. Both were ideal subjects, ideal guinea pigs.

Seria took the vial with the ova from Pallas. Carefully separating its DNA strand from the nuclei, she repeated the process with the DNA strand from one of her own ova. Gently, she took the vial containing the third ova. It, too, was from Pallas's body. She separated out the DNA which left the ova filled only with the rich nutrient within. As she added the two separate DNA strands, one of Pallas's, one of her own, she felt a thrill of tenderness almost as though she and Pallas were making love and a baby in virtual reality. The nutrient would nourish the two strands of DNA.

Seria kept close watch on the petri dish. The complete new cell began to replicate. During that time, she didn't talk much about the work and Pallas didn't want to be present in the lab while Seria was working on the embryo. Finally, after six days of division, she was ready to transplant the embryo into Pallas's womb.

"*For the first time,*" Seria thought, "*this is not cloning! This is true fertilization using only female nuclei and DNA strands from two different women!*" Excitement flooded through her. This could mean so much to their people.

Four weeks later, they knew it had taken and they exulted in the fact of Pallas's pregnancy. As Seria enfolded Pallas in her arms she found it difficult to put her feelings into words. *There was so much more to lesbian love than in male-female. They felt the same emotions, knew the moods of each other and accepted them, and they knew the completeness of fulfillment, each giving until the other was sated, continuing far beyond the physical until their souls were at peace.*

Months passed before Seria finally made a decision to bring the facts of her experiment to the Directorate. At its next meeting, she presented each member with the printed explanation of *Lesbirth*, and then after a lengthy holographic presentation, announced that she had implemented her project and it was successful. The gallery was filled, as always, with citizens and multimedia closely following legislative proposals. This openness was, after all, the balance to the Directors' power and Mytilene citizens had always been strong in their protectiveness of their individual rights. The first reaction of the audience was unmitigated joy. As the meeting progressed, the direction of the discussion took a decidedly different turn. Several questions arose which troubled Seria. Never had Dr. Seria Donner anticipated the catastrophic sociological upheaval that such a change would effect.

As Director, Lena Barkov banged her gavel for order. First Director Mason rose. "These will be the first *true* children of Mytilene," she stated. "Just as the Presidency of Earth is by Earthborn origin only, so the election to the Directorate on Mytilene should be reserved for *true* children of the Lesbian population, the *Lesborns!*" She continued, "Children born by parthenogenesis would be First-Class Citizens." A gasp went through the hall. This was a term never before heard on Mytilene. "This is the only way to ensure the continuation of our way of life and the knowledge that every law enacted will be of vital consequence to us as a Lesbian nation. We must ensure complete loyalty. Preferred entrance to schools will be given to *Lesborns*. I therefore declare that only *Lesborn* children will hereafter be eligible for admission to the Directorate!"

First Director Mason had not spoken the words as a proposal, nor opened the subject for discussion. In had been in the form of an order!

As Seria stood to state her objections, she was prevented by Director Gena Sardo, her face red with fury. "I cannot see how you can even state such a motion! What about our children, born on Mytilene and even those who were not, have grown up here since infancy! You cannot be saying what I think you are saying!" Gena's face was white with shock. Seria believed that if she could see her own face in a mirror at that very moment, it would be the same.

Many of the colonists had babies by insemination. Science had long ago been able to separate the sex of a child to be predetermined. Other citizens had adopted their daughters. If the child grew up to be heterosexual, upon

A SMALL PLANET OF OUR OWN

adulthood they followed their careers offworld. Most remembered with deep love the caring of their two mothers and kept close contact with them. The children who shared the Lesbian lifestyle returned to Mytilene, after pursuing advanced education offworld in their chosen fields.

The babble of voices grew to hysterical tones as first one, then another of the Directors and citizens expounded their views. It seemed to be the younger women, both on the Directorate and in the balcony, who seemed to find value in Director Mason's statement.

Seria tried to take back control of the floor, but it was impossible. Finally, she was able to plead that the proposed rule be tabled until further discussions could be held more fairly.

Seria drove home, her stomach in knots. As she opened the door, Pallas ran to her arms. She was large with child now and Seria put her arms around her protectively as she wiped the tears streaming down Pallas's cheeks.

"How did you hear?" she asked gently.

"They have already broken the news over the videocom. Oh, God, Seria . . . this is what I was afraid of! It's like a civil war and even Committed and Life partners are arguing among themselves."

Seria led Pallas to the sofa. She kissed her eyes, her neck, her mouth. Both watched as the videocom showed a woman slapping another in a grocery. The second woman grabbed a bottle off the shelf and struck the first over the head with it. Blood gushed from the cut.

"I wouldn't believe this if I hadn't seen what happened at the Directorate today! Instead of taking this as a great aid to our planet, it has turned into a political football. Everything dreamt would be such a boon to Lesbian women has turned into a nightmare. You warned me this might happen!"

The weeks that followed brought no end to the chaos. No agreement could be found by the mediation team that had been formed. The transvideo daily blared news of rioting and burning in the large cities.

One night, with security agents outside protecting the Directors' home and shades pulled down inside, Pallas began to moan.

"What's happening, Pallas?" Seria asked.

"It's coming! The baby is coming!" Another cry broke from her lips.

Seria went to look outside. Citizens were roaming the streets carrying weapons of any sort they could find. Angry murmurs and shouts bellied forth. "We can't get out to the clinic in this uproar. They're even overturning transit-trams. I'll get everything ready here. Thank God, I'm on the Directorate. The Security guards will protect our home and might be able to get a Medicar here."

"But the baby is early! Will it be all right? Do we have what we'll need for an early baby?"

"Pallas, listen to me! The baby is only early by three weeks. That's nothing. She'll be fine! You just concentrate on keeping calm, breathing correctly so you'll keep your blood pressure down and let me get everything set up. I'll be right back . . ." Seria ran quickly to gather medical and surgical supplied from her home dispensary and lab. "We'll set you up with clean sheets on the sofa where we made love so often. What better memories to surround ourselves with!"

The night was long and so was Pallas's birthing. Seria was surprised. The doctor in her had appraised Pallas's build and found it superb for giving birth. She had healthy tissue internally. So the sudden onset of labor pains seemed out of the ordinary. But the mate in her panicked each time she heard Pallas scream. The sac broke into the clean towels Seria had waiting. It was just as the dawning of the new day broke, that Pallas gave a last push, followed instantly by the wail of a newborn baby. Seria's cheeks were wet with empathy . . . but she smiled through them as she proceeded to do all the necessary things due a newborn. The baby was beautiful, each feature perfect. Seria minimally cleansed her and wrapped her in the soft baby blanket, and turned to place the baby in her beloved Pallas's arms.

"Oh, Pallas, look at her! This is our beloved child! Our child! Oh, Pallas . . . *Pallas!*"

The sheets were red with blood. But as red as the sheets were, was the contrasting whiteness of Pallas's face. Seria placed the baby quickly in the bassinet beside the bed, then turned back to Pallas, reaching quickly for her pulse. Faint, fluttery . . . but still there. Seria was all doctor now. She took the stairs two at a time. Grabbing plasma and any other life-saving items she could find, Seria returned to the living room. She even resented the microseconds it took to defrost the plasma. *"What went wrong?"* he mind screamed. *". . . an artery must have torn; could one have caught in the expulsion of the afterbirth? . . . How could this have happened?"* The mewling sound of the baby attacked her heart as well as assailing her ears. But she would be all right for now. Pallas needed her more, and first! She looked so beautiful lying there, features relaxed from relief of pain now, a faint smile on her lips. But when Seria knelt beside her to examine her, the coldness of her skin brought ice to Seria's heart. Seria was too late . . . *Pallas was gone!*

Finally, the raging torment in her eased and her tears stopped. She felt numb, but bending over the bassinet, she gathered the baby to her breast. Their baby—their child. They had named it Hannah even before its birth. She walked around the room crooning to the baby, *". . . Oh, how much Pallas and I loved you even before you were conceived. We both so wanted to welcome you to the world. I won't let you forget Pallas. I will never forget her and you shall*

A SMALL PLANET OF OUR OWN 61

know the love she had for you . . . the love for the whole world of Mytilene, too!"

Seria had developed hormone shots to produce milk in herself so she and Pallas could both nurse the baby, but the baby's early arrival precipitated increasing the dose today. Now, she let the baby suckle her breast to satisfy its instinctive need and its mewling quieted. Seria returned Hannah to the bassinet. Then she returned to the loving care she had ahead of her with Pallas, readying her for the Med-staff that had been called earlier. The night had quieted. Security had the crowds under control and daylight was in full splendor as she released the lockgate when the Med-staff came for Pallas.

The birth of the baby, Hannah, was celebrated by the entire population. There was still some rioting, but things were quieter now. Videocasts had one program after another debating the issues. Commonsense and thought-provoking discussions returned Mytilene to near normalcy. Directors and leaders of the communities of the planet debated the issues. At least people were talking now. Some anger was still directed at Seria Donner for having taken such a drastic step forward without realizing the consequences. Grief kept Seria from interviews or confrontations.

Drafts of various proposals were drawn up. But the lines were being established. 'Special class' designation for the new named breed of *Lesborns* seemed destined to become the rule.

Hannah lay in her bassinet by Seria's side each day as she worked. Pain mixed with joy crowded the scientist's days; that beloved child along with Seria's work kept her sane. She returned home each night, exhausted, to rest in the big chair cradling Hannah until she awoke in the small hours and laid her in the bassinet beside her as she fell into bed, to sleep and dream sporadically and restlessly.

The Directorate Board Placement Nomination took place on Hannah's first birthday. It was to be videocast planet-wide. Dr. Seria Donner was looking forward to it. The square was lined with citizens. The crowd was beyond quiet, it was silent, almost menacingly so, made more so by the occasional angry outburst from the citizens. The day had become symbolic of leaving Earth after centuries of brutal inequities, but it was tradition and traditions were emotionally clung to for constancy's sake. But Dr. Seria Donner had something to say. Indeed, she had a lot to say. She stood at the podium in the Great Hall of The Directorate, waiting patiently until all angry invocations stilled.

"I have isolated myself most of these past months. My grief was overwhelming and selfishly, I let it come first. But it has been months of horror, intrigue and fear for this, our planet. It will still be a year of horrendous decision that confronts us. I want you to return in your mind to the very beginning of reaching our planet, our colony.

"Throughout their existence on Earth, our foremothers, Lesbians, were much maligned. We were not tolerated at all until after the first two thousand years. Socially, even then, we were accepted by very few . . . mostly in the sports, film and music industry. Female glass ceilings entered into every accomplishment compared to male businesses. We might be allowed to progress only if we kept our sexual preferences hidden. Even though technology grew with fantastic speed, the leaps didn't include the freedom of choice of sexuality. For years, uninformed or ignorant heterosexuals thought of dangers to their young if exposed to us, wrongly mixing up pedophile perversion with homosexual or lesbian identities. It took many decades before the fact that we considered pedophiles perverted and that, in reality, the majority of pedophiles were heterosexual. We also knew that a child reared by Lesbians would have no greater chance of being Lesbian that a child born and reared by a heterosexual couple so we could bear or adopt a child freely.

When the opportunity came to form our own planet, we leapt at the chance. We were desperate to find a planet where each would be judged on their own accomplishment, their own fiber.

We, of all peoples, should know the cruel string of intolerance. A mother isn't someone who gives birth to a child. Biological mothers have given away their children throughout the centuries. Biological mothers have physically, emotionally and mentally abused their own children. The woman who wakes night after night to tend to the needs of a child is the true mother. She answers every call the child makes whether she has carried that baby in her womb or not. Years of dedication, of teaching it to take responsibility for its actions, preparing it to take its place in society constructively . . ."

The crowd was uniting now, swinging into line of thought behind her. Smatterings of applause were heard throughout the audience.

"We came to Mytilene so we would never again have to fight for our just freedoms. The horror of a proposal such as was made by the First Director that dooms any woman because of class or creed is enormous. Only a person's actions and deeds should determine their worthiness or unworthiness. The Judaic-Christian Bible used the example of Solomon deciding that two women, each claiming a child to be theirs, should cleave the child in two so that each could have half.

"His wisdom quickly unmasked the false claimant. She agreed to his proposal. The real mother begged the other woman to "take the baby" in order to save it from death. Truly, she wore Motherhood like a cloak around her shoulders. Don't let what we left join unto us now! This is Mytilene and, if such a horrible proposal does pass, I will not, cannot place Pallas's and my child in line for the Directorate!

"We are equal and free! I say *"So be it here!"*

Her passion turned the tide. The audience in its entirety erupted in cheers. The roar swept over Seria Donner. Director Lena Barkov, carrying Hannah in her arms, rushed to her side and they embraced, the baby laughing and gurgling in the midst of their warmth.

The First Director, Mason, stood on the other side of the podium. At first, her applause was tentative, but suddenly, it grew stronger and stronger. She heaved a sigh and looked skyward. Striding toward Seria, she loudly exclaimed, "Oh, Sappho! If I could only speak like that I could rule *ten* worlds!" She smiled sadly. "But, would I really want to?"

It was she who had chosen Seria when she was just a young Tech Med student and groomed her, arranging additional tutorial lessons for her. Mason remembered the sincere hug and tears shed when Seria finally graduated with full honors, and Mason's pride with each promotion Seria achieved. Director Mason hadn't considered race nor caste then. She gave her heart completely to the strong young woman who had succeeded so well and who had been her cherished friend for many years now.

"Seria," she whispered through tears. "Seria, you make me ashamed of myself, and so proud of you. I don't know what happened to me. I am the one who is supposed to lead for the good of all, and yet, it was I who lost my way so completely, so suddenly. I've made such a terrible mess of things!"

Dr. Seria Donner removed an arm from around Lena and Hannah's bodies and clasped her old friend to her. Her eyes, too, were filled with tears. "I made a terrible mistake, too!" she thought. *"Pallas always knew that scientific progress must always be tempered with its emotional effect on those who are to receive its benefits. Unless it adds totally to the well-being of a society, it is not progress! Oh, Pallas! I lost my way, too, without you!"*

Then, both laughing and crying at the same time, Seria admonished the First Director.

"Hush now, Ella! We all have a time of crisis in our lives and we all make mistakes. Besides, after all . . . it is never to late to teach an old Lesbian new tricks!"

Kiki

by Laurajean Ermayne

This, the world's first lesbian science fiction story was published in 1947, beating me (FJA) into print by one year. I had written "The Radclyffe Effect" (aka "World of Loneliness" and "For Women Only") and got it rejected during 1947, one perceptive editor delighting me by saying "I would give a limb to be able to publish this unusual story [I'd have settled for printer's ink and the distinction of being the first author of a sapphic sci-fi story] but alas it would be too shocking for our middle-of-the-road readers." So Laurajean Ermayne, made an Honorary Lesbian 53 years ago in 1949 by the Daughters of Bilitis, had the honor of having been published one year before me by editrix Lisa Ben in her legendary pioneering publication *Vice Versa*. Several years ago during a Gaylaxicon convention in Washington/DC, "Kiki" was read to an enchanted audience of Uranians who gave it a great round of applause. Whether straight or gay, we think all female readers of this volume will find the story fascinating.

—FJA

*N*ote: any similarity to persons either sad or gay is strictly coincidental.

The Cosmic Registrar chuckled the day Kiki was born. The Book of Time lay wide open before his x-ray eyes, and he could look into the future, see Kiki as a grown girl. Kiki's parents gave her that odd name because when their little bundle of joy came into the world Mary Pickford (America's Sweetheart) was then starring on the screen in a hit called *Kiki*, and Mr. and Mrs. MacFarland fondly hoped that their little daughter would grow up to have many sweethearts.

She did.

She had *too many* sweethearts, and that was the problem that was perplexing Kiki right now. Boys held no attraction for her. She had realized that since she was 13 and had fallen in love with Manuela, who in turn was in love with her teacher in the film *Mädchen in Uniform*.

Then, when she was 16, Kiki had met Pat. Pat had made her heart go like that: Pat-pat-pitter-pat. Kiki had heard her name in the rain on her window pane, that melancholy afternoon she had sat weeping because her parents were sending her off to college and Pat was staying behind. Tall, raw-boned, masterful Pat—a Gary Cooper in feminine form—whose hard lips crushed on hers and brought the blood to her heart in a rush that threatened to burst it.

Kiki sat morosely in the observation car of the train, and watched the wicked rails clicking off the miles behind her, and sullenly hated them for their callousness, for they would not keep quiet, they kept clacking "Pat . . . Pat . . . Pattity-Pat . . . Pat . . . Pat . . . Pat . . ."

But at college Kiki experienced a different emotion when she met Flora. Everything about Flora was flower-like, from the botany in which she was majoring to the prints of her dresses, the carnation she always wore in her flaxen hair. With Pat, Kiki had been a clinging vine. Flora made her feel differently, herself masterful. Kiki bewildered herself. She had known of her nature for four years now, but at first she had believed herself to be a fluff. Now she felt she was a butch. She did not know that Fate had named her for what she was: Kiki—the kind of Radclyffe girl with a dual nature; now masculine, now feminine.

Flora fascinated Kiki like a tiny hummingbird. Kiki admitted to herself that she was infatuated with Flora. And Flora responded to her ministrations. Like a carefully cultivated American Beauty rose, she blossomed forth with Kiki's attention: Fragile, perfumed, and—thornless. Kiki was superbly happy in her romance with Flora until one day a letter came for her, a letter in a familiar bold backhand script that took her back to nights parked on Hollywood Heights, the feel of a starched shirt pressed against her thin dress, possessive hands clasped on her shoulders, hard white teeth grating against her own in cohesive moments of overpowering desire. A letter from Pat! Pat was coming to visit her over the Christmas holidays!

Nature stretched Kiki on her rack and tortured her more exquisitely in the ensuing 3 days than many a witch in the agonizing era of the Inquisition. Night and day, there was no surcease for Kiki: Her innermost being was assaulted by forces beyond her control; she fought a losing battle of indecision, of turmoil, terror, and trepidation.

She felt weak and watery and very, very fluff when she thought of rough, domineering Pat.

She felt very competent, commanding herself, when she contemplated that dear little elf, that sprite, that fey forest-baby, Flora, who basked in her protective embrace.

Perhaps she merely meant to drug herself into the sleep she desperately needed, to escape for a few blessed hours of relief from the insoluble problem which preyed upon her mind and loosed a migraine monster there to trample with spiked boots over her naked, quivering brain. Or maybe, subconsciously the death-impulse in her mastered her personality. At any rate, Kiki took too many sleeping tablets.

THE COSMIC Registrar had not thought about Kiki for quite some time. He was idly flipping through his book of births and destinies—Kathryn MacFarland—Katrina MacFarland—Kenneth MacFarland—when the name of Kiki MacFarland was forcibly drawn to his attention by the red star opposite it. This indicated a crisis in her life. Adjusting his telescopic eye and tuning his mentality for the wave-band of planet Earth, he projected his vision and mind into the room where Kiki lay unconscious. Death, in his black shroud, stood at her door, about to pass through.

But the end was not yet for Kiki. The red-for-danger disappeared from the Registrar's book, being replaced by a peaceful safe green, as Death was brushed aside from Kiki's door by Life, Life in the person of Nurse Edwina Kincaid, hastily summoned by an alarmed Flora. The Cosmic Registrar focused his power of clairvoyance on the near future, and was mildly puzzled by what he saw there. Curious, he checked the record on Edwina Kincaid.

"Ah," the Registrar nodded in understanding. It would be a happy Christmas for Kiki. Santa had sent her a real present, the solution to her dilemma. Some of Edwina's friends—and Kiki was destined to become the most intimate of them—called her "Eddie." Nurse Kincaid was a "kiki" too.

"Smith leaned forward breathlessly."

Nyusa, Nymph of Darkness

by Catherine L. Moore
and Forrest J Ackerman

"Nymph of Darkness" was first published in the printed fan magazine *Fantasy Magazine*, in April 1935, and professionally published, in an expurgated form, in the December 1939 *Weird Tales*. There is no truth to the rumor that Nyusa was initially known as NY, USA. The January-February 1948 club organ of the Los Angeles Science Fantasy Society, *Shangri-LA*, featured an article by me on the story behind the story "of a collaboration in which I was honored to have my name linked some years ago with the lovely and talented Catherine Moore . . ." To read this article and other information about this Northwest Smith tale, see the "Bonus" material following the story in the *Expanded Science Fiction Worlds of FJA and Friends Plus*, Sense of Wonder Press, 2002.

—FJA

THE THICK VENUSIAN dark of the Ednes waterfront in the hours before dawn is breathless and tense with a nameless awareness, a crouching danger. The shapes that move murkily thru its blackness are not daylight shapes. Sun has never shone upon some of those misshapen figures, and what happens in the dark is better left untold. Not even the Patrol ventures there after the lights are out, and the hours between midnight and dawn are outside the law. If dark things happen there the Patrol never knows of them, or desires to know. Powers move thru the darkness along the waterfront to which even the Patrol bows low.

Thru that breathless blackness, along a street beneath which the breathing waters whispered, Northwest Smith strolled slowly. No prudent man ventures out after midnight along the waterfront of Ednes unless he has urgent business abroad, but from the leisurely gait that carried Smith soundlessly thru the dark he might have been some casual sightseer. He was no stranger to the Ednes waterfront. He knew the danger thru which he strolled so slowly, and under narrowed lids his colorless eyes were like keen steel probes that searched the dark. Now and then he passed a shapeless shadow that dodged aside to give him way. It might have been no more than a shadow. His no-colored eyes did not waver. He went on, alert and wary.

He was passing between two high warehouses that shut out even the faint reflection of light from the city beyond when he first heard that sound of bare, running feet which so surprised him. The patter of frantically fleeing steps is not uncommon along the waterfront, but these were—he listened closer—yes, certainly the feet of a woman or a young boy. Light and quick and desperate. His ears were keen enough to be sure of that. They were coming nearer swiftly. In the blackness even his pale eyes could see nothing, and he drew back against the wall, one hand dropping to the ray gun that hung low on his thigh. He had no desire to meet whatever it was which pursued this fugitive.

But his brows knit as the footsteps turned into the street that led between the warehouses. No woman, of whatever class or kind, ventures into this quarter by night. And he became certain as he listened that those feet were a woman's. There was a measured rhythm about them that suggested the Venusian woman's lovely, swaying gait. He pressed flat against the wall, holding his breath. He wanted no sound to indicate his own presence to the terror from which the woman fled. Ten years before he might have dashed out to her—but ten years along the spaceways teaches a man prudence. Gallantry can be foolhardy sometimes, particularly along the waterfront, where any of a score of things might be in close pursuit. At the thought of what some of those things might be the hair prickled faintly along his neck.

The frantic footsteps came storming down the dark street. He heard the rush of breath thru unseen nostrils, the gasp of laboring lungs. Then those desperate feet stumbled a bit, faltered, turned aside. Out of the dark a hurtling figure plunged full-tilt against him. His startled arms closed about a woman—a girl—a young girl, beautifully made, muscular and firmly curved under his startled hands—and quite naked.

He released her rather quickly.

"Earthman!" she gasped in an agony of breathlessness. "Oh, hide me, hide me! Quick!"

There was no time to wonder how she knew his origin or to ask from what she fled, for before the words had left her lips a queer, greenish glow appeared around the corner of the warehouse. It revealed a pile of barrels at Smith's elbow, and he shoved the exhausted girl behind them in one quick motion, drawing his gun and flattening himself still further against the wall.

Yet it was no nameless monster which appeared around the corner of the building. A man's dark shape came into view. A squat figure, broad and misshapen. The light radiated from a flash-tube in his hand, and it was an oddly diffused and indirect light, not like an ordinary flash's clear beam, for it lighted the man behind it as well as what lay before the tube, as if a greenish, luminous fog were spreading sluggishly from the lens.

The man came forward with a queer, shuffling gait. Something about him made Smith's flesh crawl unaccountably. What it was he could not be sure, for the green glow of the tube did not give a clear light, and the man was little more than a squat shadow moving unevenly behind the light tube's luminance.

He must have seen Smith almost immediately, for he came straight across the street to where the Earthman stood against the wall, gun in hand. Behind the glowing tube-mouth Smith could make out a pale blur of face with two dark splotches for eyes. It was a fat face, unseemly in its puffy pallor, like some grub that has fed too long upon corruption. No expression crossed it at the sight of the tall spaceman in his leather garb, leaning against the wall and fingering a ready gun. Indeed, there was nothing to arouse surprise in the Earthman's attitude against the wall, or in his drawn gun. It was what any nightfarer along the waterfront would have done at the appearance of such a green, unearthly glow in the perilous dark.

Neither spoke. After a single long glance at the silent Smith, the newcomer began to switch his diffused light to and fro about the street in obvious search. Smith listened, but the girl had stilled her sobbing breath and no sound betrayed her hiding place. The sluggish searcher went on slowly down the street, casting his foggy light before him. Its luminance faded by degrees as he receded from view, a black, misshapen shadow haloed in unholy radiance.

When utter dark had descended once more Smith holstered his gun and called to the girl in a low voice. The all but soundless murmur of bare feet on the pavement heralded her approach, the hurrying of still unruly breath.

"Thank you," she said softly. "I—I hope you need never know what horror you have saved me from."

"Who are you?" he demanded. "How did you know me?"

"They call me Nyusa. I did not know you, save that I think you are of Earth, and perhaps—trustworthy. Great Shar must have guided my flight along the streets tonight, for I think your kind is rare by the sea edge, after dark."

"But—can you see me?"

"No. But a Martian, or one of my own countrymen, would not so quickly have released a girl who dashed into his arms by night—as I am." In the dark Smith grinned. It had been purely reflexive, that release of her when his hand realized her nudity. But he might as well take credit for it. "You had better go quickly now," she went on, "there is such danger here that—"

Abruptly the low voice broke off. Smith could hear nothing, but he sensed a tensing of the girl by his side, a strained listening. And presently he caught a faraway sound, a curious muffled wheezing, as if something short-winded and heavy were making laborious haste. It was growing nearer. The girl's caught breath was loud in the stillness at his elbow.

"Quick!" she gasped. "Oh, hurry!"

Her hand on his arm tugged him on in the direction the squat black searcher had taken. "Faster!" And her anxious hands pulled him into a run. Feeling a little ridiculous, he loped thru the dark beside her with long, easy strides, hearing nothing but the soft fall of his own boots and the scurrying of the girl's bare feet, and far behind the distant wheezing breath, growing fainter.

Twice she turned him with a gentle push into some new byway. Then they paused while she tugged at an unseen door, and after that they ran down an alley so narrow that Smith's broad shoulders brushed its walls. The place smelled of fish and decayed wood and the salt of the seas. The pavement rose in broad, shallow steps, and they went thru another door, and the girl pulled at his arm with a breathed,

"We're safe now. Wait."

He heard the door close behind them, and light feet pattered on boards.

"Lift me," she said after a moment. "I can't reach the light."

Cool, firm fingers touched his neck. Gingerly in the dark he found her waist and swung her aloft at arm's length. Between his hands that waist was supple and smoothly muscled and slim as a reed. He heard the fumble of uncertain fingers overhead. Then in an abrupt dazzle light sprang up about him.

He swore in a choked undertone and sprang back, dropping his hands. For he had looked to see a girl's body close to his face, and he saw nothing. His hands had gripped—nothing. He had been holding aloft a smooth and supple—nothingness.

He heard the fall of a material body on the floor, and a gasp and cry of pain, but still he could see nothing, and he fell back another step, lifting an uncertain hand to his eyes and muttering a dazed Martian oath. For look tho he would, he could see no one but himself in the little bare room the light had revealed. Yet the girl's voice was speaking from empty air. "What— why did—Oh, I see!" and a little ripple of laughter. "You have never heard of Nyusa?"

The repetition of the name struck a chord of remote memory in the Earthman's mind. Somewhere lately he had heard that word spoken. Where and by whom he could not recall, but it aroused in his memory a nebulous chord of night peril and the unknown. He was suddenly glad of the gun at his side, and a keener awareness was in the pale gaze he sent around the tiny room.

"No," he said. "I have never heard the name before now."

"I am Nyusa."

"But where are you?"

She laughed again, a soft ripple of mirth honey sweet with the Venusian woman's traditionally lovely voice.

"Here. I am not visible to men's eyes. I was born so. I was born—" Here the rippling voice sobered, and a tinge of solemnity crept in. "—I was born of a strange mating, Earthman. My mother was a Venusian, but my father my father was Darkness. I can't explain . . . But because of that strain of Dark in me, I am invisible. And because of it I—I am not free."

"Why? Who holds you captive? How could anyone imprison an invisibility?"

"The—Nov." Her voice was the faintest breath of sound, and again, at the strange word, a prickle of nameless unease ran thru Smith's memory. Somewhere he had heard that name before, and the remembrance it roused was too nebulous to put into words, but it was ominous. Nyusa's breathing whisper went on very softly at his shoulder. It was a queer, unreal feeling, that, to be standing alone in a bare room and a girl's sweet, muted murmur in his ears from empty air.

"The Nov—they dwell underground. They are the last remnant of a very old race. And they are the priests who worship That which was my father. The Darkness. They prison me for purposes of their own.

"You see, my heritage from the lady who bore me was her own lovely human shape, but the Thing which was my father bequeathed to his child stranger things than invisibility. I am of a color outside the range of human eyes. And I have entry into—into other lands than this. Strange lands, lovely and far—Oh, but so damnably near! If I could only pass by the bars the Nov have set to shut me away. For they need me in their dark worship, and here I must stay, prisoned in the hot, muddy world which is all they themselves can ever know. They have a light—you saw it, the green glow in the hands of the Nov who pursued me thru the dark tonight—which makes me visible to human eyes. Something in its color combines with that strange color which is mine to produce a hue that falls within man's range of vision. If he had found me I would have been—punished—severely, because I fled tonight. And the Nov's punishments are—not nice.

"To make sure that I shall not escape them, they have set a guardian to dog my footsteps—the thing that wheezed on my track tonight—Dolf. He sprang from some frightful union of material and immaterial. He is partly elemental, partly animal. I can't tell you fully. And he is cloudy, nebulous—but very real, as you would have discovered had he caught us just now. He has a taste for human blood which makes him invaluable, tho I am safe, for I am only half human, and the Nov—well, they are not wholly human either. They—"

She broke off suddenly. Outside the door Smith's keen ears had caught a shuffle of vague feet upon the ground, and thru the cracks came very clearly the snuffle of wheezing breath. Nyusa's bare feet pattered swiftly across the boards, and from near the door came a series of low, sibilant hissings and whistlings in a clearer tone than the sounds the great Dolf made. The queer noise crescendoed to a sharp command, and he heard a subdued snuffling and shuffling outside and the sound of great, shapeless feet moving off over flagstones. At his shoulder Nyusa sighed.

"It worked that time," she said. "Sometimes I can command him, by virtue of my father's strength in me. The Nov do not know that. Queer, isn't it—they never seem to remember that I might have inherited more from their god than my invisibility and my access to other worlds. They punish me and prison me and command me to their service like some temple dancing girl—me, the half divine! I think—yes, I think that someday the doors will open at my own command, and I shall go out into those other worlds. I wonder—could I do it now?"

The voice faded into a murmurous undertone. Smith realized that she had all but forgotten his presence at the realization of her own potentialities. And again that prickle of unease went over him. She was half human, but half only. Who could say what strange qualities were rooted in her, springing from no human seed? Qualities that might someday blossom into—into—well, he had no words for what he was thinking of, but he hoped not to be there on the day the Nov tried her too far.

Hesitant footsteps beside him called back his attention sharply. She was moving away, a step at a time. He could hear the sound of her bare feet on the boards. They had almost reached the opposite wall now, one slow step after another. And then suddenly those hesitating footfalls were running, faster, faster, diminishing in distance. No door opened, no aperture in the walls, but Nyusa's bare feet pattered eagerly away. He was aware briefly of the vastnesses of dimensions beyond our paltry three, distances down which a girl's bare feet could go storming in scornful violation of the laws that held him fast. From far away he heard those steps falter. He thought he heard the sound of fists beating against resistance, the very remote echo of a sob. Then slowly the patter of bare feet returned. Almost he could see a dragging head and hopelessly slumped shoulders as the reluctant footfalls drew nearer, nearer, entered the room again. At his shoulder she said in a subdued voice,

"Not yet. I have never gone so far before, but the way is still barred. The Nov are too strong—for a while. But I know, now. I know! I am a god's daughter, and strong too. Not again shall I flee before the Nov's pursuit, or fear because Dolf follows. I am the child of Darkness, and they shall know it! They—"

Sharply into her exultant voice broke a moment of blackness that cut off her words with the abruptness of a knife stroke. It was of an instant's duration only, and as the light came on again a queer wash of rosy luminance spread thru the room and faded again, as if a ripple of color had flowed past. Nyusa sighed.

'That's what I fled," she confided. "I am not afraid now—but I do not like it. You had best go—or no, for Dolf still watches the door I entered by. Wait—let me think."

Silence for a moment, while the last flush of rose faded from the air, to be followed by a ripple of fresh color that faded in turn. Three times Smith saw the tide of red flow thru the room and die away before Nyusa's hand fell upon his arm and her voice murmured from emptiness,

"Come. I must hide you somewhere while I perform my ritual. That color is the signal that the rites are to begin—the Nov's command for my presence. There is no escape for you until they call Dolf away, for I could not guide you to a door without having him sense my presence there and follow. No, you must hide—hide and watch me dance. Would you like that? A sight which no eyes that are wholly human have ever seen before! Come."

Invisible hands pushed open the door in the opposite wall and pulled him thru. Stumbling a little at the newness of being guided by an unseen creature, Smith followed down a corridor thru which waves of rosy light flowed and faded. The way twisted many times, but no doors opened from it nor did they meet anyone in the five minutes or so that elapsed as they went down the hallway thru the pulsing color of the air.

At the end a great barred door blocked their passage. Nyusa released him for an instant, and he heard her feet whisper on the floor, her unseen hands fumble with something metallic. Then a section of the floor sank. He was looking down a shaft around which narrow stairs spiraled, very steeply. It was typically a Venusian structure, and very ancient. He had descended other spiraled shafts before now, to strange destinations. Wondering what lay in store for him at the foot of this, he yielded to the girl's clinging hands and went down slowly, gripping the rail.

He had gone a long way before the small, invisible hands plucked at his arm again and drew him thru an opening in the rock thru which the shaft sank. A short corridor led into darkness. At its end they paused, Smith blinking in the queer, pale darkness which veiled the great cavern that lay before them.

"Wait here," whispered Nyusa. "You should be safe enough in the dark. No one ever uses this passage but myself. I will return after the ceremony." Hands brushed his briefly, and she was gone. Smith pressed back against the wall and drew his gun, flicking the catch experimentally to be sure it would answer any sudden need. Then he settled back to watch.

Before him a vast domed chamber stretched. He could see only a little of it in the strange dark pallor of the place. The floor shone with the deep sheen of marble, black as quiet water underground. And as the minutes passed he became aware of motion and life in the pale dark. Voices murmured, feet shuffled softly, forms moved thru the distance. The Nov were taking their places for the ceremony. He could see the dim outlines of their mass, far off in the dark.

After a while, a deep, sonorous chanting began from nowhere and everywhere, swelling and filling the cavern and echoing from the domed ceiling in reverberant monotones. There were other sounds whose meaning he could not fathom, queer pipings and whistlings like the voice in which Nyusa had commanded Dolf, but invested with a solemnity that gave them depth and power. He could feel fervor building up around the dome of the cavern, the queer, wild fervor and ecstasy of an unknown cult for a nameless god. He gripped his gun and waited.

Now, distantly and very vaguely, a luminance was forming in the center of the arched roof. It strengthened and deepened and began to rain downward toward the darkly shining floor in long streamers like webs of tangible light. In the mirrored floor replicas of light reached upward, mistily reflecting. It was a sight of such weird and enchanting loveliness that Smith held his breath, watching. And now green began to flush the streaming webs, a strange, foggy green like the light the Nov had flashed thru the waterfront streets in pursuit of Nyusa. Recognizing the color, he was not surprised when a shape began to dawn in the midst of that raining light. A girl's shape, half transparent, slim and lovely and unreal.

In the dark pallor of the cavern, under the green luminance of the circling light, she lifted her arms in a long, slow, sweeping motion, lighter than smoke, and moved on tiptoe, very delicately. Then the light shimmered, and she was dancing. Smith leaned forward breathlessly, gun hanging forgotten in his hand, watching her dance. It was so lovely that afterward he could never be sure he had not dreamed.

She was so nebulous in the streaming radiance of the light, so utterly unreal, so fragile, so exquisitely colored in the strangest tints of violet and blue and frosty silver, and queerly translucent, like a moonstone. She was more unreal now, when she was visible, than she had ever seemed before his eyes beheld her. Then his hands had told him of her firm and slender roundness—now she was a wraith, transparent, dream-like, dancing soundlessly in a rain of lunar color.

She wove magic with her dancing body as she moved, and the dance was more intricate and symbolic and sinuous than any wholly human creature could have trod. She scarcely touched the floor, moving above her reflection in the polished stone like a lovely moonlight ghost floating in mid-darkness while green moon-fire rained all about her.

With difficulty Smith wrenched his eyes away from that nebulous creature treading her own reflection as she danced. He was searching for the sources of those voices he had heard, and in the green, revealing light he saw them ringing the cavern in numbers greater than he had dreamed. The Nov, intent as one man upon the shimmering figure before them. And at what he saw he was glad he could not see them clearly. He remembered Nyusa's words, "—the Nov are not wholly human either." Veiled tho they were in the misty radiance and the pallor of the dark, he could see that it was so. He had seen it, unrealizing, in the face of that squat pursuer who had passed him in the street.

They were all thick, shapeless, all darkly robed and white-faced as slugs are white. Their formless features, intent and emotionless, had a soft, unstable quality, not shaped with any human certainty. He did not stare too long at any one face, for fear he might make out its queer lack of contour, or understand the portent of that slug-white instability of feature.

Nyusa's dance ended in a long, floating whirl of unhuman lightness. She sank to the floor in deep obeisance, prostrate upon her own reflection. From the front ranks of the assembled Nov a dark figure stepped with upraised arms. Obediently Nyusa rose. From that dark form, from the sluglike, unfeatured face, a twittering whistle broke, and Nyusa's voice echoed the sounds unerringly, her voice blending with the other's in a chant without words.

Smith was so intent upon watching that he was not aware of the soft shuffling in the dark behind him until the wheeze of labored breath sounded almost upon his neck. The thing was all but on him before that sixth sense which had saved him so often before now shrieked a warning and he whirled with a choked oath of surprise and shock, swinging up his gun and confronting a dim, shapeless immensity out of which a dull glow of greenish light stared at him. His gun spat blue flame, and from the imponderable thing a whistling scream rang quaveringly, echoing across the cavern and cutting short that wordless chant between the Nov and the girl.

Then the dark bulk of Dolf lurched forward and fell smotheringly upon Smith. It bore him to the floor under an engulfing weight which was only half real, but chokingly thick in his nostrils. He seemed almost to be breathing Dolf's substance, like heavy mist. Blinded and gasping, he fought the curiously nebulous thing that was smothering him, knowing he must win free in a few seconds' time, for Dolf's scream must bring the Nov upon him at any moment now. But for all his efforts he could not break away, and something indescribable and nauseous was fumbling for his throat. When he felt its blind searching his struggles redoubled convulsively, and after a frantic moment he staggered free, gulping in clean air and staring out into the dark with wide eyes, trying to make out what manner of horror he had grappled with. He could see nothing but that dull flare, as of a single eye, glowing upon him from an imponderable bulk which blended with the dark.

Dolf was coming at him again. He heard great feet shuffling, and the wheezing breath came fast. From behind the shouts of the Nov rose loud, and the noise of running men, and above all the high, clear call of Nyusa, screaming something in a language without words. Dolf was upon him. That revolting, unseen member fumbled again at his throat. He thrust hard against the yielding bulk and his gun flared again, blue-hot in the dark, full into the midst of Dolf's unstable blackness.

He felt the mass of the half-seen monster jerk convulsively. A high, whistling scream rang out, shrill and agonized, and the sucking organ dropped from his throat. The dim glow of vision dulled in the shape's cloudy midst. Then it flickered, went out. Somehow there was a puff of blackness that dissolved into misty nothing all about him, and the dark shape that had been Dolf was gone. Half elemental, he had gone back into nothingness as he died.

Smith drew a deep breath and swung round to front the first of the oncoming Nov. They were almost upon him, and their numbers were overwhelming, but his flame-gun swung its long arc of destruction as they swarmed in and almost a dozen of the squat, dark figures must have fallen to that deadly scythe before he went down under the weight of them. Pudgily soft fingers wrenched the gun from his hand, and he did not fight hard to retain it, for he remembered the blunt-nosed little flame-thrower in its holder under his arm and was not minded that they should discover it in any body-to-body fight.

Then he was jerked to his feet and thrust forward toward the pale radiance that still held Nyusa in its heart, like a translucent prisoner in a cage of light. A little dazed by the swiftness of events, Smith went on unsteadily in their midst. He towered head and shoulders above them, and his eyes were averted. He tried not to flinch from the soft, fish white hands urging him forward, not to look too closely into the faces of the squat things swarming so near. No, they were not men. He knew that more surely than ever from this close sight of the puffy, featureless faces ringing him round.

At the brink of the raining light which housed Nyusa the Nov who had led the chanting stood apart, watching impassively as the tall prisoner came forward in his swarm of captors. There was command about this Nov, an air of regality and calm, and he was white as death, luminous as a corpse in the lunar reflections of the light.

They halted Smith before him. After one glance into that moveless, unfeatured face, slug pale, the Earthman did not look again. His eyes strayed to Nyusa, beyond the Nov who fronted him, and at what he saw took faint hope again. There was no trace of fear in her poise. She stood straight and quiet, watching, and he sensed a powerful reserve about her. She looked the god's daughter she was, standing there in the showering luminance, translucent as some immortal.

Said the leader Nov, in a voice that came deeply from somewhere within him, tho his unfeatured face did not stir.

"How came you here?"

"I brought him," Nyusa's voice sounded steadily across the space that parted them.

The Nov swung round, amazement in every line of his squatness.

"You?" he exclaimed. "You brought an alien to witness the worship of the god I serve? How dared—"

"I brought one who had befriended me to witness my dance before my father," said Nyusa in so ominously gentle a tone that the Nov did not realize for a moment the significance of her words. He spluttered Venusian blasphemy in a choked voice.

"You shall die!" he yelled thickly. "Both of you shall die by such torment—"

"S-s-s-zt!"

Nyusa's whistling hiss was only a sibilance to Smith, but it cut the Nov's furious flow abruptly short. He went dead quiet, and Smith thought he saw a sicker pallor than before spreading over the slug face turned to Nyusa.

"Had you forgotten?" she queried gently. "Forgotten that my father is That which you worship? Dare you raise your voice to threaten Its daughter? Dare you, little worm-man?"

A gasp ran over the throng behind Smith. Greenish anger suffused the pallid face of the priest. He spluttered wordlessly and surged forward, short arms clawing toward the taunting girl. Smith's hand, darting inside his coat, was quicker than the clutch of his captors. The blue flare of his flamethrower leaped out in a tongue of dazzling heat to lick at the plunging Nov. He spun round dizzily and screamed once, high and shrill, and sank in a dark, puddly heap to the floor.

There was a moment of the deepest quiet. The shapeless faces of the Nov were turned in one stricken stare to that oddly fluid lump upon the floor which had been their leader. Then in the pack behind Smith a low rumble began to rise, the mutter of many voices. He had heard that sound before— the dawning roar of a fanatic mob. He knew that it meant death. Setting his teeth, he spun to face them, hand closing firmer about the butt of his flamethrower.

The mutter grew deeper, louder. Someone yelled, "Kill! Kill!" and a forward surge in the thick crowd of faces swayed the mass toward him. Then above that rising clamor Nyusa's voice rang clear.

"Stop!" she called. In sheer surprise the murderous mob paused, eyes turning toward the unreal figure in her cage of radiance. Even Smith darted a glance over his shoulder, flame gun poised in mid-air, his finger hesitating upon the catch. And at what they saw the crowd fell silent, the Earthman froze into stunned immobility as he watched what was happening under the rain of light.

Nyusa's translucent arms were lifted, her head thrown back. Like a figure of triumph carved out of moonstone she stood poised, while all about her in the misty, lunar colors of the light a darkness was forming like fog that clung to her outstretched arms and swathed her half-real body. And it was darkness not like any night that Smith had ever seen before. No words in any tongue could describe it, for it was not a darkness made for any vocal creature to see. It was a blasphemy and an outrage against the eyes, against all that man hopes and believes and is. The darkness of the incredible, the utterly alien and opposed.

Smith's gun fell from shaking fingers. He pressed both hands to his eyes to shut out that indescribably awful sight, and all about him heard a long, soft sighing as the Nov sank to their faces upon the shining floor. In that deathly hush Nyusa spoke again, vibrant with conscious godhood and underrun with a queer, tingling ripple of inhumanity. It was the voice of one to whom the unknown lies open, to whom that utterly alien and dreadful blackness is akin.

"By the Darkness I command you," she said coldly. "Let this man go free. I leave you now, and I shall never return. Give thanks that a worse punishment than this is not visited upon you who paid no homage to the daughter of Darkness."

NYUSA, NYMPH OF DARKNESS

Then for a swift instant something indescribable happened. Remotely Smith was aware that the Blackness which had shrouded Nyusa was spreading thru him, permeating him with the chill of that blasphemous dark, a hideous pervasion of his innermost being. For that instant he was drowned in a darkness which made his very atoms shudder to its touch. And if it was dreadful to him, the voiceless shriek that rose simultaneously from all about him gave evidence how much more dreadfully their god's touch fell upon the Nov. Not with his ears, but with some nameless sense quickened by that moment of alien blackness, he was aware of the scream of intolerable anguish, the writhing of extra human torment which the Nov underwent in that one timeless moment.

Out of his tense awareness, out of the spreading black, he was roused by a touch that startled him into forgetfulness of that dreadful dark. The touch of a girl's mouth upon his, a tingling pressure of sweet parted lips that stirred delicately against his own. He stood tense, not moving a muscle, while Nyusa's mouth clung to his in a long, close kiss like no kiss he had ever taken before. There was a coldness in it, a chill as alien as the dark that had gathered about her translucency under the light, a shuddering cold that struck thru him in one long, deep-rooted shock of frigid revulsion. And there was warmth in it, headily stirring the pulse which that cold had congealed.

In that instant while those clinging lips melted to his mouth, he was a battleground for emotions as alien as light and dark. The cold touch of Darkness, the hot touch of love. Alienity's shuddering, frozen stab, and humanity's blood-stirring throb of answer to the warm mouth's challenge. It was a mingling of such utter opposites that for an instant he was racked by forces that sent his senses reeling. There was danger in the conflict, the threat of madness in such irreconcilable forces that his brain blurred with the effort of compassing them.

Just in time the clinging lips dropped away. He stood alone in the reeling dark, that perilous kiss burning upon his memory as the world steadied about him. In that dizzy instant he heard what the rest, in their oblivious agony, could not have realized. He heard a girl's bare feet pattering softly along some incline, up and up, faster and faster. Now they were above his head. He did not look up. He knew he would have seen nothing. He knew Nyusa walked a way that no sense of his could perceive. He heard her feet break into an eager little run. He heard her laugh once, lightly, and the laugh cut off by the sound of a closing door. Then quiet.

Without warning, on the heels of that sound, he felt a tremendous release all about him. The darkness had lifted. He opened his eyes upon a dimly lighted cavern from which that rain of light had vanished. The Nov lay in quivering windrows, about his feet, their shapeless faces hidden. Otherwise the whole vast place was empty as far as his eyes could pierce the dark. Smith bent and picked up his fallen gun. He kicked the nearest Nov ungently.

"Show me the way out of this place," he ordered, sheathing the flamethrower under his arm.

Obediently the sluggish creature stumbled to his feet.

The Miracle of the Lily

by Clare Winger Harris

In person Mrs. Harris was the typical American housewife. But what an imagination! She first came to the attention of the "scientifiction" world of 1927 by winning the third prize for a story based on a Frank R. Paul cover, "The Fate of the Poseidonia". "The Miracle of the Lily" is her acknowledged masterpiece and she went on to collaborate with Dr. Miles J. Breuer, a pioneering sf author, on a work worthy of Olaf Stapledon, "A Baby on Neptune". A book of her short stories was published during her lifetime, *Away from the Here & Now*.

—FJA

I.

*S*ince the comparatively recent résumé of the ancient order of agriculture I, Nathano, have been asked to set down the extraordinary events of the past two thousand years, at the beginning of which time the supremacy of man, chief of the mammals, threatened to come to an untimely end.

Ever since the dawn of life upon this globe, life which it seemed had crept from the slime of the sea, only two great types had been the rulers; the reptiles and the mammals. The former held undisputed sway for eons, but gave way eventually before the smaller, but intellectually superior mammals. Man himself, the supreme example of the ability of life to govern and control inanimate matter, was master of the world with apparently none to dispute his right. Yet, so blinded was he with pride over the continued exercise of his power on earth over lower types of mammals and the nearly extinct reptiles, that he failed to notice the slow but steady rise of another branch of life, different from his own; smaller, it is true, but no smaller than he had been in comparison with the mighty reptilian monsters that roamed the swamps in the Mesozoic times.

These new enemies of man, though seldom attacking him personally, threatened his downfall by destroying his chief means of sustenance, so that by the close of the twentieth century, strange and daring projects were laid before the various governments of the world with an idea of fighting man's insect enemies to the finish. These pests were growing in size, multiplying so rapidly and destroying so much vegetation, that eventually no plants would be left to sustain human life. Humanity suddenly woke to the realization that it might suffer the fate of the nearly extinct reptiles. Would mankind be able to prevent the encroachment of the insects? And at last man *knew* that unless drastic measures were taken *at once*, a third great class of life was on the brink of terrestrial sovereignty.

Of course no great changes in development come suddenly. Slow evolutionary progress had brought us up to the point, where, with the application of outside pressure, we were ready to handle a situation that, a century before, would have overwhelmed us.

I reproduce here in part a lecture delivered by a great American scientist, a talk which, sent by radio throughout the world, changed the destiny of mankind: but whether for good or for evil I will leave you to judge at the conclusion of this story.

"Only in comparatively recent times has man succeeded in conquering natural enemies; flood, storm, inclemency of climate, distance, and now we face an encroaching menace to the whole of humanity. Have we learned more and more of truth and of the laws that control matter only to succumb to the first real danger that threatens us with extermination? Surely, no matter what the cost, you will rally to the solution of our problem, and I believe, friends, that I have discovered the answer to the enigma.

"I know that many of you, like my friend Professor Fair, will believe my ideas too extreme, but I am convinced that unless you are willing to put behind you those notions which are old and not utilitarian, you cannot hope to cope with the present situation.

"Already, in the past few decades, you have realized the utter futility of encumbering yourselves with superfluous possessions that had no useful virtue, but which, for various sentimental reasons, you continue to hoard, thus lessening the degree of your life's efficiency by using for it time and attention that should have been applied to the practical work of life's accomplishments. You have given these things up slowly, but I am now going to ask you to relinquish the rest of them *quickly*; everything that interferes in any way with the immediate disposal of our enemies, the insects."

At this point, it seems that my worthy ancestor, Professor Fair, objected to the scientist's words, asserting that efficiency at the expense of some of the sentimental virtues was undesirable and not conducive to happiness, the real goal of man. The scientist, in his turn, argued that happiness was available only through a perfect adaptability to one's environment, and that efficiency *sans* love, mercy and the softer sentiments was the short cut to human bliss.

It took a number of years for the scientist to put over his scheme of salvation, but in the end he succeeded, not so much from the persuasiveness of his words, as because prompt action of some sort was necessary. There was not enough food to feed the people of the earth. Fruit and vegetables were becoming a thing of the past. Too much protein food in the form of meat and fish was injuring the race, and at last the people realized that, for fruits and vegetables, or their nutritive equivalent, they must turn from the field to the laboratory; from the farmer to the chemist. Synthetic food was the solution to the problem. There was no longer any use in planting and caring for food stuffs destined to become the nourishment of man's most deadly enemy.

The last planting took place in 2900, but there was no harvest, the voracious insects took every green shoot as soon as it appeared, and even trees, that had previously withstood the attacks of the huge insects, were by this time, stripped of every vestige of greenery.

The vegetable world suddenly ceased to exist. Over the barren plains, which had been gradually filling with vast cities, man-made fires brought devastation to every living bit of greenery, so that in all the world there was no food for the insect pests.

II

Extract from the diary of Delfair, a descendent of Professor Fair, who had opposed the daring scientist.

From the borders of the great state-city of Iowa, I was witness to the passing of one of the great kingdoms of earth—the vegetable, and I cannot find words to express the grief that overwhelms me as I write of its demise, for I loved all growing things. Many of us realized that Earth was no longer beautiful; but if beauty meant death; better life in the sterility of the metropolis.

The viciousness of the thwarted insects was a menace that we had foreseen and yet failed to take into adequate account. On the city-state borderland, life is constantly imperiled by the attacks of well organized bodies of our dreaded foe.

(*Note:* The organization that now exists among the ants, bees and other insects, testifies to the possibility of the development of military tactics among them in the centuries to come.)

Robbed of their source of food, they have become emboldened to such an extent that they will take any risks to carry human beings away for food, and after one of their well organized raids, the toll of human life is appalling.

But the great chemical laboratories where our synthetic food is made, and our oxygen plants, we thought were impregnable to their attacks. In that we were mistaken.

Let me say briefly that since the destruction of all vegetation which furnished a part of the oxygen essential to human life, it became necessary to manufacture this gas artificially for general diffusion through the atmosphere.

I was flying to my work, which is in Oxygen Plant No. 21, when I noticed a peculiar thing on upper speedway near Food Plant No. 3,439. Although it was night, the various levels of the state-city were illuminated as brightly as by day. A pleasure vehicle was going with prodigious speed westward. I looked after it in amazement. It was unquestionably the car of Erci, my co-worker at Oxygen Plant No. 21. I recognized the gay color of its body, but to verify my suspicion beyond the question of a doubt, I turned my volplane in pursuit and made out the familiar license number. What was Eric doing away from the plant before I had arrived to relieve him from duty?

In hot pursuit, I sped above the car to the very border of the state-city, wondering what unheard of errand took him to the land of the enemy, for the car came to a sudden stop at the edge of what had once been an agricultural area. Miles ahead of me stretched an enormous expanse of black sterility; at my back was the teeming metropolis, five levels high—if one counted the hangar-level, which did not cover the residence sections.

I had not long to wait, for almost immediately my friend appeared. What a sight he presented to my incredulous gaze! He was literally covered from head to foot with two-inch ants, that next to the beetles, had proved the greatest menace in their attacks upon humanity. With wild incoherent cries he fled over the rock and stubble-burned earth.

As soon as my stunned senses permitted, I swooped down toward him to effect a rescue, but even as my plane touched the barren earth, I saw that I was too late, for he fell, borne down by the vicious attacks of his myriad foes. I knew it was useless for me to set foot upon the ground, for my fate would be that of Eric. I rose ten feet and seizing my poison-gas weapon, let its contents out upon the tiny black evil things that swarmed below. I did not bother with my mask, for I planned to rise immediately, and it was not a moment too soon. From across the wasteland, a dark cloud eclipsed the stars and I saw coming toward me a horde of flying ants interspersed with larger flying insects, all bent upon my annihilation. I now took my mask and prepared to turn more gas upon my pursuers, but alas, I had used every atom of it in my attack upon the non-flying ants! I had no recourse but flight, and to this I immediately resorted, knowing that I could outdistance my pursuers.

When I could no longer see them, I removed my gas mask. A suffocating sensation seized me. I could not breathe! How high had I flown in my endeavor to escape the flying ants? I leaned over the side of my plane expecting to see the city far, far below me. What was my utter amazement when I discovered that I was scarcely a thousand feet high! It was not an altitude that was depriving me of life-giving oxygen.

A drop of three hundred feet showed me inert specks of humanity lying about the streets. Then I knew; *the oxygen plant was not in operation!* In another minute I had on my oxygen mask, which was attached to a small, portable tank for emergency use, and I rushed for the vicinity of the plant. There I witnessed the first signs of life. Men equipped with oxygen masks were trying to force entrance into the locked building. Being an employee, I possessed knowledge of the combination of the great lock, and I opened the door, only to be greeted by a swarm of ants that commenced a concerted attack upon us.

The floor seemed to be covered with a moving black rug, the corner nearest the door appearing to unravel as we entered, and it was but a few seconds before we were covered with the clinging, biting creatures, who fought with a supernatural energy born of despair. Two very active ants succeeded in getting under my helmet. The bite of their sharp mandibles and the effect of their poisonous formic acid became intolerable. Did I dare remove my mask while the air about me was foul with the gas discharged from the weapons of my allies? While I felt the attacks elsewhere upon my body gradually diminishing as the insects succumbed to the deadly fumes, the two upon my face waxed more vicious under the protection of my mask. One at each eye, they were trying to blind me. The pain was unbearable. Better the suffocating death-gas than the torture of lacerated eyes! Frantically I removed the headgear and tore at the black fiends. Strange to tell, I discovered that I could breathe near the vicinity of the great oxygen tanks, where enough oxygen lingered to support life at least temporarily. The two vicious insects, no longer protected by my gas-mask, scurried from me like rats from a sinking ship and disappeared behind the oxygen tanks.

This attack of our enemies, though unsuccessful on their part, was dire in it significance, for it had shown more cunning and ingenuity than anything that had ever preceded it. Heretofore, their onslaughts had been confined to direct attacks upon us personally or upon the synthetic-food laboratories, but in this last raid they had shown an amazing cleverness that portended future disaster, unless they were checked at once. It was obvious that they had ingeniously planned to smother us by the suspension of work at the oxygen plant, knowing that they themselves could exist in an atmosphere containing a greater percentage of carbon-dioxide. Their scheme, then, was to raid our laboratories for food.

III

A Continuation Delfair's Account

Although it was evident that the cessation of all plant-life spelled inevitable doom for the insect inhabitants of Earth, their extermination did not follow as rapidly as one might have supposed. There were years of internecine warfare. The insects continued to thrive, though in decreasing numbers, upon stolen laboratory foods, bodies of human beings and finally upon each other; at first capturing enemy species and at last even resorting to cannibalistic procedure. Their rapacity grew in inverse proportion to their waning numbers, until the meeting of even an isolated insect might mean death, unless one were equipped with poison gas and prepared to use it upon a second's notice.

I am an old man now, though I have not yet lived quite two centuries, but I am happy in the knowledge that I have lived to see the last living insect which was held in captivity. It was an excellent specimen of the stag-beetle (*Lucanus*) and the years have testified that it was the sole survivor of a form of life that might have succeeded man upon this planet. This beetle was caught weeks after we had previously seen what was supposed to be the last living thing upon the globe, barring man and the sea-life. Untiring search for years has failed to reveal any more insects, so that at last man rests secure in the knowledge that he is monarch of all he surveys.

I have heard that long, long ago man used to gaze with a fearful fascination upon the reptilian creatures which he displaced, and just so did he view this lone specimen of a type of life that might have covered the face of the earth, but for man's ingenuity.

It was this unholy lure that drew me one day to view the captive beetle in his case in district 404 at Universapolis. I was amazed at the size of the creature, for it looked larger than when I had seen it by television, but I reasoned that upon that occasion there had been no object near with which to compare its size. True, the broadcaster had announced its dimensions, but the statistics concretely given had failed to register a perfect realization of its prodigious proportions.

As I approached the cage, the creature was lying with its dorsal covering toward me and I judged to measured fourteen inches from one extremity to the other. Its smooth horny sheath gleamed in the bright artificial light. (It was confined to the third level.) As I stood there, mentally conjuring a picture of a world overrun with billions of such creatures as the one before me, the keeper approached the case with a meal-portion of synthetic food. Although the food has no odor, the beetle sensed the man's approach, for it rose on its jointed legs and came toward us, its horn-like prongs moving threateningly; then apparently remembering its confinement, and the impotency of an attack; it subsided and quickly ate the food which had been placed within its prison.

The food consumed, it lifted itself to its hind legs, partially supported by a box, and turned its great eyes upon me. I have never been regarded with such utter malevolence before. The detestation was almost tangible and I shuddered involuntarily. As plainly as if he spoke, I knew that Lucanus was perfectly cognizant of the situation and in his gaze I read the concentrated hatred of an entire defeated race.

I had no desire to gloat over his misfortune, rather a great pity toward him welled up in me. I pictured myself alone, the last of my kind, held up for ridicule before the swarming hordes of insects who had conquered my people, and I knew that life would no longer be worth living.

Whether he sensed my pity or not I do not know, but he continued to survey me with unmitigated rage, as if he would convey to me the information that his was an implacable hatred that would outlast eternity.

Not long after this he died, and a world long since intolerant of ceremony, surprised itself by interring the beetle's remains in a golden casket, accompanied by pomp and splendor.

I have lived many long years since that memorable event, and undoubtedly my days here are numbered, but I can pass on happily, convinced that in this sphere man's conquest of his environment is supreme.

IV

In a direct line of descent from Professor Fair and Delfair, the author of the preceding chapter, comes Thanor, whose journal is given in this chapter.

Am I a true product of the year 2928? Sometimes I am convinced that I am hopelessly old-fashioned, an anachronism, that should have existed a thousand years ago. In no other way can I account for the dissatisfaction I feel in a world where efficiency has at last reached a maximum.

I am told that I spring from a line of ancestors who were not readily acclimated to changing conditions. I love beauty, yet I see none of it here. There are many who think our lofty buildings that tower two and three thousand feet into the air are beautiful, but while they are architectural splendors, they do not represent the kind of loveliness I crave. Only when I visit the sea do I feel any satisfaction for a certain yearning in my soul. The ocean alone shows the handiwork of God. The land bears evidence only of man.

As I read back through the diaries of my sentimental ancestors I find occasional glowing descriptions of the world that was; the world before the insects menaced human existence. Trees, plants and flowers brought delight into the lives of people as they wandered among them in vast open spaces, I am told, where the earth was soft beneath the feet, and flying creatures, called birds, sang among the greenery. True, I learned that many people had not enough to eat, and that uncontrollable passions governed them, but I do believe it must have been more interesting than this methodical, unemotional existence. I cannot understand why many people were poor, for I am told that nature as manifested in the vegetable kingdom was very prolific; so much so that year after year quantities of food rotted on the ground. The fault, I find by my reading, was not with Nature but with man's economic system which is now perfect, though this perfection really brings few of us happiness, I think.

Now there is no waste, all is converted into food. Long ago man learned how to reduce all matter to its constituent elements, of which there are nearly a hundred in number, and from them to rebuild compounds for food. The old axiom that nothing is created or destroyed, but merely changed from one form to another, has stood the test of ages. Man, as the agent of God, has simply performed the miracle of transmutation himself instead of waiting for natural forces to accomplish it as in the old days.

At first humanity was horrified when it was decreed that it must relinquish its dead to the laboratory. For too many eons had man closely associated the soul and body, failing to comprehend the body as merely a material agent, through which the spirit functioned. When man knew at last of the eternal qualities of spirit, he ceased to regard the discarded body with referential awe, and saw in it only the same molecular constituents which comprised all matter about him. He recognized only material basically the same as that of stone or metal; material to be reduced to its atomic elements and rebuilt into matter that would render service to living humanity; that portion of matter wherein spirit functions.

The drab monotony of life is appalling. Is it possible that man had reached his height a thousand years ago and should have been willing to resign Earth's sovereignty to a coming order or creatures destined to be man's worthy successor in the eons to come? It seems that life is interesting only when there is a struggle, a goal to be reached through an evolutionary process. Once the goal is attained, all progress ceases. The huge reptiles of preglacial ages rose to supremacy by virtue of their great size, and yet was it not the excessive

THE MIRACLE OF THE LILY

bulk of those creatures that finally wiped them out of existence? Nature, it seems, avoids extremes. She allows the fantastic to develop for a while and then wipes the slate clean for a new order of development. Is it not conceivable that man could destroy himself through excessive development of his nervous system, and give place for the future evolution of a comparatively simple form of life, such as the insects were at man's height of developmental? This, it seems to me, was the great plan; a scheme with which man dared to interfere and for which he is now paying by the boredom of existence.

The earth's population is decreasing so rapidly, that I fear another thousand years will see a lifeless planet hurtling through space. It seems to me that only a miracle will save us now.

The Original Writer, Nathano, Resumes the Narrative

My ancestor, Thanor, of ten centuries ago, according to the records he gave to my great-grandfather, seems to voice the general despair of humanity which, bad enough in his times, has reached the *nth* power in my day. A soulless world is gradually dying from self-inflicted boredom.

As I have ascertained from the perusal of the journals of my forebears, even antedating the extermination of the insects, I come of a stock that clings with sentimental tenacity to the things that made life worthwhile in the old days. If the world at large knew of my emotional musings concerning past ages, it would scarcely tolerate me, but surrounded by my thought-insulator, I often indulge in what fancies I will, and such meditation, coupled with a love for a few ancient relics from the past, have led me to a most amazing discovery.

Several months ago I found among my family relics a golden receptacle two feet long, one and a half in width and one in depth, which I found, upon opening, to contain many tiny square compartments, each filled with minute objects of slightly varying size, texture and color.

"Not sand!" I exclaimed as I closely examined the little particles of matter.

Food? After eating some, I was convinced that their nutritive value was small in comparison with a similar quantity of the products of our laboratories. What were the mysterious objects?

Just as I was about to close the lid again, convinced that I had one oversentimentalized ancestor, whose gift to posterity was absolutely useless, my pocket-radio buzzed and the voice of my friend Stentor, the interplanetary broadcaster, issued from the tiny instrument.

"If you're going to be home this afternoon," said Stentor, "I'll skate over. I have some interesting news."

I consented, for I thought I would share my "find" with this friend whom I loved above all others, but before he arrived I had again hidden my golden chest, for I had decided to await the development of events before sharing its mysterious secret with another. It was well that I did this for Stentor was so filled with the importance of his own news that he could have given me little attention at first.

"Well, what is your interesting news?" I asked after he was comfortably seated in my adjustable chair.

"You'd never guess," he replied with irritating leisureliness.

"Does it pertain to Mars or Venus?" I queried. "What news of our neighbor planets?"

"You may know it has nothing to do with the self-satisfied Martians," answered the broadcaster, "but the Venusians have a very serious problem confronting them. It is in connection with the same old difficulty they have had every since interplanetary radio was developed forty years ago. You remember, that, in their second communication with us, they told us of their continual warfare on insect pests that were destroying all vegetable food? Well, last night after general broadcasting had ceased, I was surprised to hear the voice of the Venusian broadcaster. He is suggesting that we get up a scientific expedition to Venus to help the natives of his unfortunate planet solve their insect problem as we did ours. He says the Martians turn a deaf ear to their plea for help, but he expects sympathy and assistance from Earth who has so recently solved these problems for herself."

I was dumbfounded at Stentor's news.

"But the Venusians are farther advanced mechanically than we," I objected, "though they are behind us in the natural sciences. They could much more easily solve the difficulties of space-flying than we could."

"That is true," agreed Stentor, "but if we are to render them material aid in freeing their world from devastating insects, we must get to Venus. The past four decades have proved that we cannot help them merely by verbal instructions."

"Now, last night," Stentor continued, with warming enthusiasm, "Wanyana, the Venusian broadcaster, informed me that scientists on Venus are developing interplanetary television. This, if successful, will prove highly beneficial in facilitating communication, and it may even do away with the necessity of interplanetary travel, which I think is centuries ahead of us, yet."

"Television, though so common here on Earth and on Venus, has seemed an impossibility across the ethereal void," I said, "but if it becomes a reality, I believe it will be the Venusians who will take the initiative, though of course they will be helpless without our friendly cooperation. In return for the mechanical instructions they have given us from time to time, I think it no more than right that we should try to give them all the help possible in freeing their world, as ours has been freed, of the insects that threaten their very existence. Personally, therefore, I hope it can be done through radio and television rather than by personal excursions."

"I believe you are right," he admitted, "but I hope we can be of service to them soon. Ever since I have served in the capacity of official interplanetary broadcaster, I have liked the spirit of goodfellowship shown by the Venusians through their spokesman, Wanyana. The impression is favorable in contrast to the superciliousness of the inhabitants of Mars."

We conversed for some time, but at length he rose to take his leave. It was then I ventured to broach the subject that was uppermost in my thoughts.

"I want to show you something, Stentor," I said, going into an adjoining room for my precious box and returning shortly with it. "A relic from the days of an ancestor named Delfair, who lived at the time the last insect, a beetle, was kept in captivity. Judging from his personal account, Delfair was fully aware of the significance of the changed times in which he lived, and contrary to the majority of his contemporaries, possessed a sentimentality of soul that has proved an historical asset to future generations. Look, my friend, these he left to posterity!"

I deposited the heavy casket on a table between us and lifted the lid, revealing to Stentor the mystifying particles.

The face of Stentor was eloquent of astonishment. Not unnaturally his mind took somewhat the same route as mine had followed previously, though he added atomic-power units to the list of possibilities. He shook his head in perplexity.

"Whatever they are, there must have been a real purpose behind their preservation," he said at last. "You say this old fellow Delfair witnessed the passing of the insects? What sort of fellow was he? Likely to be up to any tricks?"

"Not at all," I asserted rather indignantly, "he seemed a very serious minded chap; worked in an oxygen-plant and took and active part in the last warfare between men and insects."

Suddenly Stentor stooped over and scooped up some of the minute particles into the palm of his hand—and then he uttered a maniacal shriek and flung them into the air.

"Great God, man, do you know what they are?" he screamed, shaking violently.

"No, I do not," I replied quietly, with an attempt at dignity I did not feel.

"Insect eggs!" he cried, and shuddering with terror, he made for the door.

I caught him on the threshold and pulled him forcibly back into the room.

"Now see here," I said sternly, "not a word of this to anyone. Do you understand? I will test out your theory in every possible way but I want no public interference."

At first he was obstinate, but finally yielded to threats when supplications were impotent.

"I will test them," I said, "and will endeavor to keep hatchlings under absolute control, should they prove to be what you suspect."

It was time for the evening broadcasting, so he left, promising to keep our secret and leaving me regretting that I had taken another into my confidence.

VI

For days following my unfortunate experience with Stentor, I experimented upon the tiny objects that had so terrified him. I subjected them to various tests for the purpose of ascertaining whether or not they bore evidence of life, whether in egg, pupa or larva stages of development. And to all my experiments, there was but one answer. No life was manifest. Yet I was not satisfied, for chemical tests showed that they were composed of organic matter. Here was an inexplicable enigma! Many times I was on the verge of consigning the entire contents of the chest to the flames. I seemed to see in my mind's eye the world again over-ridden with insects, and that calamity due to the indiscretions of one man! My next impulse was to turn over my problem to scientists, when a suspicion of the truth dawned on me. These were seeds, the germs of plant-life, and they might grow. But alas, where? Over all the earth man has spread his artificial dominion. The state-city has been succeeded by what could be termed the nation-city, for one great floor of concrete or rock covers the country.

I resolved to try an experiment, the far-reaching influence of which I did not at that time suspect. Beneath the lowest level of the community edifice in which I dwell, I removed, by means of a small atomic excavator, a slab of concrete large enough to admit my body. I let myself down into the hold and felt my feet resting on a soft dark substance that I knew to be dirt. I hastily filled a box of this, and after replacing the concrete slab, returned to my room, where I proceeded to plant a variety of the seeds.

Being a product of an age when practically to wish for a thing in a material sense is to have it, I experienced the greatest impatience, while waiting for any evidence of plant-life to become manifest. Daily, yes, hourly, I watched the soil for signs of a type of life long since departed form the earth, and was about convinced that the germ of life could not have survived the centuries, when a tiny blade of green proved to me that a miracle, more wonderful to me than the works of man through the ages, was taking place before my eyes. This was an enigma so complex and yet so simple, that one recognized it in a direct revelation of Nature.

Daily and weekly I watched in secret the botanical miracle. It was my one obsession. I was amazed at the fascination it held for me—a man who viewed the marvels of the thirty-fourth century with unemotional complacency. It showed me that Nature is manifest in the simple things which mankind has chosen to ignore.

Then one morning, when I awoke, a white blossom displayed its immaculate beauty and sent forth its delicate fragrance into the air. The lily, a symbol of new life, resurrection! I felt within me the stirring of strange emotions I had long believed dead in the bosom of man. But the message must not be for me alone. As of old, the lily would be the symbol of life for all!

With trembling hands, I carried my precious burden to a front window where it might be witnessed by all who passed by. The first day there were few who saw it, for only rarely do men and women walk; they usually ride in speeding vehicles of one kind or another, or employ electric skates, a delightful means of locomotion, which gives the body some exercise. The fourth city level, which is reserved for skaters and pedestrians, is kept in a smooth glass-like condition. And so it was only the occasional pedestrian, walking on the outer border of the fourth level, upon which my window faced, who first carried the news of the growing plant to the world, and it was not long before it was necessary for civic authorities to disperse the crowds that thronged to my window for a glimpse of a miracle in green and white.

When I showed my beautiful plant to Stentor, he was most profuse in his apology and came to my rooms every day to watch it unfold and develop, but the majority of people, long used to business-like efficiency, were intolerant of the sentimental emotions that swayed a small minority, and I was commanded to dispose of the lily. But a figurative seed had been planted in the human heart, a seed that could not be disposed of so readily, and this seed ripened and grew until it finally bore fruit.

VII

It is a very different picture of humanity that I paint ten years after the last entry in my diary. My new vocation is farming, but it is farming on a far more intensive scale than had been done two thousand years ago. Our crops never fail, for temperature and rainfall are regulated artificially. But we attribute our success principally to the total absence of insect pests. Our small agricultural areas dot the country like the parks of ancient days and supply us with a type of food, no more nourishing, but more appetizing than that produced in the laboratories. Truly we are living in a marvelous age! If the earth is ours completely, why may we not turn our thoughts toward the other planets in our solar-system? For the past ten or eleven years the Venusians have repeatedly urged us to come and assist them in their battle for life. I believe it is our duty to help them.

Tomorrow will be a great day for us and especially for Stentor, as the new interplanetary television is to be tested, and it is possible that for the first time in history, we shall see our neighbors in the infinity of space. Although the people of Venus were about a thousand years behind us in many respects, they have made wonderful progress with radio and television. We have been in radio communication with them for the last half century and they shared with us the joy of the establishment of our Eden. They have always been greatly interested in hearing Stentor tell the story of our subjugation of the insects that threatened to wipe us out of existence, for they have exactly that problem to solve now; judging from their reports, we fear that theirs is a losing battle. Tomorrow we shall converse face to face with the Venusians! It will be an event second in importance only to the first radio communications interchanged fifty years ago. Stentor's excitement exceeds that displayed at the time of the discovery of the seeds.

Well it is over and the experiment was a success, but alas for the revelation!

The great assembly halls all over the continent were packed with humanity eager to catch a first glimpse of the Venusians. Prior to the test, we sent our message of friendship and good will by radio, and received a reciprocal one from our inter-planetary neighbors. Alas, we were ignorant at that time! Then the television receiving apparatus was put into operation, and we sat with breathless interest, our eyes intent upon the crystal screen before us. I sat near Stentor and noted the feverish ardor with which he watched for the first glimpse of Wanyana.

At first hazy mist-like specters seemed to glide across the screen. We knew these figures were not in correct perspective. Finally, one object gradually became more opaque, its outlines could be seen clearly. Then across that vast assemblage, as well as thousands of others throughout the world, there swept a wave of speechless horror, as its full significance burst upon mankind.

The figure that stood facing us was a huge six-legged beetle, not identical in every detail with our earthly enemies of past years, but unmistakably an insect of gigantic proportions! Of course it could not see us, for our broadcaster was not to appear until afterward, but it spoke, voice of Wanyana, the

The figure that stood facing us was a huge six-legged beetle ... an insect of gigantic proportions ... Suddenly, the Venusian was joined by another being, a colossal ant, who bore in his forelegs a tiny light-colored object, which he handed to the beetle-announcer, who took it and held it forward for our closer inspection. It seemed to be a tiny ape, but was so small, we could not ascertain for a certainty.

leading Venusian radio broadcaster. Stentor grabbed my arm, uttered an inarticulate cry and would have fallen but for my timely support.

"Friends of Earth, as you call your world," began the object of horror, "this is a momentous occasion in the annals of the twin planets, and we are looking forward to seeing one of you, and preferably Stentor, for the first time, as you are now viewing one of us. We have listened many times, with interest, to your story of the insect pests which threatened to follow you as lords of your planet. As you have often heard us tell, we are likewise molested with insects. Our fight is a losing one, unless we can soon exterminate them."

Suddenly, the Venusian was joined by another being, a colossal ant, who bore in his forelegs a tiny light-colored object which he handed to the beetle-announcer who took it and held it forward for our closer inspection. It seemed to be a tiny ape, but was so small we could not ascertain for a certainty. We were convinced, however, that it was a mammalian creature, an "insect" pest of Venus. Yet in it we recognized rudimentary man as we know him on earth!

There was no question as to the direction in which sympathies instinctively turned, yet reason told us that our pity should be given to the intelligent reigning race who had risen to its present mental attainment through eons of time. By some quirk or freak of nature, way back in the beginning, life had developed in the form of insects instead of mammals. Or (the thought was repellent) had insects in the past succeeded in displacing mammals, as they might have done here on earth?

There was no more television that night. Stentor would not appear, so disturbed was he by the sight of the Venusians, but in the morning, he talked to them by radio and explained the very natural antipathy we experienced in seeing them or in having them see us.

Now they no longer urge us to construct etherships and go to help them dispose of their "insects." I think they are afraid of us, and their very fear has aroused in mankind an unholy desire to conquer them.

I am against it. Have we not had enough of war in the past? We have subdued our own world and should be content with that, instead of seeking new worlds to conquer. But life is too easy here. I can plainly see that. Much as he may seem to dislike it, man is not happy unless he has some enemy to overcome, some difficulty to surmount.

Alas my greatest fears for man were groundless!

A short time ago, when I went out into my field to see how my crops were faring, I found a six-pronged beetle voraciously eating. No—man will not need to go to Venus to fight "insects."

The Three Marked Pennies

by Mary Elizabeth Counselman

> The most amazing thing about this story to us is that in the last 68 years since its first publication it has not been anthologized to death or made as a twilight zone-type TV show or an Academy Award-winning short film. No special effects at all are required for its production or hair-raising denouement.
>
> The author was born in 1911, so it is not impossible that she is still alive; Jack Williamson, Lloyd Arthur Eshbach, and David Ackerman Kyle are (we're happy to say) still with us. But when she was last sent a check it was never cashed: a mystery. As far as is known, she never married and has spent most of her life on a houseboat in Alabama. If Mary's still alive, we'll be happy to send her some unmarked dollar bills; otherwise her share of the royalties will be donated to Andre Norton's High Hallack project.
>
> —FJA/PK

Everyone agreed, after it was over, that the whole thing was the conception of a twisted brain, a game of chess played by a madman—in which the pieces, instead of carved bits of ivory or ebony, were human beings.

It was odd that no one doubted the authenticity of the "contest." The public seems never for a moment to have considered it the prank of a practical joker, or even a publicity stunt. Jeff Haverty, editor of the *News*, advanced a theory that the affair was meant to be a clever, if rather elaborate, psychological experiment—which would end in the revealing of the originator's identity and a big laugh for every one.

Perhaps it was the glamorous manner of announcement that gave the thing such wide-spread interest. Blankville (as I shall call the Southern town of about 30,000 people in which the affair occurred) awoke one April morning to find all its trees, telephone poles, house-sides and store-fronts plastered with a strange sign. There were scores of them, written on yellow copy-paper on an ordinary typewriter. The sign read:

"During this day of April 15, three pennies will find their way into the pockets of this city. On each penny there will be a well-defined mark. One is a square; one is a circle; and one is a cross. These three pennies will change hands often, as do all coins, and on the seventh day after this announcement (April 21) the possessor of each marked penny will receive a gift.

"To the first: $100,000 in cash.

"To the second: A trip around the world.

"To the third: Death.

"The answer to this riddle lies in the marks on the three coins: circle, square, and cross. Which of these symbolizes wealth? Which, travel? Which, death? The answer is not an obvious one.

"To him who finds it and obtains the first penny, $100,000 will be sent without delay. To him who has the second penny, a first-class ticket for the earliest world-touring steamer to sail will be presented. But to the possessor of the third marked coin will be given—death. If you are afraid your penny is the third, give it away—but it may be the first or the second!'

"Show your marked penny to the editor of the 'News' on April 21, giving your name and address. He will know nothing of the contest until he reads one of these signs. He is requested to publish the names of the three possessors of the coins April 21, with the mark on the penny each holds.

"It will do no good to mark a coin of your own, as the dates of the true coins will be sent to Editor Haverty."

BY NOON every one had read the notice, and the city was buzzing with excitement. Clerks began to examine the contents of cash register drawers. Hands rummaged in pockets and purses. Stores and banks were flooded with customers who wanted silver changed to coppers.

Jeff Haverty was the target for a barrage of queries, and his evening edition came out with a lengthy editorial embodying all he knew about the mystery, which was exactly nothing. A note had come that morning with the rest of his mail—a note unsigned, and typewritten on the same yellow paper in a plain stamped envelope with the postmark of that city. It said merely: "Circle—1920. Square—1909. Cross—1928. Please do not reveal these dates until after April 21."

Haverty complied with the request, and played up the story for all it was worth.

The first penny was found in the street by a small boy, who promptly took it to his father. His father, in turn, palmed it off hurriedly on his barber, who gave it in change to a patron before he noted the deep cross cut in the coin's surface.

The patron took it to his wife, who immediately paid it to the grocer. "It's too long a chance, honey!" she silenced her mate's protests. "I don't like the idea of that death-threat in the notice . . . and this certainly must be the third penny. What else could that little cross stand for? Crosses over graves—don't you see the significance?"

And when that explanation was wafted abroad, the cross-marked penny began to changes hands with increasing rapidity.

The other two pennies bobbed up before dusk—one marked with a small perfect square, the other with a neat circle.

The square-marked penny was discovered in a slot-machine by the proprietor of the Busy Bee Café. There was no way it could have got there, he reported, mystified and a little frightened. Only four people, all of them old patrons, had been in the café that day. And not one of them had been near the slot-machine—located at the back of the place as it was, and filled with stale chewing gum, which at a glance, was worth nobody's penny. Furthermore, the proprietor had examined the thing for a chance coin the night before and had left it empty when he locked up; yet there was the square-marked penny nestling alone in the slot-machine at closing time on April 15.

He had stared at the coin a long time before passing it in change to an elderly spinster.

"It ain't worth it," he muttered to himself. "I got a restaurant that's makin' me a thin livin', and I ain't in no hurry to get myself bumped off, on the long chance I might get that hundred thousand or that trip instead. No-sirree!"

The spinster took one look at the marked penny, gave a short mouse-like squeak, and flung it into the gutter as though it were a tarantula.

"My land!" she quavered. "I don't want that thing in my pocket-book!"

But she dreamed that night of foreign ports, of coolies jabbering in a brittle tongue, of barracuda fins cutting the surface of deep blue water, and the ruins of ancient cities.

A Negro workman picked up the penny next morning and clung to it all day, dreaming of Harlem, before he succumbed at last to gnawing fear. And the square-marked penny changed hands once more.

The circle-marked penny was first noted in a stack of coins by a teller of the Farmer's Trust.

"We get marked coins every now and then," he said. "I didn't notice this one especially—it may have been here for days."

He pocketed it gleefully, but discovered with a twinge of dismay next morning that he had passed it out to some one without noticing it.

"I wanted to keep it!" he sighed. "For better or worse!"

He glowered at the stacks of some one else's money before him, and wondered furtively how many tellers ever really escaped with stolen goods.

A fruit-seller had received the penny. He eyed it dubiously. "Mebbe you bring-a me those mon, heh?" He showed it to his fat, greasy wife, who made the sign of the horns against the "evil eye."

"T'row away!" she commanded shrilly. "She iss bad lock!"

Her spouse shrugged and sailed the circle-marked coin across the street. A ragged child pounced on it and scuttered away to buy a twist of licorice. And the circle-marked penny changed hands once more—clutched at by avaricious fingers, stared at by eyes grown sick of familiar scenes, relinquished again by the power of fear.

Those who came into brief possession of the three coins were fretted by the drag and shove of conflicting advice.

"Keep it!" some urged. "Think! It may mean a trip around the world! Paris! China! London! Oh, why couldn't I have got the thing?"

"Give it away!" others admonished. "Maybe it's the third penny—you can't tell. Maybe the symbols don't mean what they seem to, and the square one is the death-penny! I'd throw it away, if I were you."

"No! No!" still others cried. "Hang on to it! It may bring you $100,000. A *hundred thousand dollars!* In these times! Why, fellow, you'd be the same as a millionaire!"

The meaning of the three symbols was on every one's tongue, and no one agreed with his neighbor's solution to the riddle.

"It's as plain as the nose on my face," one man would declare. "The circle represents the globe—the travel-penny, see?"

"No, no. The cross means that. 'Cross' the seas, don't you get it? Sort of a pun effect. The circle means money—shape of a coin, understand?"

"And the square one—?"

"A grave. A square hole for a coffin, see? Death. It's quite simple. I wish I could get hold of that circle one!"

"You're crazy! The cross one is for death—everybody says so. And believe me, everybody's getting rid of it as soon as they get it! It may be a joke of some kind . . . no danger at all . . . but I wouldn't like to be the holder of that cross-marked penny when April 21 rolls around!"

"I'd keep it and wait till the other two had got what was due them. Then, if mine turned out to be the wrong one, I'd throw it away!" one man said importantly.

"But he won't pay up till all three pennies are accounted for, I shouldn't think," another answered him. "And maybe the offer doesn't hold good after April 21—and you'd be losing $100,000 or a world tour just because you're scared to find out!"

"That's a big stake, man," another murmured. "But frankly, I wouldn't like to take the chance. He might give me his third gift!"

"He," was how every one designated the unknown originator of the contest; though, of course, there was not more clue to his sex than to his identity.

"He must be rich," some said, "to offer such expensive prizes."

"And crazy!" others exploded, "threatening to kill the third one. He'll never get away with it!"

"But clever," still others admitted, "to think up the whole business. He knows human nature, whoever he is. I'm inclined to agree with Haverty—it's all a sort of psychological experiment. He's trying to see whether desire for travel or greed for money is stronger than fear of death."

"Does he mean to pay up, do you think?"

"That remains to be seen!"

ON THE sixth day, Blankville had reached a pitch of excitement amounting to almost hysteria. No one could work for wondering about the outcome of the bizarre test on the morrow.

It was known that a grocer's delivery boy held the square-marked coin, for he had been boasting of his indifference as to whether or not the square did represent a yawning grave. He exhibited the penny freely, making jokes about what he intended to do with his hundred thousand dollars—but on the morning of the last day he lost his nerve. Seeing a blind beggar woman huddled in her favorite corner between two shops, he passed close to her and surreptitiously dropped the cent piece into her box of pencils.

"I had it!" he wailed to a friend after he had reached the grocery. "I had it right here in my pocket last night, and now it's gone! See, I've got a hole in the darn' thing—the penny must have dropped out!"

It was also known who held the circle-marked penny. A young soda clerk, with the sort of ready smile that customers like to see across a marble counter, had discovered the coin and fished it from the cash drawer, exulting over his good fortune.

"Bud Skinner's got the circle penny," people told one another, wavering between anxiety and gladness. "I hope the kid *does* get that world tour—it'd tickle him so! He seems to get such a kick out of life; it's a sin he has to be stuck in this slow burg!"

Finally, it was found who held the cross-marked cent piece. "Carlton . . . poor devil!" people murmured in subdued tones. "Death would be a godsend to him. Wonder he hasn't shot himself before this. Guess he just hasn't the nerve."

The man with the cross-marked penny smiled bitterly. "I hope this blasted little symbol means what they all think it means!" he confided to a friend.

At last the eagerly awaited day came. A crowd formed in the street outside the newspaper office to see the three possessors of the three marked coins show Haverty their pennies and give him their names to publish. For their benefit the editor met the trio on the sidewalk outside the building, so that all might see them.

The evening edition ran the three people's photographs, with the name, address, and the mark on each one's penny under each picture. Blankville read . . . and held its breath.

ON THE morning of April 22, the old blind beggar woman sat in her accustomed place, musing on the excitement of the previous day, when several people had led her—she knew by the odor of fish from the market across the street—to the newspaper office. There some one had asked her name and many other puzzling things which had bewildered her until she had almost burst into tears.

"Let me alone!" she had whimpered. "I ask only enough food to keep from starving, and a place to sleep. Why are you pushing me around like this and yelling at me? Let me go back to my corner! I don't like all this confusion and strangeness that I can't see—it frightens me!"

Then they had told her something about a marked penny they had found in her alms-box, and other things about a large sum of money and some impending danger that threatened her. She was glad when they led her back to her cranny between the shops.

Now as she sat in her accustomed spot, nodding comfortably and humming a little under her breath, a paper fluttered down into her lap. She felt the stiff oblong, knew it was an envelope, and called a bystander to her side.

"Open this for me, will you?" she requested. "Is it a letter? Read it to me."

The bystander tore open the envelope and frowned. "It's a note," he told her. "Typewritten, and it's not signed. It just says—what the devil?—just says: 'The four corners of the earth are exactly the same!' And . . . hey! look at this! . . . oh, I'm sorry; I forgot you're . . . it's a steamship ticket for a world tour! Look, didn't you have one of the marked pennies?"

The blink woman nodded drowsily. "Yes, the one with the square, they said." She sighed faintly. "I had hoped I would get the money, or . . . the other, so I would never have to beg again."

"Well, here's your ticket." The bystander held it out to her uncertainly. "Don't you want to take it?" as the beggar made no move to take it.

"No," snapped the blind woman. "What good would it be to me?" She seized the ticket in sudden rage, and tore it into bits.

THE THREE MARKED PENNIES

At nearly the same hour, Kenneth Carleton was receiving a fat manila envelope from the postman. He frowned as he squinted at the local postmark over the stamp. His friend Evans stood beside him, paler than Carleton.

"Open it, open it!" he urged. "Read it—no, don't open it, Ken. I'm scared! After all . . . it's a terrible way to go. Not knowing where the blow's coming from, and—"

Carlton emitted a macabre chuckle, ripping open the heavy envelope. "It's the best break I've had in years, Jim. I'm glad! Glad, Jim, do you hear? It will be quick, I hope . . . and painless. What's this, I wonder. A treatise on how to blow off the top of your head?" He shook the contents of the letter onto a table, and then, after a moment, he began to laugh . . . mirthlessly . . . hideously.

His friend stared at the little heap of crisp bills, all of a larger denomination than he had ever seen before. "The money! You get the hundred thousand, Ken! I can't believe . . . " He broke off to snatch up a slip of yellow paper among the bills. *"Wealth is the greatest cross a man can bear,"* he read aloud the typewritten words. "It doesn't make sense . . . wealth? Then . . . the cross-mark stood for wealth? I don't understand."

Carlton's laughter cracked. "He has depth, that bird—whoever he is! Nice irony there, Jim—wealth being a burden instead of the blessing most people consider it. I suppose he's right, at that. But I wonder if he knows the really ironic part of this act of his little play? A hundred thousand dollars to a man with—cancer. Well, Jim, I have a month or less to spend it in . . . one more damnable month to suffer through before it's all over!"

His terrible laughter rose again, until his friend had to clap hands to ears, shutting out the sound.

But the strangest part of the whole affair was Bud Skinner's death. Just after the rush hour at noon, he had found a small package, addressed to him, on a back counter in the drug store. Eagerly he tore off the brown paper wrappings, a dozen or so friends crowding about him.

A curiously wrought silver box was what he found. He pressed the catch with trembling fingers and snapped back the lid. An instant later his face took on a queer expression—and he slid noiselessly to the tile floor of the drug store.

The ensuing police investigation unearthed nothing at all, except that young Skinner had been poisoned with *crotalin*—snake venom—administered through a pin-prick on his thumb when he pressed the trick catch of the little silver box.

This, and the typewritten note in the otherwise empty box: *"Life ends where it began—nowhere,"* were all they found as an explanation of the clerk's death. Nor was anything else ever brought to light about the mysterious contest of the three marked pennies—which are probably still in circulation somewhere in the United States.

The Man from Space

by L. Taylor Hanson

A Ghost-Like Alien?
An animated flower?
You've never met a "spaceman" like this one from this lady's imagination. Incidentally, when the story was published the editor didn't realize L. stood for Louise and spoke of the author as being a man.
Forry Ackerman assures me he spoke to her over the phone during World War II and she was definitely female.
We thought the illustrations by Wesso (Hans Waldemar Wessolowski) worth reprinting.

—PK

"From the days of superstition when the sudden appearance of a new star portended the birth of a great man or a terrible destruction by war and plague, up to the present time when these phenomena are studied with telescope and spectroscope, the brilliant flashing bursts of novae continue to interest mankind."

Professor Kepling hesitated and glanced suspiciously over his class. It was a warm afternoon—languorously warm. I yawned and looked at my frat brother, Jim Turner. We had been to the same dance the night before and I was wondering if he would manage to fight off the tendency to go to sleep, as well as I was doing so far. To my surprise Jim was leaning forward eagerly, drinking in every word. I remembered then that he was a sort of "bug" on astronomy, nursing a hopeless wish that he had been born a century or two later so that he might travel to other worlds. I shrugged my shoulders as the cultured voice of the gray-haired professor droned on.

"History has recorded many instances of the appearance of novae, but the first one to be studied by a mind more scientifically than superstitiously inclined was observed by Tycho on the evening of November 11, 1572. It seems that in going toward his home on that night, the celebrated Danish astronomer saw people standing out in the streets, staring and pointing at the sky directly overhead, where he was astonished to see an unknown star of surpassing brilliance. The new star even outshone the planet Jupiter. In fact, there was not another star in the whole heavens that could be compared to it.

"He had of course, only imperfect instruments with which to study it, but with these he determined as best he could its exact location, and faithfully followed its subsequent changes. It kept on brightening until at last it even shone in the daytime. Finally, however, it began to fade, turning red as it did so. In March it disappeared from the interested astronomer's searching sight and has never been seen since."

My eyelids were getting heavy. I jerked them open, determined to get the points of the lecture for I knew by Jim's fascinated stare that he would be "raring to go" for a good discussion as soon as the bell rang.

"There have been others of less brilliance," the well-modulated tones droned on, "but the next famous nova occurred on the evening of February 22, 1901. An amateur astronomer in Edinburgh was the first man to see the new star blazing in the constellation of Perseus. He telegraphed the news all over the world. Luckily, the heavens had been photographed on February 19th and the spot where the star now shone, showed no trace in the photograph.

"Within a few hours of its discovery, however, it was ablaze—outshining Capella and exceeding first magnitude. But like a terrible conflagration, it burned only a few days and then began to die away with a red glow, its light diminishing and then flaring up again spasmodically every few days, though none of these revivals equaled the splendor of the first outburst. Finally it died away to ninth magnitude.

"This time, however, there was a sequel to the story. Some six months later photographs showed that this star was now surrounded by a spiral nebula which spread from it like an expanding wave. Four condensations seemed to gather in this fiery ring and revolve about the main nucleus of the sun, but in time these condensations faded from sight and the novae became only a faintly nebulous star of less than ninth magnitude.

I CAUGHT myself nodding and straightened quickly. If only that man could speak more roughly, but the combination of late hours and a lulling voice was liable to get me yet. . . .

"The question naturally arises—how do these terrible conflagrations come about? In answer, several theories have been advanced. The first one proposed was that two suns traveling in opposite directions through the uncharted realms of space had collided. A direct head-on collision would of course be rather rare, though quite possible. But novae are not rare spec-

THE MAN FROM SPACE

tacles. Every year the telescope brings us the tale of more novae, even though most of them are at far too great a distance to be seen with the naked eye.

"Let us suppose, however, that some of these suns, instead of actually colliding with each other, simply pass a little too close. Large bodies such as suns are extremely dangerous to each other. They have terrible tidal pulls. Suppose that each should come close enough for the tidal pull of the other to tear open its photospheric envelope. The result would be that the incandescent central masses would collide like two terrific clashing waves of fire.

"A second theory, advanced by Seelinger of Munich, was that a collision between a blazing star or sun and a vast dark nebula or swarm of meteors—remnants of some destroyed system—would cause such a spectacle as a nova presents. This theory underwent modifications from others until it was finally proposed that a dark or burnt-out sun, plunging into a swarm of meteors, would have its dead surface heated to incandescence, and if the sun was of vast size, it would then appear as a new star.

"A third theory supposed that a huge dark star had struck a sun surrounded by planets and that each successive rekindling of the blaze was the running down of a new unfortunate planet.

"In a fourth theory, however, the French astronomer Janssen discards all collision theories and puts forward the idea of an explosion of the sun caused by chemical changes within the sun itself. If oxygen exists in the sun's chromosphere, and we know that it does, then should the temperature tend to drop to a critical point, the combination of oxygen and hydrogen would cause a terrific explosion. We know that the temperature of our own sun keeps varying from day to day. It makes us shudder to think what would happen if our sun should be suddenly transformed into such a laboratory."

Jim was leaning forward with strained attention. I didn't blame him. Those last words made me glance almost involuntarily at a shaft of sunlight which was lazily streaming across the floor . . . The soft voice continued:

"In any event we can imagine a terrific flash, blinding all human sight forever, and then within ten minutes a wave of all-enveloping flame . . ."

I glanced back at the lazy yellow shaft of sunlight—but this time my eyelids drooped in spite of me as I heard the lulling voice droning on from a greater and greater distance. Finally I shook off the tendency to doze and opened my eyes. The first thing which they fell upon was the lazy shaft of sunlight. Somehow it looked different. I rubbed my eyes and stared again. There was certainly something queer about the color, but when I touched Jim's sleeve, he only shook me off impatiently. I did not have long to puzzle over it, however, when the bell rang and Jim fairly leapt over the space between us, grabbing my arm and jerking me to my feet.

"What a lecture! But what do you think caused the nebulous ring and the condensations?"

"Don't know," I murmured as we pressed out past the other students into the hall. "But I do know that I was sleepy. I had to fairly fight myself, and that in spite of the interesting facts of the lecture."

"You would," he laughed. "But what a sight that would be from a ringside seat."

"Might have an uncomfortable resemblance to those warm regions some of us are supposed to visit sometime without the wishing."

"But joking aside Bob, that would put a sure and sudden end to our little planetary system, wouldn't it?" he laughed.

"By the way," I remarked as casually as possible, "doesn't the sun look a little peculiar?"

Jim snorted.

"So old Kepling has you worried?"

"I mean it. I didn't go to lab yesterday, so I'm asking you if there is some unusual atmospheric condition such as a big fire somewhere near that would cast an ash veil. It just looks—well—strange."

"Then the trouble is with your eyes. If you took a sip from Brown's hip flask last night, I would advise you to lay off."

We walked the rest of the way toward the house in silence. I did not have a class for the rest of the day, but Jim, I remembered, had mentioned a quiz in calculus. Finally, on the porch, I touched his arm.

"I suppose you will be studying instead of playing a set of tennis with me as usual?"

"No, the quiz has been called off."

"Called off?"

"Yep. Somebody stole the questions."

"Holy cats! Who'd be fool enough to do a thing like that? Somebody doesn't care much about his diploma."

"Don't know. Lots of things have been disappearing around the laboratories. Kenny says that it is a ghost."

"Well he's kind of nutty anyway. I suppose that he claims to have seen it?"

"Yes he did. He says that he came upon something silverish and shining the other day hanging over the botany microscopes, and that the thing, which he could see right through, just faded out when he came into the room."

"Well whoever heard of a ghost taking up its residence in a scientific laboratory, and stealing calculus questions? Evidently my eyes are not the only ones around this place that are in need of an examination!"

IT WAS toward midnight that evening when I next saw Jim. Then he came bursting into my room with his eyes fairly popping out of his head.

"You remember what I told you about the calculus questions?" he asked when he could get his breath.

"Yeah," I yawned.

"Well, I can't tell you about it, but you must come with me right away. Kepling's in his office, waiting for you."

"Say, now listen. I don't know anything about those questions. Besides that, I don't take calculus."

"Oh dry up! No one is accusing you. Kepling isn't a mathematician."

"All right," I grinned with better humor. "I suppose it's about the ghost then."

For all my teasing, however, the information that I could get out of Jim as to why Kepling had sent for me was extremely unsatisfactory. I simply had to smother my curiosity and follow my friend in silence as he made his way past the night watchman and through the darkened halls of the science building to where the light shone through the transom of Kepling's office.

"Come in," answered the cultured voice behind the door, in response to Jim's knock.

"Did you see it again, Doc?" my friend's voice inquired anxiously as he stepped through the doorway in front of me.

The silver hair of Kepling's head tossed in a negative answer as he turned around in the glow of the student lamp that streamed down upon him and motioned us to a seat.

"Mr. Hunt," looking from Jim's anxious face to my puzzled one. "I asked Mr. Turner here to bring me his most trusted friend, but to give him no information as to why he had been summoned."

"He was mum all right," I grunted, hardly realizing in that moment the great compliment Jim had paid me.

"He told me that he had already informed you about the strange presence which seems to have been hovering about this science building for some time."

I nodded silently.

"He also told me that he had informed you about the main irregularities that have been discovered."

I nodded again, wondering what the man was driving at.

"It was not until tonight that I saw the creature. In fact, we both saw it.

Mr. Turner was discussing the subject of novae with me here at my desk—and in particular the most interesting Nova Persei. I had just been sketching the star with its nebula and the condensations, in illustrating what is to my belief a theory of planetary conception, when we were disturbed by the feeling that we were not alone. Glancing up, we were both somewhat startled to see a tall, shining, indescribable thing before us.

"I put out my hand and touched it.

"My fingers were resisted by a soft, damp or clammy substance which moved away sharply under my hand as if that touch had hurt it, though the movement of my hand was exceedingly gentle.

"It is my belief now that the creature would undoubtedly have tried to get into communication with us, if I had not taken the initiative. Instead, it faded from our astonished sight—leaving the room absolutely empty."

"But surely, sir, you do not believe . . ."

"That it was a ghost? No. But I do believe that we are entertaining an extra-terrestrial visitor."

"You mean," I gasped, a thrill creeping coldly up my spine, "you mean a man from . . . space?"

"Yes."

"But why?"

"Because of the strange composition of the creature in the first place, its method of locomotion, and its ability to fade from sight. In the second place, I would say because of the interest which it takes in such things as microscopes, astronomy charts, calculus questions and my poor drawings of Nova Persei."

I nodded slowly.

"Cast here among the creatures of an unknown civilization, this being is just as cautious, as curious and as half-frightened as we would be in similar circumstances."

"Did it look man-like?" I asked thoughtfully.

"No. Not at all. But that does not mean that it lacks intelligence. Remember that we are entirely the product of our own planet, from our lung capacity to the pressure which we can bear upon our bodies. Then take note of all the types of life which this single earth has evolved. We are forced to the conclusion that nature is very generous with her patterns. By the law of averages alone, we would probably search far among types of life on other planets for a pattern just like ours."

"Of course, I hadn't thought of that."

"But let's figure out a plan, Doc," Jim's voice put in impatiently.

"Yes, what shall we do about it?" I asked. I was never very long on arguments. That was Jim's strong point. Mine was action. And here he was voicing my sentiments.

"I have not outlined a very definite plan . . ." Kepling began.

"Suppose Jim and I catch it!"

The white hair tossed a quick negative.

"Such a proceeding would not only destroy all the confidence which it has gained by watching us, but would be liable to be highly dangerous as well, because we do not know what weapons it might have."

I NODDED regretfully. It was good advice, but I couldn't help wishing that he hadn't thought of that.

"Besides," he continued, "I have an odd feeling that this thing may know the secret of invisibility, thought-reading or possibly the fourth dimension. In fact, young gentlemen, when dealing with extra-terrestrial intelligence we must expect to meet with something beyond or undiscovered by our present knowledge-limit. For we are but the ignorant offspring of our own planet and once out of that pale we are adrift on an unknown sea."

"Then what shall we do?" I asked.

"In view of the fact that this being was attracted by our little discussion of Nova Persei, I propose that we continue the talk and further it by more charts and drawings. Possibly this will bring him back."

"But after he gets here?" I persisted.

"We will attempt to communicate with him."

I nodded slowly, noting that the doors were closed. Kepling had said something about the fourth dimension. I looked at Jim skeptically, but his eyes were on the old professor, and he seemed to have forgotten my presence utterly in that rapt mood, which I had seen come over him so often during an interesting lecture.

"It won't be hard for me to talk about Nova Persei, for that is one of my hobbies. Perhaps it will become more fixed in your mind if I point out on our large chart, while the action of so doing may also serve the double purpose of attracting our strange visitor."

Adjusting his glasses, Kepling peered through some charts scattered over his desk and selected one of the largest, unrolling it slowly and running one thin, sensitive finger along the Milky Way.

"Here it is in the constellation of Perseus," he nodded, the finger stopping over a dot and then dropping back to another dot.

"This is Argol. You remember my lecture on Argol, sometimes called the 'Demon Sun' because of the huge planet that eclipses its full light at regular intervals?"

I nodded, recalling the interesting discussion that Jim had hurled at me right after that lecture.

"The ancients thought, of course, that Argol winked—in fact . . ."

The sensitive finger curled up from the chart and the white head was raised slightly as if listening . . . Then suddenly I noticed a strange silvery light that seemed to shine on the wall above the desk, over the shaded portion of the student lamp.

"Slowly . . . turn slowly!" Kepling warned me as I started to whirl around in response to that instinct which made one search immediately for the cause of an unexplained fact. "Remember, it must not be frightened away again."

I checked my startled movement with an effort, and turned slowly only to gasp in amazement. For the thing which glowed just beyond the circle of light rays from the lamp, was one of the most grotesque creatures that one could conceive. It stood perhaps seven feet high—or rather, I should say floated, because apparently it had no method of support, but moved as if our atmosphere had been so much heavy liquid. Like one of those beautiful, self-luminous denizens of the deep seas, it glinted with a faint silvery light, its nine tentacles hanging down like a drooping flower whose long, faintly-waving petals faded out into shadow. At the same moment, I was aware of a strange, heavy perfume that seemed to suddenly fill the air of the little room and engulf me like a tidal wave from the sea. I put out a hand to touch Jim's sleeve to warn him about that peculiar odor, but my arm seemed to become unbearably heavy. It dropped limply back to my side, Jim leaning forward in his chair, the white head of Kepling lit by the streaming rays of the student lamp, and the silvery thing which floated just beyond the circle of light, all became fixed like figures of wax or the sketches of a madman on an illumined canvas and then suddenly swam together in a crazy whirl, as I fell forward into the dark pit of unconsciousness.

It must have been days before I again came to. Perhaps because of my unexpected movement, I received more of the mysterious drug than either of my two companions. At any rate, when I next opened my eyes, their anxious faces were bending over me. I glanced at them and smiled, when suddenly I caught sight of our strange surroundings, and the smile faded into an expression of wonder.

"Yes, we looked the same way when we first glanced around," Jim grinned.

"But . . ."

"See, Doc, he is getting interested. I said he would come around all right."

"The coming around isn't the point in question!" I answered, sitting up

THE MAN FROM SPACE

I checked my startled movement with an effort, and turned slowly only to gasp in amazement. For the thing which glowed just beyond the circle of light rays from the lamp, was one of the most grotesque creatures that one could conceive.

and staring at the glass palace surrounding us—my eyes roving from the lustrous, silver mattress-like rug upon whose tufted fibers of moon-lit cobwebs I had been resting, to the glowing draperies above our heads that twined backwards like so much gossamer-thin spun glass, glistening as they moved in an unfelt breeze.

"Doc thinks that the machinery which propels her is up there, but we can't find any way of getting up," Jim volunteered.

My eye dropped back down the sheer glass-like walls which glowed with the same weird silvery light that our visitor had emitted in the office of Dr. Kepling.

"But how in . . ."

"We know nothing more than you do," the cultured voice of the old professor assured me. "We were also drugged in the office. We both saw you fall but were already powerless ourselves. During our state of unconsciousness we were evidently kidnapped."

"He might have invited us to go," I grunted resentfully. "I have a notion to smear him up."

"That would be most unwise," Kepling said quickly. "In the first place, he has not harmed us, and in the second place, even if you should succeed in overpowering him with his strange drugs, we have not the remotest chance of getting back to earth."

"You mean that we are in space right now—off the earth?"

"Exactly."

"And this thing is a space-ship?"

"Nothing else but!" Jim grinned gleefully.

"But where did he have it when he was hanging around the Science Building?"

"Undoubtedly he had it stationed in the upper atmosphere, and he conveyed us to it in some mysterious manner."

"Suppose we ask him?"

"I have tried to communicate with him by my efforts have been unsuccessful. However, I believe I can enlighten you both on one point. My observations tend to the prophecy that we are speeding toward the constellation of Perseus or Andromeda at a terrific rate."

"Well that is the best news I have heard since the calculus questions were stolen," Jim grinned.

"But what about our earth?" I asked. "Is it still visible?"

"No, the earth dwindled away some time ago and now even our sun has shrunk to a star of the first magnitude."

"That ought to be an interesting sight," I said, starting to rise.

THE MAN FROM SPACE

"Take it easy, Mr. Hunt, the sensation of weightlessness may not make you any too steady on your feet for awhile."

I AROSE awkwardly. Outside of being slightly dizzy, which I laid to the lack of gravity, I managed to follow the white-haired figure of Kepling without any mishaps, although my eyes were busily roving over the fantastic building which Jim later told that he had nicknamed "The Temple of the Stars." It was formed of a type of composition that at first glance resembled glass, but although it was transparent, yet it glowed with a silver luminosity, giving the effect of diffused moonlight.

As soon as Kepling reached the edge of this strange palace, and pointed back to a bright yellow star below us the luminosity of the floor and walls, which I will continue to call glass for the want of a better name, faded out, and the stars glowed through the black abysses of space at us from all sides like millions of vari-colored lights. How aptly Jim had named the ship! I was so awe-struck at the gorgeous spectacle which they presented, that I failed to note the puzzled frown that had crept over the placid features of the white-haired scientist.

"Something is the matter with the sun—I mean our sun," he announced, his usually quiet voice vibrating with a note of alarm.

"I expected as much," I heard myself saying.

"What?"

"Well, I mean it's a hunch that came to me yesterday or day before, or last week—or whenever it was that you gave your lecture on Nova Persei."

"Then why didn't you mention it in the office?"

"Forgot it, I suppose. So much was happening. Then too, Jim had kidded me. He had suggested . . . oh, certain disagreeable possibilities."

But Kepling was no longer listening to me.

"Look!" he cried, his voice trembling with excitement.

My eyes turned unwillingly—almost fearfully back to that little yellow star. It was ablaze. Its dazzling glory seemed to expand—eclipsing the more feeble lights of its nearest neighbors.

Then again I felt that strange presence near me, and turning around, I saw the flower-like being floating near us in all its ghostly, silver beauty. One long, radiant tentacle slowly separated itself from the others and point to a great opaque globe which began to glow with a ruby light.

"Look, a new type of telescope, I suppose," I said as Kepling's horror-stricken eyes followed my pointing finger.

Slowly the ruby light began to shrink, turning to a glaring white as it concentrated in a spot of terrific brilliance.

"He is showing us the sun—our sun . . ." The old astronomer's voice ended with a groan.

Then suddenly I saw it—that wave of fire—spreading . . . on every side . . . spreading. Jim covered his eyes as if to shut out the horror of it. Beside me the flower thing floated silently, his phosphorescence touching the scene with a detached, unearthly shimmer. Perhaps he lingered there with unexpressed and inexpressible sympathy!

The wave of flame spread on and succeeding waves followed it, until the glare of the flaming disc became unbearable. But the globe followed the first wave of fire, and slowly the gleaming nucleus drifted to the edge and out of sight.

Jim uncovered his eyes again and stared as a hypnotized man might stare at the globe.

Flashing in a trillion sparkles, the wave of white-hot gas was reaching for its first planet . . .

"Mercury!" Kepling gasped, even as the wave engulfed it and turned it into a tiny torch.

The light of the conflagration seemed to intensify as it spread, and again the globe followed its expanding edge. I felt my throat tighten as Venus swept into view. But almost immediately it was caught up in the veil of fire, seemed to actually explode in hissing steam and slowly swung toward the edge of the globe as the third planet accompanied by its tiny silver bubble of a moon came into the path of the fiery death.

Kepling groaned, while Jim stared like one turned to stone. In that moment of horror, as we watched in helpless misery the luminescent wave creeping upon our little world, I seemed to be able to see with my mind's eye the streets of the cities with their floods of terror-stricken faces turned skyward—some groping with blind stares from which sight had been forever blasted, and others glaring with pupils from which the light of reason had vanished . . .

But the wave of death swept on—engulfing the planet and causing it to gleam suddenly like a large diamond thrown into a strong light.

Kepling slumped limply to the floor. That movement startled Jim from his frozen state, and he bent over the old gentleman with white, drawn features. But I staggered back away from the globe, closing my hands over my face as if to shut out its terrible message. My foot struck a bench and on this I sank, dropping my head into my hands.

Infinite moments went by. Finally I felt a hand on my shoulder and heard Kepling's voice murmuring:

"I know, my boy, that it is easier to face the most horrible death oneself, than to realize that everything one has loved and lived for has been swept

THE MAN FROM SPACE

away in one moment of unspeakable terror, but the past is past while we are still alive and must go on."

"As wanderers of space."

"Yes, as wanderers of space," he nodded, gripping my shoulder harder with his slender fingers. "For without the need of words it has been revealed to us why we were kidnapped."

"Perhaps he too . . . he seemed sort of helplessly sympathetic when it happened," I murmured, noting that the globe had turned black and that the silver luminosity had come back into the floor and the walls.

"Perhaps," the white head nodded. "It is a cruel, unbelievable fact to face but we must realize that not only our friends, but also all art, all history and literature, all the sciences—everything which we call our civilization has been swept like a gnat into nothingness. For when we three die, our race will be no more."

"Don't!" Jim begged in a whisper, instinctively using the hushed tones that one falls into in the presence of death.

SO IT WAS that our great adventure was begun upon the ashes of tragedy, and this was why the bitterness of that tragedy never entirely forsook our minds. For though in the days which followed, we did much to regain our zest for life, yet behind it always loomed that terrible knowledge that the past was blotted out making the future but a hopeless blank, even as the dark apertures torn in the star-clouds of the heavens are a blank, through which we seem to look into endless nothingness . . .

And now time slipped by, almost without the realization that it was passing. Kepling worked almost unceasingly upon copying what he could remember of scientific books, while Jim and I spent hours at the glass wall looking out at the stars which gleamed around us like endless swarms of fireflies.

We saw our host but seldom, although he seemed to anticipate our wishes in a most extraordinary manner, the objects we had desired always appearing to materialize from nowhere. He himself, however, kept out of sight—either preferring to stay invisible or else remaining on the upper part of the palace-ship which we had not seen. We often commented upon him, wondering where he had come from, where he was going and again, if he too, was the victim of one of those catastrophes that astronomers had called novae—an exile without a parent civilization—a wanderer through space.

This feeling was intensified, when passing near Algol, he distracted our attention from the "Demon Sun" by pointing one gleaming tentacle to the nebulous rotating ring of Nova Persei, which was looming like a strange Saturn among the stars, and then slowly fading away again into darkness. Jim was the first to voice his opinion.

"You were right, Doc. This man from space is certainly interested in Nova Persei."

Kepling nodded thoughtfully.

"Wanted: one Sherlock Holmes." I grinned.

"Well, I don't know why it should, but it gives me the creeps to think that he might have come from Nova Persei," Jim murmured with a shrug.

"And the way he has of fading away into nothing gives me the creeps," I added.

"It is equally possible that our methods of locomotion give him the creeps," Kepling smiled. "Personally, I am of the opinion that his method has innumerable advantages."

Jim laughed.

"Especially in some of the exploring expeditions that we probably have in store for us!"

"Look!" Kepling interrupted. "The nebula around Nova Persei is pretty plain now because of our nearness—but the condensations—they are easily distinguished."

"You know, Doc," Jim said thoughtfully, "they do look like the remains of planets. Not that I'm upholding the theory that they were run down by a dark star, but merely overtaken by the wave of fire."

Kepling's eyes sparkled suddenly as the idea took hold of him.

"Possibly they are. I wish I could turn the globe back to our sun and observe what has happened," he said earnestly, the scientist of him fully aroused over the conception of a new theory.

He had no sooner uttered the wish than the globe clouded with showers of stars and comets, until at an immeasurably further distance that we had viewed it before, a flaming sun flashed upon the screen. Surrounding it was a very faint nebulous haze and dimly marked were four tiny condensations— somewhat brighter than the luminescent veil which surrounded them.

"Why only four?" I asked in surprise.

"We are evidently too far away to see the four minor planets and those are the major four."

"Good reasoning, Jim," Kepling smiled affectionately.

"But it does have an uncanny resemblance to Nova Persei," I put in.

"Except that the positions are about reversed," Jim added.

"Of course, there is no need of forming theories any more, but the habits of a life-time are hard to break." The white-haired figure smiled wistfully as I turned away from the globe. Somehow, the sight of that gloriously beautiful funeral pyre hurt me more than the lash of a whip. Disconsolately I turned away, walking toward the opposite wall and looking off through the myriad swarms of stars that glowed in through the darkened sides of the ship. Then suddenly I stopped and stared. For out of the tail of my eye I had caught sight of an enormous colored light ahead of us that loomed up like a vast comet. I looked up quickly. The new object, which seemed to have appeared from behind the hidden prow of our spaceship as if we had been steering toward it and now were swerving to one side, was a brilliant blue sun, the lower third of which was covered by its reddish-yellow companion. I had often viewed binary or double stars back in the old University telescope, so the sight was not unusual, but the nearness of this pair made me gasp at the splendor of the spectacle they presented.

"Come quickly!" I called out in excitement.

Jim was the first one to reach my side, but the white-haired astronomer was not far behind him.

"Look at the blue sun up there with its companion that looks like a huge luminous orange."

"Must be Almack," Kepling said thoughtfully

"Almack?" I asked, trying to place the familiar name.

"Yes. You will remember that in my lecture on multiple suns, I mentioned this group of three."

"Three?" I said quizzically, taking another look at the apparent double.

"Yes, three. Behind the orange sun, you will see the thin green outline of the third. Like all multiple suns, you will remember that they revolve around their common center of gravity."

"Did you say the third sun was green?" I asked, trying to separate it from the red corona of the orange.

"Don't you remember our discussion on that very group?" Jim grinned at me. "You were trying to figure out the sunset effects."

"Sounds more like your ideas. You were the interplanetary bug of our group."

"Perhaps so. But oh how I would like to take a peek at a world lit by this trio of colored suns!"

"That is a wish that I have secretly nursed all of my life," Kepling admitted softly.

HARDLY HAD the words left his lips, than the three jewel-like suns swung back toward the prow, becoming eclipsed at last by the forepart of the ship.

"He is going to take us there," I laughed. "How's that for thought reading?"

"Well, the wish was double," Kepling smiled, "and therefore doubly strong."

"Triple," I corrected.

Jim laughed as the silver luminosity came back into the walls. It was the first real laugh I had heard from him since the days on earth.

"I am only hoping that our entertaining host has adequate means of breaking the speed of the ship," the old professor murmured with a worried frown.

"But if we really wanted to worry, Doc, we wouldn't have to go very far. A whole host of funny ideas would come trooping in," Jim grinned. "For instance, we might begin to wonder about the air and if its content would agree with our lungs; or we might wonder if the planet is too small and the atmospheric pressure would burst us, as the deep sea fish burst when they come into the air; or we might wonder if the planet is so large and the atmosphere so dense that we would be crushed . . . or . . ."

"That will do for the present," I put in.

"Besides, we haven't any weapons . . ." he continued.

"Young gentlemen, I for one have full confidence in the good judgment of our host."

"So have I. Even if I did start out wanting to kill him off."

"I tell you—he's a great animated flower," Jim agreed.

"But the most practical thing," I interrupted, "would be to get some sleep before we get too close, because we will be too interested in the landing of the ship to even think about such a thing later on, while we do not know what dangers or hardships may await us on the new world."

Both of my companions agreed on the wisdom of this suggestion, each throwing himself down on his particular tufted mattress-like rug. For a long time, however, sleep would not come to me. I lay awake wondering to what weird civilizations this man from the unknown was carrying us. To what destinations were we ultimately bound? What adventures waited us on the morrow? How long would we stay on this world with its colored suns—and after that—what?

The first thing I noticed after I had awakened, was the glow of the colored suns upon the silver luminosity of the walls. A green light blended into lavender and then purple was followed by orange in unending splendor.

I sat up and drank in the cubistic beauty of the crystal palace under these changing rays. When I stirred, Jim immediately sat up and called out:

"How are these for stage effects? If I could transport them to Broadway, we'd both be rich."

But my laugh that followed this apparently thoughtless remark died in my throat.

THE MAN FROM SPACE

"Come now. I'm sorry. No gloomy thoughts today."

I nodded with a smile, walking over toward the walls. As usual, this movement on our part was the signal for the luminosity to die out, but this time the light which shone through from the colored suns was even more intense than the silver which up to now had seemed to act as a screen.

Suddenly Kepling's voice sounded softly behind us.

"Look toward the prow of the ship."

We turned our faces upward almost simultaneously, and gasped to see the disc of a planet swinging between us and the star-spangled blackness of space. It was tinted green and orange—one side of a mountain chain being of a greenish hue and the other a reddish orange.

"What about the pressure?" Jim asked anxiously.

The cultured voice droned a low reply that might have been the part of a class-room lecture.

"The size of the body is close to that of our own earth and so the pressure is about right, while it is far enough from its suns to give a very pleasant temperature."

"What did I say about our ghost-like friend?"

"Was it you that said it," I teased Jim. We hadn't completely overcome our earthly habit of annoying each other's peace of mind, even with the ever-present example of gentle manners we had in the old professor.

"I didn't believe that our host would knowingly lead us into danger," Kepling put in innocently. "Concerning the contents of the atmosphere, however, we can only take a chance."

"I am only waiting for the opportunity to take it," Jim grinned.

"Don't be so sure about the chance," I nodded. "It looks very much as if our engineer has decided to give the planet a go-by."

Indeed, the disc was rapidly swinging toward our stern. Kepling watched for a few moments in silence and then smiled.

"He is turning the ship around. In other words, he is going to lower us stern first upon the planet."

"But what is the idea, Doc?"

"He probably has noted our interest and intends to allow us unobstructed observation."

After a moment it was quite plain that this was indeed just what was happening. As the great globe rushed up toward us, lit by its sinking green and rising orange sun, we kneeled down and finally threw ourselves prone upon the floor as the mountain chains took more definite form. Kepling was the first to point out that vast moon-like craters that dotted the face of the planet, and lifted jagged crags skyward from the level of what appeared to be a dead plain.

"Evidently very little water," the astronomer commented tersely.

"The seas do appear to be dried up—very much like the state on the moon," Jim agreed.

The green sun had dropped from sight when at last we decided that the light patches on the mountain tops were snow. It was an orange world that we now rapidly lowered ourselves upon, hovering sometimes and again seeming to waver along sideways as if seeking a particular spot which the engineer had admired during a previous visit. Jim was the first one to suggest this possibility, and once the idea was planted, it grew upon us.

We finally passed a part of the wildly mountainous country which began to be lit by the blue sun on one side and the orange on the other. At this point the ship ceased to waver and began to drop rapidly toward the mountains, landing with a scarcely perceptible jar on a level plateau that was just opposite a tremendous talon-like range of peaks. The little plateau upon which we found ourselves seemed to be itself the peak of a mountain, though not as high as the chain opposite—nor could we look down the other side, for another glance showed us that our resting place was not quite the top, but a small ridge had to be climbed first. For a moment now, we rested in shadow, but it was a weird twilight, the greenish tint lingering in the heavens only as a kind of afterglow, giving the effect of strangeness which I have sometimes noted on earth, after a wild storm has momentarily torn a cleft in the clouds for the zodiacal light to peer through.

Then as we stood there by the glass walls, our spectre-like host floated down toward us from the shimmering upper drapes, and pointing with one of his lustrous tentacles, he called our attention to an open doorway, through which a cool breeze sprang into the ship.

JIM WAS the first one through, landing in the moss-like growth of the plateau with one long jump. I followed. Bounding along like a puppy that has been held in confinement, he ran with long leaps and jumps toward the edge of the cliff where he stopped and waved like a maniac. I caught up with him with such a leap that I almost went over the cliff, while the white-haired figure of the scientist followed with more dignity. But when I looked down into the valley, the unearthly character of this moon-scape left me gasping.

Imagine, if you can, a range of huge silt mountains from which ever-tumbling veils of snow and rock dropped intermittently into a gorge four times deeper than the Grand Canyon, with a dull roar. It seemed as I stood there that I was gazing upon a staircase for giants leading down to a bottom-

THE MAN FROM SPACE 125

less pit of half-fluid mud, and then over it all that weirdly-changing sky and finally the first gleams of the blue sun, as it climbed through a knife-slashed pass.

I was still looking in awe-struck silence when Kepling's voice murmured:

"I believe that the scene on the other side just over the ridge, is perhaps equally interesting."

"How can it be?" Jim gasped.

"Such is the judgment of our host at any rate. He pointed up that way but you two rushed off too vigorously to even notice his instructions."

"Well, we can go up there; but Doc, just look at that pit."

"The region is evidently still volcanic," Kepling mused, picking up a rock.

"Some push certainly heaved up those mountains. But look at that swamp," Jim persisted.

Kepling nodded thoughtfully.

"I bet it's full of funny-looking monsters," I laughed.

"Not so funny close up," Jim interrupted. "But let's take that look at the other side. Personally, I feel like getting some exercise. The only trouble with space-travel is that there are so few stop-overs and those are so far apart!"

So with Jim leading the way, we climbed up the rocks leading toward the ridge. Once over the top, however, our leader did a war dance to convince us of his approval of the view, while I turned and smiled at Kepling. The old scientist waved away my offer of assistance, and I, too, leaped over the intervening rocks, where I stopped and slumped down with awe-struck eyes. For yawning below us was the cavernous depths of a vast crater where a molten lake boiled and bubbled—the living lava splashing up with livid spurts of hellish splendor in the glowing pit—miles below us. Across from us the opposite walls of the crater were outlined blackly against a carmine sky, the sinking rays of the setting orange sun giving the appearance of a huge conflagration raging down the unseen slopes of the other side, which, having swept through the crater, had left this lake of glowing embers behind.

Overhead the sky was turning a reddish-purple, while over to one side a huge purplish moon, half ruby and half blue, was rising.

Kepling stopped for a moment on top and then stepped over to the very edge and looked down. I was just admiring the old scientist's nice sense of balance when I heard him give a sharp cry, saw him throw his body around as if to catch himself, and then go plunging down through the darkness toward that glowing pit. I started to my feet in horror when a sudden convulsion of the rocks made me look down. Imagine my terror to realize that what we had mistaken for a ridge of rock in our delight at the scene before us was a sleeping dragon—a huge armored creature which had been taking a nap on the crater's rim. Kepling had been standing on the thing's back, and therefore had been the first to fall as it moved. So perfectly matched to the rocks had been his protective coloring that we had not noticed him!

I leapt to his tail, intending to then jump to some lava projections and try to get a glimpse of the old professor, before the monster turned on me, but I was too slow. He swished his tail, hurling me unceremoniously into space when I dashed helplessly against some rocks and started to slide down the cliffs toward that red, bubbling horror. Miraculously, I don't know how, I kept my senses, digging my heels and fingers into the earth to stop me and clutching what plants I could grasp. At last I caught a gnarled plant growing at the very edge of the long drop into the cauldron. There I swung between the lava cliff and the burning lake, with only one toe-hold with which to climb back.

When at last, shivering and perspiring, I finally pulled myself up and lay limply on the black rock, a wail and a roar sent my eyes back to the monster.

Something was being pulverized into nothingness under the maddened stamps of the great beast whose gleaming red eyes did not note that a new menace flew through the air at him, until it was too late, and a silvery-gleaming, flower-like creature with shimmering tentacles lit upon his back like a giant insect of some terrible, malignant type. With a roar of agony that reverberated from cliff to cliff through that glowing crater, the great animal leaped into the air and headed straight for me—maddened into frenzy by the stinging thing which he could not shake off. Each leap shook the whole mountain as those tons of animal flesh crashed to earth.

Then, suddenly, with a more ominous roar, I felt the whole cliff tremble, and leaped back just as the entire face of the mountain gave way, carrying with its rush of rocks like a struggling ant, the brown dragon and the silver thing that still clung to its quivering flanks like a phosphorescent flower . . .

For a moment I was too much concerned with racing the breaking rocks on the top of the slide to catch more than a glance of the dragon that rolled under the thunder of the avalanche, but after the dust had at last cleared away from the freshly-glowing lava lake, I sat down on the top of the rim and stared with unseeing eyes into the caldron.

Behind me, with its glass walls glittering in the rising rays of the blue sun the palace ship which Jim had nicknamed "The Temple of the Stars" stood peacefully, waiting for the gleaming master, which would never return. Before me, the ruby color of the cauldron changed subtly through all the shades of lavender to purple as the blue sun climbed higher and the orange sun deepened its glow to the red of a deep garnet. Before me, a few loosened rocks still bounded hollowly down the cliffs . . .

Of my companions who had accompanied me over the rim in such high spirits, not a shred remained to tell that they had ever lived. Indeed, seated here upon a giant crater—like a gnat that surveys a mountain gorge—to what end had I struggled so madly to preserve my life, doomed as I was to die on this wild, weird world—or in case I did learn the secret of the ship's propulsion and fuel—then to wander through space forever alone—the last living creature of my kind?

With a roar of agony that reverberated from cliff to cliff through that glowing crater, the great animal leaped into the air and headed straight for me.

****

"Bob Hunt! Will you wake up, or shall I have to carry you out of here?" I heard Jim's voice asking impatiently.

I opened my eyes suddenly, looking in consternation from the streak of yellow sunshine that was lazily streaming over the classroom floor, back to the very amused eyes of Dr. Kepling.

"But I thought . . ."

"Never mind what you thought! Come on and get moving!"

"But Jim! We're still on earth! And our sun . . . why it's all right! It's normal—isn't it?"

A deep horse-laugh greeted this statement from the vicinity of the doorway where a number of amused students were lingering.

"Make a fool of yourself it you wish—but count me out!" Jim snapped starting toward the door.

I picked up my books sheepishly and followed him, apparently deaf to a number of wise-cracks that were hurled at me. Only when we were nearing the house did he deign to notice me.

"You picked out one of the most interesting lectures of the year to sleep on, you poor nut."

"I know—it was about Nova Persei."

"Oh, you did hear some of it, did you?"

"Of course I did." Then after a moment, "You know, Jim I have funny hunch that those condensations were the remains of planets which were consumed by the wave of fire which the main sun threw off when it exploded."

"Sleep all the way through a lecture and then presume to know something about it, eh? Well, Mr. Would-be Scientist, get this—the collision theories fit the facts of Nova Persei better than the explosion theory."

After that I subsided. Only in front of the house, I laid a hand on his arm.

"Are you still too peeved to play our usual set of tennis this afternoon?"

"Sorry, old sleep-head, but I have that calculus quiz coming off this afternoon."

"Oh, the questions—no one stole them?"

"Well, aren't you just brimming over with the most amazing ideas! Who would be fool enough to steal the calculus questions?" Then with a laugh— "Say, boy, I only wish that I could answer that dumb question in the affirmative—but there is *no such luck.*"

[AUTHOR'S NOTE: I realize that there are inconsistencies in this dream of Bob Turner's, but who has ever heard of an entirely consistent dream?]

The Tunnel Ahead
by Alice Glaser

The late Rod Serling phoned me and said he wanted to locate a story he had read years ago about a tunnel. Could I find it for him? Well, I remembered Frederik Pohl's "The Tunnel Under the World" offhand but that wasn't it. So I checked various indexes 'til I had three stories starting out with Tunnel. I got them out, read portions to Rod over the phone. "No, not that . . . no . . . yes! yes! That's it—can you get it for me?" Well, the story was already 10 years in the past and the only one by an author never heard of before or since. Fortunately, the editor, Anthony Boucher, had noted in the blurb that the lady worked for *Esquire* magazine. But a decade ago? In New York she had probably changed positions 5 times already and in the meantime got married and changed her name. But I had to start somewhere, so I phoned Esquire. "Alice Glaser, please," I said, as though I expected to find her there. "One moment, please," and the next thing I knew I was speaking to Alice Glaser! "Don't look now," I said, "but Rod Serling is interested in acquiring your story "The Tunnel" for *The Twilight Zone*. I'm an agent, would you like me to handle it for you?" She was breathless. "Why, yes, yes!"

Ten days later the dear lady died!

I hope she & Rod are there now in the Twilight Zone enjoying the revival of her story.

—FJA

The floor of the Topolino was full of sand. There was sand in Tom's undershorts, too, and damp sand rubbing between his toes. Damn it, he thought, here they build you six-lane highways right on down to the ocean, a giant three hundred car turntable to keep traffic moving over the beach, efficiency and organization and mechanization and cooperation and what does it get you? Sand. And inside the car, the sour smell of sun-dried salt water.

Tom's muscles ached with their familiar cramp. He ran his hands uselessly around the steering wheel, wishing he had something to do, or that there were room to stretch in the tiny car, then felt instantly ashamed of his antisocial wish. Naturally there was nothing for him to do because the drive, as on all highways, was set at "Automatic." That was the law. And although he had to sit hunched over so that his knees were drawn nearly to his chin, and the roof of the car pressed down on the back of his neck like the lid of a box, and his four kids crammed into the rear seat seemed to be breathing down his shirt collar—well, that was something you simply had to adjust to, and besides, the Topolino had all the five foot wheelbase the law allowed. So there was nothing to complain about.

Besides, it hadn't been a bad day, all things considered. Five hours to cover the forty miles out to the beach, then of course a couple of hours waiting in line *at* the beach for their turn in the water. The trip home was taking a little longer: it always did. The Tunnel, too, was unpredictable. Say ten o'clock, for getting home. Pretty good time. As good a way as any of killing a leisureday, he guessed. Sometimes there seemed to be an awful lot of leisuretime to kill.

Jeannie, in the seat beside him, was staring through the windshield. Her hair, almost as fair as the kids', was pulled back into pigtails, and although she was pregnant again she didn't look very much older than she had ten years before. But she had stopped knitting, and her mind was on the Tunnel. He could always tell.

"*Ouch!*" Something slammed into the back of Tom's neck and he ducked forward, banging his forehead on the windshield.

"Hey!" He half-turned and clutched at the spade that four-year-old Pattie was waving.

"I swimmed," she announced, blue eyes round. "I swimmed good and I din't hit nobody."

"Anybody," Tom corrected. He confiscated the spade, thinking tiredly that "swim" these days meant "tread water," all there was room to do in the crowded bathing-area.

Jeannie had turned too, and was glowing at her daughter, but Tom shook his head.

"Over and out," he said briefly. He knew a car ride was an extra strain on kids, and lord knew he saw them seldom enough, what with their school-shifts and play-shifts and his own job-shift. But his brood was going to be properly brought up. See a sign of extroversion, squelch it at the beginning, that was his theory. Save them a lot of pain later on.

Jeannie leaned forward and pressed a dashboard button. The tranquilizer drawer slid open; Jeannie selected a pink one, but by the time she had turned around Pattie had subsided with her hands folded patiently in her lap and her eyes fixed on the rear TV screen. Jeannie sighed and slipped the pill into Pattie's half-open mouth anyway.

THE TUNNEL AHEAD

The other three hadn't spoken for hours which, of course, was as it should be. Jeannie had fed them a purposely heavy lunch in the car, steakopop and a hot, steaming bowl of rehydrated algaesoup from the thermos, and they had each had an extra dose of tranquillizers for the trip. Six-year old David, who was having a particularly hard time learning to introvert, was watching the TV screen and breathing hard. David, his first-born son, born in the supermarket delivery booth in the year twenty-one hundred on the third of April at 8:32 in the morning. The year the population of the United States hit the billion mark. And the fifth child to arrive in that booth that morning. But his own son. The tow-headed twins, Susan and Pattie, sat upright and watched the screen with expressions of great seriousness on their faces, and the baby, two-year-old Betsy, had her fat legs stuck out straight in front of her and was obviously going to be asleep in minutes.

The car crawled forward at its allotted ten mph, just one in a ribbon of identical bright bubble cars, like candy buttons, that stretched along the New Pulaski Skyway under a setting sun. The distance between them, strictly rationed by Autodrive, never changed.

Tom felt the dull ache of tension settled behind his eyes. All of his muscles were protesting now with individual stabs of cramp. He glanced apologetically at Jeannie, who disliked sports, and switched on the dashboard TV. Third game in the World Series, and the game had already begun. Malenkovsky on red. Malenkovsky moved a checker and sat back. The cameras moved to Saito, on black. It was going to be a good game. Faster than most.

They were less than a mile from the Tunnel when the line of cars came to a halt. Tom said nothing for a minute. It might just be an accident, or even somebody, driving illegally on Manual, out of line. Another minute passed. Jeannie's hands were tense on the yellow blanket she was knitting.

It was a definite halt. Jeannie regarded the motionless lines of cars, frowning a little.

"I'm glad it's happening now. That gives us a better chance of getting through, doesn't it?"

Her question was rhetorical, and Tom felt his usual stir of irritation. Jeannie was an intelligent girl; he couldn't have loved her so much otherwise. But explaining the laws of chance to her was hopeless. The Tunnel averaged ten closings a week. All ten could happen within seconds of each other, or on the hour, or not at all on a given day. That was how things were. The closing now affected their own chance of getting through not one iota.

Jeannie said, thoughtfully, "We'll be caught sometime, Tom."

He shrugged without answering. Whatever might happen in the future, they were obviously going to be held up for a good half-hour now.

David was wriggling a little, his face apologetic.

"Can I get out, Daddy, if the Tunnel's closed? I *ache.*"

Tom bit his lip. He could sympathize as well as anyone, remembering the cramped misery of the years when his own body was growing and all he wanted to do was run fast, just run headlong, anyplace. Kids. Extros, all of them. Maybe you could get away with that kind of wildness back in the Twentieth Century, when there were no crowds and plenty of space, but not these days. David was just going to have to learn to sit still like everybody else.

David had begun to flex his muscles rhythmically. Passive exercise, it was called, one of the new pseudo-sports that took up no room, and it was very scientifically taught in the playshifts. Tom eyes his son enviously. Great to be in condition like that. No need to wait in line to get your ration of gym time when you could depend on yourself like that.

"Dad, no kidding, now I gotta go." David wriggled in his seat again. Well, that sounded valid. Tom looked through the windshield. The thousands of cars in sight were still motionless, so he swung the door open. Luckily there was a chemjohn a few yards away, and only a short line in front of it. David slipped quickly out of the car. Tom watched him start to stretch his arms over his head, released from the low roof, then sheepishly remember decent behavior and tighten into the approved intro-walk. "He's getting tall," Tom thought, with a sudden accession of hopelessness. He had been praying that David would inherit Jeannie's height instead of his own six feet. The more area you took up the harder everything was, and it was getting worse. Tom noticed that, already, people would sometimes stare resentfully at him in the street.

There was an Italian family in the bright blue Topolino behind his own; they too had a car full of children. Two of the boys, seeing David in front of the chemjohn, burst out and dashed into the line behind him. The father was grinning; Tom caught his eye and looked away. He remembered seeing them pass a large bottle of expensive reclaimed-water around the car, the whole family guzzling it as though water grew on trees. Extros, that whole family. Almost criminal, the way people like that were allowed to run loose and increase the discomfort of everyone else. Now the father had left the car too. He had curly black hair; he was very plump. When he saw Tom watching him he grinned broadly, waved towards the Tunnel and lifted his shoulders with a kind of humorous resignation.

Tom drummed on the wheel. The extros were lucky. You'd never catch them worrying unduly about the Tunnel. They had to get the kids out of the city, once in a while, like everybody else; the Tunnel was the only way in and out, so they shrugged and took it. Besides, there were so many rules and regulations now that it was hard to question them any more. You can't fight City Hall. The extros would neither dread the trip, the way Jeannie did, nor . . . Tom's fingers were rigid on the wheel. He clamped down, hard, on the thought in his mind. He had been about to say, *needed* it, the way he did.

David emerged from the chemjohn and slid back into his seat. The cars had just begun to move; in a moment they had resumed their crawl.

On the left of the Skyway they were coming to the development that was already called, facetiously, "Beer Can Mountain." So far there was nothing there except the mountainous stacks of shiny bricks, the metal bricks that had once been tin cans, and would soon be constructed into another badly-needed housing development. Probably, with even lower ceilings and thinner walls. Tom winced, involuntarily. Even at home, in a much older residential section, the ceilings were so low that he could never stand up without bending his head. Individual area-space was being cut down and cut down all the time.

On the flatlands, to the right of the Skyway, stretched mile after garish mile of apartment buildings, interspersed with gasoline stations and parking lots. And beyond these flatlands were the suburbs of Long Island, cement-floored and stacked with gay-colored skyscrapers.

Here, as they approached the city, the air was raucous with the noise of transistor radios and TV sets. Privacy and quiet had disappeared everywhere, of course, but this was a lower-class unit and so noisy that the blare penetrated even the closed windows of the car. The immense apartment buildings, cement block and neon-lit, came almost to the edge of the Skyway, with ramps between them at all levels. The ramps, originally built for cars, were swarming now with people returning from their routing job-shifts or from marketing, or just carrying on the interminable business of leisuretime. They looked pretty apathetic, Tom thought. You couldn't blame them. There was so much security that none of the work anybody did was really necessary, and they knew it. Their jobs were probably even more monotonous and futile than his own. All he did, on his own job-shift, was verify figures in a ledger, then copy them into another ledger. Time-killing, like everything else. These people looked as though they didn't care, one way or the other. But as he watched there was a quick scuffle in the crowd, a sudden, brief outbreak of violence. One man's shoe had scraped the heel of the woman ahead of him; she turned and swung her shopping bag, scraping a bloody gash down his cheek. He slammed his fist at her stomach. She kicked. A man behind them rammed his way past, his face contorted. The pair separated, both muttering.

Around them other knots of people were beginning to mutter. The irritation was spreading, as it seemed to do from time to time, as though nobody wanted anything so much as the chance to strike out.

Jeannie had seen the explosion too. She gasped and turned away from the window, looking quickly back at the children, who were all asleep now. Tom pulled one of her pigtails, gently.

The skyline loomed ahead of them, one vast unified glass-walled cube of Manhattan. Light rays shot from it into the sunset; the spots of foliage that were the carefully planned block gardens, one at each level of the ninety-eight floors of the United, glowed dark green. Tom, as he always did, blessed the foresight that had put them there. Each one of his children had been allotted his or her weekly hour on the grass and a chance to play near the tree. There was even a zoo on each level, not the kind of elaborate one they had in Washington and London and Moscow, of course, but at least it had a cat and a dog and a really large tank of goldfish. When you came down to it, luxuries like that almost made up for the crowds and the noise and tiny rooms and feeling that there was never quite enough air to breathe.

They were just outside the Tunnel. Jeannie had put her knitting down; she was looking intently ahead, but as though she were listening rather than looking. In spite of his own arguments, Tom felt his fingers thudding on the dashboard. On the TV screen, Malenkovsky triumphantly moved a king.

They had reached the Tunnel entrance. Jeannie was silent. She glanced at her watch, irrationally. Tom pressed the tranquillizer button and the drawer shot out, but Jeannie shook her head.

"I hate this, Tom. I think it's an absolutely *lousy* idea."

Her voice sounded almost savage, for Jeannie, and Tom felt a little shocked.

"It's the fairest thing," he argued. "You know it perfectly well."

Jeannie's mouth had set in a stubborn line. "I don't care. There must be another way."

"This is the only fair way," Tom said again. "We take our chances along with everybody else."

His own heart was pounding, now, and his hands felt cold. It was the feeling he always had on entering the Tunnel, and he had never decided whether it was dread or elation, or both. He was no longer bored. He glanced at the children on the back seat. David was watching television again and gnawing on a fingernail; the three little ones were still asleep, sitting up as they had been taught to do, hands folded properly in their laps. Three blind mice.

The Tunnel was echoing and cold. White light slipped off the white tile walls that were clean and polished and air-tight. Wind rushed past, sounding as though the car were moving faster than it actually was. The Italian family was still behind them, following at a constant speed. Huge fans were set into the Tunnel ceiling; their roar reverberated over the roar of the giant invisible air-conditioning units, over the slow wind of the moving cars.

Jeannie had put her head down on the seat back as though she were asleep. The cars stopped for an instant, started again. Tom wondered if Jeannie felt the same vivid thrill that he felt. Then he looked at the line of her mouth and saw the fear.

The Tunnel was 8500 feet long. Each car took up seven feet, bumper to bumper, allow five feet between cars. About seven hundred cars in the Tunnel, then: more than three thousand people. It would take each car about fifteen minutes to go through. Their car was halfway through now.

They were three-quarters of the way through. Automatic signal lights were flashing at them from the catwalk under the Tunnel roof. Tom's foot moved to the gas pedal before he remembered the car was set on Automatic. It was an atavistic gesture: his hands and feet wanted a job to do. His body, for a minute, wanted to control the direction of its plunge. It was the way he always felt, in the Tunnel.

They were almost through. His scalp felt as though tiny ants were running along the hairs. He moved his toes, feeling the scratch of sand on the nerves between them. He could see the far end of the Tunnel. Maybe two minutes more. A minute.

They stopped again. A car, somewhere ahead, had swerved out of line to search for the right exit. Once out of the Tunnel it was legal to switch back to Manual Drive, since it was necessary to pick the right exit out of ten, and all too easy to find yourself carried to the top level of Manhattan Unit before finding a place to turn off.

Tom's hand drummed at the wheel. The maverick ahead had edged back into line. They started movement again. They picked up speed. They were out of the Tunnel.

Jeannie picked up her knitting and shook it, sharply. Then she dropped it as though it had bitten her fingers. A bell was clanging over their heads, not too loud, but clear. Just behind their rear bumper a gate swung smoothly into place.

Jeannie turned to look back at the space behind them where the Italian family in the bright blue car, and others, had been. There were no cars there now. She turned back, to stare whitely through the windshield.

Tom was figuring. Two minutes for the ceiling sprays to work. Then the seven hundred cars in the Tunnel would be hauled out and emptied. Ten minutes for that, say. He wondered how long it was supposed to take for the giant fans to blow the cyanide gas away.

"Depopulation without Discrimination," they called it at election time. Nobody would ever admit voting for it, but almost everybody did. Aloud, you had to rationalize: it was the fairest way to do a necessary thing. But in the unadmitted places of your mind you knew it was more than that. A gamble, the one unpredictable element in the long, dreary process of survival. A game. Russian Roulette. A game you played to win? Or, maybe, to lose? The answer didn't matter, because the Tunnel was excitement. The only excitement left.

Tom felt, suddenly, remarkably wide awake. He switched to Manual Drive and angled the round nose of the Topolino over the Fourth Level exit.

He began to whistle between his teeth. "Beach again next weekend, sweetie, huh?"

Jeannie's eyes were on his face. Defensively, he added, "Good for all of us, get out of the city, get a little fresh air once in a while."

He nudged her and pulled a pigtail gently, with affection.

Time Enough At Last
by Lyn Venable

> Marilyn R. Venable hit the jackpot (and I as her agent hit the Ackpot) with "Time Enough At Last", which became one of Rod Serling's most popular Twilight Zone episodes starring the late lamented Burgess Meredith. I have never met Ms. Venable and know virtually nothing about her except I've sold every womanuscript she ever sent me and wish she'd write more of the caliber of the story you are about to read or re-read.
> —FJA

For a long time, Henry Bemis had had an ambition. To read a book. Not just the title or the preface, or a page somewhere in the middle. He wanted to read the whole thing, all the way through from beginning to end. A simple ambition perhaps, but in the cluttered life of Henry Bemis, an impossibility.

Henry had no time of his own. There was his wife, Agnes, who owned that part of it that his employer, Mr. Carsville, did not buy. Henry was allowed enough to get to and from work—that in itself being quite a concession on Agnes' part.

Also, nature had conspired against Henry by handing him a pair of hopelessly myopic eyes. Poor Henry literally couldn't see his hand in front of his face. For a while, when he was very young, his parents had thought him an idiot. When they realized it was his eyes, they got glasses for him. He was never quite able to catch up. There was never enough time. It looked as though Henry's ambition would never be realized. Then something happened which changed all that.

Henry was down in the vault of the Eastside Bank & Trust when it happened. He had stolen a few moments from the duties of his teller's cage to try to read a few pages of the magazine he had bought that morning. He'd made an excuse to Mr. Carsville about needing bills in large denominations for a certain customer, and then, safe inside the dim recesses of the vault he had pulled from inside his coat the pocket size magazine.

He had just started a picture article cheerfully entitled "The New Weapons and What They'll Do To YOU," when all the noise in the world crashed in upon his eardrums. It seemed to be inside of him and outside of him all at once. Then the concrete floor was rising up at him and the ceiling came slanting down toward him, and for a fleeting second Henry thought of a story he had started to read once called "The Pit and The Pendulum." He regretted in that insane moment that he had never had time to finish that story to see how it came out. Then all was darkness and quiet and unconsciousness.

WHEN HENRY came to, he knew that something was desperately wrong with the Eastside Bank & Trust. The heavy steel door of the vault was buckled and twisted and the floor tilted up at a dizzy angle, while the ceiling dipped crazily toward it. Henry gingerly got to his feet, moving arms and legs experimentally. Assured that nothing was broken, he tenderly raised a hand to his eyes. His precious glasses were intact, thank God! He would never have been able to find his way out of the shattered vault without them.

He made a mental note to write Dr. Torrance to have a spare pair made and mailed to him. Blasted nuisance not having his prescription on file locally, but Henry trusted no-one but Dr. Torrance to grind those thick lenses into his own complicated prescription. Henry removed the heavy glasses from his face. Instantly the room dissolved into a neutral blur. Henry saw a pink splash that he knew was his hand, and a white blob come up to meet the pink as he withdrew his pocket handkerchief and carefully dusted the lenses. As he replaced the glasses, they slipped down on the bridge of his nose a little. He had been meaning to have them tightened for some time.

He suddenly realized, without the realization actually entering his conscious thoughts, that something momentous had happened, something worse than the boiler blowing up, something worse than a gas main exploding, something worse than anything that had ever happened before. He felt that way because it was so quiet. There was no whine of sirens, no shouting, no running, just an ominous and all pervading silence.

HENRY WALKED across the slanting floor. Slipping and stumbling on the uneven surface, he made his way to the elevator. The car lay crumpled at the foot of the shaft like a discarded accordion. There was something inside of it that Henry could not look at, something that had once been a person, perhaps several people, it was impossible to tell.

Feeling sick, Henry staggered toward the stairway. The steps were still there, but so jumbled and piled back upon one another that it was more like climbing the side of a mountain than mounting a stairway. It was quiet in the huge chamber that had been the lobby of the bank. It looked strangely cheerful with the sunlight shining through the girders where the ceiling had fallen. The dappled sunlight glinted across the silent lobby, and everywhere there were huddled lumps of unpleasantness that made Henry sick as he tried not to look at them.

"Mr. Carsville," he called. It was very quiet. Something had to be done, of course. This was terrible, right in the middle of a Monday, too. Mr. Carsville would know what to do. He called again, more loudly, and his voice cracked hoarsely. "Mr. Carrrrsville!" and then he saw an arm and shoulder extending out from under a huge fallen block of marble ceiling. In the buttonhole was the white carnation Mr. Carsville had worn to work that morning, and on the third finger of that hand was a massive signet ring, also belonging to Mr. Carsville. Numbly, Henry realized that the rest of Mr. Carsville was under that block of marble.

Henry felt a pang of real sorrow. Mr. Carsville was gone, and so was the rest of the staff—Mr. Wilkinson and Mr. Emory and Mr. Prithard, and the same with Pete and Ralph and Jenkins and Hunter and Pat the guard and Willie the doorman. There was no one to say what was to be done about the Eastside Bank & Trust except Henry Bemis, and Henry wasn't worried about the bank. There was something he wanted to do.

He climbed carefully over piles of fallen masonry. Once he stepped down into something that crunched and squashed beneath his feet and he set his teeth on edge to keep from retching. The street was not much different from the inside, bright sunlight and so much concrete to crawl over, but the unpleasantness was much, much worse. Everywhere there were strange, motionless lumps that Henry could not look at.

Suddenly, he remembered Agnes. He should be trying to get to Agnes, shouldn't he? He remembered a poster he had seen that said, "In event of an emergency do not use the telephone, your loved ones are as safe as you." He wondered about Agnes. He looked at the smashed automobiles, some with their four wheels pointed skyward like the stiffened legs of dead animals. He couldn't get to Agnes now anyway, if she was safe, then she was safe, otherwise ... of course, Henry knew Agnew wasn't safe. He had a feeling that there wasn't anyone safe for a long, long way, maybe not in the whole state or the whole country, or the whole world. No, that was a thought Henry didn't want to think, he forced it from his mind and turned his thoughts back to Agnes.

SHE HAD been a pretty good wife, now that it was all said and done. It wasn't exactly her fault if people didn't have time to read nowadays. It was just that there was the house, and the bank, and the yard. There was the Jones' for bridge and the Graysons' for canasta and charades with the Bryants'. And the television, the television Agnes loved to watch, but would never watch alone. He never had time to read even a newspaper. He started thinking about last night, that business about the newspaper.

Henry had settled into his chair, quietly, afraid that a creaking spring might call to Agnes' attention that fact that he was momentarily unoccupied. He had unfolded the newspaper slowly and carefully, the sharp crackle of the paper would have been a clarion call to Agnes. He had glanced at the headlines of the first page. "Collapse Of Conference Imminent." He didn't have time to read the article. He turned to the second page. "Solon Predicts War Only Days Away." He flipped through the pages faster, reading brief snatches here and there, afraid to spend too much time on any one item. On a back page was a brief article entitled, "Prehistoric Artifacts Unearthed In Yucatan." Henry smiled to himself and carefully folded the sheet of paper into fourths. That would be interesting, he would read all of it. Then it came, Agnes' voice. "Henrrreee!" and then she was upon him. She lightly flicked the paper out of his hands and into the fireplace. He saw the flames lick up and curl possessively around the unread article. Agnes continued, "Henry, tonight is the Jones' bridge night. They'll be here in thirty minutes and I'm not dressed yet, and here you are . . . *reading.*" she had emphasized the last word as though it were an unclean act. "Hurry and shave, you know how smooth Jasper Jones' chin always looks, and then straighten up this room." she glanced regretfully toward the fireplace. "Oh, dear, that paper, the television schedule . . . oh well, after the Jones leave there won't be time for anything but the late-late movie and . . . Don't just sit there, Henry, hurrreeee!"

Henry was hurrying now, but hurrying too much. He cut his leg on a twisted piece of metal that had once been an automobile fender. He thought about things like lockjaw and gangrene and his hand trembled as he tied his pocket-handkerchief around the wound. In his mind, he saw the fire again, licking across the face of last night's newspaper. He thought that now he would have time to read all the newspapers he wanted to, only now there wouldn't be any more. That heap of rubble across the street had been the Gazette Building. It was terrible to think there would never be another up to date newspaper. Agnes would have been very upset, no television schedule. But then, of course, no television. He wanted to laugh but he didn't. That wouldn't have been fitting, not at all.

He could see the building he was looking for now, but the silhouette was

TIME ENOUGH AT LAST

strangely changed. The great circular dome was now a ragged semi-circle, half of it gone, and one of the great wings of the building had fallen in upon itself. A sudden panic gripped Henry Bemis. What if they were all ruined, destroyed, every one of them? What if there wasn't a single one left? Tears of helplessness welled in his eyes as he painfully fought his way over and through the twisted fragments of the city.

HE THOUGHT of the building when it had been whole. He remembered the many nights he had paused outside its wide and welcoming doors. He thought of the warm nights when the doors had been thrown open and he could see the people inside, see them sitting at the plain wooden tables with the stacks of books beside them. He used to think then, what a wonderful thing a public library was, a place where anybody, anybody at all could go in and read.

He had been tempted to enter many times. He had watched the people through the open doors, the man in greasy work clothes who sat near the door, night after night, laboriously studying, a technical journey perhaps, difficult for him, but promising a brighter future. There had been an aged, scholarly gentleman who sat on the other side of the door, leisurely paging, moving his lips a little as he did so, a man having little time left, but rich in time because he could do with it as he chose.

Henry had never gone in. He had started up the steps once, got almost to the door, but then he remembered Agnes, her questions and shouting, and he had turned away.

He was going in now though, almost crawling, his breath coming in stabbing gasps, his hands torn and bleeding. His trouser leg was sticky red where the wound in his leg had soaked through the handkerchief. It was throbbing badly but Henry didn't care. He had reached his destination.

Part of the inscription was still there, over the now doorless entrance. P-U-B—C L-I-B-R—. The rest had been torn away. The place was in shambles. The shelves were overturned, broken, smashed, tilted, their precious contents spilled in disorder upon the floor. A lot of the books, Henry noted gleefully, were still intact, still whole, still readable. He was literally knee deep in them, he wallowed in books. He picked one up. The title was "Collected Works of William Shakespeare." Yes, he must read that, sometime. He laid it aside carefully. He picked up another. Spinoza. He tossed it away, seized another, and another, and still another. Which to read first . . . there were so many.

He had been conducting himself a little like a starving man in a delicatessen—grabbing a little of this and a little of that in a frenzy of enjoyment.

But now he steadied away. From the pile about him, he selected one volume, sat comfortably down on an overturned shelf, and opened the book.

Henry Bemis smiled.

There was the rumble of complaining stone. Minute in comparison with the epic complaints following the fall of the bomb. This one occurred under one corner of the shelf upon which Henry sat. The shelf moved; threw him off balance. The glasses slipped from his nose and fell with a tinkle.

He bent down, clawing blindly, and found, finally, their smashed remains. A minor, indirect destruction stemming from the sudden, wholesale smashing of a city. But the only one that greatly interested Henry Bemis.

He stared down at the blurred page before him.

He began to cry.

Yvala

by Catherine L. Moore
and Amaryllis Ackerman

It is a practically unknown fact that I created the character (pronounced Ee-vah-lah) in this excellent Northwest Smith tale. Herewith, the story of a beautiful woman as dangerous and cruel as any monster ever encountered!
—FJA

*N*orthwest Smith leaned against a pile of hemp-wrapped bales from the Martian drylands and stared with expressionless eyes, paler than pale steel, over the confusion of the Lakkdarol space-port before him. In the clear Martian day the tatters of his leather spaceman's garb were pitilessly plain, the ray-burns and the rents of a hundred casual brawls. It was evident at a glance that Smith had fallen upon evil days. One might have guessed by the shabbiness of his clothing that his pockets were empty, the charge in his ray-gun low.

Squatting on his heels beside the lounging Earthman, Yarol the Venusian bent his yellow head absently over the thin-bladed dagger which he was juggling in one of the queer, interminable Venusian games so pointless to outsiders. Upon him too the weight of ill fortune seemed to have pressed heavily. It was eloquent in his own shabby garments, his empty holster. But the insouciant face he lifted to Smith was as careless as ever, and no more of weariness and wisdom and pure cat-savagery looked out from his sidelong black eyes than Smith was accustomed to see there. Yarol's face was the face of a seraph, as so many Venusian faces are likely to be, but the set of his mouth told a tale of dissoluteness and reckless violence which belied his features' racial good looks.

"Another half-hour and we eat," he grinned up at his tall companion.

Smith glanced at the tri-time watch on his wrist.

"If you haven't been having another dope dream," he grunted. "Luck's been against us so long I can't quite believe in a change now."

"By Pharol I swear it," smiled Yarol. "The man came up to me in the *New Chicago* last night and told me in so many words how much money was waiting if we'd meet him here at noon."

Smith grunted again and deliberately took up another notch in the belt that circled his lean waist. Yarol laughed softly, a murmur of true Venusian sweetness, as he bent again to the juggling of his knife. Above his bent blond head Smith looked out again across the busy port.

Lakkdarol is an Earthman's town upon Martian soil, blending all the more violent elements of both worlds in its lawless heart, and the scene he watched had under-currents that only a ranger of the spaceways could fully appreciate. A semblance of discipline is maintained there, but only the space-rangers know how superficial that likeness is. Smith grinned a little to himself, knowing that the bales being trundled down the gangplank from the Martian liner *Inghti* carried a core of that precious Martian "lamb's-wool" on which the duties ran so high. And a whisper had run through the *New Chicago* last night as they sat over their *segir*-whisky glasses that the shipment of grain from Denver expected in at noon on the *Friedland* would have a copious leavening of opium in its heart. By devious ways, in whispers running from mouth to mouth covertly through the spacemen's rendezvous, the outlaws of the spaceways glean more knowledge than the Patrol ever knows.

Smith watched a little air-freight vessel, scarcely a quarter the size of the monstrous ships of the Lines, rolling sluggishly out from the municipal hangar far across the square, and a little frown puckered his brows. The ship bore only the non-committal numerals which are all the freighters carry by way of identification, but that particular sequence was notorious among the initiate. The ship was a slaver.

This dealing in human freight had received a great impetus at the stimulation of space-travel, when the temptation presented by the savage tribes on alien planets was too great to be ignored by unscrupulous Earthmen who saw vast fields opening up before them. For even upon Earth slaving has never died entirely, and Mars and Venus knew a small and legitimate traffic in it before John Willard and his gang of outlaws made the very word "slaving" anathema on three worlds. The Willards still ran their pirate convoys along the spaceways three generations later, and Smith knew he was looking at one now, smuggling a cargo of misery out of Lakkdarol for distribution among the secret markets of Mars.

FURTHER MEDITATIONS ON the subject were cut short by Yarol's abrupt rise to his feet. Smith turned his head slowly and saw a little man at their elbow, his rotundity cloaked in a long mantle like those affected by the lower class of Martian shopkeepers in their walks abroad. But the face that peered up into his was frankly Celtic. Smith's expressionless features broke reluctantly into a grin as he met the irrepressible good-humor on that fat Irish face from home. He had not set foot upon Earth's soil for over a year now—the price on his liberty was too high in his native land—and curious pricks of homesickness came over him at the oddest moments. Even the toughest of space-rangers know them sometimes. The ties with the home planet are strong.

"You Smith?" demanded the little man in a rich Celtic voice.

Smith looked down at him a moment in cold-eyed silence. There was much more in that query than met the ear. Northwest Smith's name was one too well known in the annals of the Patrol for him to acknowledge it incautiously. The little Irishman's direct question implied what he had been expecting—if he acknowledged the name he met the man on the grounds of outlawry, which would mean that the employment in prospect was to be as illegal as he had thought it would be.

The merry blue eyes twinkled up at him. The man was laughing to himself at the Celtic subtlety with which he had introduced his subject. And again, involuntarily, Smith's straight mouth relaxed into a reluctant grin.

"I am," he said recklessly.

"I've been looking for you. There's a job to be done that'll pay you well, if you want to risk it."

Smith's pale eyes glanced about them warily. No one was within earshot. The place seemed as good as any other for the discussion of extra-legal bargains.

"What is it?" he demanded.

The little man glanced down at Yarol, who had dropped to one knee again and was flicking his knife tirelessly in the intricacies of his queer game. He had apparently lost interest in the whole proceeding.

"It'll take both of you," said the Irishman in his merry, rich voice. "Do you see that air freighter loading over there?" and he nodded toward the slaver.

Smith's head jerked in mute acknowledgment.

"It's a Willard ship, as I suppose you know. But the business is running pretty low these days. Cargoes too hot to ship. The Patrol is shutting down hard, and receipts have slackened like the devil in the last year. I suppose you've heard that too."

Smith nodded again without words. He had.

"Well, what we lose in quantity we have to make up in quality. Remember the prices the Minga girls used to bring?"

Smith's face was expressionless. He remembered very well indeed, but he said nothing.

"Along toward the last, kings could hardly pay the price they were asking for those girls. That's really the best market, if you want to get into the 'ivory' trade. Women. And there you come in. Did you ever hear of Cembre?"

Blank-eyed, Smith shook his head. For once he had run across a name whose rumors he had never encountered before in all the tavern gossip.

"Well, on one of Jupiter's moons—which one I'll tell you later, if you decide to accept—a Venusian named Cembre was wrecked years ago. By a miracle he survived and managed to escape; but hardships he'd undergone unsettled his mind, and he couldn't do much but rave about the beautiful sirens he'd seen while he was wandering through the jungles there. Nobody paid any attention to him until the same thing happened again, this time only about a month ago. Another man came back half-cracked from struggling through the jungles, babbling about women so beautiful a man could go mad just from looking at them.

"Well, the Willards heard of it. The whole thing may sound like a pipedream, but they've got the idea it's worth investigating. And they can afford to indulge their whims, you know. So they're outfitting a small expedition to see what basis there may be for the myth of Cembre's sirens. If you want to try it, you're hired."

Smith slanted a non-committal glance downward into Yarol's uplifted black gaze. Neither spoke.

"You'll want to talk it over," said the little Irishman comprehendingly. "Suppose you meet me in the *New Chicago* at sundown and tell me what you've decided."

"Good enough," grunted Smith. The fat Celt grinned again and was gone in a swirl of black cloak and a flash of Irish merriment.

"Cold-blooded little devil," murmured Smith, looking after the departing Earthman. "It's a dirty business, Yarol."

"Money's clean," observed Yarol lightly. "And I'm not a man to let my scruples stand in the way of my means. I say take it. Someone'll go, and it might as well be us."

Smith shrugged.

"We've got to eat," he admitted.

"THIS," MURMURED YAROL, staring downward on hands and knees at the edge of the space-ship's floor-port, "is the prettiest little hell I ever expect to see."

The vessel was arching in a long curve around the Jovian moon as its pilot braked slowly for descent, and a panorama of ravening jungle slipped by in an unchanging wilderness below the floorport.

Their presence here, skimming through the upper atmosphere of the wild little satellite, was the end of a long series of the smoothest journeying either had ever known. The Willard network was perfect over the three planets and the colonized satellites beyond, and over the ships that ply the spaceways. This neat little exploring vessel, with its crew of three coarse-faced, sullen slavers, had awaited them at the end of their journey outward from Lakkdarol, fully fitted with supplies and every accessory the most modern adventurer could desire. It even had a silken prison room for the hypothetical sirens whom they were to carry back for the Willard approval and the Willard markets if the journey proved successful.

"It's been easy so far," observed Smith, squinting downward over the little Venusian's shoulder. "Can't expect everything, you know. But that *is* a bad-looking place."

The dull-faced pilot at the controls grunted in fervent agreement as he craned his neck to watch the little world spinning below them.

"Damn' glad I'm not goin' out with you," he articulated thickly over a mouthful of tobacco.

Yarol flung him a cheerful Venusian anathema in reply, but Smith did not speak. He had little liking and less trust in this sullen and silent crew. If he was not mistaken—and he rarely made mistakes in his appraisal of men—there was going to be trouble with the three before they completed their journey back into civilization. Now he turned his broad back to the pilot and stared downward.

From above, the moon seemed covered with the worst type of semi-animate, ravenous super-tropical jungle, reeking with fertility and sudden death, hot under lurid Jupiter's blaze. They saw no signs of human life anywhere below as their ship swept in its long curve over the jungle. The tree-tops spread in an unbroken blanket over the whole sphere of the satellite. Yarol, peering downward, murmured:

"No water. Somehow I always expect sirens to have fish-tails."

Out of his queer, heterogeneous past Smith dragged a fragment of ancient verse, "—gulfs enchanted, where the sirens sing . . ." and said aloud, "They're supposed to sing, too. Oh, it'll probably turn out to be a pack of black-faced savages, if there's anything but delirium behind the story."

The ship was spiraling down now, and the jungle rushed up to meet them at express-train speed. Once again the little moon spun under their searching eyes, flower-garlanded, green with fertile life, massed solid in tangles of ravening growth. Then the pilot's hands closed hard on the controls and with a shriek of protesting atmosphere the little spaceship slid in a long dive toward the unbroken jungle below.

In a great crashing and crackling they sank groundward through smothers of foliage that masked the ports and plunged the interior of the ship into a green twilight. With scarcely an impact the jungle floor received them. The pilot leaned back in his seat and heaved a tobacco-redolent sigh. His work was done. Incuriously he glanced at the forward port.

Yarol was scrambling up from the floor-glass that now showed nothing but crushed vines and branches and the reeking mud of the moon's surface. He joined Smith and the pilot at the forward port.

They were submerged in jungle. Great serpentine branches and vines like cables looped downward in broken lengths from the shattered trees which had given way at their entrance. It was an animate jungle, full of hungry, reaching things that sprang in one wild, prolific tangle from the rich mud. Raw-colored flowers, yards across, turned sucking mouths blindly against the glass here and there, trickles of green juice slavering down the clear surface from their insensate hunger. A thorn-fanged vine lashed out as they stood staring and slid harmlessly along the glass, lashed again and again blindly until the prongs were dulled and green juice bled from its bruised surfaces.

"Well, we'll have some blasting to do after all," murmured Smith as he looked out into the ravenous jungle. "No wonder those poor devils came back a little cracked. I don't see how they got through at all. It's—"

"Well—Pharol take me!" breathed Yarol in so reverent a whisper that Smith's voice broke off in mid-sentence and he spun around with a hand dropping to his gun to front the little Venusian, who had sought the stern port in his exploration.

"It's a road!" gasped Yarol. "Black Pharol can have me for dinner if there isn't a road just outside here!"

THE PILOT REACHED for a noxious Martian cigarette and stretched luxuriously, quite uninterested. But Smith had reached the Venusian's side before he finished speaking, and in silence the two stared out upon the surprising scene the stern port framed. A broad roadway stretched arrow-straight into the dimness of the jungle. At its edges the hungry green things ceased abruptly, no encroaching by so much as a tendril or a leaf into the clearness of the path. Even overhead the branches had been forbidden to intrude, their vine-looped greenery forming an arch above the road. It was as if a destroying beam had played through the jungle, killing all life in its path. Even the oozing mud was firmed here into a smooth pavement. Empty, enigmatic, the clear way slanted across their line of vision and on into the writhing jungle.

"Well," Yarol broke the silence at last, "here's a good start. All we've got to do is follow the road. It's a safe bet there won't be any lovely ladies wandering around through this jungle. From the looks of the road there must be some civilized people on the moon after all."

"I'd be happier if I knew what made it," said Smith. "There are some damned queer things on some of the moons and asteroids."

Yarol's cat-eyes were shining.

"That's what I like about this life," he grinned. "You don't get bored. Well, what do the readings say?"

From his seat at the control panel the pilot glanced at the gages which gave automatic report on air and gravity outside.

"O.K." he grunted. "Better take blast-guns."

Smith shrugged off his sudden uneasiness and turned to the weapon rack. "Plenty of charges, too," he said. "No telling what we'll run into."

The pilot rolled his poisonous cigarette between thick lips and said, "Luck. You'll need it," as the two turned to the outer lock. He had all the indifference of his class to anything but his own comfort and the completion of his allotted tasks with a minimum of effort, and he scarcely troubled to turn his head as the lock swung open upon an almost overwhelming gush of thick, hot air, redolent of green growing things and the stench of swift decay.

A vine-tip lashed violently into the opened door as Smith and Yarol stood staring. Yarol snapped a Venusian oath and dodged back, drawing his blast-gun. An instant later the eye-destroying blaze of it sheered a path of destruction through the lush vegetable carnivora straight toward the slanting roadway a dozen feet away. There was an immense hissing and sizzling of annihilated green stuff, and an empty path stretched before them across the little space which parted the ship's outer lock from the road. Yarol stepped down into reeking mud that bubbled up around his boots with a stench of fertility and decay. He swore again as he sank knee-deep into its blackness. Smith, grinning, joined him. Side by side they floundered through the ooze toward the road.

Short though the distance was, it took them all of ten minutes to cover it. Green things whipped out toward them from the walls of sheared forest where the blast-gun had burned, and both were bleeding from a dozen small scratches and thorn-flicks, breathless and angry and very muddy indeed before they reached their goal and dragged themselves into the firmness of the roadway.

"Whew!" gasped Yarol, stamping the mud from his caked boots. "Pharol can have me if I stir a step off this road after this. There isn't a siren alive who could lure me back into that hell again. Poor Cembre!"

"Come on," said Smith, "Which way?"

Yarol slatted sweat from his forehead and drew a deep breath, his nostrils wrinkled distastefully.

"Into the breeze, if you ask me. Did you ever smell such a stench? And hot! God! I'm soaked through already."

Without words Smith nodded and turned to the right, from where a faint breeze stirred the heavy, moisture-laden air. His own lean body was impervious to a great variation in climate, but even Yarol, native of the Hot Planet, dripped with sweat already and Smith's own leather-tanned face glistened and his shirt clung in wet patches to his shoulders.

The cool breeze struck gratefully upon their faces as they turned into the wind. In a gasping silence they plodded muddily up the road, their wonder deepening as they advanced. What had made the roadway became more of a mystery at every step. No vehicle tracks marked the firm ground, no footprints. And nowhere by so much as a hair's breadth did the forest encroach upon the path.

On both sides, beyond the rigid limits of the road, the lush and cannibalistic life of the vegetation went on. Vines dangled great sucking disks and thorn-toothed creepers in the thick air, ready for a deadly cast at anything that wandered within reach. Small reptilian things scuttling through the reeking swamp mud squeaked now and then in the toils of some thorny trap, and twice they heard the hollow bellowing of some invisible monster. It was raw primeval life booming and thrashing and devouring all about them, a planet in the first throes of animate life.

But here on the roadway that could have been made by nothing less than a well-advanced civilization the ravening jungle seemed very far away, like some unreal world enacting its primitive dramas upon a stage. Before they had gone far they were paying little heed to it, and the bellowing and the lashing, hungry vines and the ravenous forest growths faded into half-heard oblivion. Nothing out of that world entered upon the roadway.

As they advanced the sweltering heat abated in the steady breeze that was blowing down the road. There was a faint perfume upon it, sweet and light and utterly alien to the fetor of the reeking swamps which bordered their way. The scented gusts of it fanned their hot faces gently.

Smith was glancing over his shoulder at regular intervals, and a pucker of uneasiness drew his brows together.

"If we don't have trouble with that crew of our before we're through," he said, "I'll buy you a case of *segir*."

"It's a bet," agreed Yarol cheerfully, turning up to Smith his sidelong cat-eyes as insouciantly savage as the raving jungle around them. "Though they were a pretty tough trio, at that."

"They may have the idea they can leave us here and collect our share of the money back home," said Smith. "Or once we get the girls they may want to dump us and take them on alone. And if they haven't thought of anything yet, they will."

"Up to no good, the whole bunch of 'em," grinned Yarol. "They—they—" His voice faltered and faded into silence. There was a sound upon the breeze. Smith had stopped dead-still, his ears straining to recapture the echo of that murmur which had come blowing toward them on the breeze. Such a sound as that might had come drifting over the walls of Paradise.

In the silence as they stood with caught breath it came again—a lilt of the loveliest, most exquisitely elusive laughter. From very far away it came floating to their ears, the lovely ghost of a woman's laughing. There was in it a caress of kissing sweetness. It brushed over Smith's nerves like the brush of lingering fingers and died away into throbbing silence that seemed reluctant to let the exquisite sound of it fade into echoes and cease.

THE TWO MEN faced each other in rapt bewilderment. Finally Yarol found his voice.

"Sirens!" he breathed. "They don't have to sing if they can laugh like that! Come on!"

At a swifter pace they went on up the road. The breeze blew fragrantly against their faces. After a while its perfumed breath carried to their ears another faint, far-away echo of that heavenly laughter, sweeter than honey, drifting on the wind in fading cadences that died away by imperceptible degrees until they could no longer be sure if it was the lovely laughter they heard or the quickened beating of their own hearts.

Yet before them the road stretched emptily, very still in the green twilight under the low-arching trees. There seemed to be a sort of haze here, so that though the road ran straight the green dimness veiled what lay ahead and they walked in a queer silence along the roadway through ravening jungles whose sights and sounds might almost have been on another world for all the heed they paid them. Their ears were straining for a repetition of that low and lovely laughter, and the expectation of it gripped them in an unheeding spell which wiped out all other things but its own delicious echoes.

When they first became aware of a pale glimmer in the twilight greenness ahead, neither could have told. But somehow they were not surprised that a girl was pacing slowly down the roadway toward them, half veiled in the jungle dimness under the trees.

To Smith she was a figure walking straight out of a dream. Even at that distance her beauty had a still enchantment that swallowed up all his wondering in a strange and magical peace. Beauty flowed along the long, curved lines of her body, alternately cloaked and revealed by the drifting garment of her hair, and the slow, swinging grace of her as she walked was a potent enchantment that gripped him helpless in its spell.

Then another glimmer in the dimness caught his eyes away from the bewitchment that approached, and in bewilderment he saw that another girl was pacing forward under the low-hanging trees, her hair swinging about her in slow drifts that veiled and unveiled the loveliness of a body as exquisite as the first. That first was nearer now, so that he could see the enchantment of her face, pale golden and lovelier than a dream with its subtly molded smoothness and delicately tilted planes of cheek-bone and cheek smoothing deliciously upward into a broad, low forehead whence the richly colored hair sprang back in tendrils like licking flames. There was a subtle Slavic tilting to those honey-colored features, hinted in the breadth of the cheeks and the sweet straightness with which their planes slanted downward to a mouth colored like hot embers, curving now in a smile that promised—heaven.

She was very near. He could see the peach-like bloom upon her pale gold limbs and the very throb of the pulse beating in her round throat, and the veiled eyes sought his. But behind her that second girl was nearing, every whit as lovely as the first, and her beauty drew his gaze magnet-like to its own delicate flow and ripple of enchantment. And beyond her—yes, another was coming, and beyond her a fourth; and in the green twilight behind these first, pale blurs bespoke the presence of yet more.

And they were identical. Smith's bewildered eyes flew from face to face, seeking and finding what his brain could still not quite believe. Feature by feature, curve by curve, they were identical. Five, six, seven honey-colored bodies, half veiled in richly tinted hair, swayed toward him. Seven, eight, nine exquisite faces smiled their promise of ecstasy. Dizzy and incredulous, he felt a hand grip his shoulder. Yarol's voice, bemused, half whispered, murmured:

"Is this Paradise—or are we both mad?"

The sound of it brought Smith out of his tranced bewitchment. He shook his head sharply, like a man half-awake and striving for clarity, and said, "Do they all look alike to you?"

"Every one. Exquisite—exquisite—did you ever see such satin-black hair?"

"Black—black?" Smith muttered that over stupidly, wondering what was so wrong with the word. When realization broke upon him at last, the shock of it was strong enough to jerk his eyes away from the enchantment before him and turn them sharply around to the little Venusian's rapt face.

Its stainless clarity was set in a mask of almost holy wonder. Even the wisdom and weariness and savagery of its black eyes were lost in the glamor of what they gazed on. His voice murmured, almost to itself, "And white—so white—like lilies, aren't they? —blacker and whiter than—"

"Are you crazy?" Smith's voice broke harshly upon the Venusian's rapture. That trance-like mask broke before the impact of his exclamation. Like a man awaking from a dream, Yarol turned blinking to his friend.

"Crazy? Why—why—aren't we both? How else could we be seeing a sight like this?"

"One of us is," said Smith grimly. "I'm looking at red-haired girls colored like—like peaches."

Yarol blinked again. His eyes sought the bevy of bewildering loveliness in the roadway. He said, "It's you, then. They've got black hair, every one of them, shiny and smooth and black as so many lengths of satin, and nothing in creation is whiter than their bodies."

SMITH'S PALE EYES turned again to the road. Again they met honey-pale curves and planes of velvet flesh half veiled in hair like drifting flames. He shook his head once more, dazedly.

The girls hovered before him in the green dimness, moving with little restive steps back and forth on the hard-beaten road, their feet like the drift of flower-petals for lightness, their hair rippling away from the smoothly swelling curves of their bodies and furling about them again in ceaseless motion. They turned lingering eyes to the two men, but they did not speak.

Then down the wind again came drifting the far echo of that exquisite, lilting laugh. The sweetness of it made the very breeze brush light against their faces. It was a caress and a promise and a summoning almost irresistible, floating past them and drifting away into the distance in low, far-off cadences that lingered in their ears long after its audible music had ceased.

The sound of it woke Smith out of his daze, and he turned to the nearest girl, blurting, "Who are you?"

Among the fluttering throng a little shiver of excitement ran. Lovely, identical faces turned to him from all over the whole group, and the one addressed smiled bewilderingly.

"I am Yvala," she said in a voice smoother than silk, pitched to caress the ear and ripple along the very nerve fibers with a slow and soothing sweetness. And she had spoken in English! It was long since Smith had heard his mother tongue. The sound of it plucked at some hidden heart-string with intolerable poignancy, the home language spoken in a voice of enchanted sweetness. For a moment he could not speak.

The silence broke to Yarol's low whistle of surprise.

"I know now we're crazy," he murmured. "No other way to explain her speaking in High Venusian. Why, she can't ever have—"

"High Venusian!" exclaimed Smith, startled out of his moment of silence. "She spoke English!"

They stared at each other, wild suspicions rising in their eyes. In desperation Smith turned and hurled the question again at another of the lovely throng, waiting breathlessly for her answer to be sure his ears had not deceived him.

"Yvala—I am Yvala," she answered in just that silken voice with which the first had answered. It was English unmistakably, and sweet with memories of home.

Behind her among the bevy of curved, peach-colored bodies and veils of richly tinted hair other full red lips moved and other velvety voices murmured, "Yvala, Yvala, I am Yvala," like dying echoes drifting from mouth to mouth until the last syllable of the strange and lovely name faded into silence.

Across the stunned quiet that fell as their murmurs died the breeze blew again, and once more that sweet, low laughter rang from far away in their ears, rising and falling on the wind until their pulses beat in answer, and falling, fading, dying away reluctantly on the fragrant breeze.

"What—who was that?" demanded Smith softly of the fluttering girls, as the last of it faded into silence.

"It was Yvala," they chorused in caressing voices like multiple echoes of the same rich, lingering tones. "Yvala laughs—Yvala calls . . . Come with us to Yvala . . ."

Yarol said in a sudden ripple of musical speech.

"*Geth norri a'Yvali?*" at the same moment that Smith's query broke out. "Who is Yvala, then?" in his own seldom-used mother tongue.

But they got no reply to that, only beckonings and murmurous repetitions of the name, "Yvala, Yvala, Yvala—" and smiles that set their pulses beating faster. Yarol reached out a tentative hand toward the nearest, but she melted like smoke out of his grasp so that he no more than grazed the velvety flesh of her shoulder with a touch that left his fingers tingling delightfully. She smiled over her shoulder ardently, and Yarol gripped Smith's arm.

"Come on," he said urgently.

IN A PLEASANT dream of low voices and lovely warm bodies circling just out of reach they went slowly on down the road in the midst of that hovering group, walking up-wind whence that tantalizing laughter had rung, and all about them the golden girls circled on restless, drifting feet, their hair floating and furling about the loveliness of their half-seen bodies, the echoes of that single name rising and falling in cadences as rich and smooth as cream. Yvala—Yvala—Yvala—a magical spell to urge them on their way.

How long they walked they never knew. The changeless jungle slid away behind them unnoticed; the broad, enigmatic pavement stretched ahead, a mysterious, green gloom shadowing the whole length of that laughter-haunted roadway. Nothing had any meaning to them outside the circle the murmurous girls were weaving with their swaying bodies and swinging hair and voices like the echoes of a dream. All the wonder and incredulity and bewilderment in the minds of the two men had sunk away into nothingness, drowned and swallowed up in the flagrant magic of their enchantresses.

After a long, rapt while they came to the roadway's end. Smith lifted dreaming pale eyes and saw as if through a veil, so remotely that the scene had little meaning to him, the great park-like clearing stretching away before them as the jungle walls fell away on either side. Here the primeval swamplands and animate green life ceased abruptly to make way for a scene that might have been lifted straight over a million years. The clearing was columned with great patriarchal trees ages removed in evolution from the snake things which grew in the hungry jungle. Their leaves roofed the place in swaying greenery though which the light sifted with twilight softness upon a carpet of flower-starred moss. With one step they spanned ages of evolution and entered into the lovely dim clearing that might have been lifted out of a world a million years older than the jungle that raved impotently around its borders.

The moss was velvety under their pacing feet. With eyes that but half comprehended what they saw, Smith gazed out across the twilight vistas through the green gloom brooding beneath the trees. It was a hushed place, mystical, very quiet. He thought sometimes he saw the flash of life through the leaves overhead, the stir of it among the trees as small wild things crossed their path and birds fluttered in the foliage, but he could not be sure. Once or twice it seemed to him that he had caught an echo of bird-song, somehow as if the melody had rung in his ears a moment before, and only now, when the sound was fading, did he realize it. But not once did he hear an actual song note or see any animate life, though the presence of it was rife in the green twilight beneath the leaves.

They went on slowly. Once he could have sworn he saw a dappled fawn staring at him with wide, unhappy eyes from a covert of branches, but when he looked closer there was nothing but leaves swaying emptily. And once upon his inner ear, as if with the echo of a just-past sound, he thought he heard a stallion's high whinny. But after all it did not greatly matter. The girls were shepherding them on over the flowery moss, circling like hollow-throated doves whose only music was "Yvala—Yvala—Yvala . . ." in unending harmony of rising and falling notes.

They paced on dreamily, the trees and mossy vistas of park sliding smoothly away behind them in unchanging quiet. And more and more strongly that impression of life among the trees nagged at Smith's mind. He wondered if he might not be developing hallucinations, for no arrangement of branches and shadows could explain the wild boar's head that he could have sworn thrust out among the leaves to stare at him for an instant with small, shamed eyes before it melted into patterned shadow under his direct gaze.

HE BLINKED AND rubbed his eyes in momentary terror lest his own brain was betraying him, and an instant later was peering uncertainly at the avenue between two low-hanging trees where from the corner of his eye he thought he had seen a magnificent white stallion hesitating with startled head upflung and the queerest, urgent look in its eyes, somehow warning and afraid—and ashamed. But it faded into mere leaf-cast shadows when he turned.

And once he started and stumbled over what was nothing more than a leafy branch lying across their path, yet which an instant before had looked bewildering like a low-slung cat-beast slinking across the moss with sullen, hot eyes upturned in hate and warning and distress to him.

There was something about these animals that roused a vague unrest in his mind when he looked at them—something in their eyes that was warning and agonized and more hotly aware than are the eyes of beasts—something queerly dreadful and hauntingly familiar about the set of their heads upon their shoulders—hinting horribly at another gait than the four-footed.

At last, just after a graceful doe had bounded out of the leaves, hesitated an instant and flashed away with a fleetness that did not look like the fleetness of a quadruped, turning upon him as she vanished a great-eyed agony that was warning as a cry, Smith halted in his tracks. Uneasiness too deep to be magicked away by the crooning girls urged him of danger. He paused and looked uncertainly around. The doe had melted into leaf-shadows flickering on the moss, but he could not forget the haunting shame and the warning of her eyes.

He stared about the dim greenness of the tree-roofed clearing. Was all this a lotus-dream, an illusion of jungle fever, or a suddenly unstable mind? Could he have imagined those beasts with their anguished eyes and their terribly familiar outlines of head and neck upon four-footed bodies? Was any of it real at all?

More for reassurance than for any other reason he reached out suddenly and seized the nearest honey-colored girl in a quick grip. Yes, she was tangible. His fingers closed about a firm and rounded arm, smoothly soft with the feel of peach-bloom velvet over its curving surface. The girl did not pull away. She stopped dead-still at his touch, slowly turning her head, lifting her face to his with a dream-like easiness, tilting her chin high until the long, full curve of her throat was arched taut and he could see the pulse beating hard under her velvet flesh. Her lips parted softly, her lids drooped low.

His other arm went out of its own accord, drawing her against him. Then her hands were in his hair, pulling his head down to hers, and all his uneasiness and distress and latent terror spun away at the kiss of her parted lips.

The next thing he realized was that he was strolling on under the trees, a girl's lithe body moving in the bend of his arm. Her very nearness was a delight that sent his senses reeling, so that the green woodland was vague as a dream and the only reality dwelt in the honey-color loveliness in the circle of his arm.

Dimly he was aware that Yarol strolled parallel with them a little distance away through the leaves, a bright head on his shoulder, another golden girl leaning against his encircling arm. She was so perfectly the counterpart of his own lovely captive that she might have been a reflection in a mirror. Uneasily, a remembrance swam up in Smith's mind. Did it seem to Yarol that a snow-white maiden walked with him, a black head leaned upon his shoulder? Was the little Venusian's mind yielding to the spell of the place, or was it his own? What tongue could it be that the girls spoke which fell upon his ears in English phrases and upon Yarol's in the musical lilt of High Venusian? Were they both mad?

Then in his arm the supple golden body stirred, the softly shadowed face turned up to his. The woodland vanished like smoke from about him in the magic of her lips.

THERE WERE DIM glades among the trees where piles of white ruins met Smith's unseeing eyes sometimes without leaving more than the merest trace of conscious remembrance. Vague wonders swam through his mind of what they might once have been, what vanished race had wrested this clearing from the jungle and died without leaving any trace save these. But he did not care. It had no significance. Even the half-seen beasts, who now turned eyes of sorrow and despair rather than warning, had lost all meaning to his enchanted brain. In a lotus dream he wandered on in the direction he was urged, unthinking, unalarmed. It was very sweet to stroll so through the dim green gloom, with purest magic in the bend of his arm. He was content.

They strolled past the white ruins of scattered buildings, past great bending trees that dappled them with shadow. The moss yielded underfoot as softly as thick-piled carpets. Unseen beasts slunk by them now and then, so that the tail<trail?> of Smith's eye was continually catching the—almost—hint of humanity in the lines of their bodies, the set of a head upon bestial shoulders, the clarity of urgent eyes. But he did not really see them.

Sweetly—intolerably sweetly—and softly, laughter rang through the woods. Smith's head flung up like a startled stallion's. It was a stronger laughter now, from near, very near among the leaves. It seemed to him that the voice indeed must come from some lovely, ardent houri leaning over the wall of Paradise—that he had come a long way in search of her and now trembled on the very brink of his journey's end. The low and lovely sound echoed through the trees, ringing down the green twilight aisles, shivering the leaves together. It was everywhere at once, a little world of music superimposed upon the world of matter, enclosing everything within its scope in a magical spell that left no room for any other thing but its lovely presence. And its command rang through Smith's mind with the sharpness of a sword in his flesh, calling, calling unbearably through the woods.

Then they came out of the trees into a little space of mossy clearing in whose center a small white temple rose. Somehow Yarol was there too—and somehow they were alone. These exquisite girls had melted like smoke into oblivion. The two men stood quite still, their eyes dazed as they stared. This building was the only one they had seen whose columns still stood upright, and only here could they tell that the architecture of those fallen walls whose ruins had dotted the wooded glades had been one at variance to anything on any world they knew. But upon the mystery of that they had no desire to dwell. For the woman those slim columns housed drove every other thought out of their dazzled minds.

She stood at the center of the tiny temple. She was pale golden, half veiled in the long cloak of her curls. And if the siren girls had been lovely, then here stood loveliness incarnate. Those girls had worn her form and face. Here was that same exquisitely molded body, colored like honey, half revealed among the drifts of hair that clung to it like tendrils of bright flames. But those bewildering girls had been mere echoes of the beauty that faced them now. Smith stared with a kindling of colorless eyes.

Here was Lilith—here was Helen—here was Circe—here before him stood all the beauty of all the legends of mankind; here on this marble floor, facing them gravely, with unsmiling eyes. For the first time he looked into the eyes that lighted that sweet, tilt-planed face, and his very soul gasped from the sudden plunge into their poignant blueness. It was not a vivid blue, not a blazing one, but its intensity far transcended anything he had words to name. In that business a man's soul could sink forever, reaching no bottom, stirred by no tides, drowned and steeped through and through with an infinity of absolute light.

When the blue, blue gaze released him he gasped once, like a drowning man, and then stared with new amazement upon a reality whose truth had escaped him until this moment. That instant of submerged ecstasy in the blue deeps of her eyes must have opened a door in his brain to new knowledge, for he saw as he stared a very strange quality in the loveliness he faced.

Tangible beauty dwelt here, an indwelling thing that could root itself in human flesh and clothe a body in loveliness as with a garment. Here was more than fleshly beauty, more than symmetry of face and body. A quality like a flame glowed all but visibly—no, more than visibly—along the peach-bloomy lines and smoothly swelling curves of her, giving a glory to the high tilt of her bosom and the long, subtly curved thigh and the exquisite line of shoulder gliding down into fuller beauty half veiled in drifting hair.

In that dazed, revealing moment her loveliness shimmered before him, too intensely for his human senses to perceive save as a dazzle of intolerable beauty before his half-comprehending eyes. He flung up his hands to shut the glory out and stood for a moment with hidden eyes in a self-imposed darkness though which beauty blazed with an intensity that transcended the visible and beat unbearably on every fiber of his being until he stood bathed in light that permeated the ultimate atoms of his soul.

THEN THE BLAZE DIED. He lowered shaking hands and saw that lovely, pale-gold face melting slowly into a smile of such heavenly promise that for an instant his senses failed him again and the world spun dizzily around a focus of honey-pale features breaking into arcs and softly shadowed curves, as the velvety mouth curled slowly into a smile.

"All strangers are very welcome here," crooned a voice like a vibration of sheerest silk, sweeter than honey, caressing as the brush of a kissing mouth. And she had spoken in the purest of earthly English. Smith found his voice.

"Who—who are you?" he asked in a queer gasp, as if his very breath were stopped by the magic he faced.

Before she could answer, Yarol's voice broke in, a little unsteady with sudden, savage anger.

"Can't you answer in the language you're addressed in?" he demanded in a violent undertone. "The least you could do is ask her name in High Venusian. How do you know she speaks English?"

QUITE SPEECHLESS, SMITH turned a blank gray gaze upon his companion. He saw the blaze of hot Venusian temper fade like mist from Yarol's black eyes as he turned to the glory in the temple. And in the lovely, liquid cadences of his native tongue, that brims so exquisitely with hyperbole and symbolism, he said:

"Oh, lovely and night-dark lady, what name is laid upon you to tell how whiter than sea-foam is your loveliness?"

For the moment, listening to the beauty of phrase and sound that dwells in the High Venusian tongue, Smith doubted his own ears. For though she had spoken in English, yet the loveliness of Yarol's speech seemed infinitely more suited to have fallen from the lyric curving of her velvet-red mouth. Such lips, he thought, could never utter less than pure music, and English is not a musical tongue.

But explain Yarol's visual illusion he could not, for his own steel-pale eyes were steadfast upon richly colored hair and pale gold flesh, and no stretch of imagination could transform them into the black and snow-whiteness his companion claimed to see.

A hint of mirth crept into the smile that curled up the softness of her mouth as Yarol spoke. She answered them both in one speech that to Smith was pure English, though he guessed that it fell upon Yarol's ears in the music of High Venusian cadences.

"I am Beauty," she told them serenely. "I am incarnate Beauty. But Yvala is my name. Let there be no quarrel between you, for each man hears me in the tongue his heart speaks, and sees me in the image which spells beauty to his own soul. For I am all men's desire incarnate in one being, and there is no beauty but Me."

"But—those others?"

"I am the only dweller here—but you have known the shadows of myself, leading you through devious ways into the presence of Yvala. Had you not gazed first upon the reflections of my beauty, its fullness which you see now would have blinded and destroyed you utterly. And later, perhaps, you shall see me even more clearly . . ..

"But no, Yvala alone dwells here. Save for yourselves there is in this park of mine no living creature. Everything is illusion but myself. And am I not enough? Can you desire anything more of life or death than you gaze on now?"

The query trembled into a music-ridden silence, and they knew that they could not. The heaven-sweet murmur of that voice was speaking sheerest magic, and in the sound of it neither of them was capable of any emotion but worship of the loveliness they faced. It beat out in waves like heat from that incarnate perfection, wrapping them about so that nothing in the universe had existence but Yvala.

Before the glory that blazed in their faces Smith felt adoration pouring out of him as blood gushes from a severed artery. Like life-blood it poured, and like life-blood draining it left him queerly weaker and weaker, as if some essential part of him were gushing away in great floods of intensest worship.

But somewhere, down under the lowest depths of Smith's subconsciousness, a faint disquiet was stirring. He fought it, for it broke the mirror surfaces of his tranced adoration, but he could not subdue it, and by degrees that unease struggled up through layer upon layer of rapt enchantment until it burst through into his conscious mind and the little quiver of it ran disturbingly through the exquisite calm of his trance. It was not an articulate disquiet, but it was somehow bound up with the scarcely seen beasts he had glimpsed—or had he glimpsed?—in the wood. That, and the memory of an old Earth legend which, try as he would, he could not quite exorcize: the legend of a lovely woman—and men turned into beasts . . . He could not grasp it, but the elusive memory pricked at him with little pinpoint goads, crying danger so insistently that with infinite reluctance his mind took up the business of thinking once more.

Yvala sensed it. She sensed the lessening in that life-blood gush of rapt adoration poured out upon her loveliness. Her fathomless eyes turned upon his in a blaze of transcendent blueness, and the woods reeled about him at the impact of their light. But somewhere in Smith, under the ultimate layer of conscious thought, under the last quiver of instinct and reflex and animal cravings, lay a bedrock of savage strength which no power he had ever met could wholly overcome, not even this—not even Yvala. Rooted deep in that immovable solidity the little uneasy murmur persisted. "There is something wrong here. I mustn't let her swallow me up again—I must know what it is . . ."

That much he was aware of. Then Yvala turned. With both velvety arms she swept back the curtain of her hair, and all about her in a glory of tangible loveliness blazed out the radiance that dwelt in such terrible intensity here. Smith's whole consciousness snuffed out before it like a blown candle-flame.

REMOTELY, AFTER EONS it seemed, awareness overtook him again. It was not consciousness, but a sort of dumb, blind knowledge of processes going on around him, in him, through him. So an animal might be aware, without any hint of real self-consciousness. But hot above everything else the tranced adoration of sheer beauty was blazing now in the center of his universe, and it was devouring him as a flame devours fuel, sucking out his worship, draining him utterly. Helpless, unbodied, he poured forth adoration into the ravenous blaze that held him; and as he poured it out he felt himself fading, somehow sinking below the level of a human being. In his dumb awareness he made no attempt to understand, but he felt himself—degenerating.

It was as if the insatiable appetite for admiration which consumed Yvala and was consuming him sucked him dry of all humanity. Even his thoughts were sinking now as she drained him, so that he no longer fitted words to his sensations, and his mind ran into figures and pictures below the level of human minds . . .

He was not tangible. He was a dark, inarticulate memory, bodiless, mindless, full of queer, hungry sensations . . . He remembered running. He remembered the dark earth flowing backward under his flying feet, wind keen in his nostrils and rife with the odors of a thousand luscious things. He remembered the pack baying around him to the frosty stars, his own voice lifting in exultant, throat-filling clamor with the rest. He remembered the sweetness of flesh yielding under fangs, the hot gush of blood over a hungry tongue. Little more than this he remembered. The ravenous craving, the exultation of the chase, the satisfying reek of hot flesh under ripping fangs—all these circled through his memory round and round, leaving room for little else.

But gradually, in dim, disquieting echoes, another realization strengthened beyond the circle of hunger and feeding. It was an intangible thing, nothing but the faint knowledge that somehow, somewhere, in some remote existence, he had been—different. He was little more than a recollection now, a mind that circled memories of hunting and killing and feeding which some lost body in long-ago distances had performed. But even so—he had once been different. He had—

Sharply through that memory-circle broke the knowledge of presences. With no physical sense was he aware of them, for he possessed no physical senses at all. But his awareness, his dumb, numb mind, knew that they had come—knew what they were. In memory he smelled the rank, blood-stirring scent of man, felt a tongue lolling out over suddenly dripping fangs; remembered hunger gushed up through his sensations.

Now he was blind and formless in a formless void, recognizing these presences only as they impinged upon his. But from the man-presences realization reached out and touched him, knowing his presence, realizing his nearness. They sensed him, lurking hungrily so close. And because they sensed him so vividly, their minds receiving the ravenous impact of his, their brains must have translated that hungry nearness into sight for just an instant; for from somewhere outside the gray void where he existed a voice said clearly:

"Look! Look—no, it's gone now, but for a minute I thought I saw a wolf..."

The words burst upon his consciousness with all the violence of a gun-blast; for in that instant, he *knew*. He understood the speech the man used, remembered that once it had been his speech—realized what he had become. He knew too that the men, whoever they were, walked into just such danger as had conquered him, and the urgency to warn them surged up in his dumbness. Not until then did he know clearly, with a man's word-thoughts, that he had no being. He was not real—he was only a wolf-memory drifting through the dark. He had been a man. Now he was pure wolf—beast—his soul shorn of its humanity down to the very core of savagery that dwells in every man. Shame flooded over him. He forgot the men, the speech they used, the remembered hunger. He dissolved into a nothingness of wolf-memory and man-shame.

Through the dizziness of that a stronger urge began to beat. Somewhere in the void sounded a call that reached out to him irresistibly. It called him so strongly that his whole being whirled headlong in response along currents that swept him helpless into the presence of the summoner.

A blaze was burning. In the midst of the universal emptiness it flamed, calling, commanding, luring him so sweetly that with all his entity he replied, for there was in that burning an element that wrenched at his innermost, deepest-rooted desire. He remembered food—the hot gush of blood, the crunch of teeth on bone, the satisfying solidarity of flesh under his sinking fangs. Desire for it gushed out of him like life itself, draining him—draining him ... He was sinking lower, past the wolf level, down and down ...

Through the coming oblivion terror stabbed. It was a lightning-flash of realization from his long-long humanity, one last throb that brightened the dark into which he sank. And out of that bed-rock of unshakable strength which was the core of his being, even below the wolf level, even below the oblivion into which he was being sucked—the spark of rebellion flashed.

Before now he had floundered helplessly with no firmness anywhere to give him foothold to fight; but now, in his uttermost extremity, while the last dregs of conscious life drained out of him, the bed-rock lay bare from which the well-springs of his strength and savagery spring, and at that last stronghold of the *self* called Smith he leaped into instant rebellion, fighting with all the wolf-nature that had been the soil from which his man-soul rooted. Wolfishly he fought, with a beast's savagery and a man's strength, backed by the bed-rock firmness that was the base for both. Space whirled about him, flaming with hungry fires, black with flashes of oblivion, furious and ravenous in the hot presence of Yvala.

But he was winning. He knew it, and fought harder, and abruptly felt the snap of yielding opposition and was blindingly aware again, blindingly human. He lay on soft moss as a dead man lies, terribly relaxed in every limb and muscle. But life was flowing back into him, and humanity was gushing like a river in space back into the drained hollows of his soul. For a while he lay quiet, gathering himself into one body again. His hold on it was so feeble that sometimes he thought he was floating clear and had to struggle hard to force re-entrance. Finally, with infinite effort, he tugged his eyelids open and lay there in a deathly quiet, watching.

Before him stood the white marble shrine which housed Beauty. But it was not Yvala's delirious loveliness he gazed on now. He had been through the fire of her deepest peril, and he saw her now as she really was—not in the form which spelled pure loveliness to him, and, as he guessed, to every being that gazed upon her, whether it be man or beast—not in any form at all, but as a blaze of avid light flaming inside the shrine. The light was alive, quivering and trembling and animate, but it bore no human form. It was not human. It was a life so alien that he wondered weakly how his eyes could ever have twisted it into the incarnate loveliness of Yvala. And even in the depths of his peril he found time to regret the passing of that beauty—that exquisite illusion which had never existed save in his own brain. He knew that as long as life burned in him he could never forget her smile.

IT WAS A thing of some terribly remote origin that blazed here. He guessed that the power of it had fastened on his brain as soon as he came within its scope, commanding him to see it in that lovely form which meant heart's-desire to him alone. It must have done the same thing to countless other beings—he remembered the beast wraiths that had brushed his brain in the forest with the faint, shamed contact of theirs. Well, he had been one of them—he knew, now. He understood the warning and the anguish in their eyes. He remembered too the ruins he had seen in the woods. What race had dwelt here once, imposing its civilization and its stamp of quiet glades and trees upon the ravenous forest? A human race, perhaps, dwelling in seclusion under the leaves until Yvala the Destroyer came. Or perhaps not a human race, for he knew now that to every living creature she wore a different form, the incarnation of each individual's highest desire.

Then he heard voices, and after an infinity of effort twisted his head on the moss until he could see whence they came. At what he saw he would have risen if he could, but a deathly weariness lay like the weight of worlds upon him and he could not stir. Those man-presences he had felt in his beast-form stood here—the three slavers from the little ship. They must have followed them not far behind, with what dark motives would never be known now, for Yvala's magic had seized them and there would be no more of humanity for them after the next few moments were past. They stood in a row there before the shrine with an ecstasy almost holy on their faces. Plainly he saw reflected there the incarnate glory of Yvala, though to his eyes the thing they faced was only a formless flame.

He knew then why Yvala had let him go so suddenly in that desperate struggle. Here was fresh fodder for her avidity, new worship to drink in. She had turned away from his outworn well-springs to drain new prey of its humanity. He watched them standing there, drunk with loveliness before what to them must be a beautiful woman veiled in drifting hair, glowing with more than mortal ardency where, to him, only a clear flame burned.

But he could see more. Cloudy about those three figures, rapt before the shrine, he could see—was it some queer reflection of themselves dancing in the air? The misty outlines wavered as, with eyes that in the light of what he had just passed through had won momentarily a sight which penetrated beyond the flesh, he looked upon that dancing shimmer which clearly must be the reflection of some vital part of those three men, visible now in some strange way at the evocation of Yvala's calling.

They were man-shaped reflections. They strained toward Yvala from their anchorage in the bodies that housed them, yearning, pulling as if they would forsake their fleshly roots and merge with the incarnate beauty that called them so irresistibly. The three stood rigid, faces blank with rapture, unconscious of that perilous tugging at what must be in their very souls.

Then Smith saw the nearest man sag at the knees, quiver, topple to the moss. He lay still for a moment while from his fallen body that tenuous reflection of himself tugged and pulled and then in one last great effort jerked free and floated like a smoke-wreath into the white-hot intensity at the shrine. The blaze engulfed it, flaring brighter as if at the kindling of new fuel.

WHEN THAT SUDDEN brightness died again the smoke-wreath drifted out, trailing through the pillars in a form that even to Smith's dimmed eyes wore a strange distortion. It was no longer man-formed. All of humanity had burned out from it to feed the blaze that was Yvala. And that beast foundation which lies so close under the veneer of civilization and humanity in every human creature was bared and free. Cold with understanding, Smith watched the core of beast instinct which was all that remained now that the layer of man-veneer had been stripped away, a core of animal memories rooted eons deep in that far-away past when all man's ancestors ran on four paws.

It was a cunning beast that remained, instinct with foxy slyness. He saw the misty thing slink away into the green gloom of the woods, and he realized afresh why it was he had seen fleeting glimpses of animals in the park as he came here, wearing that terrible familiarity in the set of their heads, the line of shoulder and neck that hinted at other gaits than four-footed. They must have been just such wraiths as this, drifting through the woods, beast-wraiths that wore still the tatters and rags of their doffed humanity, brushing his mind with the impact of theirs until their vividness evoked actual sight of the reality of fur and flesh, just for a glimpse, just for a hint, before the wraith blew past. And he was cold with horror at the thought of how many men must have gone to feed the flame, stripping off humanity like a garment and running now in the nakedness of their beast natures through the enchanted woods.

Here was Circe. He realized it with a quiver of horror and awe. Circe the Enchantress, who turned the men of Greek legend into beasts. And what tremendous backgrounds of reality and myth loomed smokily behind what happened here before his very eyes! Circe the Enchantress—ancient Earthly legend incarnate now on a Jovian moon far away through the void. The awe of it shook him to the depths. Circe—Yvala—alien entity that must, then, rove through the universe and the ages, leaving the dim whispers behind her down the centuries. Lovely Circe on her blue Aegean isle—Yvala on her haunted moon under Jupiter's blaze—past and present merged into a blazing whole.

The wonder of it held him so rapt that when the reality of the scene before him finally bore itself in upon his consciousness again, both of the remaining slavers lay prone upon the moss, forsaken bodies from which the vitality had been sucked like blood into Yvala's flame. That flame burned more rosily now, and out of its pulsing he saw the last dim wraith of the three who had fed her come hurrying, a swinish brute of a wraith whose grunts and snorts were almost audible, tusks and bristles all but visible as it scurried off into the wood.

Then the flame burned clear again, flushed with hot rose, pulsing with regular beats like the pulse of a heart, satiate and ecstatic in its shrine. And he was aware of a withdrawal, as if the consciousness of the entity that burned here were turned inward upon itself, leaving the world it dominated untouched as Yvala drowsed and digested the sustenance her vampire-craving for worship had devoured.

SMITH STIRRED A little on the moss. Now, if ever, he must make some effort to escape, while the thing in the shrine was replete and uninterested in its surroundings. He lay there, shaken with exhaustion, forcing strength back into his body, willing himself to be strong, to rise, to find Yarol, to make his way somehow back to the deserted ship. And by slow degrees he succeeded. It took a long while, but in the end he had dragged himself up against a tree and stood swaying, his pale eyes alternately clouding with exhaustion and blinking awake again as he scanned the space under the trees for Yarol.

The little Venusian lay a few steps away, one cheek pressing the ground and his yellow curls gay against the moss. With closed eyes he looked like a seraph asleep, all the lines of hard living and hard fighting relaxed and the savageness of his gaze hidden. Even in his deadly peril Smith could not suppress a little grin of appreciation as he staggered the half-dozen steps that parted them and fell to his knees beside his friend's body.

The sudden motion dazed him, but in a moment his head cleared and he laid an urgent hand on Yarol's shoulder, shaking it hard. He dared not speak, but he shook the little Venusian heavily, and in his brain a silent call went out to whatever drifting wraith among the trees housed Yarol's naked soul. He bent over the quiet yellow head and called and called, turning the force of his determination in all its intensity to that summoning, while weakness washed over him in great slow waves.

After a long time he thought he felt a dim response, somewhere from far off. He called harder, eyes turned apprehensively toward the rosily pulsing flame in the shrine, wondering if this voiceless summoning might not impinge upon the entity there as tangibly as speech. But Yvala's satiety must have been deep, and there was no changing in the blaze.

The answer came clearer from the woods. He felt it pulling in toward him along the strong compulsion of his call as a fisherman feels a game fish yielding at last to the tug of his line. And presently among the leafy solitudes of the trees a little mist-wraith came gliding. It was a slinking thing, feline, savage, fearless. He could have sworn that for the briefest instant he saw the outlines of a panther stealing across the moss, misty, low-slung, turning upon him the wise black gaze of Yarol—exactly his friend's black eyes, with no lessening in them of lost humanity. And something in that familiar gaze sent a little chill down his back. Could it be—could it possibly be that in Yarol the veneer of humanity was so thin over his savage cat-nature that even when it had been stripped away the look in his eyes was the same?

Then the smoke-beast was hovering over the prone Venusian figure. It curled round Yarol's shoulders for an instant; it faded and sank, and Yarol stirred on the moss. Smith turned him over with a shaking hand. The long Venusian lashes quivered, lifted. Black, sidelong eyes looked up into Smith's pale gaze. And Smith, in a gush of chilly uncertainty, did not know if humanity had returned into his friend's body or not, if it was a panther's gaze looking up into his or if that thin layer of man-soul veiled it, for Yarol's eyes had always looked like this.

"Are—are you all right?" he choked in a breathless whisper.

Yarol blinked dizzily once or twice, then grinned. A twinkle lighted up his black cat gaze. He nodded and made a little effort to rise. Smith helped him sit up. The Venusian was not a fraction so weak as the Earthman had been. After a little interval of hard breathing he struggled to his feet and helped Smith up, apprehension in his whole demeanor as he eyed the flame that pulsed in its white shrine. He jerked his head urgently.

"Let's get out of here!" his silent lips mouthed. And Smith in fervent agreement turned in the direction he indicated, hoping the Yarol knew where he was going. His own exhaustion was still too strong to permit him anything but acquiescence.

They made their way through the woods, Yarol heading unerringly in a swerveless course toward the roadway they had left such a long time ago. After a while, when the flame-housing shrine had vanished among the trees behind them, the Venusian's soft voice murmured, half to itself.

"—wish, almost, you hadn't called me back. Woods were so cool and still—remembering such splendid things—killing and killing—taste of hot blood—I wish—"

The voice fell quiet again. But Smith, stumbling on beside his friend, understood. He knew why the woods seemed familiar to Yarol, so that he could head for the roadway unerringly. He knew why Yvala in her satiety had not even wakened at the withdrawal of Yarol's humanity—it was so small a thing that the loss of it meant nothing. He gained a new insight in that moment into Venusian nature that he remembered until the day he died.

Then there was a gap in the trees ahead, and Yarol's shoulder was under his supportingly, and the road to safety shimmered in its tree-arched green gloom ahead.

Creatures of the Light

by Sophie Wenzel Ellis

My collaborator, Pam Keesey, wasn't even born when this story appeared in the second issue (February, 1930) of *Astounding Stories of Super-Science* (now known as *Analog*). From my collection she read this story by Ms. Ellis and also "Slaves of the Dust" and "Shadow World" and liked this one best. I know nothing about SWE and even the great Tasmanian bibliographer Donald Tuck in his monumental *Encyclopedia of Science Fiction & Fantasy* has no record of her. It would be fantastic if, as the result of this publication, I should hear from someone saying, "Why, she was my great Aunt Sophie!" or "She was my great grandmother!" or something of that sort, shedding a little light on the creator of "Creatures of the Light".

—FJA

In a night club of many lights and much high-pitched laughter, where he had come for an hour of forgetfulness and an execrable dinner, John Northwood was suddenly conscious that Fate had begun shuffling the cards of his destiny for a dramatic game.

First, he was aware that the singularly ugly and deformed man at the next table was gazing at him with an intense, almost malevolent scrutiny. But, more disturbing than this, was the scowl of hate on the face of another man, as handsome as the other was hideous, who sat in a far corner hidden behind a broad column, with his elbows on the table, gazing first at Northwood and then at the deformed, almost hideous man.

Northwood's blood chilled over the expression on the handsome, fair-haired stranger's perfectly carved face. If a figure in marble could display a fierce, unnatural passion, it would seem no more eldritch than the hate in the in the icy blue eyes.

It was not a new experience for Northwood to be stared at. He was not merely a good looking young fellow of twenty-five, he was scenery, magnetic and compelling. Furthermore, he had been in the public eye for years, first as a precocious child and later as a brilliant young scientist. Yet, for all his experience with hero worshipers to put an adamantine crust on his sensibilities, he grew warm-eared under the gaze of these two strangers—this hunchback with a face like a grotesque mask in a Greek play, this other who, even handsomer than himself, chilled the blood queerly with the cold perfection of his godlike masculine beauty.

Northwood sensed something familiar about the hunchback. Somewhere he had seen that huge, round, intelligent face splattered with startling features. The very breadth of the man's massive brow was not altogether unknown to him, nor could Northwood look into the mournful, near-sighted black eyes without trying to recall when and where he had last seen them.

But this other of the marble-perfect nose and jaw, the blond, thick-waved hair, was totally a stranger, whom Northwood fervently hoped he would never know too well.

Trying to analyze the queer repugnance that he felt for this handsome, boldly staring fellow, Northwood decided, "He's like a newly-made wax figure endowed with life."

Shivering over his own fantastic thought, he again glanced swiftly at the hunchback, who he noticed was playing with his coffee, evidently to prolong the meal.

One year of calm-headed scientific teaching in a famous old eastern university had not made him callous to mysteries. Thus, with a feeling of high adventure, he finished his supper and prepared to go. From the corner of his eye, he saw the hunchback leave his seat, while the handsome man behind the column rose furtively, as though he, too, intended to follow.

Northwood was out in the dusky street about thirty seconds, when the hunchback came from the foyer. Without apparently noticing Northwood, he hailed a taxi. For a moment, he stood still, waiting for the taxi to pull up at the curb. Standing thus, with the street light limning every unnatural angle of his twisted body and every queer abnormality of his huge features, he looked almost repulsive.

On his way to the taxi, his thick shoulder jostled the younger man. Northwood felt something strike his foot and, stooping in the crowded street, picked up a black leather wallet.

"Wait!" he shouted as the hunchback stepped into the waiting taxi.

But the man did not falter. In a moment Northwood lost sight of him as the taxi moved away.

HE DEBATED with himself whether or not he should attempt to follow. And while he stood there in indecision, the handsome stranger approached him.

"Good evening to you," he said. His rich, musical voice, for all its deepness, held a faint hint of the tremulous, birdlike notes heard in the voice of a young child who has not used his vocal chords long enough to have lost their exquisite newness.

"Good evening," echoed Northwood, somewhat uncertainly. A sudden wave of repulsion swept coldly over him. Seen close, with the brilliant light of the street directly on his too perfect face, the man was more sinister than in the café. Yet Northwood, struggling desperately for a reason to explain his violent dislike, could not discover why he shrank from this splendid creature whose eyes and flesh had a new, fresh appearance rarely seen except in very young boys.

"I want what you picked up," went on the stranger.

"It isn't yours!" Northwood flashed back. Ah! That effluvium of hatred which seemed to weave a tangible web around him!

"Nor is it yours. Give it to me!"

"You're insolent, aren't you?"

"If you don't give it to me, you will be sorry." The man did not raise his voice in anger, yet the words whipped Northwood with almost physical violence. "If he knew that I saw everything that happened in there—that I am talking to you at this moment—he would tremble with fear."

"But you can't intimidate me."

"No?" for a long moment the cold blue eyes held his contemptuously. "No? I can't frighten you—you were of the Black Age?"

Before Northwood's horrified eyes he vanished; vanished as though he had turned suddenly to air and floated away.

The street was not crowded at that time, and there was no pressing group of bodies to hide the splendid creature. Northwood gawked stupidly, mouth half open, eyes searching wildly everywhere. The man was gone. He had simply disappeared, in this sane, electric-lighted street.

Suddenly, close to Northwood's ear, grated a derisive laugh. "I can't frighten you?" From nowhere came that singularly young-old voice.

As Northwood jerked his head around to meet blank space, a blow struck the corner of his mouth. He felt the warm blood run over his chin.

"I could take that wallet from you, worm, but you may keep it, and see me later. But remember this—the thing inside will never be yours."

The words fell from empty air.

For several minutes Northwood waited at the spot, expecting another demonstration of the abnormal but nothing else occurred. At last, trembling violently, he wiped the thick moisture from his forehead and dabbed at the blood which he still felt on his chin.

But when he looked at his handkerchief, he muttered: "Well, I'll be jiggered!"
The handkerchief bore not the slightest trace of blood.

UNDER THE light in his bedroom, Northwood examined the wallet. It was made of alligator skin, clasped with a gold signet that bore the initial M. The first pocket was empty; the second yielded an object that sent a warm flush to his face.

It was the photograph of a gloriously beautiful girl, so seductively lovely that the picture seemed almost to be alive. The short, curved upper lip, the full, delicately voluptuous lower, parted slightly in a smile that seemed to linger in every exquisite line of her face. She looked as though she had just spoken passionately, and the spirit of her words had inspired her sweet flesh and eyes.

Northwood turned his head abruptly and groaned "Good Heavens!"

He had no right to palpitate over the picture of an unknown beauty. Only a month ago, he had become engaged to a young woman whose mind was as brilliant as her face was plain. Always he had vowed that he would never marry a pretty girl, for he detested his own masculine beauty sincerely.

He tried to grasp a mental picture of Mary Burns, who had never stirred in him the emotion that this smiling picture invoked. But, gazing at the picture, he could not remember how his fiancée looked.

Suddenly the picture fell from his fingers and dropped to the floor on its face, revealing an inscription on the back. In a bold, masculine hand, he read: "Your future wife."

"Some lucky fellow is headed for a life of bliss," was his jealous thought.

He frowned at the beautiful face. What was this girl to that hideous hunchback? Why did the handsome stranger warn him, *"The thing inside never will be yours"*?

Again he turned eagerly to the wallet.

In the last flap he found something that gave him another surprise: a plain white card on which a name and address were written by the same hand that had penned the inscription on the picture.

Emil Mundson, Ph. D.,
44½ Indian Court

Emil Mundson, the electrical wizard and distinguished scientific writer, friend of the professor of science at the university where Northwood was an assistant professor. Emil Mundson, whom, a week ago, Northwood had yearned mightily to meet.

CREATURES OF THE LIGHT

Now Northwood knew why the hunchback's intelligent, ugly face was familiar to him. He had seen it pictured as often as enterprising news photographers could steal a likeness from the over-sensitive scientist, who would never sit for a formal portrait.

Even before Northwood had graduated from the university where he now taught, he had been avidly interested in Emil Mundson's fantastic articles in scientific journals. Only a week ago Professor Michael had come to him with the current issue of *New Science* shouting excitedly.

"Did you read this, John, this article by Emil Mundson?" His shaking, gnarled old fingers tapped the open magazine.

Northwood seized the magazine and looked avidly at the title of the article, "Creatures of the Light."

"No, I haven't read it," he admitted. "My magazine hasn't come yet."

"Run through it now briefly, will you? And note with especial care the passages I have marked. In fact, you needn't bother with anything else just now. Read this—and this—and this." He pointed out penciled paragraphs.

Northwood read:

Man always has been, always will be a creature of the light. He is forever reaching for some future point of perfected evolution which, even when his most remote ancestor was a fish creature composed of a few cells, was the guiding power that brought him up from the first stinking sea and caused him to create gods in his own image. It is this yearning for perfection which sets man apart from all other life, which made him man even in the rudimentary stages of his development. He was man when he wallowed in the slime of the new world and yearned for the air above. He will still be man when he has evolved into that glorious creature of the future whose body is deathless and whose mind rules the universe.

Professor Michael, looking over Northwood's shoulder, interrupted the reading:

"*Man always has been man,*" he droned emphatically. "That's not original with friend Mundson, of course, yet it is a theory that has not received sufficient investigation." He indicated another marked paragraph. "Read this thoughtfully, John. It's the crux of Mundson's thought."

Northwood continued:

Since the human body is chemical and electrical, increased knowledge of its powers and limitations will enable us to work with Nature in her sublime but infinitely slow processes of human evolution. We need not wait another fifty thousand years to be god-like creatures. Perhaps even now we may be standing at the beginning of the splendid bridge that will take us to that state of perfected evolution when we shall be Creatures who have reached the Light.

Northwood looked questioningly at the professor. "Queer, fantastic thing isn't it?"

Professor Michael smoothed his thin, gray hair with his dried-out hand. "Fantastic?" His intellectual eyes behind the thick glasses sought the ceiling. "Who can say? Haven't you ever wondered why all parents expect their children to be nearer perfection than themselves, and why is it a natural impulse for them to be willing to sacrifice themselves to better their offspring?" He paused and moistened his pale, wrinkled lips. "Instinct, Northwood. We Creatures of the Light know that our race shall reach that point in evolution where, as perfect creatures we shall rule all matter and live forever." He punctuated the last words with blows on the table.

Northwood laughed dryly. "How many thousands of years are you looking forward, Professor?"

The professor made an obscure noise that sounded like a smothered sniff. "You and I shall never agree on the point that mental advancement may wipe out physical limitations in the human race, perhaps in a few hundred years. It seems as though your profound admiration for Dr. Mundson would win you over to this pet theory."

"But what sane man can believe that even perfectly developed beings, through mental control, could overcome Nature's fixed laws?"

"We don't know! We don't know!" The professor slapped the magazine with an emphatic hand. "Emil Mundson hasn't written this article for nothing. He's paving the way for some announcement that will startle the scientific world. I know him. In the same manner he gave out veiled hints of his various brilliant discoveries and inventions long before he offered them to the world."

"But Dr. Mundson is an electrical wizard. He would not be delving seriously into he mysteries of evolution, would he?"

"Why not?" The professor's wizened face screwed up wisely. "A year ago, when he was back from one of those mysterious long excursions he takes in that weirdly different aircraft of his, about which he is so secretive, he told me that he was conducting experiments to prove his belief that the human brain generates electric current, and that the electrical impulses in the brain set up radioactive waves that some day, among other miracles, will make thought communication possible. Perfect man, he says, will perform mental feats which will give him complete mental domination over the physical."

Northwood finished reading and turned thoughtfully to the window. His profile in repose had the straight-nosed, full-lipped perfection of a Greek coin. Old, wizened Professor Michael, gazing at him covertly, smothered a sigh.

"I wish you knew Dr. Mundson," he said. "He, the ugliest man in the world, delights in physical perfection. He would revel in your splendid body and brilliant mind."

Northwood blushed hotly. "You'll have to arrange a meeting between us."

"I have." The professor's thin, dry lips pursed comically. "He'll drop by in to see you within a few days."

And now John Northwood sat holding Dr. Mundson's card and the wallet which the scientist had so mysteriously dropped at his feet.

HERE WAS high adventure, perhaps, for which he had been singled out by the famous electrical wizard. While excitement mounted in his blood, Northwood again examined the photograph. The girl's strange eyes, odd in expression rather than in size or shape, seemed to hold him. The young man's breath came quicker.

"It's a challenge," he said softly. "It won't hurt to see what it's all about."

His watch showed eleven o'clock. He would return the wallet that night. Into his coat pocket he slipped a revolver. One sometimes needed weapons in Indian Court.

He took a taxi, which soon turned from the well-lighted streets into a section where squalid houses crowded against each other, and dirty children swarmed in the streets in their last games of the day.

Indian Court was little more than an alley, dark and evil smelling.

The chauffeur stopped at the entrance and said:

"If I drive in, I'll have to back out, sir. Number forty-four and a half is the end house, facing the entrance."

"You've been here before?" asked Northwood.

"Last week I drove the queerest bird here—a fellow as good-looking as you, who had me follow the taxi occupied by a hunchback with a face like Old Nick." The man hesitated and went on haltingly. "It might sound goofy, mister, but there was something funny about my fare. He jumped out, asked me the charge and, in the moment I glanced at my taxi-meter, he disappeared. Yes, sir. Vanished, owing me four dollars, six bits. It was almost ghostlike, mister."

Northwood laughed nervously and dismissed him. He found his number and knocked at the dilapidated door. He heard a sudden movement in the lighted room beyond, and the door opened quickly.

Dr. Mundson faced him.

"I knew you'd come!" he said with a slight Teutonic accent. "Often I'm not wrong in sizing up my man. Come in."

Northwood cleared his throat awkwardly. "You dropped your wallet at my feet, Dr. Mundson. I tried to stop you before you got away, but I guess you did not hear me."

He offered the wallet, but the hunchback waved it aside.

"A ruse, of course," he confessed. "It was just my way of testing what your Professor Michael told about you—that you are extraordinarily intelligent, virile, and imaginative. Had you sent the wallet to me, I should have sought elsewhere for my man. Come in."

Northwood followed him into a living room evidently recently furnished in a somewhat hurried manner. The furniture, although rich, was not placed to best advantage. The new rug was a trifle crooked on the floor, and the lamp shades clashed in color with the other furnishings.

Dr. Mundson's intense eyes swept over Northwood's tall, slim body.

"Ah, you're a man!" he said softly. "You are what all men would be if we followed Nature's plan that only the fit shall survive. But modern science is permitting the unfit to live and to mix their defective beings with the developing race!" His huge fist gesticulated madly. "Fools! Fools! They need me and perfect men like you."

"Why?"

"Because you can help me in my plan to populate the earth with a new form of godlike people. But don't question me too closely now. Even if I should explain, you would call me insane. But watch. Gradually I shall unfold the mystery before you that you will believe."

He reached for the wallet that Northwood still held, opened it with a monstrous hand and reach for the photograph. "She shall bring you love. She's more beautiful than a poet's dream."

A warm flush crept over the young man's face.

"I can easily understand," he said, "how a man could love her, but for me she comes too late."

"Pooh! Fiddlesticks!" The scientist snapped his fingers. "This girl was created for you. That other—you will forget her the moment you set eye on the sweet flesh of this Athalia. She is an houri from Paradise—a maiden of musk and incense." He held the girl's photograph toward the young man. "Keep it. She is yours, if you are strong enough to hold her."

Northwood opened his card case and placed the picture inside, facing Mary's photograph. Again the warning words of the mysterious stranger rang in his memory: *"The thing inside will never be yours."*

"Where to," he said eagerly, "and when do we start?"

"To the new Garden of Eden," said the scientist, with such a beatific smile that his face was less hideous. "We start immediately. I have arranged with Professor Michael for you to go."

NORTHWOOD FOLLOWED Dr. Mundson to the street and walked with him a few blocks to a garage where the scientist's motor car waited.

"The apartment in Indian Court is just a little eccentricity of mine," explained Dr. Mundson. "I need people in my work, people whom I must select through swift, sure tests. The apartment comes in handy, as to-night."

Northwood scarcely noted where they were going, or how long they had been on the way. He was vaguely aware that they had left the city behind and were now passing through farms bathed in moonlight.

At last they entered a path that led through a bit of woodland. For half a mile the path continued and then ended at a small, enclosed field. In the middle of this rested a queer aircraft. Northwood knew it was a flying machine only by the propellers mounted on the top of the huge ball-shaped body. There were no wings, no birdlike hull, no tail.

"It looks almost like a little world ready to fly off into space," he commented.

"It is just about that." The scientist's squat, bunched-out body, settled squarely on long, thin, straddled legs, looked gnome-like in the moonlight. "One cannot copy flesh with steel and wood, but one can make metal perform magic of which flesh is not capable. My sun-ship is not a mechanical reproduction of a bird. It is—but, climb in, young friend."

Northwood followed Dr. Mundson into the aircraft. The moment the scientist closed the metal door behind them, Northwood was instantly aware of some concealed horror that vibrated through his nerves. For one dreadful moment, he expected some terrific agent of the shadows that escaped the electric lights to leap upon him. And this was odd, for nothing could be saner than the globular interior of the aircraft, divided into four wedge-shaped apartments.

Dr. Mundson also paused at the door, puzzled, hesitant.

"Someone has been here!" he exclaimed. "Look, Northwood! The bunk has been occupied—the one in this cabin I had set aside for you."

He pointed to the disarranged bunk, where the impression of a head could still be seen on a pillow.

"A tramp, perhaps."

"No! The door was locked and, as you saw, the fence around this field was protected with barbed wire. There's something wrong. I felt it on my trip here all the way, like someone watching me in the dark. And don't laugh! I have stopped laughing at all things that seem unnatural. You don't know what is natural."

Northwood shivered. "Maybe someone is concealed about the ship."

"Impossible. Me, I thought so too. But I looked and looked and there was nothing."

All evening Northwood had burned to tell the scientist about the handsome stranger in the Mad Hatter Club. But even now he shrank from saying that a man had vanished before his eyes.

Dr. Mundson was working with a succession of buttons and levers. There was a slight jerk, and then the strange craft shot up, straight as a bullet from a gun, with scarcely a sound other than a continuous whistle.

"The vertical rising aircraft perfected," explained Dr. Mundson. "But what would you think if I told you that there is not an ounce of gasoline in my heavier-than-air craft?"

"I shouldn't be surprised. An electrical genius would seek for a less obsolete source of power."

In the bright flare of the electric lights, the scientist's ugly face flushed. "The man who harnesses the sun rules the world. He can make the sun rule the world. He can make the desert places bloom, the frozen poles balmy and verdant. You, John Northwood, are one of the very few to fly in a machine operated solely by electrical energy from the sun's rays."

"Are you telling me that this airship is operated with power from the sun?"

"Yes. And I cannot take the credit for its invention," he sighed. "The dream was mine, but a greater brain developed it—a brain that may be greater than I suspect." His face grew suddenly graver.

A little later Northwood said, "It seems that we must be making fabulous speed."

"Perhaps!" Dr. Mundson worked with the controls. "Here, I've cut her down to the average speed of the ordinary airplane. Now you can see a bit of the night scenery."

Northwood peeped out the thick glass porthole. Far below he saw two tiny streaks of light, one smooth and stationery, the other wavering as though it were a reflection in water.

"That can't be a lighthouse!" he cried.

The scientist glanced out. "It is. We're approaching the Florida Keys."

"Impossible! We've been traveling less than an hour."

"But, my young friend, do you realize that my sun-ship has a speed of over one thousand miles an hour? How much over I dare not tell you."

Throughout the night Northwood sat beside Dr. Mundson, watching his deft fingers control the simple-looking buttons and levers. So fast was their flight now that, through the portholes, sky and earth looked the same: dark gray films of emptiness. The continuous weird whistle from the hidden mechanism of the sun-ship was like the drone of a monster insect, monotonous and soporific during the long intervals when the scientist was too busy with his controls to engage in conversation.

For some reason that he could not explain, Northwood had an aversion to going into the sleeping apartment behind the control room. Then, towards morning, when the suddenly falling temperature struck a biting chill throughout the sun-ship, Northwood, going into the cabin for fur coats, discovered why his mind and body shrank in horror from the cabin.

AFTER HE had procured the fur coats from a closet, he paused a moment, in the privacy of the cabin, to look at Athalia's picture. Every nerve in his body leaped to meet the magnetism of her beautiful eyes. Never had Mary Burns stirred emotion like this in him. He hung over Mary's picture, wistfully, hoping almost prayerfully that he could react to her as he did to Athalia, but her pale, over-intellectual face left him cold.

"Cad!" he ground out between his teeth. "Forgetting her so soon!"

The two pictures were lying side by side on a little table. Suddenly an obscure noise in the room caught his attention. It was more vibration than noise, for small sounds could scarcely be heard above the whistle of the sun-ship. A slight compression of the air against his neck gave him the eery feeling that someone was standing close behind him. He wheeled and looked over his shoulder. Half ashamed of his startled gesture, he again turned to the pictures. Then a sharp cry broke from him.

Athania's picture was gone.

He searched for it everywhere in the room, in his own pockets, under the furniture. It was nowhere to be found.

In sudden, overpowering horror, he seized the fur coats and returned to the control room.

Dr. Mundson was changing the speed.

"Look out the window!" he called to Northwood.

The young man looked and started violently. Day had come, and now that the sun-ship was flying at a moderate speed, the ocean beneath was plainly visible and its entire surface was covered with broken floes of ice and small ragged icebergs. He seized a telescope and focused it below. A typical polar scene met his eyes: penguins strutting about on cakes of ice, a whale blowing in the icy water.

"A part of the Antarctic that has never been explored," said Dr. Mundson, "and there, just showing on the horizon, is the Great Ice Barrier." His characteristic smile lighted the mortal black eyes. "I am enough of the dramatist to wish you to be impressed with what I shall show you within less than an hour. Accordingly, I shall make a landing and let you feel polar ice under your feet."

After less than a minute's search, Dr. Mundson found a suitable place on the ice for a landing, and, with a few deft manipulations of the controls, brought the sun-ship swooping down like an eagle on its prey.

For a long moment after the scientist had stepped out on the ice, Northwood paused at the door. His feet were chained by a strange reluctance to enter this white, dead wilderness of ice. But Dr. Mundson's impatient, "Ready?" drew from him one last glance at the cozy interior of the sun-ship before he, too, went out into the frozen stillness.

They left the sun-ship resting on the ice like a fallen silver moon, while they wandered to the edge of the Barrier and looked at the gray, narrow stretch of sea between the ice pack and the high cliffs of the Barrier. The sun of the commencing six-months' Antarctic day was a low, cold ball whose slanted rays struck the ice with blinding whiteness. There were constant falls of ice from the Barrier, which thundered into the ocean amid great clouds of ice smoke that lingered like wraiths around the edge. It was a scene of loneliness and waiting death.

"What's that?" exclaimed the scientist suddenly.

Out of the white silence shrilled a low whistle, a familiar whistle. Both men wheeled toward the sun-ship.

Before their horrified eyes, the great sphere jerked and glided up, and swerved into the heavens.

Up it soared. Then, gaining speed, it swung into the blue distance until, in a moment, it was a tiny star that flickered out even as they watched.

Both men screamed and cursed and flung up their arms despairingly. A penguin, attracted by their cries, waddled solemnly over to them and regarded them with manlike curiosity.

"Stranded in the coldest spot on earth!" groaned the scientist.

"Why did it start itself, Dr. Mundson!" Norwood narrowed his eyes as he spoke.

"It didn't!" The scientist's huge face, red from cold, quivered with helpless rage. "Human hands started it."

"What! Whose hands?"

"*Ach!* Do I know?" His Teutonic accent grew more pronounced, as it always did when he was under emotional stress. "Somebody whose brain is better than mine. Somebody who found a way to hide away from our eyes. *Ach, Gott!* Don't let me think!"

His great head sank between his shoulders, giving him, in his fur suit, the grotesque appearance of a friendly brown bear.

"Doctor Mundson," said Northwood suddenly, "did you have an enemy, a man with the face and body of a pagan god—a great, blond creature with eyes as cold and cruel as the ice under our feet?"

"Wait!" The huge round head jerked up. "How do you know about Adam? You have not seen him, won't see him until we arrive at our destination."

"But I have seen him. He was sitting not thirty feet from you in the Mad Hatter's Club last night. Didn't you know! He followed me to the street, spoke to me, and then—" Northwood stopped. How could he let the insane words pass his lips?"

"Then, what? Speak up!"

NORTHWOOD LAUGHED nervously. "It sounds foolish, but I saw him vanish like that." he snapped his fingers.

"*Ach, Gott!*" All the ruddy color drained from the scientist's face. As though talking to himself, he continued:

"Then it is true, as he said. He has crossed the bridge. He has reached the Light. And now he comes to see the world he will conquer—came unseen when I refused him my permission."

He was silent for a long time, pondering. Then he turned passionately to Northwood.

"John Northwood, kill me! I have brought a new horror into the world. From the unborn future, I have snatched a creature who has reached the light too soon. Kill me!" He bowed his great, shaggy head.

"What do you mean, Dr. Mundson? That this Adam has arrived at a point in evolution beyond this age?"

"Yes. Think of it! I visioned god-like creatures with the souls of gods. But, Heaven help us, man always will be man, always will lust for conquest. You and I, Northwood, and all others are barbarians to Adam. He and his kind will do what men always do to barbarians—conquer and kill."

"Are there more like him?" Northwood struggled with a smile of unbelief.

"I don't know. I did not know that Adam had reached a point so near the ultimate. But you have seen. Already he is able to set aside what we call natural laws."

Northwood looked at the scientist closely. The man was surely mad—mad in this desert of white death.

"Come!" he said cheerfully. "Let's build an Eskimo snow house. We can live on penguins for days. And who knows what may rescue us?"

For three hours the two worked at cutting ice blocks. With snow for mortar, they build a crude shelter which enabled them to rest out of the cold breath of the spiral polar winds that blew from the south.

Dr. Mundson was sitting at the door of their hut, moodily pulling at his strong, black pipe. As though a fit had seized him, he leaped up and let his pipe fall to the ice.

"Look!" he shouted. "The sun-ship!"

It seemed but a moment before the tiny speck on the horizon had swept overhead, a silver comet on the grayish-blue polar sky. In another moment it had swooped down, eaglewise, scarcely fifty feet from the ice hut.

Dr. Mundson and Northwood ran forward. From the metal sphere stepped the stranger of the Mad Hatter Club. His tall, straight form, erect and slim, swung toward them over the ice.

"Adam!" shouted Dr. Mundson. "What does this mean? How dare you!"

Adam's laugh was like the happy demonstration of a boy. "So? You think you are still master? You think I returned because I reverenced you yet?" Hate shot viciously through the freezing blue eyes. "You worm of the Black Age!"

Northwood shuddered. He had heard those strange words addressed to himself scarcely more than two hours ago.

Adam was still speaking. "With a thought I could annihilate you where you are standing. But I have use for you. Get in." He swept his hand to the sun-ship.

Both men hesitated. Then Northwood strode forward until he was within three feet of Adam. They stood there eyeing each other, two splendid beings, one blond as a Viking, the other dark and vital.

"Just what is your game?" demanded Northwood.

The icy eyes shot forth a gleam like lightning. "I needn't tell you, of course, but I may as well let you suffer over the knowledge." He curled his lips with superb scorn. "I have one human weakness. I want Athalia." The icy eyes warmed for a fleeting second. "She is anticipating her meeting with you—bah! The taste of these women of the Black Age! I could kill you, of course, but that would only inflame her. And so I take you to her, throw you down her throat. When she sees you, she will fly to me." He spread his magnificent chest.

"Adam!" Dr. Mundson's face was dark with anger. "What of Eve!"

"Who are you to question my actions? What a fool you were to let me, when you forced into life thousand of years too soon, grow more powerful that you! Before I am through with all of you petty creatures of the Black Age, you will call me more terrible than your Jehovah! For see what you called forth from unborn time."

He vanished.

BEFORE THE startled men could recover from the shock of it, the vibrant, too-new voice went on.

"I am sorry for you, Mundson, because, like you, I need specimens for my experiments. What a splendid specimen you will be!" His laugh was ugly with significance. "Get in, worms!"

Unseen hands cuffed and pushed them into the sun-ship.

Inside, Dr. Mundson stumbled to the control room, white and drawn of face, his great brain seemingly paralyzed by the catastrophe.

"You needn't attempt tricks," went on the voice. "I am watching you both. You cannot even hide your thoughts from me."

And thus began the strange, continuation of the journey. Not once, in that wild half-hour's rush over the polar ice clouds, did they see Adam. They saw and heard only the weird signs of his presence: a puffing cigar hanging in midair, a glass of water swinging to unseen lips, a ghostly spite hurling threats and insults at them.

Once the scientist whispered, "Don't cross him; it is useless, John Northwood. You'll have to fight a demigod for your woman!"

Because of the terrific speed of the sun-ship, Northwood could distinguish nothing of the topographical details below. At the end of half-an-hour, the scientist slowed enough to point out a full range of snow-covered mountains, over which hovered a play of colored lights like the *aurora australis*.

"Behind those mountains," he said, "is our destination."

Almost in a moment, the sun-ship had soared over the peaks. Dr. Mundson kept the speed low enough for Northwood to see the splendid view below.

In the giant cup formed by the encircling mountain range was a green valley of tropical luxuriance. Stretches of dense forest swept half up the mountains and filled the valley cup with tangled verdure. In the center, surrounded by a broad field and a narrow ring of woods, towered a group of buildings. From the largest, which was circular, came the aurora-like radiance that formed an umbrella of light over the entire valley.

"Do I guess right," said Northwood, "that the light is responsible for this oasis in the ice?"

"Yes," said Dr. Mundson. "In your American slang, it is canned sunshine containing an overabundance of certain rays, especially the Life Ray, which I have isolated." He smiled proudly. "You needn't look startled, my friend. Some of the most common things store sunlight. On very dark nights, if you have sharp eyes, you can see the radiance given off by certain flowers, which many naturalists say is trapped sunshine. The familiar nasturtium and the marigold opened for me the way to hold sunshine against the long polar night, for they taught me how to apply the Einstein theory of bent light. Stated simply, during the polar night, when the sun is hidden over the rim of the world, we steal some of his rays. During the polar day we concentrate the light."

"But could stored sunshine alone give enough warmth for the luxuriant growth of those jungles?"

"An overabundance of the Life Ray is responsible for the miraculous growth of all life in New Eden. The Life Ray is Nature's most powerful force. Yet Nature is often niggardly and paradoxical in her use of her powers. In New Eden, we have forced the powers of creation to take ascendency over the powers of destruction."

At Northwood's sudden start the scientist laughed and continued. "Is it not a pity that Nature, left alone, requires twenty years to make a man who begins to die in another ten years? Such waste is not tolerated in New Eden, where supermen are younger than babes and—"

"Come, worms; let's land."

It was Adam's voice. Suddenly he materialized, a blond god, whose eyes and flesh were too new.

THEY WERE in a world of golden skylight, warmth and tropical vegetation. The field on which they had landed was covered with a velvety green growth of very soft, fine-bladed grass, sprinkled with tiny, star-shaped blue flowers. A balmy, sweet-scented wind, downy as the breeze of a dream, blew gently along the grass and tingled against Northwood's skin refreshingly. Almost instantly he had the sensation of perfect well being, and this feeling of physical perfection was part of the ecstasy that seemed to pervade the entire valley. Grass and breeze and golden skylight were saturated with a strange ether of joyousness.

At one end of the field was a dense jungle, cut through by a road that led to the towering building from which, while above in the sun-ship, they had seen the golden light issue.

From the jungle road came a man and a woman, large, handsome people, whose flesh and eyes had the sinister newness of Adam's. Even before they came close enough to speak, Northwood was aware that while they seemed of

Adam's breed, they were yet unlike him. The difference was psychical rather than physical. They lacked the aura of hate and horror that surrounded Adam. The woman drew Adam's head down and kissed him affectionately on both cheeks.

Adam, from his towering height, patted her shoulder impatiently and said, "Run on back to the laboratory, grandmother. We're following soon. You have some new human embryos, I believe you told me this morning."

"Four fine specimens, two of them being your sister's twins."

"Splendid! I was sure that creation had stopped with my generation. I must see them." He turned to the scientist and Northwood. "You needn't try to leave this spot. Of course, I shall know instantly and deal with you in my own way. Wait here."

He strode over the emerald grass on the heels of the woman.

Northwood asked, "Why does he call that girl grandmother?"

"Because she is his ancestress." He stirred uneasily. "She is of the first generation brought forth in the laboratory, and is no different from you or I, except that, at the age of five years, she is the ancestress of twenty generations."

"My God!" muttered Northwood.

"Don't start being horrified, my friend. Forget about so-called natural laws while you are in New Eden. Remember, here we have isolated the Light Ray. But look! Here comes your Athalia!"

Northwood gazed covertly at the beautiful girl approaching them with a rarely graceful walk. She was tall, slender, round-bosomed, and narrow-hipped, and she held her lovely body in the erect poise of splendid health. Northwood had a confused realization of uncovered bronze hair drawn to the back of a white neck in a bunch of short curls; of immense, soft black eyes, lips the color of blood, and delicate, plump flesh on which the golden skylight lingered graciously. He was instantly glad to see that while she possessed the freshness of young girlhood, her skin and eyes did not have the horrible newness of Adam's.

When she was still twenty feet distant, Northwood met her eyes and she smiled shyly. The rich, red blood went through her face and he, too, flushed.

She went to Dr. Mundson and, placing her hands on his thick shoulders, kissed him affectionately.

"I've been worried about you, Daddy Mundson." Her rich contralto voice matched her exotic beauty. "Since you and Adam had that quarrel the day you left, I did not see him until this morning when he landed the sun-ship alone."

"And you pleaded with him to return for us?"

"Yes." Her eyes drooped and a hot flush swept over her face.

Dr. Mundson smiled. "But I'm back now, Athalia, and I've brought someone whom I hope you will be glad to know."

Reaching for her hand, he placed it simply in Northwood's. "This is John, Athalia. Isn't he handsomer than the pictures of him which I televisioned to you? God bless both of you."

He walked ahead and turned his back.

A MAGICAL half hour followed for Northwood and Athalia. The girl told him of her past life, how Dr. Mundson had discovered her one year ago working in a New York sweat shop, half dead from consumption. Without friends, she was eager to follow the scientist to New Eden where he promised she would recover her health immediately.

"And he was right, John," she said shyly. "The Life Ray, that marvelous energy ray which penetrates to the utmost depths of earth and ocean, giving to the cells of all living bodies the power to grow and remain animate, has been concentrated by Dr. Mundson in his stored sunshine. The Life Ray healed me almost immediately."

Northwood looked down at the glorious girl beside him, whose eyes already fluttered away from his like shy black butterflies. Suddenly he squeezed the soft hand in his and said passionately:

"Athalia! Because Adam wants you and will get you if he can, let us set aside all the artificialities of civilization. I have loved you madly ever since I saw your picture. If you can say the same to me, it will give me courage to face what I know lies before me."

Athalia, her face suddenly tender, came closer to him.

"John Northwood, I love you."

Her red lips came temptingly close, but before he could touch them, Adam suddenly pushed his body between him and Athalia. Adam was pale, and all the iciness was gone from his blue eyes, which were deep and dark and very human. He looked down at Athalia and she looked up at him, two handsome specimens of perfect manhood and womanhood.

"Fast work, Athalia!" The new vibrant voice was strained. "I was hoping you would be disappointed in him, especially after having been wooed by me this morning. I could take you if I wished, of course, but I prefer to win you in the ancient manner. Dismiss him!" He jerked his thumb over his shoulder in Northwood's direction.

Athalia flushed vividly and looked at him almost compassionately. "I am not great enough for you, Adam. I dare not love you."

Adam laughed, and still oblivious of Northwood and Dr. Mundson, folded his arms over his breast. With the golden skylight on his burnished hair, he was a valiant, magnificent spectacle.

"Since the beginning of time, gods and archangels have looked upon the daughters of men and found them fair. Mate with me, Athalia, and I, fifty thousand years beyond the creature Mundson has selected for you, will make you as I am, the deathless overlord of life and all nature."

He drew her hand to his bosom.

For one dark moment, Northwood felt himself seared by jealousy, for, through the plump, sweet flesh of Athalia's face, he saw the red blood leap again. How could she withhold herself from this splendid superman?

But her answer, given with faltering voice, was the old, simple one, "I have promised him, Adam. I love him." Tears trembled on her thick lashes.

"So! I cannot get you in the ancient manner. Now I'll use my own."

He seized her in his arms, crushed her against him, and, laughing over her head at Northwood, bent his glistening head and kissed her on the mouth.

There was a blinding flash of blue electric sparks—and nothing else. Both Adam and Athalia had vanished.

Adam's voice came in a last mocking challenge: "I shall be what no other gods before me have been—a good sport. I'll leave you both to your own devices until I want you again."

White-lipped and trembling, Northwood groaned. "What has he done now?"

Dr. Mundson's great head drooped. "I don't know. Our bodies are electric and chemical machines—a super intelligence has discovered new laws of which you and I are ignorant."

"But Athalia . . ."

"She is safe. He loves her."

"Loves her!" Northwood shivered. "I cannot believe that those freezing eyes could ever look with love on a woman."

"Adam is a man. At heart he is as human as the first man-creature that wallowed in the new earth's slime." His voice dropped as though he were musing aloud. "It might be well to let him have Athalia. She will help to keep vigor in the new race, which would stop reproducing in another few generations without the injection of Black Age blood."

"Do you want to bring more creatures like Adam into the world?" Northwood flung at him. "You have tampered with life enough, Dr. Mundson. But, although Adam has my sympathy, I'm not willing to turn Athalia over to him."

"Well said! Now come to the laboratory for chemical nourishment and rest under the Life Ray."

They went to the great circular building from whose highest tower issued the golden radiance that shamed the light of the sun, hanging low in the northeast.

"John Northwood," said Dr. Mundson, "with that laboratory, which is the center of all life in New Eden, we'll have to whip Adam. He gave us what he called a 'sporting chance' because he knew that he is able to send us and all mankind to a doom more terrible than hell. Even now we might be entering some hideous trap that he has set for us."

THEY ENTERED by a side entrance and went immediately to what Dr. Mundson called the Rest Ward. Here, in a large room, were ranged rows of cots, on many of which lay men basking in the deep orange flood of light which poured from individual lamps set above each cot.

"It is the Life Ray!" said Dr. Mundson reverently. "The source of all growth and restoration in Nature. It is the power that bursts open the seed and brings forth the shoot, that increases the shoot into a giant tree. It is the same power that enables the fertilized ovum to develop into an animal. It creates and recreates cells almost instantly; accordingly, it is the perfect substitute for sleep. Stretch out, enjoy its power and, while you rest, eat these nourishing tablets."

Northwood lay on a cot and Dr. Mundson turned the Life Ray on him. For a few minutes a delicious drowsiness fell upon him, producing a spell of perfect peace which the cells of his being seemed to drink in. For another delirious, fleeting space, every inch of him vibrated with a thrilling sensation of freshness. He took a deep, ecstatic breath and opened his eyes.

"Enough," said Dr. Mundson, switching off the Ray. "After three minutes of rejuvenation, you are commencing again with perfect cells. All ravages from disease and wear have been corrected.

Northwood leaped up joyously. His handsome eyes sparkled, his skin glowed. "I feel great! Never felt so good since I was a kid."

A pleased grin spread over the scientist's homely face. "See what my discovery will mean to the world! In the future we shall all go to the laboratory for recuperation and nourishment. We'll have almost twenty-four hours a day for work and play."

He stretched out on the bed contentedly. "Some day, when my work is nearly done, I shall permit the Life Ray to cure my hump."

"Why not now?"

Dr. Mundson sighed. "If I were perfect, I should cease to be so overwhelmingly conscious of the importance of perfection." He settled back to enjoyment of the Life Ray.

A few minutes later, he jumped up, alert as a boy. "*Ach!*" That's fine. Now I'll show you how the Life Ray speeds up development and produces four generations of humans a year."

With restored energy, Northwood began thinking of Athalia. As he followed Dr. Mundson down a long corridor, he yearned to see her again, to be certain that she was safe. Once he imagined he felt a gentle, soft-fleshed touch against his hand, and was disappointed not to see her walking by his side. Was she with him, unseen? The thought was sweet.

Before Dr. Mundson opened the massive bronze door at the end of the corridor, he said, "Don't be surprised or shocked over anything you see here, John Northwood. This is the Baby Laboratory."

They entered a room which seemed no different from a hospital ward. On little white beds lay naked children of various sizes, perfect, solemn-eyed youngsters and older children as beautiful as animated statues. Above each bed was a small Life Ray projector. A white-capped nurse went from bed to bed.

"They are recuperating from the daily educational period," said the scientist. "After a few minutes of this they will go into the growing room, which I shall have to show you through a window. Should you and I enter, we might be changed in a most extraordinary manner." He laughed mischievously. "But, look, Northwood!"

He slid back a panel in the wall, and Northwood peered in through a thick pane of clear glass. The room was really an immense outdoor arena, its only carpet the fine-bladed grass, its roof the blue sky cut in the middle by an enormous disc from which shot the aurora of trapped sunshine which made a golden umbrella over the valley. Through openings in the bottom of the disc poured a fine rain of rays which fell constantly upon groups of children, youths and young girls, all clad in the merest scraps of clothing. Some were dancing, others were playing games, but all seemed as supremely happy as the birds and butterflies which fluttered about the shrubs and flowers edging the arena.

"I don't expect you to believe," said Dr. Mundson, "that the oldest young man in there is three months old. You cannot see visible changes in a body which grows as slowly as the human being, whose normal period of development is twenty years or more. But I can give you visible proof of how fast growth takes place under the full power of the Life Ray. Plant life, which, even when left to nature, often develops from seed to flower within a few weeks or months, can be seen making its miraculous changes under the Life Ray. Watch those gorgeous purple flowers over which the butterflies are hovering."

Northwood followed his pointing finger. Near the glass window through which they looked grew an enormous bank of resplendent violet colored flowers which literally enshrouded the entire bush with their royal glory. At first glance it seemed as though a violent wind were snatching at flower and bush, but closer inspection proved that the agitation was part of the plant itself. And then he saw that the movements were the result of perpetual composition and growth.

He fastened his eyes on one huge bud. He saw it swell, burst, spread out its passionate purple velvet, lift the broad flower face to the light for a joyous minute. A few second later a butterfly lighted airily to sample its nectar and to brush the pollen from its yellow dusted wings. Scarcely had the winged visitor flown away than the purple petals began to wither and fall away, leaving the seed pod on the stem. The visible change went on in this seed pod. It turned rapidly brown, dried out, and then sent the released seeds in a shower to the rich black earth below. Scarcely had the seeds touched the ground than they sent up tiny green shoots that grew larger each moment. Within ten minutes there was a new plant a foot high. Within half an hour, the plant budded, blossomed, and cast forth its own seed.

"You understand?" asked the scientist. "Development is going on as rapidly among the children. Before the first year has passed, the youngest baby will have grandchildren; this is, if the baby tests out fit to pass its seed down to the new generation. I know it sounds absurd. Yet you saw the plant."

"But Doctor," Northwood rubbed his jaw thoughtfully, "Nature's forces of destruction of tearing down, are as powerful as her creative powers. You have discovered the ultimate in creation and upbuilding. But perhaps—oh, Lord, it is too awful to think!"

"Speak, Northwood!" The scientist's voice was impatient.

"It is nothing!" The pale young man attempted a smile. "I was only imagining some of the horror that could be thrust on the world if a supermind like Adam's should discover Nature's secret of death and destruction and speed it up as you have sped the life force."

"*Ach Gott!*" Dr. Mundson's face was white. "He has his own laboratory where he works every day. Don't talk so loud. He might be listening. And I believe he can do anything he sets out to accomplish."

Close to Northwood's ear fell a faint, triumphant whisper: "Yes, he can do anything. How did you guess, worm?"

It was Adam's voice.

"NOW COME and see the Leyden jar mothers," said Dr. Mundson. "We do not wait for the child to be born to start our work."

He took Northwood to a laboratory crowded with strange apparatus, where young men and women worked. Northwood knew instantly that these people, although unusually handsome and strong, were not of Adam's generation. None of them had the look of newness which marked those who had grown up under the Life Ray.

"They are the perfect couples whom I combed the world to find," said the scientist. "From their eugenic marriages sprang the first children that passed through the laboratory. I had hoped," he hesitated and looked sideways at Northwood, "I had dreamed of having children of you and Athalia to help strengthen the New Race."

A wave of sudden disgust passed over Northwood.

"Thanks," he said tartly. "When I marry Athalia, I intend to have an old-fashioned home and a Black Age family. I don't relish having my children turned into—experiments."

"But wait until you see all the wonders of the laboratory! That is why I am showing you all this."

Northwood drew his handkerchief and mopped his brow. "It sickens me, Doctor! The more I see, the more pity I have for Adam—and the less I blame him for his rebellion and his desire to kill and to rule. Heavens! What a terrible thing you have done, experimenting with human life."

"Nonsense! Can you say that all life—all matter—is not the result of scientific experiment? Can you?" His black gaze made Northwood uncomfortable. "Buck up, young friend, for now I am going to show you a marvelous improvement on Nature's bungling ways—the Leyden jar mother." He raised his voice and called, "Lilith!"

The woman whom they had met on the field came forward.

"May we take a peep at Lona's twins?" asked the scientist. "They are about ready to go to the growing dome, are they not?"

"In five more minutes," said the woman. "Come see."

She lifted one of the black velvet curtains that lined an entire side of the laboratory and thereby disclosed a globular jar of glass and metal, connected by wires to a dynamo. Above the jar was a Life Ray projector. Lilith slid aside a metal portion of the jar, disclosing through the glass underneath the squirming, kicking body of a baby, resting on a bed of soft, spongy substance, to which it was connected by the naval cord.

"The Leyden jar mother," said Dr. Mundson. "It is the dream of us scientists realized. The human mother's body does nothing but nourish and protect her unborn child, a job which science can do better. And so, in New Eden, we take the young embryo and place it in the Lyden jar mother, where the Life Ray, electricity, and chemical food shorten the period of gestation to a few short days."

At that moment a bell under the Leyden jar began to ring. Dr. Mundson uncovered the jar and lifted out the child, a beautiful, perfectly formed boy, who began to cry lustily.

"Here is one baby who'll never be kissed," he said. "He'll be nourished chemically, and, at the end of the week, will no longer be a baby. If you are patient, you can actually see the processes of development taking place under the Life Ray, for babies develop very fast."

Northwood buried his face in his hands. "Lord! This is awful. No childhood; no mother to mold his mind! No parents to watch over him, to give him their tender care!"

"Awful, fiddlesticks! Come see how children get their education, how they learn to use their hands and feet so they need not pass through the awkwardness of childhood."

He led Northwood to a magnificent building whose façade of white marble was as simply beautiful as a Greek temple. The side walls, built almost entirely of glass, permitted the synthetic sunshine to sweep from end to end. They first entered a library, where youths and young girls poured over books of all kinds. Their manner of reading mystified Northwood. With a single sweep of the eye, they seemed to devour a page, and then turned to the next. He stepped closer to peer over the shoulder of a beautiful girl. She was reading "Euclid's Elements of Geometry," in Latin, and she turned the pages as swiftly as the other girl occupying her table, who was devouring "Paradise Lost."

Dr. Mundson whispered to him, "If you do not believe that Ruth here is getting her Euclid, which she probably never saw before today, examine her from the book; that is, if you are a good enough Latin scholar."

Ruth stopped her reading to talk to him and, in few minutes, had completely dumfounded him with her pedantic replies, which fell from lips as luscious and unformed as an infant's.

"Now," said Dr. Mundson, "test Rachael on her Milton. As far as she has read, she should not misquote a line, and her comments will probably prove her scholarly appreciation of Milton."

Word for word, Rachael was able to give him "Paradise Lost" from memory, except the last four pages, which she had not read. Then, taking the book from him, she swept her eyes over these pages, returned the book to him, and quoted copiously and correctly.

Dr. Mundson gloated triumphantly over his astonishment. "There, my friend. Could you now be satisfied with old-fashioned children who spend long, expensive years in getting an education? Of course, your children will not have the perfect brains of these. Yet, developed under the Life Ray they should have splendid mentality."

"These children, through selective breeding, have brains that make everlasting records instantly. A page in a book, once seen, is indelibly retained by them, and understood. The same is true of a lecture, of an explanation given by a teacher, of even idle conversation. Any man or woman in this room should be able to repeat the most trivial conversation days old."

"But what of the arts, Dr. Mundson? Surely even your supermen and women cannot instantly learn to paint a masterpiece or to guide their fingers and their brains through the intricacies of a difficult musical composition."

"No?" His dark eyes glowed. "Come see!"

Before they entered another wing of the building, they heard a violin being played masterfully.

Dr. Mundson paused at the door.

"So that you may understand what you shall see, let me remind you that the nerve impulses and the coordinating means in the human body are purely electrical. The world has not yet accepted my theory, but it will. Under superman's system of education, the instantaneous records made on the brain give immediate skill to the acting parts of the body. Accordingly, musicians are made overnight."

He threw open the door. Under a Life Ray projector, a beautiful, Junoesque woman was playing a violin. Facing her, and with eyes fastened to hers, stood a young man, whose arms and slender fingers mimicked every motion she made. Presently she stopped playing and handed the violin to him. In her own masterly manner, he repeated the score she had played.

"That is Eve," whispered Dr. Mundson. "I had selected her as Adam's wife. But he does not want her, the most brilliant woman of the New Race."

Northwood gave the woman an appraising look. "Who wants a perfect woman? I don't blame Adam for preferring Athalia. But how is she teaching her pupil?"

"Through thought vibration, which these perfect people have developed until they can record permanently the radioactive wave of the brains of others."

Eve turned, caught Northwood's eyes in her magnetic blue gaze, and smiled as only a goddess can smile upon a mortal she has marked as her own. She came toward him with out flung hands.

"So you have come!" Her vibrant contralto voice, like Adam's, held the birdlike, broken tremulo of a young child's. "I have been waiting for you, John Northwood."

HER EYES, as blue and icy as Adam's, lingered long on him, until he flinched from their steely magnetism. She slipped her arm though his and drew him gently but firmly from the room, while Dr. Mundson stood gaping after them.

They were on a flagged terrace arched with roses of gigantic size, which sent forth billows of sensuous fragrance. Eve led him to a white marble seat piled with silk cushions, on which she reclined her superb body while she regarded him from narrowed lids.

"I saw your picture that he televised to Athalia," she said. "What a botch Dr. Mundson has made of his mating." Her laugh rippled like falling water. "I want you, John Northwood!"

Northwood started and blushed furiously. Smile dimples broke around her red, humid lips.

"Ah, you're old-fashioned!"

Her large, beautiful hand, fleshed more tenderly than any woman's hand he had ever seen, went out to him appealingly. "I can bring you amorous delight that your Athalia never could offer in her few years of youth. And I'll never grow old, John Northwood."

She came closer until he could feel the fragrant warmth of her tawny, ribbon-bound hair pulse against his face. In sudden panic he drew back.

"But I am pledged to Athalia!" tumbled from him. "It is all a dreadful mistake, Eve. You and Adam were created for each other."

"Hush!" The lightning that flashed from her blue eyes changed her from seductress to angry goddess. "Created for each other! Who wants a made-to-measure lover?"

The luscious lips trembled slightly, and into the vivid eyes crept a suspicion of moisture. Eternal Eve's weapons! Northwood's handsome face relaxed with pity.

"I want you, John Northwood," she continued shamelessly. "Our love will be sublime." She leaned heavily against him and her lips were like a blood red flower pressed against white satin. "Come, beloved, kiss me!"

Northwood gasped and turned his head. "Don't, Eve!"

"But a kiss from me will set you apart from all your generation, John Northwood, and you shall understand what no man of the Black Age could possibly fathom."

Her hair had partly fallen from its ribbon bondage and poured its fragrant gold against his shoulder.

"For God's sake, don't tempt me!" he groaned. "What do you mean?"

"That mental and physical and spiritual contact with me will temporarily give you, a three-dimension creature, the power of the new sense, which you race will not have for fifty thousand years."

White-lipped and trembling, he demanded, "Explain!"

Eve smiled. "Have you not guessed that Adam has developed an additional sense? You've seen him vanish. He and I have the sixth sense of Time Perception—the new sense which enables us to penetrate which you of the Black Age call the Fourth Dimension. Even you, whose mentalities are framed by three dimensions, have this sixth sense instinct. Your very religion is based on it, for you believe that in another life you shall step into Time, or, as you call it, eternity." She leaned closer so that her hair brushed his cheek. "What is eternity, John Northwood?" Is it not keeping forever ahead of the Destroyer? The future is eternal, for it is never reached. Adam and I, through our new sense which comprehends Time and Space, can vanish by stepping a few seconds into the future, the Fourth Dimension of Space. Death can never reach us, not even accidental death, unless that which causes death could also slip into the future, which is not yet possible."

"But if the Fourth Dimension is future time, why can one in the third dimension feel the touch of an unseen presence in the Fourth Dimension—hear his voice, even?"

"Thought vibration. The touch is not really felt nor the voice heard; they are only imagined. The radioactive waves of the brain of even you Black Age people are swift enough to bridge Space and Time. And it is the mind that carries us beyond the third dimension."

Her red mouth reached closer to him, her blue eyes touched hidden forces that slept in remote cells of his being. "You are going into Eternal Time, John Northwood. Eternity without beginning or end. You understand? You feel it? Comprehend it? Now for the contact—kiss me!"

Northwood had seen Athalia vanish under Adam's kiss. Suddenly, in one made burst of understanding, he leaned over to his magnificent temptress.

For a split second he felt the sweet pressure of baby-soft lips, and then the atoms of his body seemed to fly asunder. Black chaos held him for a frightful moment before his felt sanity return.

He was back on the terrace again, with Eve by his side. They were standing now. The world about him looked the same, yet there was a subtle change in everything.

Eve laughed softly. "It is puzzling, isn't it? You're seeing everything as in a mirror. What was left before is now right. Only you and I are real. All else is but a vision, a dream. For now you and I are existing one minute in future time, or, more simply, we are invisible. Let me show you that Dr. Mundson cannot see you."

They went back to the room beyond the terrace. Dr. Mundson was not present.

"There he goes down the jungle path," said Eve, looking out a window. She laughed. "Poor old fellow. The children of his genius are worrying him."

They were standing in the recess formed by a bay window. Eve picked up his hand and laid it against her face, giving him the full, blasting glory of her smiling blue eyes.

Northwood, looking away miserably, uttered a low cry. Coming over the field beyond were Adam and Athalia. By the trimming on the blue dress she wore, he could see that she was still in the Fourth Dimension, for he did not see her as a mirror image.

A look of fear leaped to Eve's face. She clutched Northwood's arm, trembling.

"I don't want Adam to see that I have passed you beyond," she gasped. "We are existing but one minute in the future. Always Adam and I have feared to pass too far beyond the sweetness of reality. But now, so that Adam may not see us, we shall step five minutes into what-is-yet-to-be. And even he, with all his power, cannot see into a future that is more distant than that in which he exists."

She raised her humid lips to his. "Come, beloved."

Northwood kissed her. Again came the moment of confusion, of the awful vacancy that was like death, and then he found himself and Eve in the laboratory, following Adam and Athalia down a long corridor. Athalia was crying and pleading frantically with Adam. Once she stopped and threw herself at his feet in a gesture of dramatic supplication, arms out flung, streaming eyes wide open with fear.

Adam stooped and lifted her gently and continued on his way, supporting her against his side.

Eve dug her fingers into Northwood's arm. Horror contorted her face, horror mixed with rage.

"My mind hears what he is saying, understands the vile plan he has made, John Northwood. He is on his way to his laboratory to destroy not only you and most of these in New Eden, but me as well. He wants only Athalia."

Striding forward like an avenging goddess, she pulled Northwood after her.

"Hurry!" she whispered. "Remember, you and I are five minutes in the future and Adam is only one. We are witnessing what will occur four minutes from now. We yet have time to reach the laboratory before him and be ready for him when he enters. And because he will have to go back to Present Time to do his work of destruction, I will be able to destroy him. Ah!"

Fierce joy burned in her flashing blue eyes, and her slender nostrils quivered delicately. Northwood, peering at her in horror, knew that no mercy could be expected of her. And when she stopped at a certain door and inserted a key, he remembered Athalia. What if she should enter with Adam in Present Time?

THEY WERE inside Adam's laboratory, a huge apartment filled with queer apparatus and cases of live animals. The room was a strange paradox. Part of the equipment, the walls, and the floor were glistening with newness, and part was moulding with extreme age. The powers of disintegration that haunt a tropical forest seemed to be devouring certain spots of the room. Here, in the midst of bright marble, was a section of wall that seemed as old as the pyramids. The surface of the stone had an appalling mouldiness, as though it had been lifted from an ancient graveyard where it had lain in the festering ground for unwholesome centuries.

Between cracks in this stained and decayed section of stone grew fetid moss that quivered with the microscopic organisms that infest age-rotten places. Sections of the flooring and woodwork also reeked with mustiness. In one dark, webby corner of the room lay a pile of bleached bones, still tinted with the ghastly grays and pinks of putrefaction. Northwood, overwhelmingly nauseated, withdrew his eyes from the bones, only to see, in another corner, a pile of worm-eaten clothing that lay on the floor in the outline of a man.

Faint with the reek of ancient mustiness, Northwood retreated to the door, dizzy and staggering.

"It sickens you," said Eve, "and it sickens me also, for death and decay are not pleasant. Yet Nature, left to herself, reduces all to this. Every grave that has yawned to receive its prey hides corruption no less shocking. Nature's forces of creation and destruction forever work in partnership. Never satisfied with her composition, she destroys and starts again, building, building towards the ultimate of perfection. Thus, it is natural that if Dr. Mundson isolated the Life Ray, Nature's supreme force of compensation, isolation of the Death Ray should closely follow. Adam, thirsting for power, has succeeded. A few sweeps of his unholy ray of decomposition will undo all Dr. Mundson's work in this valley and reduce it to a stinking holocaust of destruction. And the time for his striking has come!"

She seized his face and drew it toward her. "Quick!" she said. "We'll have to go back to the third dimension. I could leave you safe in the fourth, but if anything should happen to me, you would be stranded forever in future time."

She kissed his lips. In a moment, he was back in the old familiar world, where right is right and left is left. Again the subtle change wrought by Eve's magic had taken place.

Eve went to a machine standing in a corner of the room.

"Come here and get behind me, John Northwood. I want to test it before he enters."

Northwood stood behind her shoulder.

"Now watch!" she ordered. "I shall turn it on one of those cages of guinea pigs over there."

She swung the projector around, pointed it at the cage of small, squealing animals, and threw a lever. Instantly a cone of black mephitis shot forth, a loathsome, bituminous stream of putrefaction that reeked of the grave and the cesspool, of the utmost reaches of decay before the dust accepts the disintegrated atoms. The first touch of seething, pitchy destruction brought screams of agony from the guinea pigs, but the screams were cut short as the little animals fell in shocking, instant decay. The very cage which imprisoned them shriveled and retreated from the hellish, devouring breath that struck its noisome rot into the heart of the wood and the metal, reducing both to revolting ruin.

Eve cut off the frightful power, and the black cone disappeared, leaving the room putrid with its defilement.

"And Adam would do that to the world," she said, her blue eyes like electric-shot icicles. "He would do it to you, John Northwood—and to me!" Her full bosom strained under the passion beneath.

"Listen!" She raised her hand warningly. "He comes! The destroyer comes!"

A hand was at the door. Eve reached for the lever, and, the same moment, Northwood leaned over her imploringly.

"If Athalia is with him!" he gasped. "You will not harm her?"

A wild shriek at the door, a slight scuffle, and then the doorknob was wrenched as though two were fighting over it.

"For God's sake, Eve!" implored Northwood. "Wait! Wait!"

"No! She shall die, too. You love her!"

Icy, cruel eyes cut into him, and a new-fleshed hand tried to push him aside. The door was straining open. A beloved voice shrieked, "John!"

Eve and Northwood both leaped for the lever. Under her tender white flesh she was as strong as man. In the midst of the struggle, her red, humid lips approached his—closer. Closer. Their merest pressure would thrust him into Future Time where the laboratory and all it contained would be but a shadow, and where he would be helpless to interfere with her terrible will.

He saw the door open and Adam stride into the room. Behind him, lying prone in the hall where she had probably fainted, was Athalia. In a mad burst of strength he touched the lever together with Eve.

The projector, belching forth its stinking breath of corruption swung in a mad arc over the ceiling, over the walls—and then straight at Adam.

Then, quicker than thought came the accident. Eve, attempting to throw Northwood off, tripped, fell half over the machine and, with a short scream of despair, dropped into the black path of destruction.

Northwood paused, horrified. The Death Ray was pointed at an inner wall of the room which, even as he looked, crumbled and disappeared, bringing down upon him dust more foul than any obscenity the bowels of the earth might yield. In an instant the black cone ate through the outer parts of the building, where crashing stone and screams that were more horrible because of their shortness followed the ruin that swept far into the fair reaches of the valley.

The paralyzing odor of decay took his breath, numbed his muscles, until of all that huge building, the wall behind him and one small section of the room by the doorway alone remained whole. He was trying to nerve himself to reach for the lever close to that quiet formless thing still partly draped over the machine, when a faint sound in the door electrified him. At first, he dared not look, but his own name spoken almost in a gasp, gave him courage.

Athalia lay on the floor, apparently untouched.

He jerked the lever violently before running to her, exultant with the knowledge that his own efforts to keep the ray from the door had saved her.

"And you're not hurt!" He gathered her close.

"John! I saw it get Adam." She pointed to a new mound of mouldy clothes on the floor. "Oh, it is hideous for me to be so glad, but he was going to destroy everything and everyone except me. He made that ray projector for that one purpose."

Northwood looked over the pile of putrid ruins which a few minutes ago had been a building. There was not a wall left intact.

"His intention is accomplished, Athalia," he said sadly. "Let's get out before more stones fall."

IN A moment they were in the open. An ominous stillness seemed to grip the very air—the awful silence of the polar wastes which lay not far beyond the mountains.

"How dark it is, John!" cried Athalia. "Dark and cold!"

"The sunshine projector!" gasped Northwood. "It must have been destroyed. Look, dearest! The gold light has disappeared."

"And the warm air of the valley will lift immediately. That means a polar blizzard." She shuddered and clung closer to him. "I've seen Antarctic storms, John. They're death."

Northwood avoided her eyes. "There's the sun-ship. We'll give the ruins the once-over in case there are any survivors; then we'll save ourselves."

Even a cursory examination of the mouldy piles of stone and dust convinced them that there could be no survivors. The ruins looked as though they had lain in those crumbling piles for centuries. Northwood, smothering his repugnance, stepped among them—among the green, slimy stones and the unspeakable revolting débris, staggering back and faint and shocked when he came upon dust that was once human.

"God!" he groaned, hands over his eyes. "We're alone, Athalia! Alone in a charnel house. The laboratory housed the entire population, didn't it?"

"Yes. Needing no sleep nor food, we did not need houses. We all worked here, under Dr. Mundson's generalship, and, lately under Adam's, like a little band of soldiers fighting for a great cause."

"Let's go to the sun-ship, dearest."

"But Daddy Mundson was in the library," sobbed Athalia. "Let's look for him a little longer."

Sudden remembrance came to Northwood. "No, Athalia! He left the library. I saw him go down the jungle path several minutes before I and Eve went to Adam's laboratory."

"Then he might be safe!" Her eyes danced. "He might have gone to the sun-ship."

Shivering, she slumped against him. "Oh, John! I'm cold."

Her face was blue. Northwood jerked off his coat and wrapped it around her, taking the intense cold against his unprotected shoulders. The low, gray sky was rapidly darkening, and the feeble light of the sun could scarcely pierce the clouds. It was disturbing to know that even the summer temperature in the Antarctic was far below zero.

"Come, girl," said Northwood gravely, "Hurry! It's snowing."

They started to run down the road through the narrow strip of jungle. The Death Ray had cut huge swatches in the tangle of trees and vines, and now areas of heaped débris, livid with the colors of recent decay, exhaled a mephitic humidity altogether alien to the snow that fell in soft, slow flakes. Each hesitated to voice the new fear; had the sun-ship been destroyed?

By the time they reached the open field, the snow stung their flesh like sharp needles, but it was not yet thick enough to hide from them a hideous fact.

The sun-ship was gone.

IT MIGHT have occupied one of several black, foul areas on the green grass, where the searching Death Ray had made the very soil putrefy, and the rock crumble into shocking dust.

Northwood snatched Athalia to him, too full of despair to speak. A sudden terrific flurry of snow whirled around them, and they were almost blown from their feet by the icy wind that tore over the unprotected field.

"It won't be long," said Athalia faintly. "Freezing doesn't hurt, John, dear."

"It isn't fair, Athalia! There never would have been such a marriage as ours. Dr. Mundson searched the world to bring us together."

"For scientific experiment!" she sobbed. "I'd rather die, John. I want an old-fashioned home, a Black Age family. I want to grow old with you and leave the earth to my children. Or else I want to die here now under the kind, white blanket the snow is already spreading over us." She dropped in his arms.

Clinging together, they stood in the howling wind, looking at each other hungrily, as though they would snatch from death this one last picture of the other.

Northwood's freezing lips translated some of the futile words that crowded against them. "I love you because you are not perfect. I hate perfection!"

"Yes. Perfection is the only hopeless state, John. That is why Adam wanted to destroy, so that he might build again."

They were sitting in the snow now, for they were very tired. The storm began whistling louder, as though it were only a few feet above their heads.

"That sounds almost like the sun-ship," said Athalia drowsily.

"It's only the wind. Hold your face down so it won't strike your flesh so cruelly."

"I'm not suffering. I'm getting warm again." She smiled at him sleepily.

Little icicles began to form on their clothing, and the powdery snow frosted their uncovered hair.

Suddenly came a familiar voice. *"Ach Gott!"*

Dr. Mundson stood before them, covered with snow until he looked like a polar bear.

"Get up!" he shouted. "Quick! To the sun-ship!"

He seized Athalia and jerked her to her feet. She looked at him sleepily for a moment, and then threw herself at him, and hugged him frantically.

"You're not dead?"

Taking each by the arm, he half dragged them to the sun-ship, which had landed only a few feet away. In a few minutes he had hot brandy for them.

While they sipped greedily, he talked, between working the sun-ship's controls.

"No, I wouldn't say it was a lucky moment that drew me to the sun-ship. When I saw Eve trying to charm John, I had what you American slangists call a hunch, which sent me to the sun-ship to get it off the ground so that

Adam couldn't commandeer it. And what is a hunch but a mental penetration into the Fourth Dimension?" For a long moment, he brooded, absent-minded. "I was in the air when the black ray, which I suppose is Adam's deviltry, began to destroy everything it touched. From a safe elevation I saw it wreck all my work." A sudden spasm crossed his face. "I've flown over the entire valley. We're the only survivors—thank God!"

"And so at last you confess that it is not well to tamper with human life?" Northwood, warmed with hot brandy, was his old self again.

"Oh, I have not altogether wasted my efforts. I went to elaborate pains to bring together a perfect man and a perfect woman of what Adam called our Black Age." He smiled at them whimsically.

"And who can say to what extent you have thus furthered natural evolution?" Northwood slipped his arms around Athalia. "Our children might be more than geniuses, Doctor!"

Dr. Mundson nodded his huge, shaggy head gravely.

"The true instinct of a Creature of the Light," he declared.

The Man Who Fought A Fly
by Leslie F. Stone

From all of Leslie's works I read for this anthology I selected this one as the most powerful. From different time periods it echoes elements of Henry Hasse's "He Who Shrank", Bob Olsen's "Ant with a Human Soul", Ray Cummings' "The Insect Invasion", Richard Matheson's "The (Incredible) Shrinking Man" ("Insects Extraordinary", Walter Kateley, "The Insect World", Thos. S. Gardner"—FJA) but all with a perspective of Leslie's own. Her short-short story in this volume was selected by my collaborator and I feel there is room for two tales by the same talented woman.
—PK

There was no reminder of the medieval alchemist with his dust-laden tomes, his belching force, his stuffed crocodile and empty skulls, in the bright, pleasant chamber that housed Professor Duncan Trent's laboratory. It was a converted conservatory in the old home he maintained as his residence and workshop. Three sides were of glass, the roof a skylight pouring sunlight down upon the healthy flowering plants set in boxes in a ring around the floor under the windows or on stands. Even when the sun was not shining it was a pleasant room. Only the low tables with their clear glass receptacles of every size and shape, the chest of shelves along the back wall, with its rows of bottles tagged with strange scientific names and an occasional strange pungent odor told one that this was a room devoted to science.

It was the duty of Mike Turey to keep his laboratory neat and clean. Each day he swabbed the red and blue tile floor with sudsy water, ran his duster over tables and machines, and washed out the glasses the professor ordered to be ready for his ministrations. Then carefully he watered the potted plants, brought in cut-flowers from the garden to set in the many vases and bowls about, weeded and trimmed the flower boxes. Mike was also the some-time assistant to the professor, helping the scientist when a second hand was needed at some delicate task. A crippled war veteran, he had found congenial surroundings in the professor's pleasant employ, for himself and his wife. Trent liked him and often discussed his latest discoveries or failures with the ex-service man.

Today everything was finished in the laboratory except for the watering of the plants. Mike was a little late with the watering because he had taken time out to wash the flower vases and bowls. Now he came stumping into the laboratory weighted down with his watering cans, his limp just barely noticeable. It was a darkish, cloudy day in April, and on such days his leg ached a bit more than usual.

"*Mary!*" A crash, the gurgling splash of water on the tiles as the watering cans dropped from nerveless hands and Mike, the efficient, stood rooted to the ground just within the French window of the laboratory, staring agape at his wife settled in one of his master's chintz-covered chairs, hands folded in her lap, her head and body bathed in the golden glow of a light from a lamp over her head.

That the lamp was not an ordinary one was evident at first glance. Its shade was a bowl-shaped affair of shiny metal on a tall stand, the golden light issuing from it seemed to have a malevolent gleam in its depths. It cut the grayness of the room like a knife.

"*Mary!*" Mike's second cry was a shriek, for it is not given every man to see his plump wife shrinking into a child again, which was exactly what was happening. From a big-bosomed, comfortable sort of a woman of five feet four inches tall, she had already shrunk to a woman four feet five inches when her husband first caught sight of her, and from his first to second cry, she had shrunk even more. Nor did she stir at his calls and Mike saw her eyes were closed; her breathing spasmodic.

His second cry aroused Mike from the apathy of his first fright and the next instant he was a hurtling body that crossed the intervening space between himself and his wife in an astounding shortness of time. But the lamp-cord was his undoing. It caught his bad foot and sent him crashing forward, the momentum of his body overturning his wife's chair and the lamp in one blow, cracking his head upon the tile floor with such force that he lost consciousness for several minutes.

The cataclysm that had carried the lamp and chair to the floor with Mike, had acted as a catapult upon the woman's diminishing form, flinging her across the nearest flower box. And there she hung, her head upon the box's edge, her feet dropping over the side, only, as she continued to shrink in size, it could be seen that the box would soon be large enough to contain all of her. And the spreading fan of the golden ray from the lamp still shone upon her, as it now shone upon the prone body of her husband huddled close to the flower box!

SOME MINUTES later, Mike raised his aching head, but that was not the only part of him that ached; every bone, every muscle ached as if he had indulged in some new sort of bodily exercise that brought every muscle in his body into play, more than he knew he possessed. A groan pushed its way up his throat, then another; he found he enjoyed groaning. For several minutes he practiced this until he found the groans cost him unnecessary effort and he desisted. Instead, he tried sitting up and was surprised to find he could do it. But what strange place was this?

All around him, for what seemed miles, was a red plain, a deep red, a plain that might have been called flat, though of exceeding roughness. He could not call them hills; they were more like rough pits, crater pits such as he had known in the war, only his mind was too stunned now to associate such ideas. He could only think of his immediate present, and try to place it in his memory. The plain seemed to have a glossy finish at one time, but now it was dulled, roughened, only the high points of the craters retained a reminiscent polish from the past. A sort of diffused gray light hung over him, and by placing a hand above his eyes and squinting, he could see strange, undefinable shapes in the far distances.

But what was this? Out of the heavens was falling a strange rain. He called it rain for want of a better word, but he could not remember such a rain as this, for from all sides was a continuous falling of strange particles, boulders of every size and shape from the size of a baseball to several times the size of his head—sticks, long and short, of every color, every hue dropping around him on all sides, obscuring the landscape partly, making it necessary to dodge their blows. He could hear them falling to the ground, click, crash, boom. One hit his shoulder, another fell across his extended legs. Luckily they were not heavy and did not hurt him, but he knew the large boulder coming down through the air toward him would hurt unless he dodged it. He rolled to one side under it and got to his feet. The mass plopped into the spot where he had been sitting, lightly, as if gravity did not matter much here. He looked at it carefully. It was cube-shaped and had the appearance of iron. It was smooth to his touch and cold.

The air cleared a moment of the falling débris and he gazed around him. Far to his right was the dark line of a crevice in the plain, grayish in color, a ravine of shallow depth. On its opposite side lay a second plain, blue in color, a dull grayish blue. Looking to the left, he could discern a second ravine more distant than the one on his right, and beyond it lay a second plain of blue. Before him the red plain was wide and he could just make out the crack that enclosed it. But turning on his heel, he saw that less than forty yards from where he stood was a fourth crevice and a fourth blue plain. It seemed the most natural thing in the world to him that he should be standing on a red plain cut by four straight dikes with blue plains on their other sides. He tried to recall where he had seen that pattern before, but so strange seemed his awakening, he could not quite recall the past beyond the point of his awakening here on the red plain. It was an effort to try to think. He could feel a bump on the side of his head and he attributed his loss of memory to it.

With the idea of orientating himself still further, he studied the landscape beyond the four coulees. All the blue plains seemed identical, as far as he could see, but for the fourth, where he discerned in the middle distance a great thick column sloping upward from the ground at about a thirty degree angle, rising so high into the air that he was unable to see its end; it seemed to go right up into the indistinguishable blue of the heavens themselves. And beyond that he could just make out, in the hazy distance, what was apparently a high wall, but that did not interest him yet. It was the column set alone in all the vastness of this great pattern that attracted him; it was his whole future for the present.

Amid the falling things from the air he started to pick his way toward the column, half-consciously dodging the débris that piled itself up on the ground in a hotch-potch, varying the natural color of the red plain with their own shades. They seemed for the most part fragments of animal, vegetable and mineral matter. They blocked his path making it necessary to circle them where it was impossible to climb over them. They were unstable, rolling under his feet, and what with jumping out of the way of those still falling, it was enough to drive a man out of his senses, but Mike was unusually phlegmatic, able to take everything as a matter of course, at the same time realizing how unnatural this new place was.

THE GROUND under foot did not seem like a soil, but a vitrified substance from which the original life had been decarbonized. Perhaps that accounted for the remaining gloss that clung to the pitted surfaces. But at last he was able to leave the red plain behind, as he stood on the edge of his first canyon, the dividing line between red and blue plain. Carefully he made his way down the side of the ravine which seemed sanded, altogether different from the surface of the plain he had just left behind, and it was different in color. In the bottom of the depression, he saw half a dozen odd structures, each a great round globe many times his own size. They seemed balls of some transparent matter, held in a state of balance; bright things in which light seemed at play, changing into all the colors of the rainbow as he stared at them. He dared reach out to touch the side of the nearest sphere, it was elastic; it dented at his touch. He pushed hard upon it with the full force of his hand, and to his horror the sphere bulged outward and became a round sticky mouth that sucked him to the sphere's surface. In the next instant he found himself dragged over the surface, spun around in miniature whirlpool! One foot and hand remained free of the stuff, but for the rest of him he was caught like a fly on a sticky paper, unable to move, unable to grasp anything by which to pull himself free.

After his first fright was over, he ceased struggling long enough to consider what this strange ball might be. He noticed that whereas the stuff was sticky, elastic, it did not seem to wet him at all; there appeared to be some sort of skin over the surface of the globe that held its contents together, protected it against contact with him, while it held him prisoner. Minutes, hours seemed to pass, and then he noticed how cold he was. It was the sphere that was cold; however, it seemed to be losing some of its original size. At the same time, it was animated with a strange interior force that lifted and stretched it with terrific power. Then the man felt himself falling. There was a violent shock, as if an explosion had taken place quite near him and he found himself on the ground. The ball had disappeared.

Without a minute's pause Mike picked himself up and ran wildly up the slope of the gulch to the blue plain regardless of the bruises he had sustained from his fall. He stopped, breathless, on its edge to look backward at the transparent spheres below. Not one was left. All were gone, exploded!

The surface of the blue plain hardly differed from that of the red plain. It also looked as if it were ossified, and there were the irregular piles of débris fallen from the sky, mounting as more came down. His crippled leg began to pain him as he pushed on and on toward the strange tilted pillar set over in one corner of the blue plain, and after what had seemed an indeterminable length of time he reached it. He was tired, weary and hungry, but there was nothing edible to be found hereabouts, nothing in this wild dreary land, nothing in the pockets of his blue working jeans. He stood gazing at the column for a while, trying to peer upward to its end. It was several times his own girth, its surface of no material he could place. It seemed fibrous, filled with hundreds of little cracks, rough, pitted. He decided the pillar must be very ancient.

It was, however, he concluded, hardly worth the bother of coming to see. He turned his back upon it and gazed off in the distance to the high precipice etched across the far sky. It seemed a great unbroken wall of a mighty mountain range, rising several thousand feet into the air, stretching further than the eye could see in both directions. Mountains suggested trees, verdure, water, food perhaps. It suggested something else beside. For on his trek across the plains a single word had seemed to crop persistently into his mind. "Mary, Mary," his sluggish brain had repeated. Now something was suggesting that Mary was to be found on the mountain top, though for the life of him he could not tell where that odd thought came from, and exactly who Mary was!

He decided to start off immediately, but then he realized how tired and worn out he was. First he must sleep, must rest his weary bones, his crippled leg. He noticed suddenly that the rain of particles from the sky was less heavy on the opposite side of the leaning pillar from that which he had come. At its foot, practically no débris fell at all. He would lie there, huddled against the pillar's foot and sleep awhile.

MIKE NEVER KNEW exactly what had awakened him but suddenly he was wide awake and frightened. He felt eyes upon him; the hair on the nape of his neck was rising. He gasped when he saw the *thing* facing him, a great black creature with six hairy legs and two eyes that were divided and subdivided into a thousand different parts, each part carrying a reflection of himself. And never had he seen an uglier or more gruesome face. Between the eyes the face was flat but below them it bulged out into a most fearsome mouth with heavy jaws that seemed more like tusks. In size it was as big as an elephant, while on its back was a pair of gorgeous, transparent wings, half-open now as if the thing was prepared for flight at a moment's notice. It exuded a strong penetrating odor that reminded Mike of decaying flesh, putrefaction.

How long the creature had been surveying him he did not know. A scream rose to his throat as it took a step toward him. A step backward brought Mike's back against the great leaning column. Its solidity felt good there behind him. It was safety of a sort, and he took another step backward, pressed against the pillar away from the creature. The beast, in consequence, took a step toward him, trying to outstare him with its many eyes while two long horns that Mike had not noticed before waved in front of its face. His own eyes darted this way and that in search of a weapon of some sort, and he saw a long rough stick that could serve him as a club lying close by. It meant, however, taking a step toward the elephantine animal, and in his extremity, Mike even dared this. He was surprised to see the beast take a step backward as he moved forward. Ah, the thing was cowardly.

The club was heavy, almost too heavy for Mike, but by grasping it with two hands he succeeded in lifting it above his head. The beast watched him

The beast watched him closely. With all his might he brought the stick downward in a great circle toward the beast's glistening eyes . . .

dumbly, and Mike took the offensive. With all his might he brought the stick downward in a great circle toward the beast's glistening eyes, but when the stick landed, the thing wasn't there. He heard the hum of its wings as it took to the air, then around him grew the sound of a roar, a deep booming noise like thunder coming from its thorax. He wheeled about to see the creature dropping to the ground on the other side of him, and again he struck out with his club.

This time the club caught one of the creature's wings, tearing it across so it could never use it again. It started back from him, but changing its mind, charged upon the man. Again Mike raised his heavy club, to bring it down on the beast's clumsy head. One of the waving horns was broken, and the jagged head of the stick cut a furrow through the left eye of the beast, half-blinding it. The roar of the beast grew louder and again it charged and again Mike struck out with his club. A hairy claw raked his back, but it did not touch skin, merely tearing the cloth of his jeans off his shoulder. He lost count of its charges as he placed his heavy blows with precision, and each blow counted against the beast. One eye was entirely gone, the other had only half its sight, two legs were crippled, the second wing was frayed. It seemed to have lost all sense of direction when another blow tore the other horn away from the top of the beast's head. Now it no longer roared, and suddenly gave up the battle, crawling hastily away from the enraged man. But Mike, with the lust of battle in his veins, was not through yet. Bringing the club high above his head and as far back as his arms would go, he gave a mighty heave that sent it after the retreating creature. The point entered the hard black body just between the sagging wings, carrying it to the ground. It lay where it fell, legs twitching, a low murmur issuing from its body.

It was a gruesome sight with red sticky blood oozing from its many wounds, but Mike did not have it in his heart to pity it. He stood off to survey it, wondering what it was, what was so familiar about it.

"Why! It's a fly," he said at last, and after he had spoken the words, he wondered at them. A fly? What was a fly? Why, What? Why should he recognize the creature? Why was he here? What was he doing in this oddly familiar land that after all was unfamiliar?

One after another the man put these questions to himself, but he was at a loss to answer them. His mind was in a queerly muddled state. Faint, dim memories came to him; he was always on the verge of understanding things, yet on the other hand, his mind refused him the answers, was unable to collect them properly and catalogue them for himself. He was aware of the fact that something untoward had happened to him, that this was not his natural world, that nothing around him was natural. He remembered falling asleep here on this blue plain beside the leaning column; he remembered the ravine he had left behind, but he could not remember what lay there before his awakening on the red plain.

And here was this fly incident. He seemed to recall that in the past he had killed other flies, many flies, that it was his business to kill flies. He could turn his back on it and leave it to kick away the rest of its life without compunction, but that did not explain what a fly was, why he knew it for what it was.

SHRUGGING HIS shoulders, he turned his back on the pillar, his eyes toward the mountain range dimly visible in the distance. The queer rain from the skies was less now, and rarely a boulder came within touching distance of him and he could see it falling toward him long before it reached the point where he had been. A second coulee opened to him and across it lay a second red plain like the first he had left behind. In his mind he called the plains, squares, but like the fly incident, he could not find the source of his knowledge. He was suddenly thirsty and that desire transcended every other thought.

Standing on the edge of the ravine, a shout welled to his lips, for in the bottom of the crevice was a shining river. Water! He fairly ran down the side of the ravine, but at the water's edge he came to an abrupt halt. Certainly he had never seen an odder stream of water. It had no movement, it did not appear to flow, yet it wasn't stagnant; it was clear. It just lay there in the hollow, inert, and wherever it touched the shore, its edges curled up, hollowed out rather, and it became concave. A large boulder lay in the stream a half a dozen feet from where Mike stood, and the water also seemed to repel it; it was, in fact, indented all around the boulder, forming a hollow depression around it!

Strange, strange world!

Puzzled, Mike bent down toward the water, determined to taste it, to learn if it were truly water. But no—as he bent toward it, it moved, came forward to meet him! He drew back, frightened and suddenly remembered the antics of the sphere in the bottom of the first canyon. In his mind he was able to associate the two, but he could not explain them. A sigh escaped him. Was there no succor for him in this hard land where all natural laws seemed topsy turvy? Just how long was he going to be able to exist without drink or food?

And how was he to bridge this unique river? Could he throw enough débris to form a bridge to cross on? Stopping, he picked up a small boulder close at hand. The river received it without a splash, but the thing did not sink immediately. It was a slow process before the water-stuff sucked it below the surface. He shook his head wearily, realizing it would take hours to fill in a causeway at that rate. Instead, he decided to walk on and discover if he could not find a bridge already prepared.

Ten minutes of walking brought him to a place where the river came to an end. Although the canyon floor was no higher, the river simply ended abruptly. He concluded it was a lake instead of a river. The climb up the other side of the ravine was difficult, for here was a heavy mass of sky-débris that impeded his progress, but at last he climbed to the surface of the second red plain. He lost all count of time as he headed for the mountain range. His body appeared to be a number of individuals all crying for attention. There was his thirst, together with hunger and the lame leg all clamoring for service. He stumbled on and on until the red plain suddenly came to an end. He was ready to stop there and lie down to die, but on lifting his head his blurred eyes showed him that this was the last ravine before he should reach the foot of the mountains. He thought he could descry something green a few hundred feet above him, on the side of the mountain. In that bit of green he saw promise of food and maybe of drink.

Only, God! What was that thing hurrying down the ravine toward him! So might a dinosaur have appeared to primitive man. He saw a long yellowish green serpentine body, several times his own length, topped by a massive, hideously ugly head, while set along the length of the body were small upright bunches of bristles at intervals. Although the beast walked along the bottom of the coulee, the bristles showed above the edge of the gulch.

Mike started back, frightened almost out of his wits, as the Thing suddenly turned toward his side of the ravine and started up the side! Its head was on the level with his own, before he could control his shaking knees, but before he could take a step backward, the beast switched from his path and passed the frightened man without a second glance his way. Mike smelt the heavy, earthy odor the beast exuded as it passed him by.

"Lord! It's a caterpillar!" he found himself ejaculating and he was recalling that caterpillars after all were harmless creatures, herbivorous. He scurried down the bank of the depression and up the other side.

On, on he trudged over the rough terrain of the plain, his head sunk between sagging shoulders, only occasionally lifting his head to see how much of the distance toward the mountain he had covered. He glanced back only once, but found he could no longer see the leaning pillar that had been his first goal. Distances were strangely deceptive in this weird land, possibly due to the quality of the light, but he was beyond questioning anything. He could only think of that patch of green far up on the mountain side, which he could make out more plainly now, but he eyed the mountain itself in fear. It seemed a great perpendicular cliff, rising straight up to the heavens, impossible for a man to climb. The plain appeared to end abruptly at the cliff's foot, as if the mountain was not part and parcel of the land, but had been placed there at some later period than placing of the plains, but as he drew nearer and stood at the mountain foot, he realized it was not as unscalable as it had appeared at first. The surface was fibrous and pitted with irregularities, where boulders and soil had taken footing, and he could make out a number of long crevices mounting upward. There were innumerable hand and foot holds in which he could find easy purchase. He wondered at the queer structure of the cliff itself. It was certainly different from any mountain he had ever known; at places it was soft to the touch, giving under hand or foot, breaking under him sometimes and sending flakes of tissue falling behind him.

Thirst and hunger were forgotten as he began to make his way upward, but every few feet he had to take time to rest. Then, after an indeterminable passage of time, he reached the green verdure that had beckoned to him from afar. It was a small plot of moss and lichen clinging to the mountain wall. A small, green bush, covered with red and yellow berries, had taken root in the moss. Food!

He knew it was food, for here were two bright green creatures hardly four feet in length, ugly, but harmless as they proved, feeding on the berries. They scurried away at his approach and immediately he appropriated their dinner. The berries were sweet, juicy and filling. Practically all the berries were gone before he filled his stomach. They gave him a new life, they quenched his thirst. Almost regretfully he deserted them, but the mountain was calling him upward.

HE WAS MORE than three quarters of the way up the mountain, when he glanced backward. Now he saw the regular pattern of the red and blue plains he had left behind with their geometrically straight crevices, crossing and recrossing as far as eye could see. Dimly he could discern great shapes in the greater distances, but he was at a loss to name them; yet, again he felt their familiarity, felt that he had known them in his past. He felt a yearning to be back in the life he could not recall, a yearning for his own kind, for life as he had once known it.

But now he was tired, weary, too weary to go on. He needed sleep more than he needed anything else. He looked about seeking a safe spot where he might stow himself, while renewing life's forces. A shelf a dozen feet or so above his head jutted a few feet over the cliff's edge. It offered haven. Hand over hand he pulled himself toward it head down as he picked out safe holds for hands and feet. Thus he was unaware of the creature emerging from a cave that opened upon the ledge he sought. The creature, however, saw him!

And what a creature. More than six feet high it stood, reddish brown in color, with an abnormally long body separated into three segments—head, thorax and abdomen, the thorax and abdomen being separated by an incredibly narrow waist. It was six-legged and it had a pair of multi-faceted eyes that had the power of seeing in practically every direction, but it depended more upon the finer selectivity of the pair of antennas sticking out from the head just over the eyes that waved constantly in the air. Its mouth was a most savage one, great heavy mandibles that looked as if they might bite the climbing man in two at one stroke. It stood perfectly still in the cave mouth, eyeing the unwarned climbing man. And although not a sound issued from its throat, it was suddenly joined by a fellow creature, who came likewise from the cave and now stood beside the first peering over its shoulder at the oncoming prey.

Poor Mike! It was an unfair fight from the first. Tired and weary, he did not raise his eyes until he had climbed over the abutment. Then it was too late and though he gave a good account of himself, the pair of ants had the advantage as they rushed from two sides at once. The first ant lost one of its antenna horns in the struggle, the second lost one of its middle legs. Then Mike felt the first ant plunge its mandibles into his shoulder and as soon as the sting bit his flesh, all fight departed. He was a prisoner.

Although the first of the two red ants was larger than its fellow, it was the second creature who picked up Mike's sudden limp form and tossed him over its shoulder. Mike knew nothing of the journey through the dark tunnels of the Hill. It was the bump that occurred when his captor dropped him on a hard packed floor that shook him back into consciousness. But consciousness did not bring movement in its train and Mike found his body numb, paralyzed from the bite of the insect that left only his mind awake.

After a while he could make out indefinite shapes in the darkness around him and realized that he lay on some soft decaying stuff that hurt his nostrils with its fetid odors. He felt rather than saw the comings and goings of his captors through the chamber in which he lay. Something dropped across the small of his back and lay there heavily, adding its heavy smell to the others that nauseated him. Lying there, he tried to piece together the events that had brought him here, but the poison the beasts had injected into his blood seemed to dull the edge of his brain.

He was unaware of the fact that now he was "cold storage" in the warehouse the red ants—"preserved" against the time when he should become "provisions" in the ant vernacular (if they had such a thing). Nature has a number of tricks up her sleeve, and, lacking proper refrigerant methods as devised by Man, she nevertheless has provided her pets, the ants, with a means of their own to preserve food against the time when it is needed. This is a mild poison injected into the body of the victims, which paralyzes the nerve centers so that whereas they are still alive, they are incapable of crawling away again, and must simply await the hour of their doom.

The paralysis of his nerves had caused Mike to lose all sense of time and he did not know how long he had lain in his quiescent state. He slept intermittently, awakening every now and then to the ugly odor of the nest and decaying life around him, but at last he believed he could feel a loosening up of his muscles. He could move a finger, then his head. Possibly, the fact that he came of a more highly developed genus than the ordinary victim of the ant was the reason why the paralysis was deserting him. He flexed the muscles of one arm, then of the other and tried to sit up, but the weight lying across his hips held him down. It took a number of squirms to release him, but at least he was free.

Stretching his body, he took several deep breaths, only to be nauseated anew by the thick odors surrounding him. He wondered heavily how he was to get out of this noxious place. Something told him he must be away before the next returning forage came with its burden. Dimly, he made out the faintly illuminated circle that was the doorway from this chamber. Cautiously he crawled toward it, hoping to escape from his prison.

THERE SEEMED to be some sort of faint light filtering down the tunnel that opened to him, so he could see the passage walls losing themselves somewhere ahead. If only he had a weapon of some sort, he thought; but he was unarmed. Moving forward about a hundred feet in the tunnel he heard a noise coming his way. There was a dry scratching, as of feet upon the hard packed floor, and of something being dragged along. A new odor came to his nostrils. It was an ant bringing part of a butterfly wing. Mike backed up slowly away from the approaching sound and so he stumbled and fell heavily. Something hard lay under him, and he felt for it with his hands. It was a fragment of rock that he had tripped over. He wrapped his fingers around it, hefted it and felt better because of it. A darker blot in the darkness of the tunnel told him the on-coming ant was almost abreast of where he crouched against the wall. The thing stopped. There was an almost illusionary gleam of light where its eyes were, and he heard a slithering sound as the ant dropped its burden. Mike heaved his rock where the eye had been. He heard its scrunch against something brittle, then panic seized him. It gave momentum to his feet carrying him swiftly up the tunnel in the direction from which the ant had come. And he was in the midst of a half dozen beasts before he knew it. Two tunnels crossed each other at this juncture, the party was herding a number of aphides (ant-cows) back to their stables, but when the creatures found a new being in their midst, the combined thought was to recapture him. This time Mike used hands and feet to full advantage. A hairy leg snapped under one hand, and it in turn became a bludgeon against his enemies. For several moments he crouched under the abdomen of an ant, and here it proved difficult for the others to reach him, until the ant itself managed to twist its body about so as to make his strategy of no avail. Fighting with flaying arms and feet he managed to reach the nearest wall. The tunnel seemed to overflow with ants, and the herd of cows increased the mêlée, so that the beasts became so jammed they found it impossible to move one way or the other as more and more came piling in from all directions.

It was almost a noiseless battle with only the scraping and grating of dry feet on the soil or of chiton-covered bodies rubbing against each other, and the deep, panting breath of the man fighting for life and freedom.

Mike's greatest care was to keep the mandibles of the beasts from any part of his body, to prevent a second injection of the formic acid into his system, but though mandibles snapped around him, they were poorly aimed, so closely packed were their wielders. Only those ants on the edge of the pack against the wall of the tunnel could reach the man who was creeping as close to the floor as the forest of legs would permit.

As he battled, he crept forward, an inch at a time, leaving a trail of broken legs, twisted antenna and maimed bodies behind him. His clothing hung to him in tatters, his face and hands were scratched and torn, blood flowed from a wound on one temple, getting into his eyes, and there were several long scratches on back and chest. His breath wheezed as it came through his clenched teeth, blood trickled from one distended nostril, and his blows were growing weaker. It was only a question of minutes now before the very weight of numbers would pull him down. He hardly knew what happened when the wall crumbled behind him and he fell headlong into the narrow opening thus revealed. A pair of mandibles snapped harmlessly over his head as he fell, and there was a scraping of rough feet as the beast tried to widen the mouth of the hole into which Mike had fallen.

Hardly aware of what had saved him so providentially, the man sought to rise only to bang his head sharply against the low ceiling of the chamber in which he found himself, bringing kindly oblivion. He awakened to a new sense of motion to find he was being dragged along the low tunnel into which the crumbling wall had catapulted him, for his cave turned out to be a tunnel

THE MAN WHO FOUGHT A FLY   217

running at right angles to the one in which he had fought. Even now the ants were trying with feet and mandibles to widen the tunnel mouth for their bulky bodies, but the passage proved too low and narrow for them. The ant, who had been behind Mike when he fell, even now lay crushed by the numbers in the opening behind it, and the others were trying to remove it piecemeal.

For a moment the darkness here seemed blacker than in the tunnel he had just left behind, but after a few moments of concentration, Mike managed to make out the shapes of the creatures dragging him. They seemed a smaller edition of the ants he had left behind. One had him by the hair, the other had caught its mandibles in the shoulder strap of his overalls. The pain of being dragged by the hair had restored him to consciousness. With a mighty effort he managed to twist his body around so that he could put his hands upon the floor of the tunnel even though the movement caused him frightful pain and he was ready to do battle again. But he was saved that. The first ant dropped its hold upon his hair at his first upheaval, and the other little fellow was frantically trying to tear its mandibles from the shoulder strap. It succeeded just as Mike gained his hands and feet, and he could hear the pair running hurriedly from his proximity.

CAREFULLY MIKE felt the tunnel walls about him, and learned that nowhere was the diameter of the tunnel more than two feet. It meant he would have to crawl on hands and feet its entire length, but considering the inclination of the floor, he gathered that the passage eventually rose to the surface. He guessed that he was safe from his erstwhile six-foot enemies, but it was a back-breaking task to crawl along for what seemed like hours on hands and knees. Twice he came to cross-tunnels, and he grew aware of small creatures scurrying away from his lumbering approach. Only their ant-like appearance gave him clue to what his rescuers were, but he knew too little of ant-life to guess at how the tiny robber-ant constructs its nest to dovetail with that of the large red ant. Like the mice preying on a human household, these tiny foragers made their excursions into the storerooms and granaries of their unwilling hosts, fleeing to their narrow tunnels where the larger ants could not follow when their thieving proclivities were discovered.

As he continued upward, Mike noticed the tunnel growing brighter as light filtered in from some source far ahead. Then he thought he descried a pin-point of gray light, and it gave him new life. The pin-point of light grew steadily larger and at last he reached an opening. A guardsman ant stood in the entrance, but it scurried away at his approach, and he was free to step into the green world of the mountain top. The robber tunnel had led him directly up to the plateau of the mountain-range!

Before him lay a wide land beyond which he could see a mighty forest of every sort of tree and plant imaginable bedecked with flowers and swept by sweet fresh clean breezes. Paradise after Hell!

Cautiously he crawled forth, peering on every side for lurking enemies. His first thought was a weapon. A round dry stick lay close to the tunnel opening and this he quickly appropriated. A small, round stone that fitted to his hand tempted him next, and he dropped it into his pocket for safekeeping. He saw that here again the air was filled with falling rocks, fibrous woody sticks of débris, blocks of solid metal. The forest offered protection from the attack from the skies, but it was a long way off. Still there was no reason to linger here, and he feared that the nest of the red ants might have their exit somewhere near.

The way across the barren-lands, as he named the space lying between him and the forest, was exceedingly difficult. The ground was spongy under foot, and the landscape almost mountainous. He had to pick his way carefully, usually following an arroyo that seemed the remains of a dry watercourse, using every out-jutting promontory as a protection from the raining skies.

He was hungry, thirsty and weak from his past experiences and loss of blood. At times, everything went black before his eyes, he grew dizzy and went reeling and stumbling along, not caring what should happen. Then when he thought he could not take another step, when his tongue felt like flannel-cloth in his mouth, he came upon a bed of moss in which grew a bush covered with red and yellow berries like those he had found on the mountain side. Again he feasted ravenously and thought of lying down for some sleep, but twice when he sought rest he had been attacked by the horrible beasts of this terrible world, and besides there was no cover from the skies, and he had to go on, on to the trees.

Climbing to the top of a tor, or small hill that stood higher than the surrounding country to take his bearings, he was suddenly elated by the sight of a monstrous statue set alone in all this wilderness. It reminded him of the leaning pillar that had interested him back on the plains. There was no path leading to it, but he felt that, if he could reach it, many things would be explained.

The statue represented an ugly, foreign, yellow face with squinty almond-shaped eyes. Its garments were strange, foreign looking, and there was something familiar about it. He tried to remember where he had seen a like statue. A vague glimmering of the truth assaulted his brain, but again he was unable to trace out its meaning; his mind seemed to refuse to function past a certain point. The statue, however, was a sign, a sign that there must be creatures somewhere around who had built it. He climbed to the pedestal and gazed in all directions, and thus he caught a gleam of water in the distance, and a great high bridge crossing it! Now far beyond the water, lay the outpost of the forest.

He started to run toward the lake, but his muscles rebelled, so he was forced to take it at a walk that was hardly more than a crawl, as he was creeping painfully around the obstructions that filled his path, sometimes losing his direction, continually dodging the débris from the skies. Then he came to the lake.

Chagrined, he stared with popping eyes. It wasn't a lake after all, but a hard clear surface that reflected his image. He gazed at himself in disappointment. What a sight he was. An inch long stubble covered his face, his hair was a sweaty mass caked with dried blood, dirt streaked his face and hands where they were not scratched and bruised, his jeans were in tatters, hanging to him by threads. His face was thin, haggard.

Getting to his feet, he stared at the bridge crossing the mirror lake. He sneered. What sort of people were they who built a bridge over a surface of such a type. He disdained to use the bridge and stepped upon the imitation lake instead. It was not so smooth as it appeared a first glance; it was bumpy with irregularities in its surface, bubbles showed just under the skin, and it was difficult to walk upon, like ice. But anything was better than the surrounding country, and he wanted to reach the trees. Sky débris fell upon the mirror as on everything else, adding to his difficulties; pebbles rolled under his feet as he walked.

The mirror-lake did not reach to the edge of the woods, and carefully he began picking his way anew over the rough, uneven ground. There it was that he heard the first call.

"Help, Help. For God's sake, someone, save me. Mike! Mike!"

A voice, a living voice! And wonder of wonders he knew the voice. It was calling him. "Mike, Mike, save me!"

"Mary, I'm coming, I'm coming!" He was surprised to hear his own voice answer.

It came from the middle of the trees ahead. Mary needed *him*. He did not stop to question who Mary was. He knew. Mary was part of him; Mary was his, and she needed him.

He was running now between hillocks, unconsciously dodging the falling fragments from the sky. Everything was forgotten. His weariness was of the past; he forgot his lame foot. He reached the trees, great, thick-stalked trees many times his own girth, that had queer, straight branches out of which grew giant leaves many yards across. Then there were strange blade-like growths rising straight from the ground to unguessed heights. Gargantuan flowers topped the strange trees, and filled him again with a sense of his own puniness, but this was not the time to consider such things.

"Mike, Oh Mike, will you never come?"

"I'm coming, *I'M COMING!*"

HERE THE trees were at well spaced intervals, but as he hurried on toward the voice, he found himself plunging into a wild tangle of rank undergrowth—the like of which he had never seen. Saw-toothed grasses, taller than his own head, brambles, spine-covered vines tore at him, held him back, and every step he took was a fight in itself. He had only made a few feet of progress toward the moaning voice, when a great shadow swept over him and the air was filled with a roaring thunder of sound.

He ducked to the left without looking, into a thicket of brambles that cut him cruelly, but the brambles were better than the death swooping upon him in the shape of a long, snake-shaped body upheld by twin pairs of wide transparent wings, iridescent wings, each yards across. He cowered among the thick, fleshy leaves of the bramble-bush, realizing he was safe from the monstrous flying thing. It seemed ages before the dragonfly gave up hope of an easy meal and departed with an ear-crushing whoosh of its lovely wings.

Mike did not climb from the brambles for several minutes after the fly was gone, then he painfully extracted himself from the thorns, leaving a good part of what remained of his clothing adhering to the vicious spikes. Again he heard the beckoning, terrified voice call. And he renewed his efforts to push through the clinging jungle.

Then he saw her. She was almost in his path, and at first glance he thought she was merely standing there, looking at him, but the second glance showed her a prisoner, a strange shapeless bundle, hanging in a cocoon within a foot or so of the ground, wrapped around with thick heavy cords, as thick as his thumb. There were other ropes, dirty white ropes caught to the leaves and branches of two great trees, and he traced them upward to a spot high above him, where they seemed joined in a hub with innumerable other ropes coming from all directions. On one of the ropes, high above the hub, was the round, black, eight-legged figure of the owner of the web. He knew it for a spider immediately and realized that Mary was the spider's prisoner.

She saw him as soon as he saw her, and tears sprang into her eyes. "Mike, where have you been? Come, get me out of here before that devil from hell comes this way. I . . . I . . ." she began to sob pitifully, uncontrollably.

The man's heart was full at the sight of her. He wanted to take her in his arms, to soothe her fears, but first she must be freed. He came to her side and

THE MAN WHO FOUGHT A FLY 221

grasped one of the ropes to try its strength, only to find it horribly sticky so his hand adhered to it. It took real effort to pull the hand away. If only he had a knife! But in lieu of that, he looked for a sharpened stick. The ropes he found were quite elastic, their real strength lying in their sticky covering.

"He's coming, he's coming. Quick, Mike, he will stab me again!"[1]

He looked to see the spider hurrying down a rope towards them. It had felt the shaking of the rope and was coming to investigate. Mike remembered the stone in his pocket and let it fly at the oncoming arachnid. The missile seemed to stun the creature for a moment, but again it came on. Mike espied a long pole lying in a tangle of brambles. He could use it as a spear to keep the spider away from Mary at least. Mary was moaning, then suddenly she was filling the air with one prolonged shriek after another.

PROFESSOR Duncan Trent ushered his eminent friend and guest, Dr. Yowell Morely, entomologist, into his pleasant laboratory after the long drive from the station. Dr. Morely had hurried from New York to see his friend on receiving a note, requesting his presence there in regard to a new ray Trent had just discovered. They came into the bright room laughing and talking, wholly unprepared for the sight to meet their eyes.

"My T-Ray Lamp!" It was Trent who cried out as he pointed a shaking finger at the spot where his latest invention lay on the floor beside a fallen chair. His friend was forgotten as he rushed to pick up the lamp, examining it to see if it were damaged.

"Someone's been using it," he ejaculated; "the bulb is still warm, though it has burnt out. They were here less than ten minutes ago, for the ray burns out the filament in that time. Oh, the vandals, the . . . oh Mike, MIKE! MIKE!" And calling the name of his man-of-all-work, the professor ran out of the laboratory. Morely could hear his voice resonate throughout the house. Then it came from the garden.

The doctor, left to his own devices, shrugged his shoulders, smiling a little to himself. He bent over and picked up the fallen chair that lay against one of the window flower boxes. He dropped into the chair and sat there, his eyes ranging over the flower-boxes so artfully arranged. Pains had been taken to make the box appear like a Japanese garden with little men and women, pretty bridges and what not set about among the plants. With the aid of a small mirror a lake had been formed. A dragon fly hovered over some blossoms and there was the open door of an ant-hill to be contemplated by the

---
[1] Spiders, like ants, anaesthetize their victims against the time when they need them for food.

entomologist. An ugly little weed caught his eye, and reaching down, he removed it. Then there was something else that drew his wandering attention.

He saw a tiny, newly constructed spider's web stretching across two small ferns, amid a tangle of some more weeds that had been neglected. He could make out the agitation of the web's tiny owner, and, because his vocation was also his hobby, he drew out his magnifying glass to see what troubled the tiny home-maker. He brought it close to the scene, taking place there among the weeds, and a whistling exclamation escaped his lips.

At that moment Professor Trent reentered the room talk-talking to himself. "Can't find that confounded fellow anywhere, or his wife either. Well, of all the blankety-blank . . ." Coming in through the French window he had not noticed where he was going and the air was suddenly blue, as the man of science shook water out of his shoes. He had stepped on the edge of one of the fallen water cans, tipping the remaining water over his feet.

"Dunc, old man, come here. You had better identify these . . ."

Trent recognized the excitement in his friend's voice and the next instant was peering with unbounded wonder at the spectacular drama taking place under the lens of the magnifying glass. He saw an incredibly tiny man battling what to him must have seemed a monstrous spider, while in a cocoon in the spider's web hung an hysterical woman.

"Good Lord! Mike and Mary. The ray! A complete success! But whatever possessed Mike to . . ."

Morely interrupted as he drew forth a pair of pincers from an inner pocket. "No matter why they're there, we've got to rescue them. He'd never kill that spider with that straw!" As he spoke, he picked the spider from the nest with his pincers and crushed it. "A piece of paper, please," he added to Trent as carefully now he drew the threads of the spider silk away from around the woman. A few moments later, he was placing the frightened, almost microscopic woman on the broad expanse of white paper Trent had brought. The man was placed beside the woman and under the magnifying glass, the two saw the tiny man take the woman's fainting form into his arms.

Carefully transferring the paper to a table-top nearby, the doctor looked at Trent with twinkling eyes. "Indubitably, my friend, your new rays are a success, but have you the means of returning these unusual specimens of *homo sapiens* to their original size?"

"That will be simple. You see, I perfected the s-ray, or enlarging ray, before I ever thought about this reducing ray at all. In fact, the t-ray is simply a by-product of the s-ray I have already mentioned to you. But what I can't understand, is what led Mike to do such a thing. He's a steady sort of fellow. Never did a prank like this before in his life."

Morley inclined his head toward the spilled watering cans. "I'd hardly attribute this 'prank,' as you call it to the man. According to the position of the ray-lamp and the chair and that can over there, I should suppose the man was in the act of rescuing his wife when he fell, carrying everything to floor with him. You see . . ."

"By George, you're right. But Mary is supposed never to come in here. She has none of the intelligence of Mike, and I don't like her fussing around in my laboratory."

"Has she a touch of rheumatism or something of the sort?"

"Why, perhaps. I've never inquired," said Trent stiffly, not seeing where this questioning was leading to.

"But haven't you noticed, my friend, that you have mounted the t-ray apparatus in a lamp shade similar to those sold on the market for dispensing the beneficial ultra-violet ray? If I'm not mistaken, there's its mate in the corner!"

"By George, that is a sun-ray lamp over there. I used it on some cultures with which I wanted to prove my experiment to you . . ."

"Um, and your Mary must have gotten them mixed."

"You're right. I see it all now. Here, help me rig up this s-ray paraphernalia. Better put them on the floor, hadn't we?" As the pair discoursed, Trent had been putting together an odd-looking machine with which he intended to "bring back" Mary and Mike.

IT WAS a matter of minutes before the now unconscious man and woman were almost back to their original size. Morely watched them grow with a scientific eye, exclaiming at their rapid return to normalcy, noticing that as they grew larger their bodily growth seemed to slow down correspondingly.

"There," exclaimed Trent, "that seems to be about right. I think that is Mike's normal size. Don't want to make a giant of him," and he turned off the red ray of the apparatus from the pair.

Morely sucked in his breath. "Your man looks like very much of a tramp, Dunc. I think he might shave occasionally. And what a slattern his wife is." The pair still under the coma induced by the ray, could not hear his biting slander.

"What's that? Why, they are a sight, aren't they? But Mike was clean-shaven this morning, and I've never seen Mary with a hair out of place, let alone a soiled apron. By George, of course. Let me see. You remember I said the bulb of the t-ray was still warm when I picked it up. That means that they were under the influence of the ray not ten minutes before we appeared on the scene, but think of it, Yo, those two had endured all sorts of hardships in that two minutes. What seems minutes to us must have been days, if not weeks, to them in their reduced state, for naturally with the reduction of size, came the speeding up of heart-beats and of bodily actions. That accounts for Mike's unshaven appearance. And look, how tired and haggard he looks. I bet he's lost some weight, too."

"Quiet, Mike's coming out of it." That was Morely.

A deep groan came from the man on the floor. He winked his eyes against the light, closing them quickly again as if it made him dizzy. But he opened them directly, and tried to sit up. Trent said not a word as he permitted the man to get his bearings. Now the woman was moaning, making mumbling sounds under her breath.

Morely helped Mike to sit up, feeling his pulse as he did so. The man became aware of those administering to him, tried to get to his feet. "Take your time, Mike, it's all right," put in Trent.

It was some time before the pair were fully cognizant of their surroundings, however. Trent and Morely had gotten Mary to a couch against a far wall, and left her there to recover herself; then they were helping Mike to orientate himself once more. But gradually it was coming back to him. He wanted to speak and, after the men had insisted upon him seating himself in the chair Morely had quitted earlier, he began to talk, first in disjointed sentences, then more rationally, and they heard his story as he relived his experiences of the past ten minutes or so.

In the middle of the telling he suddenly drew in his breath sharply. "The spider—you saved Mary and me from, sir?" That part seemed vague to him.

"We'll tell you about that later," observed Trent. "Tell us all you remember from the beginning while it's still alive in your mind. Do you recall everything?"

"Everything, sir. It's all clear now. Now I understand all I could not comprehend . . . down there . . ."

"You know what happened to you? How it happened?"

"Why yes, sir. It was Mary, begging your pardon for her, sir. She's had a touch of neuritis, though I told her she wasn't to use your sun-ray light for it. Well, I was late in watering the flowers, and I came in to see her sitting under your new-ray lamp, shrinking . . ."

"Yes, what did you do when you saw her under the ray?"

"I knew immediately that she had switched lamps, sir. I dropped my cans and made a dash for her, only I must have tripped and the next thing I knew I was sitting in the middle of a red plain . . ."

"A red plain?" The professor stared at the floor, his face bright. "You mean one of those tiles there?"

THE MAN WHO FOUGHT A FLY 225

"Yes, sir, I was in the middle of one of those red tiles and it looked like a vast plain, all rough and hilly and when I stood up, I could see the blue plains beyond the cracks. Then I saw a great leaning pillar. Good Heavens, sir, that must have been a leg of this very chair in which I'm sitting," and he went on to describe the appearance of the "pillar."

From this point Mike told the whole story, his discovery of the transparent spheres in the first coulee, his fight with the fly, the strange stream of water, the appearance of the caterpillar, *et cetera*. The others heard him through to the end, and now Mike insisted on rising and placing the chair as it was when Morely found it. They located the exact spot where the chair leg had stood, when the body of the dead fly was found unmolested, where it had fallen, and there was still a tiny trickle of water in the "canyon" where he had found his "lake."

"That's one of the things I could not understand, sir, the queer action of the water. I seemed to know it was water, and yet it acted so strangely . . . ." and he explained about the surface skin of the sphere and the "river."

Trent explained to him the law of capillary attraction, together with the law of expansive forces. The body of water, which Mike discovered in the cement between the tiles, lay on an absorbent substance, therefore, the edges had appeared concave, although had it been an non-absorbent substance, it would have appeared just the opposite. The surface tension of the "skin" was due to the molecular forces in liquids, that tend to bring about cohesion of all parts.

"And those spheres that grabbed me up and then exploded?"

"Water droplets, nothing less. You'd just finished mopping the floor, you know, and those droplets had not yet evaporated. When they did evaporate into vapor, the expansion force produced your 'terrific explosion.'"

"Then, there were those falling particles in the air. At first they were troublesome, but beyond the chair-leg, the fall was lessened, until I reached the top of the mount—er flower-box."

"They were dust-motes, Mike. You can appreciate the fact that our air is filled with dust particles. We see them more readily when falling through a beam of sunlight, but we know they are falling continually because of the manner in which they collect on surfaces, our bodies, furniture, *et cetera*. Under the microscope, these dust motes appear to consist of organic, mineral and metallic particles. That you did not find so many beyond your 'pillar,' was because you were under the chair seat, which partially protected you!"

Continuing to trace his pilgrimage across the tiles, Mike found the spot where he had begun to mount the side of the flower-box, which he had taken for a mountain-cliff. By using the magnifying glass, they could find the cracks and crevices that had been his footholds, the bit of lichen that had taken root in the moss where he had dined on microscopic berries. Morely plucked the tiny plant and put it away carefully for later analyses. Next, they found Mike's ledge and the ant-hill entrance. They even saw an ant on duty at the entrance. Neither man spoke when Mike put out his finger and squashed the little beast. It was revenge!

He laughed when he saw the wilderness through which he had wandered. The statue was one of the Japanese statesmen he himself put in place. And the mirror caused him to chuckle. How it had fooled him! And what idiots he had thought the giants were, who had placed a bridge over the imitation lake! And his trees were the small plants he had set out. Had he but cleared away those tiny weeds yesterday, he would not have had such a struggle through the morass to get to Mary. Shreds of the spider web were found scarcely two inches from Mirror Lake. How far it had been to the poor, flea-high man that he had been!

MORLEY WAS most interested in the events in the ant-hill. He told Mike what the tiny creatures were to whom he owed his life. It was Trent, however, who brought up a point in Mike's story that seemed most puzzling. "It seems strange, Mike," he observed, "that you appeared to have no cognizance of the fact that you had been so reduced in size. You speak of your adventures as if you imagined you had been transplanted to some strange land with only the hazard, unreal remembrances of your true life. Surely that crack on your head wasn't enough to . . ."

"Wait, Dunc, I think I could explain that better," put in Morely. "It's this way. 'By rather elaborate algebraic calculations, Cuvier and Eugéne Dubois, the learned physiologist, celebrated for discovering the Pithecanthropus of Java, when he was in the Colonial service there, afterwards Professor in the University of Amsterdam, have established the fact that the specific brain-weight of a species of animal cannot fall below a certain proportion in relation to the weight of the body, if the normal intelligence of the species is to be maintained. Among the monkeys, which are the most intelligent groups of anthropoid mammals, the individual cannot be smaller than an ouistit, which has a brain one twenty-fourth the weight of his total body-weight of ten and one-half ounces. Imagine this monkey one-third the size and you find that he will need a brain one-sixteenth of his body to enjoy the same degree of intelligence. On the other hand, less intelligent animals, like certain insectivora, have a weight of barely one-tenth of an ounce and a brain one-fortieth their weight, which is sufficient for their slight mental

THE MAN WHO FOUGHT A FLY 227

activity. By the same calculation, it is shown that a man, to possess average intelligence, can not weight less than thirty-three and a half pounds.'[2]

"Now in Mike's case, his reduction in size meant a relative loss of brain-activity, thereby giving him just enough intelligence to safeguard him in the new world he found himself in, and of consequence memory and constructive, rational thinking were practically beyond him. He could name things he saw, because they were so thoroughly impressed upon his brain, but when he tried to use his thinking processes, they simply rebelled. He was more animal than man, unable to hold to abstract thought-process long enough to comprehend things clearly. He was motivated to climb the 'mountain' because reason told him there he would find food, water and shelter. He was, however, enough man to hold to his original purpose once it developed in his dulled brain. There was also the sub-conscious desire for his own kind; as he has already told you, this thought reoccurred at intervals. That was the reason he could not visualize Mary or remember her clearly until he actually came into physical contact with her."

"Ah, but Mary remembered Mike. She called *him!*"

"Mary recalled Mike's name because he was the only protector she knew, and she used his name as a child, frightened in the dark or hurt accidentally, voices a call for its mother, its protector."

There was more said before the two scientists realized that Mike was in no condition to sit talking. His cuts and bruises needed immediate attention. Then Mary awoke from a nap she had taken, herself once more, puzzled by her untidy appearance. The men came to her side and when she saw her husband's condition, her face went white. "Then . . . it really happened! I didn't dream about the jungle and—the spider?"

Piecemeal they got her story out of her, how she had awakened in a topsy-turvy world where sticks and boulders larger than her head fell instead of rain. She had not moved from the spot where she first found herself for some time, too frightened to move, she was. Then hunger drove her searching for food. She found some berries to eat, but she was disturbed by a fly. The fly paid her no heed but she went running wildly over a ragged country, dodging through the dust motes, stumbling over every irregularity of the soil, a grain was hill-high to her then. She had come to "Mike's lake," but she climbed the bridge and found a large building (a tiny summerhouse on top of the miniature bridge) which she took for some sort of temple. There was already

---

[2]Quoted from fourth chapter of UNSUSPECTED MARVELS OF THE UNIVERSE TO BE UNFOLDED IF OUR EYES, NOSE AND BRAIN WERE IMPROVED by Professor Rene Thevenin appearing in the *Sunday American Weekly*, December 22, 1929.

an inhabitant there, a green aphid, and she fled, running and tumbling down the bridge. She had gone on to the jungle Mike had found, only she discovered a way where the weeds were not so thick and then she had scrambled into the spider's web. The spider anaesthetized her with its sting and, when she came to, she was wrapped around and around by the heavy cords of spider-silk. She had called for help from the only source she knew, Mike, and when she thought she could not keep up her courage any longer, he came to her. She had shrieked when she saw Dr. Morley's pincers descending upon her from the heavens.

She admitted this had not been the first time she had used the professor's "sun-lamp" for her neuritis. Mike had mentioned the professor's new ray, but he had failed to say it was operated as the sun-ray was operated. She was duly contrite over her offense and began to assure Trent she would never make use of his laboratory again, but the professor waived aside her apologies.

"You've done me a greater favor than you know, Mary. I would never have dared use a human being under the ray. I knew how it would react upon organic matter, and I was content to experiment with mice, *et cetera*. You've done science a great turn today at the expense of your own nerves, and I shall see that you get a sun-ray lamp for your own use."

That was not all that Professor Trent did for Mike and Mary. He put a substantial sum of money in the bank in their name, and sent the pair on what he called a second honeymoon to Niagara. The results of the ten-minute sojourn in microscopia was written up in scientific journals and was consequently pounced upon by a tabloid editor, who played with the story for several weeks to the great enjoyment of the public, so that for a long while after Mike was known as the Man-who-Fought-a-Fly. Mike, however, went on as if nothing had happened, though the affair left its mark upon him. In the first place, he discovered that he was an inch taller than his normal height, and he had what amounted to a fanatical antipathy toward flies, ants and dragon-flies!

Earthlight on the Moon
by Lilith Lorraine

She was one of those pioneering "scientifiction" authors of the 30s ("The Celestial Visitor", "Into the 28th Century"), who, like Stanton A. Coblentz and "The Planet Prince" (J. Harvey Haggard) had a reputation as a poet. We have just room for one by her here.
—FJA

Yes, we shall see them, men against the stars,
A federated planet, proud and free;
When grown aweary of their pygmy wars,
They hurl their legions through eternity.

Yes, we shall see their silver star-ships daring
Wherever worlds are waiting to be won,
Against the battlements of darkness faring,
Against the flaming fortress of the sun.

And when at last their gods of greed they leaven,
And glorify the man of simple worth,
Then we shall see them pluck the stars from heaven,
And set them in the diadem of earth.

Yes, poets at last shall sing and lovers croon
Beneath the emerald earth-light on the moon.

A Peculiar People
by Betsy Curtis

Nee Elizabeth McGee, Betsy, one year younger than I, is a respectable grandma. Because her husband Ed was researching bats at the time her daughter Mary (Molly) was born, the first word he taught her was "bat". In 1951, she says "*F&SF* editor Tony Boucher requested it be published under my own name as he hoped to increase the interest of women in science fiction [good for you, Tony!—PK] by publishing a female author." At this point I interrupt the bio of Betsy to include Boucher's introduction for the story you are about to read.

In our last issue we were expatiating again on one of our editorial obsessions: the unlikelihood of humanoid robots. We have usually, we said, failed to see any functional reason why independent machines should be designed in the all-purpose form of Man when they could be so much more usefully constructed each for its given purpose. But we promised you a coming story which would, perhaps for the first time, fully justify the android; and here it is. You'll certainly remember Betsy Curtis' *Divine Right*; and you'll be as pleased as we are to learn that in the year since we published her first story she has definitely established herself as one of the leading new science fiction writers. We're happy to welcome her back with another example of her distinctive skill at blending ingenious future-fiction ideas with warmly human treatment, seeing broad social patterns in terms of their intimate and moving small-scale impact. And we think you'll want, as we do, to hear more about her strangely human humanoids.

Eventually she had 3 daughters and one son. From 1950 on she entertained me in half a dozen of the sci-fi magazines of the day. "The Protector" in the 1951 *Galaxy* is her favorite among her short stories (most of her work was long) but I prefer this selection. Grandma Betsy has written "quite a number of hymns and anthems for Christ Church choir" and in 1986 "began writing daily letters to Robert Heinlein and then to 16 (now 18) friends after his death in 1988." A remarkable woman!

—FJA

In the momentary privacy of the gentlemen's room, Fedrik Spens loosened the neck cord of his heavy white toga and reached for the threadlike platinum chain of his tiny adjuster key. Pulling back the pale plastissue skin from the almost invisible slit at the center of his chest, he inserted the key in the orifice of the olfactory intensificator and gave it two full turns. Three full turns for the food receptacle grinder. These official banquets could be murder. Removing the key, he retied the cord and approached the mirror, as the ambassador had insisted in last minute instruction to the several robots on the embassy staff.

"Normal respiration, human body temperature—" Fedrik could still hear the stentorian tones of the ambassador—"as there may be dancing after dinner. Check appearance carefully with a mirror. Martian security demands Terran ignorance of your mechanical nature!" (As if all of them hadn't lived like humans all their lives. It might be true, as some of the boys said, that the ambassador was subconsciously prejudiced.)

Coming out of the gentlemen's room, Spens found the ceremonial dinner procession already forming. His searching eyes found the little knot of attachés and he hurried to join his dinner partner, a statuesque blonde swathed in an ice-blue tissue tunic, and offered her his arm with appropriate compliments.

THE GREAT dinner was well under way when Fedrik, a little weary of small talk about Earth politics and fashions, let his gaze wander down and up the long resplendent table and saw the girl. Her head, demurely inclined to listen attentively to the man on her left, showed hair black and smooth as a Martian dove's wing, drawn softly back to a great Spanish knot. He stared at the gently rounded cheek and chin, proud neck and exquisitely modeled shoulders rising from folds of shiny deep green stuff—shoulders, neck, and face of the color and texture of the brown yornith blossom.

Trying to seem casual, he asked the blonde who she was, and received the noncommittal reply that she was probably the wife of one of the undersecretaries, who, she stated flatly before returning to the succulent *ambaut roatel*, were seldom invited to State Department functions.

Attaché Spens turned from his uninformative dinner partner to the imposing lady on his left and wondered at the towering mass of white hair piled on her head before he looked at her eyes and asked his question again.

"Who?" she replied. "The girl in bottle-green sataffa? Sitting this side of your Martian Emissary of Finance? Why she's Gordon Lowrie's daughter—the Minister of Terran Agriculture, you know. He's sitting down there between Alice Farwell and Teresita Morgan." The white tower nodded almost imperceptibly down and across the table to Fedrik's left.

Fedrik looked covertly down the table where she gestured and noticed for the first time Gordon Lowrie's ageless face, the keen dark eyes, the smooth skin so dark a brown that the white, close-cropped hair seemed assumed for dramatic contrast. But not so dramatic as the daughter, Spens thought, as he stole a glance at the other end of the table.

He smoothed the magenta ribbon that crossed the glistening white folds of his chest, the ribbon that marked him as an attaché of the Martian Embassy, and smiled at the grande dame of the white hair-do. "The men in our department were jealous as anything when they found out I was coming to Earth. You earthwomen certainly outdo any of the rumors that reach us on Mars."

The lady inclined her white tower graciously, pleased. "We do have some pretty girls. But I'm sure," she added deprecatingly, "that half the effect is just seeing them in a different setting."

"No, I hate to say it, but our girls are mostly homely, like me. Attractive as anything, but homely." He grinned as she looked appraisingly at his straight red hair, craggy red brows, hawk nose and wide mouth. "You women all have a delicacy of feature that is a great pleasure to see."

White tower's nose was tiny, straight, patrician. Spens looked down at his plate. "And the cooking. Is it always this good? I'm beginning to be sorry that I'm slated for only a year here."

"Randole is the treasure of the State Department," she informed him. "Good cooks are probably just as hard to come by here as on Mars. I hope some day you'll have a chance to eat with us at the Transport Hall. My husband, as you know, is Undersecretary Breton of Transport. We think our Ashil Blake as good as Randole, although Randole's *ambaut* . . ."

Fedrik stopped listening and began scheming.

FINDING HIS quarry in the throng milling about the great silver ballroom was much easier than he had expected. His dinner partner had been claimed by her mustachioed husband as soon as they left the banquet hall; and as Spens circled the ballroom, he caught sight of Gordon Lowrie's white hair just beyond the shoulder of Bartok Borrl, the Martian finance chief. He joined the group casually, remarking deferentially to Borrl that the Terrans certainly put on a mighty splendid party and that "we'll have to work extra hard to give them a taste of Martian hospitality soon, won't we sir?"

Borrl's eye searched the crowd for an instant, and it seemed to Fedrik that he performed the introductions with more than his usual enthusiasm. In fact, Fedrik had hardly begun to explain to Gordon Lowrie that he had wanted to meet him than his superior was excusing himself to the smiling girl and disappearing in the melee.

"My father," Fedrik continued, "was a tweedle and bradge farmer south of Jayfield and I grew up on the farm. He took his agricultural training here on Earth while the irrigation projects in his area were under construction; and I've always had a consuming curiosity about the Earth farms. Dad used to tell me and my brothers stories about cowboys and cattle ranching and miles of tall corn and plains of wheat rippling in the wind till we dreamt of it nights. We even used to have 'roundups' with bands of hoppy little tweedles and then throw them handfuls of bradge and tell 'em to eat their corn and get fat now."

Anna Lowrie's laugh was a gay arpeggio.

"This part of the country is going to be a disappointment to you. Dad," she turned to Gordon, "has a few acres of choice tobacco and a prize dairy, but no prairies and no cowboys. When he's on the warpath, he insists he's part Indian, but he never gets very wild."

"We have garden corn, too, but it's Dwarf Pearl and we wouldn't think of casting it before swine," added Lowrie's rich baritone.

"Well anyhow, maybe you'll give me the address of a cow so I can tell my brothers, Donnel and Rone, that I've really seen one when I get back," Fedrik requested.

"Anna," said Gordon, "I wonder if this poor, ignorant, earnest, young man . . ."

"This seeker for wider experience, Father?"

"Exactly! Isn't it our duty to broaden his knowledge as well as to behave toward the stranger in our midst with diplomatic hospitality?"

"Mr. Spens," Anna's smile was infectious, "Daddy would like to invite you to become personally acquainted with one or several of our cows. Klover Korzybski Kreamline Garth would be charmed to know you, though you may prefer Altamont Daybird Fennerhaven, she being the petite Jersey type."

Gordon Lowrie frowned thoughtfully, "Of course, you'll have to meet them at their hours. Early morning, that is. What time do you have to be at the office?"

Fedrik was suddenly aware of his internal food chopper grinding away at speed three. "Oh, not much before eleven," he said as nonchalantly as he could.

"Then you could come right home with us now and visit with their highnesses at crack of day tomorrow and still have plenty of time to get back to stern realities by eleven." Anna was persuasive.

Fedrik could feel something, his little plans jumping up and down in his head. "Oh but . . ." he gestured toward the great shining floor where couples were turning in the slow ellipses of the xerxia, "I couldn't think of taking you away from here so early. Wouldn't you really like to dance?" He could even sacrifice the pleasure of looking at her for the pleasure of hearing more of her delicate contralto voice.

"Not tonight," she responded at once. "And everybody's used to my leaving early. I'm a government sculptress and my studio opens at eight, not eleven."

"You mean you do busts for halls of fame and bas-reliefs for post-offices and things like that?"

"Well . . . that's close enough. Anyhow, do come. We practically promised Mother to bring home something or someone from the party, didn't we, Dad?"

"Solemn promise, Annie. You're trapped, Mr. Spens. Trapped by two fiendishly exacting women. We'll meet you up at the copter stage as soon as we can find our robes," and Lowrie took his daughter's hand to leave the room as if there were no more to be said.

Fedrik hurried to the gentlemen's room where he had left his downy black fur robe. Fortunately the room was again empty, and he turned off the empty grinder with considerable relief. Then out and up the ramp to the copter stage.

THE THIRTY-MINUTE copter trip seemed like ten to the young Martian as Anna and Gordon drew out the story of his winters at Jayfield Union School and Donnel's phoenix fair and Rone and Betha's trip to deep space.

At the house, Anna and her father left him to find her mother. Fedrik had only a few moments to look about at the deep, walnut-paneled room and notice the many stringed instruments lying about on tables and the top of the great black piano, the books, looking in the glow of many lamps like jewels, ruby, ultramarine, garnet, in their cases set into the paneling, the sedate smile of an old portrait, and the high, many-arched window. Anna entered almost as once, followed by a wheel chair pushed by Gordon Lowrie, which contained, feather-wool afghan across her knees, a lady in a rose sataffa wrap. Gordon eased the chair down the two broad steps to the lower level and Fedrik approached the chair.

"Mother," Lowrie bent over the chair, "this is Fedrik Spens from the Martian Embassy." He straightened. "Fedrik, this is my wife, Janet Lowrie."

Spens looked down into the sweet dark face. "So very glad, Mrs. Lowrie . . ."

"My name is Janet." The fine lines of a smile spread to her thin dark cheeks from the corners of clear brown eyes as she held out her hand. Fedrik took it and found the gentle pressure drawing him down to a chair beside her. "I won't ask you for your first impressions of Earth or what you think of Terran women." Fedrik grinned. "Gordon tells me that your father was a farmer; and presently we should like to hear about the Martian farm, but first let's have some real Brazilian coffee. Gordon?"

"At once, dear." He went back up the steps and out through the wide doorway.

Anna came to the other side of the chair and took her mother's other hand. "Mother's a sculptress, too, Fedrik, not a chronic invalid. She had a little accident at the studio a few weeks ago, but she's almost through with the wheel chair."

"A dangerous profession?" he asked, grave-faced, looking at the perfect modeling of Anna's head and shoulders.

"Oh no," she answered quickly. "A beaker of . . . of . . . solution fell and broke on her foot and an infection set in. By the way," her free hand waved about the room, "do you like music, and do you play a viol by any strange chance?"

"I could probably wring a tune out of this one." He rose and crossed to lift a viola d'aubade from the top of the piano. "I was the star," he bowed to the ladies, "of our grade-school orchestra. Though I'm afraid I haven't played a note since."

"Daddy wrote a lovely xerxia for three viols the other day," Anna was setting up stands and handed Janet a tiny violette whose pale patina shone from use. "Let's surprise him with it."

The sweet sonority of the trio greeted Gordon's return. When the piece was finished, he set the tray before Anna and said, "Bravo, Fed. I like that even if I did write it myself. Do you know any of those rousing Martian frontier songs? *Out Along the Rim*, *In Ellberg Town*, or *Her Six-Ton Boots?*"

"Sure, but it's been so long since I held a viol that I don't think I could sing them and accompany at the same time."

Janet laughed. "Well, drink your coffee now and afterwards Anna can fake the harmony on the piano while you roar out those wonderful words."

Despite the cows and Anna's studio, it was one-thirty when Gordon showed Fedrik his room. An evening to remember for its fullness.

SKILLFULLY AS usual, Fedrik maneuvered the copter he had rented by the month, for the express purpose of bringing Anna home from the studio, down to the stage on the roof of the George Willis public school to pick up Bud and Sukie, Anna's younger brother and sister.

Bud waved from the crowd of children at the top of the ramp and bounded over to the copter yelling, "Hi Fed, hi Annie," at the top of his seven-year-old lungs. Sukie, six, as tall as Bud, followed more demurely and had to be boosted in, clutching a coloring book in one hand and holding a bright splashy painting on newsprint in the other.

"Hi kids. Home James, huh?" greeted Fedrik.

"Give her fifty gees and slam for the ranch!" hooted Bud from the back seat, while Sukie cuddled down on Anna's lap in the front and began a long "D'ya know what . . ." description of her school day to her older sister, who sat smiling and listening carefully.

Fed was glad he did not have to make talk as the copter carried them swiftly toward the Lowries'. This was probably the last trip, though the kids didn't know it. Neither did Anna. Nobody but himself had heard his going-over from the ambassador only an hour before.

"The Lowrie girl, Mr. Spens," the ambassador always came straight to the point with his subordinates in spite of his reputation as an interplanetary diplomat, "you're seeing a great deal of her these days."

"Yes, indeed, sir."

"That's hardly fair, Spens. Not fair to her if she's a tenth as sweet and affectionate as I imagine she is; not fair to us because there's an ever present danger that anyone who knows you too well will find out that we have robots on our staff and draw the obvious conclusion that there are many of your kind on Mars. It's only human nature, you know, to be afraid of machines and what men fear they fight."

"Yes, sir, but . . ."

"Interplanetary suspicion isn't likely to be around by a girl's being jilted by a young man; but I don't want it to go even that far. Lowrie's an important man to us, you know. We're still importing more than a fifth of our food, thanks to the fact that Earth farmers feel they can trust us. He's got to trust us."

"But sir, Miss Lowrie's not in love with me. It's true of course that I"ve been going out there to see her, but I want to be with her family, too. It's a family, sir, and they do things together—sing and talk and plan things like . . . like a garden . . . or a new cow barn . . . it's so . . . well . . . unlonely. It's more like having a new father and mother. I'm sure they don't suspect anything." He hoped wildly that the ambassador couldn't suspect how much he needed Anna's incredibly friendly self.

The ambassador's face softened for a moment, his eyes looked far out the window. "Father and mothers have very sharp eyes, son. You love your Mars family too well to threaten their existence by a war, don't you? If I can't convince you that nobody on earth can hold your secret safely and that you must give up the Lowries, I'll have to ship you back home on the next flight. You'll have to get your music at concerts and your talk at receptions or not at all around here. That's all."

"Yes, sir. But may I take Miss Lowrie home this afternoon? She's expecting me."

"Of course. But make it brief. You can tell them that you've got a new assignment that's going to take a lot of time. Thank them nicely. Remember, we need Lowrie's good will."

FEDRIK LANDED landed the copter gently in the plot by the house. The children dashed off into the interior and he followed Anna slowly into the paneled music room as usual. Anna flipped into her favorite chair and he brought her a frosty green glass of minth from the kulpour on a side-table.

Before he could get the words in order, Sukie popped into the room around the corner of the door, barefooted in a tattered old red plaid dress. "Look at me quick," she giggled and danced and bobbed about, then back to the door. "Just wait a minute now. You don't have to shut your eyes." She popped out.

In a moment she was back, resplendent in a ballet frock of spangled net, a star in her ebony curls, shining silveglas slippers on her twinkling feet. Bud followed her in reluctantly, swathed in a long mauve cape which did not entirely hide mauve knee-breeches. Sukie laughed at him gently, trillingly. "Daddy says I'm his queen of the starlings—and Bud and I are playing Cinderella. Do you like me?"

"I couldn't help myself, your majesty," Fedrik dropped gallantly to one knee and held out his hand as the little girl twirled about him.

Anna ran to the piano and added a few bars of the *Butterfly Étude* to the fun. Bud grinned condescendingly down at the kneeling Fedrik. Sukie stopped her whirling and laughed at Bud.

"You look so silly for a prince with all those teeth out," she said.

Fedrik got awkwardly to his feet. "Why Sukie, you'll look just as silly in a year or so when yours begin to drop," he observed.

"Oh no I shan't. Mine aren't going to drop," she stated saucily.

Anna got up. Her voice seemed cold. "Susan Lowrie, you know better than to say such things. Tell Bud you're sorry you teased him and then run along and play Cinderella in the nursery."

"I'm sorry Bud," Sukie was half penitent. She followed him to the door, then turned back to Fedrik defiantly. "Just the same, I'm never going to look silly and my teeth aren't ever going to drop," and she was gone.

"Kids," Fedrik smiled, returning to the sofa, "always so jealous of their dignity."

Anna went back to her chair, stood behind it grasping the back. "Sukie mustn't learn to enjoy teasing Bud," she said quietly. "Everybody has some dignity. Bud's a right guy, but he can get perfectly miserable when he thinks he's not living up to what that little minx expects of him. Sue's got to learn to be fair."

That word *fair* again. Fed looked about the room and seemed to feel a wrench somewhere in the vicinity of his grinder. He search his synapses for the thing to say and heard his voice, wistful, "You love children, don't you, Anna?"

Her face went blank. Her eyes stared at him. Her voice was empty. "Yes, Fedrik, I suppose I do." She walked around the tapestried chair and continued toward the steps and the door. "Please excuse me." Her voice seemed faint, confused. When she reached the door she was moving rapidly; and Fed imagined that she was running after she turned into the hall.

He had not had a chance to rise before she was gone; and he leaned forward to put his head in his hands, an unconscious imitation of Gerel Spens, who had sat like this when he was baffled.

His fingers had barely met at his temples when Janet Lowrie came through the door and down the steps, steadying herself on her husband's arm. Fedrik pulled himself off the sofa and stood up.

Gordon Lowrie assisted Janet to a tall carved chair and sat down on the arm of it. "Sit down, please, Fedrik."

Fedrik sat down.

"What was the matter with Anna, Fed? She came running out of here as if something were after her." Janet's voice was full of deep concern.

"Really, Janet, I don't know. We were talking about Bud and Sukie and suddenly she just said 'excuse me' and went out."

"Can you remember exactly what you said before she went?" asked Lowrie. "I have a particular reason for wanting to know."

"I . . . I . . . well, I guess I said she loved children, didn't she."

"Oh." Janet's dark face was full of pain and she reached for Gordon's hand where it lay on his knee.

Gordon took hers, clasped it. He looked at Fedrik. "I don't want to sound like the stern medieval father, Fedrik Spens, but I want to know if you are in love with Anna."

Here it was. There was no escape from finding words this time. Fed wondered what the ambassador would have said in his place. He tried to sit straight and matter of fact on the sofa, but it was too soft and he seemed to be wriggling deeper into the cushions.

"I'll tell you, Gordon, but it'll have to be in a sort of round-about way." Gordon Lowrie's white head nodded, but otherwise he sat motionless.

"My father wanted to be an artist—a painter—but Mars needed farmers and his . . . his responsibilities combined with what amounted to orders from the government made him come here for training and then move out and start a family in the thick bradge country. When I used to go around with him he was always . . . exulting over colors and shadings and forms. He even used to bring home twigs of dry bradge and put them in bowls and sketch them; and when the brown and mauve yornith blossomed in the spring we used to have expeditions to the little valleys to bring home a few for a special celebration. Well, Gordon, Anna is lovely like all the things Dad showed me, and I wanted to make a special celebration for her."

Gordon glanced proudly down at Janet, who smiled up, then both turned back to Fed.

"And when I got to know her she was such a friendly encouraging sort of person and . . . and she had you. I don't know how to put it, but there's something about this house full of things you like to use and the children who don't look at you twice except as a welcome audience and ally . . . and . . . well . . . Anna is my friend. I guess that's not exactly love but there it is." He wondered how anybody could make such a lame speech as that.

Gordon's face was still serious, but he seemed somehow relieved. "It's hard, son, but that's how we hoped it was. Not love yet. Because we're going to have to ask you to see very little of us for a while."

("For the love of . . ." thought Fed, "they're going to do the breaking off and it's out of my hands." His relief was followed by the thought of the utter absence of Anna.) "Of course, if you say so, but I don't understand . . ."

"We want you to understand," Gordon said kindly, "and we want you to know because you're like one of the family and we don't want you to feel that we've cast you out. But the story of the reason is what all our government offices call a security risk; and once you know it, we could hardly let you go back to Mars." He looked hopefully at the young Martian.

"I'm afraid you'd better not tell me, Gordon," Fedrik replied regretfully, firmly. "The ambassador told me today that I was slated for a special mission back any day. I only came this afternoon to break the news and say goodbye."

"Would you like to stay, Fed?" Janet asked sympathetically. "Even if it meant not coming here for a while . . . that is, until Anna's married or living somewhere else?"

A soft, low voice broke in. "What about Anna, Mother? Are you planning to get rid of me?" No one had noticed her come so slowly through the door and down the two shallow steps.

Fedrik jumped and turned his head. Janet raised a beckoning hand and Anna went to sit on the other arm of her mother's chair. "What about Anna?"

"Wait a bit, dear," said Janet.

Gordon addressed Fedrik again. "I have papers in my study, Fed; that need only my signature to declare you a security risk for Earth and require that you stay here. And we really need men like you. There are a dozen excellent jobs. You can have your pick. And when you understand about us you'll probably find you want to stay and help anyway."

Fedrik sat motionless for a moment, flooded with a thought of gruesome humor . . . a security risk to both sides would be . . . well . . . too great a risk. He could imagine the interminable delicate argument between the ambassador and the President of Earth as to who was to conduct the disassembly, which side would have the doubtful privilege of short-circuiting his synapses.

Gordon seemed to interpret Fedrik's silence as indecision. "There's Earth security, Fedrik, and Mars security: and then there's human security. I guess that really comes first; and that's why we need to tell you and have you understand."

Fed's memory cells flashed him a sudden picture of his father and of Betha, his father's only human child; and a feeling of affection and pity for their weakness, their kindness and their vast lovely dreams seemed mixed with the very metal of his bones. "Human security. Yes."

"So as one human being to another, I must tell you of your duties as a man as well as your privileges."

(His father had explained duty to him and Donnel and Rone so they'd understand about Betha.)

"You see, Susan and Anna here are—are our daughters, but they're not human like Bud. They're what you Martians would think of as robots. Please don't interrupt me yet," as he saw Fed's mouth open.

"Because of the emigrations to other planets and an inexplicably declining birth rate, we came to depend more and more on intelligent machines in almost all kinds of work. And when began to depend on them we began to be afraid—afraid of their alienness—afraid that they wouldn't always see things our way—afraid that some day we should have to choose between giving them up entirely, destroying them, or having them give us up entirely as poor, weak, selfish things who didn't deserve to clutter up their earth. We found out that we'd have to make friends of them, sons and daughters as well as bridge partners and copter mechanics . . . personalities that had to develop slowly like us, who understood and sympathized with us, no matter how much easier and more interesting and productive physical existence might be for them than for us. They had to love humaness. That's one reason why they look like humans. Both Janet and Anna," he smiled down, "are body sculptors. Janet made Anna almost truly as if she were her real flesh-and-blood offspring.

"You're probably wondering now where the human security comes into the picture, what you and I are bound to do. Well . . . humans are a peculiar people with peculiarly human capabilities. We're bound to be fathers if we can—fathers of human children and mechanical, to grow up together under the most intelligent and loving care we can give them. Robots may be parents of robots here, but it's not the same. That's why you have a great duty that is not to Anna."

Anna added earnestly, "That's why I scolded Sukie, you see, Fed. She mustn't ever make Bud feel inferior—a feeling he might take out on his mechanical children some day. Of course Sukie's teeth won't ever drop out, although she will change her body every year for the next ten or eleven. We have our responsibilities too, in understanding you and in doing well the things we are made so well to do."

Fed traced the pattern in the wine carpet to the wall and back with his eyes as Gordon finished his revelation.

"And last of all comes interplanetary security," Gordon concluded firmly, sadly. "Your young cultures are still expanding and you rely on men still, not machines. As you can all too easily see, Mars would fear and, when her economy is more self-sustaining, she would fight what she would think of as the alien invasion of Earth. She might try to rescue a few Janets, a few Gordons, from what she would consider the domination of unhuman interests; but most Earth humans as well as our dear foster children would be doomed. Because we humans have learned not to be type-gregarious. There are not associations here whose membership is more than about a quarter human. Janet and I have had two earlier families; this makes four children of our bodies, fifteen children given to us by the government. You must stay with us, Fedrik Spens, because you understand from knowing Anna what we can do here and why it must not be destroyed."

Martian stood up to face Earthman. He spoke deliberately but without feeling. "Settling the interplanetary angle will be even harder than you think . . . although I'm glad you told me. I imagine with care we can keep it between a few men at the top and me."

Gordon's dark face took on a shade of gray, not brown. "You don't mean that you're going to tell your ambassador?"

"It may be the best thing to do," was the reply, as Fedrik opened the neck of his conservative dark green toga and exposed the pale skin of his chest. He fumbled for the slit and pulled the edges back to show the adjustor orifices, the silver plate bearing his name and serial number. "I represent more than one security risk."

He retied the neck cord and smiled a little at last. "If I'm not officially disassembled, I might even marry Anna. That is, if she'll have me."

Anna rose and held out her hand, which he grasped as if never to let go.

Gordon began to laugh, convulsively, until he saw that Janet was weeping. He tightened his arm about her shoulders.

"I wouldn't worry about disassembly," he said. "I think your ambassador and I can make plans to write you into the charter? at last without having anything to hide. And do you really want to get married?"

Two human-type mechanical faced looked only at each other.

"Then Annie, you bring me home a parentage application form from the studio tomorrow. I'll qualify you as parents first class."

"Anna," Fedrik asked. "Will you make all our kids look just like you?"

"Personally, I rather fancy craggy red-haired people."

" 'People' . . . Gordon Lowrie murmured to his wife. There were tenderness and wonder and amusement in the quotation marks with which he enclosed the word.

Janet smiled up at him. "Well?" she asked.

The Last Gentleman
by Dorothea Faulkner

This was first published in *IF* magazine under the pen name Rory Magill but nearly 10 lustrums later and probably the last time it will be seen, I prefer for my dear friend "Dottie" to be remembered with her real name. Dorothea Faulkner was one of the oldest active members of the Los Angeles Science Fantasy Society. She took pride in calling herself Dottie the Demon. She had a salty sense of humor and was more "one of the boys" than a member of her own sex. A nonreligious old gal, when I visited her in the hospital for the last time she staggered me by informing me "I've converted to Catholicism." Her explanation, "Might as well improve my chances." Well, Dottie, if you're up there where you belong, put in a good word for this unregenerate secular humanist.

—FJA

The explosion brought Jim Peters upright in bed. He sat there, leaning back on the heels of his hands, blinking stupidly at the wall. His vision cleared and he looked down at Myra, just stirring beside him. Myra opened her eyes.

Jim said, "Did you feel that?"

Myra yawned. "I thought I was dreaming. It was an explosion or something, wasn't it?"

Jim's lips set grimly. After ten years of cold war, there was only one appropriate observation, and he made it. "I guess maybe this is it."

As by common agreement, they got out of bed and pulled on their robes. They went downstairs and out into the warm summer night. Other people had come out of their homes also. Shadowy figures moved and collected in the darkness.

"Sounded right on top of us."

"I was looking out the window. Didn't see no flash."

"Must have been further away than it seemed."

This last was spoken hopefully, and reflected the mood of all the people. Maybe it wasn't the bomb after all.

Oddly, no one had thought to consult a radio. The thought struck them as a group and they broke into single and double units again—hurrying back into the houses. Lights began coming on here and there.

Jim Peters took Myra's hand, unconsciously, as they hurried up the porch steps. "Hugh would know," Jim said. "I kind of wish Hugh was here."

Myra laughed lightly—a calculated laugh, meant to disguise the gravity of this terrible thing. "That's not very patriotic, Jim. If that was the bomb, Hugh will be kept busy making other bombs to send back to them."

"But he'd know. I'll bet he could tell just by the sound of it." Jim smiled quietly in the darkness—proudly. It wasn't everybody who had a genius for a brother. A nuclear scientist didn't happen in every family. Hugh was somebody to be proud of.

They turned on the radio and sat huddled in front of it. The tubes warmed with maddening slowness. Then there came the deliberately impersonal voice of the announcer:

"—on the strength of reports now in, it appears the enemy bungled badly. Instead of crippling the nation, they succeeded only in alerting them. The bombs—at this time there appear to have been 5 of them dropped—formed a straight north-south line across western United States. One detonated close to the Idaho-Utah line. The other 4 were placed at almost equidistant points to the south—the fifth bomb, according to first reports, exploding in a Mexican desert. We have been informed that Calas, Utah, a town of 900 persons, has been completely annihilated. For further reports, keep tuned to this station."

A dance band cut in. Jim got up from his chair. "They certainly did bungle," he said. "Imagine wasting 4 atom bombs like that."

Myra got up also. "Would you like some coffee?"

"That'd be a good idea. I don't feel like going back to bed. I want to listen for more reports."

But there were no more reports. An hour passed. Another and another. Jim spun the dials and got either silence or the cheerful blatherings of some inane disc jockey who prattled on as though nothing had happened.

Finally Jim snapped the set off. "Censorship," he said. "Now we're going to see what it's really like."

In the morning they gathered again in groups—the villagers in this little community of 500, and discussed the shape of things to come, as they visualized them.

"It'll take a little time to get into action," old Sam Bennett said. "Even expecting it, and with how fast things move these days—it'll take time."

"If they invade us—come down from the north—you think the government will let us know they're coming?"

"You can't tell. Censorship is a funny thing. In the last war, we knew more about what was going on in Europe than the people that lived there."

At that moment, old Mrs. Kendal fainted dead away and had to be carried home. Three men carried her and Tom Edwards was one of them. "Kind of heavy, ain't she?" Tom said. "I never thought Mary weighed much more than a hundred."

That night the village shook. In his home, Jim staggered against the wall. Myra fell to the floor. There were two tremors—the second worse than the first. Then things steadied away, and he helped Myra to her feet.

"But there wasn't any noise," Myra whispered. The whisper was loud in the silence.

"That was an earthquake," Jim said. "Nothing to worry about. Might be one of the bomb's after effects."

The quake did no great damage in the village, but it possibly contributed to old Mrs. Kendal's death. She passed on an hour later. "Poor old lady," a neighbor told Myra. "She was just plain weary. That was what she said just before she closed her eyes. 'Hazel' she said, 'I'm just plumb tuckered.' "

The neighbor wiped her face with her apron and turned toward home. "Think I'll lie down for a spell. I'm tuckered myself. Can't take things like I used to."

NOW IT WAS a week after the earthquake—2 weeks after the falling of the bombs, and the town went on living. But is was strange, very strange. Art Cordell voiced the general opinion when he said, "You know, we waited a long time for the thing to happen—we kind of visualized, maybe, how it'd be. But I didn't figure it'd be anything like this."

"Maybe there isn't any war," Jim said. "Washington hasn't said so."

"Censorship."

"But isn't that carrying censorship a little too far? The people ought to be told whether or not they're at war."

But the people didn't seem to care. A deadening lethargy had settled over them. A lethargy they felt and questioned in their own minds, but didn't talk about, much. Talking itself seemed to have become an effort.

This continued weariness—this dragging of one foot after another—was evidently the result of radiation from the bombs. What other place could it come from? The radiation got blamed for just about everything untoward that happened. It caused Jenkins' apples to fall before they were half-ripe. Something about it bent the young wheat to the ground where it mildewed and rotted.

Some even blamed the radiation for the premature birth of Jan Elman's baby, even though such things had happened before even gun powder was invented.

But it certainly was a strange war. Nothing came over the radio at all. Nobody seemed to care, really. Probably because they were just plain too tired. Jim Peters dragged himself to and from work in sort of a daze. Myra got her housework done, but it was a greater effort every day. All she could think of was the times she could drop on the lounge for a rest. She didn't care much whether a war was going on or not.

People had quit waiting for them to come down from the north. They knew that the places where the bombs had fallen were guarded like Ft. Knox. Nobody got in or out.

Jim remembered the flash, the color, the rumors, the excitement of World War 2. The grim resolution of the people to buckle down and win it. Depots jammed. Kids going off to war.

But nobody went to join this war. That was funny. Somehow Jim hadn't thought of that before. None of the kids was being called up. Did they have enough men? Washington didn't say. Washington didn't say anything.

And the people didn't seem to care. That was the strange thing, when you could get your tired mind to focus on it.

The people didn't care. They were too busily occupied with the grim business of putting one foot in front of the other.

Jim got home one evening to find Myra staring dully at a small hand-full of ground meat. "That's a pound," she said.

Jim frowned. "What do you mean? That little bit?"

Myra nodded. "I asked for a pound of hamburger and Art put that much on the scale. In fact not even that much. It said a pound. I saw it. But there was such a little bit that he felt guilty and put some more on."

Jim turned away. "I'm not hungry anyhow," he said.

AT 10 THAT night, after they were in bed, a knock sounded on the door. They had been in bed three hours, because all they could think of as soon as they had eaten was getting into bed and staying there until the last possible minute on the following morning.

But the knock came and Jim went down. He called back upstairs with more life than he'd shown in along time, "Myra—come down. It's Hugh. Hugh's come to see us."

And Myra came down quickly—something she hadn't done for a long time either.

Hugh seemed weary and drawn, but his smile was the same. Hugh hadn't changed a great deal from the gangling kid who never studied mathematics in school but always had the answers. It came natural to him.

During the coffee that Myra made, Hugh said, "Had quite a time getting here. "Trains disrupted. All air lines grounded. But I wanted to see you again before—"

"Then there *is* a war," Jim said. "We've been kind of wondering out here. With the censorship we don't get any news and the people hereabouts have almost forgotten the bombs I guess."

Hugh stared into his coffee cup for a long time. "No—there isn't any war." Hugh grinned wryly. "I don't think anybody in the world has got enough energy left to fight one."

"There *was* one then? One that's over?" Jim felt suddenly like a fool, sitting here on a world that might have gone through a war stretching from pole to pole, and asking if it had happened as though he lived on Mars somewhere—out of touch. But that's the way it was.

"No, there wasn't any war."

"You mean our government shot off those bombs themselves? You know I thought it was funny. Landing out in the desert that way like they did."

"Old Joe would have hit for Chicago or Detroit or New York. It was silly to say bombs dropped on the desert came from an enemy."

"No—the government didn't fire them."

Myra set her cup down. "Jim, stop asking Hugh so many questions. He's tired. He's come along way. The questions can wait."

"Yes—I guess they can. We'll show you where your room is, Hugh."

As she opened the window of the spare bedroom, Myra stood for a moment looking out. "Moon's certainly pretty tonight. So big and yellow. Wish I wasn't too tired to enjoy it."

They went to bed then, in the quiet home under the quiet town. A moon over a quiet country—over a weary, waiting, world.

Jim didn't go to work the next day. He hadn't planned to stay away from work, but he and Myra awoke very late and it was then that he made up his mind. For a long time, they lay in bed, not even the thought of Hugh being around and all the things they wanted to talk about, could bring them out of bed until they felt guilty about not getting up.

HUGH WAS sitting on the front porch watching the still trees in the yard. There was a breeze blowing, but it wasn't enough to move the leaves. Every leaf hung straight down, not stirring, and the grass seemed matted and bent toward the earth.

Myra got breakfast. She dropped the skillet while transferring the eggs to a platter but she got her foot out of the way so no harm was done. After breakfast the men went back outside. Jim moved automatically toward a chair.

Then he stopped and frowned. He straightened deliberately. He turned and looked at his brother. He said, "Hugh. You're a man that knows. What's wrong? What did those bombs do to us? Tell me. I've got to know."

Hugh was silent for a time. Then he said, "Feel up to a walk?"

"Certainly. Why not?"

They went to the edge of town and out into a pasture and stopped finally by a brook where the water flowed sluggishly.

After a while, Hugh said, "I'm not supposed to tell anybody anything, but somehow it doesn't seem decent—keeping the truth from your own brother. And what difference does it make—really?"

"What's happened, Hugh?"

"There weren't any bombs."

"No bombs."

"It happened this way. Long before this Earth was formed, a million light years out in space, a white dwarf died violently."

"You're talking in riddles."

Hugh looked up into the blue sky. "A dwarf star, Jim. So incredibly heavy, it would be hard for you to conceive of its weight. This star blew up—broke into five pieces and the five pieces followed each other through space. This world was formed in the meantime—maybe even this galaxy—we don't know. So the five pieces of heavy star had a rendezvous with a world unborn. The world was born and grew old and then the rendezvous was kept. Right on schedule. On some schedule so huge and ponderous we can't even begin to understand it."

"The 5 bombs."

"They hit the Earth in a line and drove deep into the ground. But that was only the beginning. It all has to do with magnetism—the way they kept right on burrowing toward the center of our earth—causing the earthquakes—causing apples to fall from trees." Hugh turned to glance at Jim. "Did you know you weigh around 600 pounds now?"

"I haven't weighed myself lately."

"We checked and found out what the stuff was. We'd never seen anything like it before. That star was a real heavyweight. All the pieces are drawing together toward the center of the earth. But they'll never get there."

"They won't."

"We're doomed, Jim. Earth is doomed. That's the way of this censorship. We didn't want panics—mass suicide—a world gone mad."

"How's it going to come?"

THE LAST GENTLEMAN

"If allowed to run its course, the world would come to a complete standstill. Nothing would grow. People would move slower and slower until they finally fell in their tracks and could not get up. Eternal night on one side of a dead planet—eternal day on the other."

"But it's not going to happen?"

Hugh's mind went off on another track. "You know, Jim—I've never been a religious man. In fact I've only had one concept of God. I believe that God—above all, is a gentleman."

Jim said nothing and after a moment, Hugh went on. "Do you know what they do when they execute a man by firing squad?"

"What do they do?"

"After the squad fires its volley, the Captain steps up to the fallen man and puts a bullet through his brain. The man is executed for a reason, but the bullet is an act of mercy—the act of a gentleman.

"We are being executed for a reason we can't understand, and the bullet has already been fired, Jim. Another 10 hours—11 hours."

"What bullet?"

"Look up there. See it? The Moon."

Jim looked dully in into the sky. "It's bigger—a way bigger."

"Hurtling in toward us at ever increasing speed. When it hits—"

Jim looked at his brother with complete understanding at last. "When it hits—we won't be here any more."

"That's right. A quick, easy death for the world—from the bullet fired by the Last Gentleman."

Servant Problem
by Thelma D. Hamm

Thel was the wife of sci-fi author E. Everett Evans and a dear dear old gal. She gave me all of Ev's books and manuscripts after his passing. I was best man at her wedding. Her best known story is "Gallie's House" and I'm annoyed I can't lay my hands on a copy of it. To read any single story in this WOMANTHOLOGY in its original publication could cost as much as several hundred dollars. So enjoy for a buck! PS: From the denouement of the story it is evident Asimov's Three Laws of Robotics were not yet common knowledge. They would have negated the O'Henry ending.
—FJA

Henry Smith stared morosely at Servo. Servo stared back at him with his eager, painted smile. (Finish guaranteed permanent.) Sometimes Henry thought he disliked the servile smirk worse than anything else about the Perfect Robot.

"It will," the salesman had said blithely, "anticipate your every wish."

And it did, too. For a while it had been exciting to reach for a cigarette and find one snatched from the box, lighted with a motion too quick for the eye to follow, and deftly inserted between his lips. Or to reach for his slippers and find his shoes gently removed and the slippers on his feet. Or to wonder where he had laid down the latest *National Geographic* and find it in his hand open to the page he had last finished. Or . . . but why go on through the depressing chronicle of perfection?

Carefully indoctrinated to remove anything that might give Henry discomfort, as well as to anticipate his wishes, the robot's delicate mechanisms were attuned to the owner's encephalographic patterns with an almost incredible minuteness that a century ago would have smacked of black magic.

Having a personal devil, Mr. Smith sometimes reflected moodily, would have been preferable; at least one could have dissolved the pentagram and seen the familiar vanish in a puff of sulphur.

There was no such easy solution here; to begin with, Servo had not been Henry Smith's own idea. Unfortunately, Mr. Smith was an essential cog in his country's security. It had not been thought advisable that a human servant should be in such close, familiar contact with the repository of such vast, secret knowledge. Human servants might conceivably be bribed or terrorized. Also it was imperative that the Great Brain should not be distracted by performing small, menial duties himself. Hence, Servo. Mr. Smith thought of the divine imperfections of the dour, tyrannical Alfred whom Servo had replaced, and sighed regretfully.

He began to struggle against his benevolent tyrant. Occasionally by humming a careless strophe and exercising a careful mind-block he would succeed in diving headlong into the bathroom and taking his own bath, while Servo tapped gently at the locked door.

For there never was any violence in Servo's reactions. Everything was done quietly, gently and perfectly. When Henry, after one of these successful sorties, would emerge, Servo would be standing there, smiling his eager smile, waiting for the next wish. Mr. Smith found himself yielding to the state of mind that impels one to kick a cringing dog.

AND THERE WAS no escaping him except at work. Every morning a magnificent, official car arrived at Mr. Smith's door and whirled him to the very entrance of the little cubicle which had come to seem to the harassed little man a haven of refuge from the comfortable apartment with its ubiquitous attending genius.

Here Henry Smith was in his true element. As the beautiful, exact equations unrolled in their unwearied perfection, he hummed happily like a fly in a bottle, a tuneless score to the magnificent libretto unrolling under his pudgy little fingers.

And all too soon the hours unfolded, the day ended, and the car whisked him back to the tender ministrations of Servo. Mr. Smith was ashamed to complain to the powers above him. How could one explain rationally that a perfect robot was driving one mad? He lit a cigarette abstractedly and cursed mildly as the flame crept unnoticed along the sliver of wood and burnt his finger. He regarded it with morose satisfaction; at least he was still permitted to burn himself outside his own room!

Invariably, since the advent of Servo, Mr. Smith's day began inauspiciously.

Breakfast and dinner were brought up on trays by the hotel staff and turned over to the eager care of Servo. A large glass of orange juice started the day (in itself a proof of his status in a country where fresh fruit was only a fond memory), followed by two hot, crisp slices of toast, and a cup—one cup—of black coffee.

This was a major irritation on each succeeding morning. Mr. Smith was very fond of coffee. Before the advent of the perfect servant it was Mr. Smith's custom to drink two large breakfast cups of the steaming brew. Gently he spooned in large helpings of sugar; tenderly he added cream to just the right amount of whiteness. The authorities, however, noticing Henry's growing state of nerves, had insisted on having him examined by an officious doctor, who declared that he was ruining his digestion with the concoction and had stipulated one cup only . . . and that without cream and/or sugar. The hotel kitchen . . . and Servo . . . had been duly appraised of this fact, and Mr. Smith each morning made a wry face as he sipped the bitter, insipid brew.

On this present morning, however, Mr. Smith surveyed his tray and his eyes widened with shock and pleasure. There in its place reposed a large silver jug . . . of cream! Mr. Smith could hardly believe his eyes. Hastily he tipped the jug generously over the waiting cup. With trembling hands he lifted it to his lips, inhaling the rich bouquet. A large plastic hand gently inserted itself between mouth and cup and lifted it out of reach. Mr. Smith went a little mad.

Nearly weeping with rage and frustration, as the precious liquid gurgled down the drain, he threw himself on the monstrosity, kicking and pummeling the servilely smiling, chrome-plated Servo. His frenzy abating, and nothing accomplished but sore toes and barked knuckles, he grabbed for his hat (which Servo neatly placed on his head), for his brief-case (which he found being tucked under his arm) and started for the door, which was being opened for him by Servo, smiling his eager smile.

THE REST OF the day went as badly as the beginning. The morning was taken up by one of the interminable conferences which he despised, and accomplished precisely as little as they always did. His emotional upset of the morning prevented his eating more than a spartan lunch of milk and crackers; and in the afternoon he made a bad error in his calculations which was duly pointed out to him by a carefully unsmiling subordinate.

Wearily that evening, he dragged up the stairs to his door, which was instantly opened by the smiling Servo, his briefcase whisked from under his arm, his hat placed on the hat-tree, his cigarette lit, his slippers placed on his feet and the paper handed to him open at the chess problem.

Angrily he rustled it over to the financial page which he never read. At least he'd have some independence! Having asserted himself for some minutes, he flapped it back noisily and, immersed in Maestro's Daily Problem, allowed Servo to lead him unprotestingly to the table and gently insinuate his chair under him. Deep in the misleading position of the white queen's bishop, he lifted his soup spoon to his mouth and instantly erupted in an outburst of heartfelt profanity.

Having relieved his feelings, he mopped his streaming eyes, took a sip of water, and prepared to return more warily to the attack. It was his favourite potage, an adaptation of bouillabaisse prepared by a chef of heart and discrimination.

It was with a roar of genuine anguish that he saw the placidly smiling Servo, bearing the offending bowl aloft, advancing inexorably toward the disposal unit. Maddened, he galloped frantically after, arriving just as the last of the monumental creation gurgled away forever.

It was too much. Dropping heavily into the nearest chair, he said sonorously: "I wish I were dead!"

And smiling his eager smile, Servo picked up the ice-mallet from the sideboard, and unhesitatingly obliged him.

The Statue
by Mari Wolf

> Forry tells me "Mari was a very attractive young blond who attended some meetings of the Los Angeles Science Fantasy Society and the Pinckard Science Fiction Writers Salon. For awhile she seemed to be the girlfriend of the late Roy Squires, gentleman and fantasy bibliophile extraordinary. She disappeared from the ken of the science fiction world nearly 50 years ago and if she is still alive and sees herself in print here, I would be delighted to hear from her."
>
> In plot, I find "The Statue" a story that Ray Bradbury might have conceived while writing his *Martian Chronicles*.
>
> —PK

"Lewis," Martha said. "I want to go home."

She didn't look at me. I followed her gaze to Earth in the east. It came up over the desert horizon, a clear, bright star at this distance. Right now it was the Morning Star. It wasn't long before dawn.

I looked back at Martha sitting quietly beside me with her shawl drawn tightly about her knees. She had waited to see it also, of course. It had become almost a ritual with us these last few years, staying up night after night to watch the earthrise.

She didn't say anything more. Even the gentle squeak of her rocking chair had fallen silent. Only her hands moved. I could see them trembling where they lay folded in her lap, trembling with emotion and tiredness and old age. I knew what she was thinking. After seventy years there can be no secrets.

We sat on the glassed-in veranda of our Martian home looking up at the Morning Star. To us it wasn't a point of light. It was the continents and oceans of Earth, the mountains and meadow and laughing streams of our childhood. We saw Earth still, though we had lived on Mars for almost 66 years.

"Lewis," Martha whispered softly. "It's very bright tonight, isn't it?"

"Yes," I said.

"It seems so near."

She sighed and drew the shawl higher about her waist.

"Only three months by rocket ship," she said. "We could be back home in three months, Lewis, if we went out on this week's run."

I nodded. For years we'd watched the rocket ships streak upward through the thin Martian atmosphere, and we'd envied the men who so casually traveled from world to world. But it had been a useless envy, something of which we rarely spoke.

Inside our veranda the air was cool and slightly moist. Earth air, perfumed with the scent of Earth roses. Yet we knew it was only illusion. Outside, just beyond the glass, the cold night air of Mars lay thin and alien and smelling of alkali. It seemed to me tonight that I could smell that ever-dry Martian dust, even here. I sighed, fumbling for my pipe.

"Lewis," Martha said, very softly.

"What is it?" I cupped my hands over the match flame.

"Nothing. It's just that I wish—I wish we *could* go home, right away. Home to Earth. I want to see it again, before we die."

"We'll go back," I said. "Next year for sure. We'll have enough money then."

She sighed. "Next year may be too late."

I looked over at her, startled. She'd never talked like that before. I started to protest, but the words died away before I could even speak them. She was right. Next year might indeed be too late.

Her work-coarsened hands were thin, too thin, and they never stopped shaking any more. Her body was a frail shadow of what it had once been. Even her voice was frail now.

She was old. We were both old. There wouldn't be many more Martian summers for us, nor many years of missing Earth.

"Why can't we go back this year, Lewis?"

She smiled at me almost apologetically. She knew the reason as well as I did.

"We can't," I said. "There's not enough money."

"There's enough for our tickets."

I'd explained all that to her before, too. Perhaps she'd forgotten. Lately I often had to explain things more than once.

"You can't buy passage unless you have enough extra for insurance, and traveler's checks, and passport tax. The company has to protect itself. Unless you're financially responsible, they won't take you on the ships."

She shook her head. "Sometimes I wonder if we'll ever have enough."

WE'D SAVED OUR money for years, but it was a pitifully small savings. We weren't rich people who could go down to the spaceport and buy passage

THE STATUE

on the rocket ships, no questions asked, no bond required. We were only farmers, eking our livelihood from the unproductive Martian soil, only two of the countless little people of the solar system. In all our lifetime we'd never been able to save enough to go home to Earth.

"One more year," I said. "If the crop prices stay up . . ."

She smiled, a sad little smile that didn't reach her eyes. "Yes, Lewis," she said. "One more year."

But I couldn't stop thinking of what she'd said earlier, nor stop seeing her thin, tired body. Neither of us was strong any more, but of the two I was far stronger than she.

When we'd left Earth she'd been as eager and graceful as a child. We hadn't been much past childhood then, either of us . . .

"Sometimes I wonder why we ever came here," she said.

"It's been a good life."

She sighed. "I know. But now that it's nearly over, there's nothing to hold us here."

"No," I said. "There's not."

If we had had children it might have different. As it was, we lived surrounded by the children and grandchildren of our friends. Our friends themselves were dead. One by one they had died, all of those who came with us on the first colonizing ship to Mars. All of those who came later, on the second and third ships. Their children were our neighbors now—and they were Martian born. It wasn't the same.

She leaned over and pressed my hand. "We'd better go in, Lewis," she said. "We need our sleep."

Her eyes were raised again to the green star that was Earth. Watching her, I knew that I loved her now as much as when we had been younger together. More, really, for we had added years of shared memories. I wanted so much to give her what she longed for, what we both longed for. But I couldn't think of any way to do it. Not this year.

Once, almost 70 years before, I had smiled at the girl who had just promised to become my wife, and I'd said: "I'll give you the world, darling. All tied up in pink ribbons."

I didn't want to think about that now.

We got up and went into the house and shut the veranda door behind us.

I COULDN'T go to sleep. For hours I lay in bed staring up at the shadowed ceiling, trying to think of some way to raise the money. But there wasn't any way that I could see. It would be at least eight months before enough greenhouse crops were harvested.

What would happen, I wondered, if I went to the spaceport and asked for tickets? If I explained that we couldn't buy insurance, that we couldn't put up the bond guaranteeing we wouldn't become public charges back on Earth . . . But all the time I wondered I knew the answer. Rules were rules. They wouldn't be broken, especially not for two old farmers who had long outlived their usefulness and their time.

Martha sighed in her sleep and turned over. It was light enough now for me to see her face clearly. She was smiling. But a minute ago she had been crying, for the tears were still wet on her cheeks.

Perhaps she was dreaming of Earth again.

Suddenly, watching her, I didn't care if they laughed at me or lectured me on my responsibilities to the government as if I were a senile fool. I was going to the spaceport. I was going to find out if, somehow, we couldn't go back.

I got up and dressed and went out, walking softly so as not to awaken her. But even so she heard me and called out to me.

"Lewis . . ."

I turned at the head of the stairs and looked back into the room.

"Don't get up, Martha," I said. "I'm going into town."

"All right, Lewis."

She relaxed, and a minute later she was asleep again. I tiptoed downstairs and out the front door to where the trike car was parked, and started for the village a mile to the west.

It was desert all the way. Dry, fine red sand that swirled upward in choking clouds, if you stepped off the pavement into it. The narrow road cut straight through it, linking the outlying district farms to the town. The farms themselves were planted in the desert. Small, glassed-in houses and barns, and large greenhouses roofed with even more glass, that sheltered the Earth plants and gave them Earth air to breathe.

WHEN I came to the second farmhouse John Emery hurried out to meet me.

"Morning, Lewis," he said. "Going to town?"

I shut off the motor and nodded. "I want to catch the early shuttle plane to the spaceport," I said. "I'm going to the city to buy some things . . ."

I had to lie about it. I didn't want anyone to know we were even thinking of leaving, at least not until we had our tickets in our hands.

"Oh," Emery said. "That's right. I suppose you'll be buying Martha an anniversary present."

I stared at him blankly. I couldn't think what anniversary he meant.

THE STATUE

"You'll have been here thirty-five years next week," he said. "That's long time, Lewis . . ."

Thirty-five years. It took me a minute to realize what he meant. He was right. That was how long we had been here, in Martian years.

The others, those who had been born here on Mars, always used the Martian seasons. We had too, once. But lately we forgot, and counted in Earth time. It seemed more natural.

"Wait a minute, Lewis," Emery said. "I'll ride into the village with you. There's plenty of time for you to make your plane."

I went up on his veranda and sat down and waited for him to get ready. I leaned back in the swing chair and rocked slowly back and forth, wondering idly how many times I'd sat here.

This was old Tom Emery's house. Or had been, until he died eight years ago. He'd built this swing chair the very first year we'd been on Mars.

Now it was young John's. Young? That showed how old we were getting. John was sixty-three, in Earth years. He'd been born that second winter, the month the parasites got into the greenhouses . . ."

He came back out onto the veranda. "Well, I'm ready, Lewis," he said.

We went down to my trike car and got in.

"You and Martha ought to get out more," he said. "Jenny's been asking me why you don't come to call."

I shrugged. I couldn't tell him we seldom went out because when we did we were always set apart and treated carefully like children. He probably didn't even realize that it was so.

"Oh," I said. "We like it at home."

He smiled. "I suppose you do, after thirty-five years."

I started the motor quickly, and from then on concentrated on my driving. He didn't say anything more.

IT TOOK ONLY a few minutes to get to the village, but even so I was tired. Lately it grew harder and harder to drive, to keep the trike car on the narrow strip of pavement. I was glad when we pulled up in the square and got out.

"I'll walk over to the plane with you," Emery said. "I've got plenty of time."

"All right."

"By the way, Lewis, Jenny and I and some of the neighbors thought we'd drop over on your anniversary."

"That's fine," I said, trying to sound enthusiastic. "Come on over."

"It's a big event," he said. "Deserves a celebration."

The shuttle plane was just landing. I hurried over to the ticket window, with him right beside me.

"I just wanted to be sure you'd be home," he said. "We wouldn't want you to miss your own party."

"Party?" I said. "But John—"

He wouldn't even let me finish protesting.

"Now don't ask questions, Lewis. You wouldn't want to spoil the surprise, would you?"

He chuckled. "Your plane's loading now. You'd better be going. Thanks for the ride, Lewis."

I went across to the plane and got in. I hoped that somehow we wouldn't have to spend that Martian anniversary being congratulated and petted and babied. I didn't think Martha could stand it. But there wasn't any polite way to say no.

IT WASN'T a long trip to the spaceport. In less than an hour the plane dropped down to the air strip that flanked the rocket field but it was like flying from one civilization to another.

The city was big, almost like an Earth city. There was lots of traffic, cars and copters and planes. All the bustle of the spaceways stations.

But although the city looked like Earth, it smelled dry and alkaline as all the rest of Mars.

I found the ticket office easily enough and went in. The young clerk barely glanced up at me. "Yes?" he said.

"I want to inquire about tickets to Earth," I said.

My hands were sweating, and I could feel my heart pounding too fast against my ribs. But my voice sounded casual, just the way I wanted it to sound.

"Tickets?" the clerk said. "How many?"

"Two. How much would they cost? Everything included?"

"Forty-two eighty," he said. His voice was still bored. "I could give them to you for the flight after next. Tourist class, of course . . ."

We didn't have that much. We were at least 300 short.

"Isn't there any way," I said hesitantly, "that I could get them for less? I mean, we wouldn't need insurance, would we?"

He looked up at me for the first time, startled. "You don't mean you want them for your yourself, do you?"

"Why yes, for me and my wife."

He shook his head. "I'm sorry," he said flatly. "But that would be impossible in any case. You're too old."

THE STATUE

He turned away from me and bent over his desk work again.

The words hung in the air. Too old . . . too old . . . I clutched the edge of the desk and steadied myself and forced down the panic I could feel rising.

"Do you mean," I said slowly, "that you wouldn't sell us tickets even if we had the money?"

He glanced up again, obviously annoyed at my persistence. "That's right. No passengers over seventy carried with special visas. Medical precaution."

I just stood there. This couldn't be happening. Not after all our years of working and saving and planning for the future. Not go back. Not even next year. Stay here, because we were old and frail and the ships wouldn't be bothered with us anyway.

Martha . . . How could I tell her? How could I say, "We can't go home, Martha. They won't let us."

I couldn't say that. There had to be some other way.

"Pardon me," I said to the clerk, "but who should I see about getting a visa?"

He swept the stack of papers away with an impatient gesture and frowned up at me.

"Over at the colonial office, I suppose," he said. "But it won't do you any good."

I could read in his eyes what he thought of me. Of me and all the other farmers who lived in the outlying districts and raised crops and seldom came to the city. My clothes were old and provincial and out of style, and so was I, to him.

"I'll try it anyway," I said.

He started to say something, then bit it back and looked away from me again. I was keeping him from his work. I was just a rude old man interfering with the operation of the spaceways.

Slowly I let go of the desk and turned to leave. It was hard to walk. My knees were trembling, and my whole body shook. It was all I could do not to cry. It angered me, the quavering in my voice and the weakness in my legs.

I went out into the hall and looked for the directory that would point the way to the colonial office. It wasn't far off.

I walked out onto the edge of the field and past the Earth rocket, its silver nose pointed up at the sky. I couldn't bear to look at it for longer than a minute.

It was only a few hundred yards to the colonial office, but it seemed like miles.

THIS OFFICE was larger than the other, and much more comfortable. The man seated behind the desk seemed friendlier too.

"May I help you?" he asked.

"Yes," I said slowly. "The man at the ticket office told me to come here. I wanted to see about getting a permit to go back to Earth . . ."

His smile faded. "For yourself?"

"Yes," I said woodenly. "For myself and my wife."

"Well, Mr. . . ."

"Farwell. Lewis Farwell."

"My name's Duane. Please sit down, won't you? . . . How old are you, Mr. Farwell?"

"Eighty-seven," I said. "In Earth years."

He frowned. "The regulations say no space travel for people past seventy, except in certain special cases . . ."

I looked down at my hands. They were shaking badly. I knew he could see them shake, and was judging me as old and weak and unable to stand the trip. He couldn't know why I was trembling.

"Please," I whispered. "It wouldn't matter if it hurt us. It's just that we want to see Earth again. It's been so long . . ."

"How long have you been here, Mr. Farwell?" It was merely politeness. There wasn't any promise in his voice.

"Sixty-five years." I looked up at him. "Isn't there some way—"

"Sixty-five years? But that means you must have come on the first colonizing ship."

"Yes," I said. "We did."

"I can't believe it," he said slowly. "I can't believe I'm actually looking at one of the pioneers." He shook his head. "I didn't even know any of them were still on Mars."

"We're the last ones," I said. "That's the main reason we want to go back. It's awfully hard staying on when your friends are dead."

DUANE GOT UP and crossed the room to the window and looked out over the rocket field.

"But what good would it do to go back, Mr. Farwell?" he asked. "Earth has changed very much in the last sixty-five years."

He was trying to soften the disappointment. But nothing could. If only I could make him realize that.

"I know it's changed," I said. "But it's *home*. Don't you see? We're Earthmen still. I guess that never changes. And now that we're old, we're aliens here."

"We're all aliens here, Mr. Farwell."

"No," I said desperately. "Maybe you are. Maybe a lot of the city people are. But our neighbors were born on Mars. To them Earth is a legend. A place where their ancestors once lived. It's not real to them . . ."

He turned and crossed the room and came back to me. His smile was pitying. "If you went back," he said, "you'd find you were a Martian, too."

I couldn't reach him. He was friendly and pleasant and he was trying to make things easier, and it wasn't any use talking. I bent my head and choked back the sobs I could feel rising in my throat.

"You've lived a full life," Duane said. "You were one of the pioneers. I remember reading about your ship when I was a boy, and wishing I'd been born sooner so that I could have been on it."

Slowly I raised my head and looked at him.

"Please," I said. "I know that. I'm glad we came here. If we had our lives to live over, we'd come again. We'd go through all the hardships of those first few years and enjoy them just as much. We'd be just as thrilled over proving that it's possible to farm a world like this, where it's always freezing and the air is thin and nothing will grow outside the greenhouses. You don't need to tell me what we've done, or what we've gotten out of it. We know. We've had a wonderful life here."

"But you still want to go back?"

"Yes," I said. "We still want to go back. We're tired of living in the past, with our friends dead and nothing to do except remember."

He looked at me for a long moment. Then he said slowly, "You realize, don't you, that if you went back to Earth you'd have to stay there? You couldn't return to Mars . . ."

"I realize that," I said. "That's what we want. We want to die at home. On Earth."

FOR A long, long moment his eyes never left mine. Then, slowly, he sat down at his desk and reached for a pen.

"All right, Mr. Farwell," he said. "I'll give you a visa."

I couldn't believe it. I stared at him, sure that I'd misunderstood.

"Sixty-five years . . ." He shook his head. "I only hope I'm doing the right thing. I hope you won't regret this."

"We won't," I whispered.

Then I remembered that we were still short of money. That was why I had come to the spaceport originally. I was almost afraid to mention it, for fear I'd lose everything.

"Is there—is there some way we could be excused from the insurance?" I said. "So we could go back this year? We're three hundred short."

He smiled. It was a very reassuring smile. "You don't need to worry about the money," he said. "The colonial office can take care of that. After all, we own your generation a great debt, Mr. Farwell. A passport tax and the fare to Earth are little enough to pay for a planet."

I didn't quite understand him, but that didn't matter. The only thing that mattered was that we were going home. Back to Earth. I could see Martha's face when I told her. I could see her tears of happiness . . .

There were tears on my own cheeks, but I wasn't ashamed of them now.

"Mr. Farwell," Duane said. "You go back home. The shuttle ship will be leaving in a few minutes."

"You mean that—" I started.

He nodded. "I'll get your tickets for you. On the first ship I can. Just leave it to me."

"It's too much trouble," I protested.

"No, it's not." He smiled. "Besides, I'd like to bring them out to you. I'd like to see your farm, if I may."

Then I remembered what John Emery had said this morning about our anniversary. It would be a wonderful celebration, now that there was something to celebrate. We could even save our announcement that we were going home until then.

"Mr. Duane," I said. "Next week, on the 10th, we'll have been here 35 Martian years. Maybe you'd like to come out then. I guess our neighbors will be giving us a sort of party."

He laid the pen down and looked at me very intently. "They don't know you're planning to leave yet, do they?"

"No. We'll wait and tell them then."

Duane nodded slowly. "I'll be there," he promised.

MARTHA WAS out on the veranda again, looking down the road toward the village. All afternoon at least one of us had been out there watching for our guests, waiting for our anniversary celebration to begin.

"Do you see anyone yet?" I called

"No," she said. "Not yet . . ."

I looked around the room hoping I'd find something left undone that I could work on, so I wouldn't have to sit and worry about the possibility of Duane's having forgotten us. But everything was ready. The extra chairs were out and the furniture all dusted, and Martha's cakes and cookies arranged on the table.

I couldn't sit still. Not today. I got up out of the chair and joined her on the veranda.

THE STATUE

"I wonder what their surprise is . . ." she said. "Didn't John give you any hint at all?"

"No," I said. "But whatever it is, it can't be half as wonderful as ours."

She reached for my hand. "Lewis," she whispered. "I can hardly believe it, can you?"

"No," I said. "But it's true. We're really going."

I put my arm around her, and she rested her head against me.

"I'm so happy, Lewis."

Her cheeks were full of color once again, and her step had a spring to it that I hadn't seen for years. It was as if the years of waiting were falling away from both of us now.

"I wish they'd come," she said. "I can hardly wait to see their faces when we tell them."

It was getting late in the afternoon. Already the sun was dipping down toward the desert horizon. It was hard to wait. In some ways it was harder to be patient these last few hours than it had been during all those years we'd wanted to go back.

"Look," Martha said suddenly. "There's a car now."

Then I saw the car too, coming quickly toward us. It pulled up in front of the house and stopped and Duane stepped out.

"Well, hello there, Mr. Farwell," he called. "All ready for the trip?"

I nodded. Suddenly, now that he was here, I couldn't say anything at all.

He must have seen how excited we were. By the time he was inside the veranda door he'd reached into his wallet and pulled out a long envelope.

"Here's your schedule," he said. "Your tickets are all made out for next week's flight."

Martha's hands crept into mine. "You've been so kind," she whispered.

WE WENT into the house and smiled at each other while Duane admired the furniture and the farming district in general and our place in particular. We hardly heard what he was saying.

When the doorbell rang we stared at each other. For a minute I couldn't think who it might be. I'd forgotten our guests and their surprise party, even the anniversary itself had slipped my mind.

"Hello in there," John Emery called. "Come on out, you two."

Martha pressed my hand once more. Then she stepped to the door and opened it.

"Happy anniversary!"

We stood frozen. We'd expected only a few visitors, some of our nearest neighbors. But the yard was full of people. They crowded up our walk and in the road and more of them were still piling out of cars. It looked as if everyone in the district was along.

"Come on out," Emery called. "You too, Duane."

The two men smiled at each other knowingly, and for just a moment I had time to wonder why.

Then Martha clutched my arm. "You tell him, Lewis."

"John," I said. "We have a surprise for you too—"

He wouldn't let me finish. He took hold of my arm with one hand and Martha's with the other and drew us outside where everyone could see us.

"You can tell us later, Lewis," he said. "First we have a surprise for you!"

"But wait—"

They crowded in around us, laughing and waving and calling "Happy anniversary." We couldn't resist them. They swept us along with them down the walk and into one of the cars.

I looked around for Duane. He was in the back seat, smiling somewhat nervously. Perhaps he thought that this was normal farm life.

"Lewis," Martha said, "where are they taking us?"

"I don't know . . ."

The cars started, ours leading the way. It was a regular procession back to the village, with everyone laughing and calling to us and telling us how happy we were going to be with our surprise. Every time we tried to ask questions, John Emery interrupted.

"Just wait and see," he kept saying. "Wait and see . . ."

AT THE END of the village square they'd put up a platform. It wasn't very big, nor very well made, but it was strung with yards of bunting and a huge sign that said "Happy Anniversary, Lewis and Martha."

We were pushed toward it, carried along by the swarm of people. There wasn't any way to resist. Martha clung to my arm, pressing against me. She was trembling again.

"What does it mean, Lewis?"

"I wish I knew."

They pushed us right up onto the platform and John Emery followed us up and held out his hand to quiet the crowd. I put my arm around Martha and looked down at them. Hundreds of people. All in their best clothes. Our friend's children and grandchildren, and even great-grandchildren.

"I won't make a speech," John Emery said when they were finally quiet. "You know why we're here today— all of you except Lewis and Martha know. It's an anniversary. A big anniversary. Thirty-five years today since our fathers—and you two—landed here on Mars . . ."

THE STATUE

He paused. He didn't seem to know what to say next. Finally he turned and swept his arm past the platform to where a big canvas-covered object stood on the ground.

"Unveil it," he said.

The crowd grew absolutely quiet. A couple of boys stepped up and pulled the canvas off.

"There's your surprise," John Emery said softly.

It was a statue. A life-size statue carved from the dull red stone of Mars. Two figures, a man and a woman, dressed in farm clothes, standing side by side and looking out across the square toward the open desert.

They were very real, those figures. Real, and somehow familiar.

"Lewis," Martha whispered. "They're—they're us!"

She was right. It was a statue of us. Neither old nor young, but ageless. Two farmers, looking out forever across the endless Martian desert . . .

There was an inscription on the base, but I couldn't quite make it out. Martha could. She read it, slowly, while everyone in the crowd stood silent, listening.

"Lewis and Martha Farwell," she read. "The last of the pioneers—" Her voice broke. "Underneath," she whispered, "it says—the first Martians. And then it lists them—us . . ."

She read the list, all the names of our friends who had come out on that first ship. The names of men and women who had died, one by one, and left their farms to their children—to the same children who now crowded close about the platform and listened to her read, and smiled up at us.

She came to the end of the list and looked out at the crowd. "Thank you," she whispered.

They shouted then. They called out to us and pressed forward and held their babies up to see us.

I LOOKED out past the people, across the flat red desert to the horizon, toward the spot in the east where the Earth would rise, much later. The dry smell of Mars had never been stronger.

The first Martians . . .

They were so real, those carved figures. Lewis and Martha Farwell . . .

"Look at them, Lewis," Martha said softy. "They're cheering us. Us!"

She was smiling. There were tears in her eyes, but her smile was bright and proud and shining. Slowly she turned away from me and straightened, staring out over the heads of the crowd across the desert to the east. She stood with her head thrown back and her mouth smiling, and she was as proudly erect as the statue that was her likeness.

"Martha," I whispered. "How can we tell them goodby?"

Then she turned to face me, and I could see the tears glistening in her eyes. "We can't leave, Lewis. Not after this."

She was right, of course. We couldn't leave. We were symbols. The last of the pioneers. The first Martians. And they had carved their symbol in our image and made us a part of Mars forever.

I glanced down, along the rows of upturned, laughing faces, searching for Duane. He was easy to find. He was the only one who wasn't shouting. His eyes met mine, and I didn't have to say anything. He knew. He climbed up beside me on the platform.

I tried to speak, but I couldn't.

"Tell him, Lewis," Martha whispered. "Tell him we can't go."

Then she was crying. Her smile was gone and her proud look was gone and her hand crept into mine and trembled there. I put my arm around her shoulders, but there was no way I could comfort her.

"Now we'll never go," she sobbed. "We'll never get home . . ."

I don't think I had ever realized, until that moment, just how much it meant to her—getting home. Much more, perhaps, than it had ever meant to me.

The statues were only statues. They were carved from the stone of Mars. And Martha wanted Earth. We both wanted Earth. Home . . .

I looked away from her then, back to Duane. "No," I said. "We're still going. Only—" I broke off, hearing the shouting and the cheers and the children's laughter. "Only, how can we tell *them*."

Duane smiled. "Don't try to, Mr. Farwell," he said softly. "Just wait and see."

He turned, nodded to where John Emery still stood at the edge of the platform. "All right, John."

Emery nodded too, and then he raised his hand. As he did so, the shouting stopped and the people stood suddenly quiet, still looking up at us.

"You all know that this is an anniversary," John Emery said. "And you all know something else that Lewis and Martha thought they'd kept as a surprise—that this is more than an anniversary. It's goodby."

I stared at him. He knew. All of them knew. And then I looked at Duane and saw that he was smiling more than ever.

"They've lived here on Mars for 35 years," John Emery. "And now they're going back to Earth."

Martha's hand tightened on mine. "Look, Lewis," she cried. "Look at them. They're not angry. They're—they're happy for us!"

John Emery turned to face us. "Surprised?" he said.

THE STATUE

I nodded. Martha nodded too. Behind him, the people cheered again.

"I thought you would be," Emery said. Then, "I'm not very good at speeches, but I just wanted you to know how much we've enjoyed being your neighbors. Don't forget us when you get back to Earth."

IT WAS a long, long trip from Mars to Earth. Three months on the ship, 35 million miles. A trip we had dreamed about for so long, without any real hope of ever making it. But now it was over. We were back on Earth. Back where we had started from.

"It's good to be alone, isn't it, Lewis" Martha leaned back in her chair and smiled up at me.

I nodded. It did feel good to be here in the apartment, just the two of us, away from the crowds and the speeches and the official welcomes and the flashbulbs popping.

"I wish they wouldn't make such a fuss over us," she said. "I wish they'd leave us alone."

"You can't blame them," I said, although I couldn't help wishing the same thing. "We're celebrities. What was it that reporter said about us? That we're part of history . . ."

She sighed. She turned away from me and looked out the window again, past the buildings and the lighted traffic ramps and the throngs of people bustling by outside, people who couldn't see in through the one-way glass, people whom we couldn't hear because the room was soundproofed."

"Mars should be up by now," she said.

"It probably is," I looked out again, although I knew that we would see nothing. No stars. No planets. Not even the moon, except as a pale half disc peering through the haze. The lights from the city were too bright. The air held the light and reflected it down again, and the sky was a deep, dark blue with the buildings about us towering into it, outlined blackly against it. And we couldn't see the stars . . .

"Lewis," Martha said slowly. "I never thought it would have changed this much, did you?"

"No." I couldn't tell from her voice whether she liked the changes or not. Lately I couldn't tell much of anything from her voice. And nothing was the same as we had remembered it.

Even the Earth farms were mechanized now. Factory production lines for food, as well as for everything else. It was necessary, of course. We had heard all the reasons, all the theories, all the latest statistics.

"I guess I'll go to bed soon," Martha said. "I'm tired."

"It's the higher gravity." We'd both been tired since we got back to Earth.

We had forgotten, over the years, what Earth gravity was like.

She hesitated. She smiled at me, but her eyes were worried. "Lewis—are you really glad we came back?"

It was the first time she had asked me that. And there was only one answer I could give her. The one she expected.

"Of course, Martha . . ."

She sighed again. She got up out of the chair and turned toward the bedroom door, and then she paused there by the window looking out at the deep blue sky.

"Are you really glad, Lewis?"

Then I knew. Or, at least, I hoped. "Why, Martha? Aren't you?"

For one long moment she stood beside me, looking up at the Mars we couldn't see. And then she turned to face me once again, and I could see the tears.

"Oh, Lewis, I want to go home!"

Full circle. We had both come full circle these last few hectic weeks on Earth.

"So do I, Martha."

"Do you, Lewis?" And then the tiredness came back to her eyes and she looked away again. "But of course we can't."

Slowly I crossed over to the desk and opened the top drawer and took out the folder that Duane had given me, that last day at the spaceport, just before our ship to earth had blasted off. Slowly I unfolded the paper that Duane had told me to keep in case we wanted it.

"Yes, we can, Martha. We can go back."

"What's that, Lewis?" And then she saw what it was. Her face came alive again, and her eyes were shining. "We're going home?" she whispered. "We're really going home?"

I looked down at the Earth-Mars half of the round trip ticket that Duane had given me, and I knew that this time she was right.

This time we'd really be going home.

Heartache
by Helen M. Urban

Read this story before or after "The Statue". And with a kleenex handy. Years ago Helen Urban was the godmother of a Greater Los Angeles sci-fi fanclub known as The Chesley Donovan Society. Ron Cobb is the one member who has risen to prominence (in the scientifilm world: ALIEN and others). Helen wrote her heart out on major sf novels that I could never sell. She did well with short stories ("The Cat and the Canaries" in my Ackermanthology). But for Charles Beaumont I made 78 submissions of his manuscripts before he caught on big in *Playboy* with "Black Country" and "The Crooked Man", the watershed work of the homogenized world of the future when heterosexual lovers were outcasts of the heterophobic society— then one of his favorite stories, "Miss Gentilbelle", became saleable. Same with Marion Zimmer Bradley and "Falcons of Narabedla" ("Aldebaran" spelled backwards, like "The Act of Retipuj"—"Jupiter"—way back in 1931!) I'm convinced if Helen could just get one of her novels published the rest would be in demand. Perhaps Sense of Wonder Press will prove to be the answer. I hope Helen is still alive; Mrs. Urban must be even older than I and I got no reply when I wrote her asking for a xopy (Xerox copy; coined by Kris Neville) of one of her unique stories I once planned to publish in my died-aborning slick magazine *SCI-FI*.

—FJA

You're seldom aware of gravity, but occasionally you see it killing someone, right before your eyes, and then it doesn't matter if that killing is dramatic and swift, or slow and relentless and subtle—the monstrous grasping force of the living planet pulling into itself the essence of its own, the living motes that have sprung up from its fertility—of that you are fully aware. It is almost as if Earth needs to earlier claim those who have defied her jealous dominance over life that she seems to deal so ruthlessly with the Marsborn.

You know how they look; so old and wrinkled in such a very short while after coming home, and though Earth is not really home to them, it seems like it. Emotional home. Racial home.

Earth is too big and the gravity is too heavy for their Mars-bred muscles. People born and reared on Mars develop those capacious lungs, but their large leg and arm muscles never develop like they do on Earth, so they walk in a slightly tipped over, hunched up, drag-footed manner, and you have to feel sorry for them. Particularly when you see one daily, as I do the woman next door.

Crouching in a patch of shade, all hunkered down and gathered in on herself, crooning a sort of rising, falling, monotonous sub-sound of eternal pain, the woman next door seeks in her indrawnness an oblivion to this Earth that is her ancestral home, but not her world. Cut off from the lightness of mars and the cold, clear, red plains where the winds are slender breezes and the dark blue sky is a twinkle of daytime stars that suddenly deepens in tone at the quick nightfall to a mind-reeling tremendousness of far-calling night beauty, the constellations obliterated with the filling in of stars never seen through Earth's heavy atmosphere.

Then you wonder why they ever come home to Earth.

"EARTH IS a glorious place," he urged, whispering his pleading love into her ear with an intensity that matched her own eagerness to link her life with his and journey across those 34,000,000 least-miles to his green planet that was her home, too. Never Martians; always Earth's people, no matter what accident of birth-place had directed her life so far.

Young and lithe and strong; full of vigor and eagerness for adventure—she could not fail to believe that she would not find on Earth the beauties and promises he whispered to her.

"No dome. We'll have a house on a proper street; flowers"—she'd never seen a flower, only pictures—"you'll meet my mother and sister and our kids will go to the school down the street and play cowboys and Indians with the other kids."

Beauty and enchantment as close as a spaceship trip, and the dome manager so disapproving and sad eyed. Saying that it was an illusion and that she could never adjust to Earth, and its monstrous pull and heavy air pressure.

But how could she stand any longer to see him gasping after any small, un-masked exertion? It tore her heart in her breast to see his strong, heavily-muscled body made impotent by the thin unfilling aridness of Martian atmosphere. The constant necessity—return to the dome or don the mask.

Reluctant permission, given with the sentence of doom that youth never accepts: "It will never work."

"It will be different with me; you'll see. I'm young and strong." Bright, eager, slender, willing girl.

HEARTACHE

THE NIGHT air that blew into my open windows was full and deep, and heavy with mid-summer sounds and smells and wet warmth. Thunder rolled deep in the mountains, and the moths and junebugs smashed themselves against the front porch light in the senseless immolation of summer insects everywhere on Earth. We sat on the porch, watching the heat lightning glow up in the distance, listening to the summer thunder storm gather itself for the rain that would come lashing quickly across the valley around midnight to lay a brief cooling hand on our summer-hot foreheads, coolness that fades too quickly into swelter.

We listened to the radio—too hot to sit inside and watch TV—and the old recording of John McCormack wove Irish heartbreak in our minds, filling our throats with a wrenching nostalgia for something that had never been ours, but still belonged to every human being. A sad loveliness of melody so spirit-enchanting that not to identify oneself with his Irish rapture seemed non-human and unthinkable.

The people next door walked down the street, slowly, for her legs were never capable of Earth-striding—she who had strode free swinging across the red sands—he, matching his Earth-born vigour to her slow, painful pace.

They stopped for a moment before our house, caught by the music, the pool of light.

"Come up and sit down," we urged. Neighbourly. Friendly—a night for neighbourliness and friendliness. A soft, warm, easing, relaxing night for us—a smothering, gasping night of hideousness for her, we knew; and the songs of the Irish tenor seemed to echo her sadness and need for home.

Oh, I will take you home, Kathleen,
To where your heart will feel no pain.

He turned to her and spoke so gently, softly, more tenderly than I had ever heard him speak—for he had a brisk gay voice that filled rooms and carried across spaces—and even though her name was Rhoda:

"I will, Kathleen."

Miracle in Three Dimensions

by Catherine L. Moore

Three stories by Queen Catherine?! Well, Mae West said, "You can't overdo a good thing." This story differs radically from "Nyusa" & "Yvala" and virtually qualifies as a "lost" story by CLM. I don't believe it has ever been collected or anthologized; if so, so long ago that it's been unreasonably forgotten.

—FJA

"I've got it, Abe! It's as near to life itself as the movies will ever come. I've done it!" Blair O'Byrne's haunted black eyes were bright with triumph.

Abe Silvers, gaunt and dark and weary-eyed, shifted the cigar to the other side of his mouth and stepped in under the doorway that made sharp division between the glare of California sunlight outside and the lofty shadows of O'Byrne's long, dim studio.

"I hope you're right," he said around the cigar. "I've waited a long time for it. And God knows you've spent more years than you ought, and more money than even you could afford. Why have you done it, Blair? A man with your money, your background, shutting yourself up here in the dark, sweating over shadows?"

"I haven't been shut up from life—I've been shut in with it!" O'Byrne's smile spread across the pallor of his delicate face. "It's life itself I've been groping after all these years, and I've found it, Abe. I've got it!"

"Got the illusion of it, maybe. A little better than Metro-Cosmic has been filming for the last few years. And if it's as good as you say we'll buy it—and so what?"

O'Byrne turned to him fiercely, his dream-haunted eyes suddenly blazing.

"I tell you this *is* life! As near as shadows can come—too near, perhaps."

'Moving pictures'! They'll have to find a new name for what I've got. It isn't pictures—it's breathing, living reality. I've worked over it until nothing else seemed to matter, nothing else seemed real. I've got it, Abe. It's—life."

ABE SILVERS shifted the cigar back across his mouth, and if his eyes were understanding, his voice was only patient. He had heard such words before, from many fiercely sincere inventors. That he had known O'Byrne for many years did not alter his accustomed attitude toward such things.

"All right," he murmured. "Show me. Where's the projection room, Blair?"

"Here." O'Byrne waved a thin, unsteady hand toward the center of the big studio where under a battery of high-hung lights a U-shaped bar of dull silver rose from a low platform to the height of a man's waist. Beyond it against the wall bulked a big rectangular arrangement of chromium and glass, behind whose face bulbs were dimly visible. Silvers snorted.

"There? That thing looks like a radio—that doubled-over pipe? But the screen, man—the seats—the—"

"I'm telling you this is utterly new, Abe. You'll have to clear your mind of all your preconceived ideas of what a moving picture should be. All that is obsolete, from this minute on. The 'moving picture' is as dead as the magic lantern. This is the new thing. These batteries of lights, that 'radio' as you call it, the platform and bar, one for each individual spectator—"

"But what is it? What happens?"

"I can't explain it to you now," said O'Byrne impatiently. "For one thing, you wouldn't believe me until after you've seen it. And it would take weeks to give you enough ground-work to understand the principles. The thing's too complex for anyone to explain in words. I can't even explain the appearance except in metaphors—there's never been anything like it before.

"Roughly, though, it's the projection of the illusion of life on a three-dimensional moving screen composed of fogged light. Other men are just beginning to fumble around with the principles of three-dimensional movies projected on a flat screen, giving the appearance of a stage with depth. That's going at it clumsily. I've approached the problem from a much new angle. My screen itself is three-dimensional—the light that bathes you when the batteries of arcs are on. You're in the midst of it, the action is projected on the light all around you from double films taken from slightly different angles, on the stereoscopic principle. I'll show you later.

"And there is in that bar you're to hold on to, sufficient current to stimulate very selectively the nerves which carry tactile impressions to the brain. You'll feel, as well as hear and see. You'll even smell. On occasion you may actually taste—it's close enough to the sensations of smelling to work out. Only that doesn't figure so much in this case, for you as a spectator will not enter into the action. You'll simply witness it from closer quarters than any audience has ever dreamed of doing before.

"Here, step up on the platform and take hold of the rod there, at the curve. That's it. No, hold tight, and don't be surprised. Remember, nothing like this has ever been done before. Ready?"

Abruptly the great banks of lights blazed into radiance that closed the dazzled Silvers about in soft, pouring brightness. There was a quality of mistiness about it that made even his own hands invisible before him on the bar. It was as if the light poured upon innumerable motes in the air, so refracting from their infinitesimal surfaces that nothing was visible but that shimmer of bright blindness. Silvers gripped the bar and waited.

Through the bright fog a voice as smooth as cream spoke in vast, clear echoes, rolling in from all around him at once, filling the little artificial world of mist wherein he stood lost. Mellowly the deep tones said:

"You are about to enter an enchanted wood outside Athens on a midsummer night, to share in a dream that Shakespeare dreamed over three hundred years ago. Titania, Queen of Faeryland, will be played by Anne Acton. Oberon, the King, is Philip Graves—"

Abe Silvers clutched the bar in amazement as that unctuous voice rolled on. Anne Acton and Philip Graves were under contract to his own Metro-Cosmic, and every one of the other names were stars of the first magnitude. The greatest actors of the day were playing in this incredible fragment of a Midsummer Night's Dream. What it had cost O'Byrne he shuddered to think.

The creamy voice died away. The mist began to clear. Silver's hands closed hard on the bar and he stared in blankest incredulity about the dim blue glades of forest stretching around him, silvery in the light of a high-riding moon. A breeze whispered through the leaves, blowing cool on his face. Save that it did not stir a hair of his head he could have believed it an actual breeze sighing through the moonlit dark.

He looked down. He was himself invisible, disembodied, no longer standing on a bare floor but in the midst of a flowering meadow whose grasses were faintly fragrant at his feet. There was no flicker, no visible light-and-shadow composition of the projection upon this incredible three-dimensional screen that surrounded him. The glade stretched away into actual distances much deeper than the studio's walls could possibly contain; the illusion of deep, starry sky overhead was perfect; the flowers in the grass were so real he thought he could have knelt and gathered them in his hands.

Then, under the trees, the mists parted like a curtain and the Queen of

Faeryland came splendidly into the moonlit glade. Anne Acton had never looked so lovely. The long veil of her silver-pale hair streamed like gossamer behind her, and every curve and shadowy roundness was as real as life itself. Yet there hovered about her a hint of unreality, so that she blended perfectly the illusion of fantasy and reality as she moved over the unbending grass, the bright wings streaming from her shoulders.

THERE WAS a blast of silvery challenge from elfin horns and into the moonlight strode Oberon, his lean features wrathful. The famous deep tones of Philip Graves resounded angrily through the moonlight. Titania answered in silvery defiance.

Then came full, rich human voices ringing through the wood. Phoebe Templeton in Hermia's rustling satin came radiantly into the glade, brushing so close by the watching Silvers that he caught a whiff of her perfume, felt the touch of her satin skirts. And he knew—almost he *knew*—that he could put out a hand and stop her, so warmly real was she at that close range. Her lovely throaty voice called to Lysander behind her.

And somehow the forest was slipping away past Abe Silver's face—somehow he had the illusion of walking as if in a dream down an enchanted forest aisle, the dim air quivering with starlight, and Helena came running and weeping through the trees, stumbling, sobbing the name of Demetrius.

She passed. Silvers started involuntarily as from a swaying branch above him pealed the wild, half-human laughter of Puck, delicate as the chatter of a squirrel, and down through the air over his very shoulders, the breeze of his passing fanning Silvers' face, the lithe little goblin sprang.

The scene clouded over as if a mist had been drawn across the moon. Silvers blinked involuntarily, and when he looked again Titania lay exquisitely asleep on the dew-spangled bank where the wild thyme grew.

Then through the magic-haunted wood suddenly shrilled a bell. Insistently, metallically it rang. Silvers glanced about the glades of the forest, trying to locate among the dew-shimmering leaves the source of that irritating noise. And suddenly the Athenian woods melted like smoke about him. Incredulously he stared around a big bare studio. It was like waking in bewilderment from a dream so vivid that reality itself paled beside its memory.

"The studio wants you on the telephone, Abe," said O'Byrne's voice. "Here, wake up! Didn't you hear the bell?"

SILVERS SHOOK himself, laughed sheepishly.

"I'm still in Athens," he admitted, blinking. "That's the damnedest thing I ever—studio, did you say? Where's the phone?"

Thinly over the wire came a worried voice.

"Hate to bother you, chief, but I think you ought to know. Anne Acton's been mumbling around in a sort of daze for half an hour. The doctor can't do a thing with her. And Philip Graves passed out on set and is just kind of whispering to himself—poetry, it sounds like."

Silvers blinked. "D-don't let the papers get it. I'll be right over."

He slammed the telephone back on its cradle and turned blankly to O'Byrne.

"Something's gone wrong with a couple of our actors you stole," he said. "I've got to get back right away. But listen, Blair—you've got something! How long will it take you to have some more of these bar and platform arrangements rigged up? Say a dozen for a starter. I'd like to have our board see it as soon as possible. This is going to be the most tremendous thing that ever happened in motion pictures. When can you have things ready to show the board?"

"I—I don't know, Abe. Somehow—I'm a little afraid of it."

"Afraid? Good God, man, what do you mean?"

"I don't know, exactly—but did you have a feeling, as you watched the action, that somehow it came—too near—to life?"

"Blair—I'm afraid you've been working too hard on this. Let me handle it from now on, will you? And stop thinking about it. I've got to get back to the studio now and see what's happened to my actors—attack of temperament, probably—but I'll see you tonight about quantity production. Until then, you won't let anyone else in on this, will you?"

"You know I won't, Abe. It's yours if you want it."

All the way back to the studio Silvers' mind was spinning with the magnitude of what lay before him. He had dared to let the inventor know how enormously impressed he was, how anxious to have the new process, because he knew O'Byrne so well. The man was wealthy in his own right, indifferent to fame, to everything, but the deep need to create which had driven him so hard for so many years toward the completion of his miracle. Miracle in three dimensions! It seemed like a dream, what he had just seen, but behind it lay the prospect for a fortune vaster than any movie magnate had ever dared to hope for. To control this was to control the whole world. Silvers clenched his cigar tighter and dreamed magnificent dreams.

Anne Acton lay on a low couch in her lavish little dressing bungalow, staring up with conscious pathos into the doctor's face as Silvers came into the room. Somehow, illogically, it was a shock to him to see her here when he had so short a time before left that perfect illusion of herself in the enchanted wood outside Athens, asleep on the bank of wild thyme.

"How are you, Anne?" he demanded anxiously, for she represented a fabulous sum to the company and an illness now, in the midst of her latest picture, would be ruinous. "Is she all right, Doc? When did she come out of it?"

"While they were phoning you, Abe," said Acton herself in a faint, pathetic voice, moving her head uneasily so that the great slipping rope of silver-pale hair moved across the brocade. "It—it was all so queer. Suddenly I felt too tired to move, as if all the strength had drained right out of me. And I must have fainted, but I wasn't really out. Kept having sort of dreams—I don't remember now—woods, somewhere, and music. And suddenly it all ended and I opened my eyes here. I'm all right now, only I feel as weak as a kitten. Look." She held up an exquisite hand to show it quivering.

"What is it, Doc?" demanded Silvers anxiously.

"Um-m-m—overwork, perhaps, general exhaustion—it's impossible to say definitely without further examination."

"Will she be okay now?"

"I see no reason why, with rest and care, she shouldn't be."

"I'll send for your car, Anne," said Silvers authoritatively. "You're going home to bed. I'll see you later."

Philip Graves, in the braid-be-decked finery of a movie caballero, was sitting up on his couch when Silvers pushed through the little knot of attendants that surrounded him.

"Feeling better, Phil?" he demanded. "What was it?"

"Nothing—nothing," said the actor impatiently. "I'm okay now. Just passed out for a few minutes. I'll be all right."

Abe Silvers lost no time in calling a meeting of the board. The 12 members of Metro-Cosmic stood about in twos and threes, murmuring incredulously in the shadows of the O'Byrne studio on the night when the first dozen bar-platforms were erected. Silvers had not dared to describe fully this modern miracle.

"It's like nothing you ever saw before," he warned them as rather sheepishly they allowed themselves to be herded forward to the platforms. When they were all at their stations and Silvers signaled O'Byrne to begin, he glanced once around the little company before the lights blazed on. Doubtfully they returned his stare with a murmur or two of protest rising.

"Feel so damn' silly," an official said, "standing here. Mean to say there isn't any screen? What are we supposed to look at?"

AND THEN like a wall of brilliant blindness the foggy light closed down upon them and every man was cut off from his fellows so that he stood alone and disembodied in the heart of that soft, misty blaze. Startled exclamations sounded through the mist, murmurs that died away as Silvers heard for the second time the creamy smoothness of the announcer's voice rolling through the dimming brightness.

"You are now about to enter an enchanted wood outside Athens on a midsummer night, to share in a dream that Shakespeare dreamed . . ."

Somehow, as the play went on, Abe Silvers began to wonder a little uneasily at the violence of the quarrel between Titania and Oberon that flamed almost tangibly through the clear dim air. Had they fought before so fiercely? Had they—

A gibber of wild inhuman laughter, the long leap of Puck over his shoulder, broke the queer thought half-formed, just as a bell began to shrill through the forest. He knew a moment of unreality. He remembered that in the previous performance the bell had not rung until Titania lay down to sleep on the bank where the wild thyme grew. But with shocking completeness the forest vanished. Silvers stared blankly around the studio's reaches that had so suddenly replaced the glades of Faeryland, blinking at the circle of dazed men in amazement.

"Telephone for you, Abe," O'Byrne's voice called through the fading mists of the dream that had so strongly gripped him. He grinned sheepishly and stepped down from the platform.

"Listen, chief," babbled a distressed voice over the wire, shrill above the rising babble of delight behind Silvers, "Acton's out like a light at the Grove!"

"Is she plastered?"

"I don't think so—but try to tell the papers that! She—wait—oh, she's just coming out of it. What'll we do?"

"Send her home," sighed Silvers. "It'll get into the papers right away. What a life!"

HE TURNED back to O'Byrne with a shrug. "Acton's passed out again," he murmured unhappily. "I wonder if she—well, if she folds now in the middle of NEVER TOMORROW, we'll lose our shirts on it. I'm going to get a doctor to—"

"Abe," said O'Byrne in a voice so quiet that the other man turned to him in surprise. "Abe, do you realize that every time we run this picture Anne Acton faints? I wonder if the other actors feel the same reaction?"

"Why—what do you mean? Why should they? Blair, are you going crazy?"

Silvers' voice was stoutly confident, but despite himself an uneasy little flicker woke in his mind. Philip Graves, who played Oberon, had been dazed and out of his head too that other time. And—yes, hadn't he noticed an item in a gossip column saying that Phoebe Templeton had collapsed at a tea in

New York. Was it the same day? Rather terrifyingly, he thought it was. But of course all this was the most flagrant nonsense. His job now was to keep Acton out of the papers. She had not endeared herself to reporters, and he knew they would make the story sound as bad as possible. They—the phone rang again.

"A wire from Philip Graves' man has just come in, Abe," his wife's voice told him worriedly. "Philip's been taken terribly sick on shipboard. His man says it will be in all the papers tomorrow, and he wants your advice."

Silvers ran a hand distractedly through his hair. "Thanks," he said a little blankly. "I'll take care of it. Be home later."

He turned to the men still grouped around the bar-platforms in their babble of amazed delight. They had not heard his low-voiced conversation at the desk.

We've got this fellow under contract, haven't we?" said someone anxiously at his elbow. "Ought to get going on production right away. This is the most tremendous thing that ever happened."

"Yes—he'll let us have it," Silvers told him abstractedly. "Blair, how's the production on the first hundred bar-platforms coming? We've got to give a larger showing right away."

"A hundred and fifty will be ready in about a week," O'Byrne admitted reluctantly. "But Abe—Abe, do you think we ought to do it?"

Silvers pulled him aside. "Look, Blair," he said gently, "you mustn't let your imagination run away with you. What possible connection can there be between the showing of this picture and the fact that a few overworked, nervous people have fainting spells? I'll admit it's a coincidence but we've got to be sensible. We can't let the biggest thing that ever happened in pictures slip through our fingers just because some dizzy actress passes out once or twice."

O'Byrne shrugged a little. "I wonder," he murmured, as if thinking aloud, "how long people have been trying to create life? Something's always prevented it—no one's been allowed to succeed. This thing of mine isn't life, but it's too near it to leave me at peace with myself. I think there's a penalty for usurping the powers of godhead—for coming too close to success. I'm afraid, Abe."

"Blair, will you do me a favor?" demanded Silvers. "Will you go to bed and forget all about this until morning? I'll see you tomorrow. Right now I'm up to my neck in trouble."

O'Byrne smiled ghostily. "All right," he said . . ..

TEMPLETON-FREDERICKS ELOPEMENT!

That was the headline the news-boys were yelling when Silvers stepped out of his car the next day. He looked twice at the headline to be sure, for the romance of Phoebe Templeton, not with Bill Fredericks but with Manfield Drake, had kept screen magazines in ecstasies for the past six months. The wedding was to have been this week, but—he bought a paper hastily, a wild thought flashing through his mind. Templeton and Fredericks had played the *lovers* in O'Byrne's photoplay!

"Bill and I have known one another for about six months," Phoebe Templeton was quoted as saying, "but we never realized until last night how much we meant to each other. It happened rather miraculously. I was on my way west and Bill was here in Hollywood. And suddenly in Denver it came over me that I simply must talk to him. I phoned long distance and—well, it's all pretty hazy to look back on, but I chartered a plane and met him in Yuma, and we were married this morning. Of course I feel badly about Manfield, but really, this was too big to fight against. We've known since ten o'clock last night that we were meant for each other."

Silvers tucked the paper under his arm and bit down hard on his cigar. It was at ten last night that they had watched Hermia and Lysander, in the actual, breathing presences of Templeton and Fredericks, murmuring passionate love under a high-floating moon. For a moment a fantastic wonder crossed his mind. "I must be going nuts," he murmured to himself.

A week later an audience of a hundred and fifty people gathered for the real preview of O'Byrne's "Midsummer Night's Dream." The bar-platforms had been set up in the big studio that had seen the first running of the miraculous illusion. It was crowded now with murmurous and skeptical people—officers and directors of Metro-Cosmic, a sprinkling of wives. Silvers conquered an inexplicable uneasiness as he sought O'Byrne in a corner near the controls. Blair was sitting on a heavy stool before the machine, and the face he turned to his friend was full of a queer, strained tension. He said, his voice a thread of sound:

"Abe—I've had the maddest notion that every time I show this the figures come back realer than before into the scenes they play. Maybe they don't always hold to the action we photographed—maybe the plot carried on beyond what Shakespeare wrote—more violently than—"

SILVERS' FINGERS gripped the other man's shoulders hard. Sharply he shook him, an absurd uneasiness darkening his memory of that impression of fiercer violence in the quarrel between Oberon and Titania the last time he saw the play, even as he said firmly:

"Snap out of it, Blair! You've been working too hard. Maybe someone else could run the picture tonight—you need rest."

O'Byrne looked up at him apathetically, his alarm gone suddenly flat.

"No, I'll do it. If you're really determined to run the whole thing, maybe I'd better. Maybe I can control them better than an assistant could. After all, I created them . . ."

Silvers looked down at him for a moment in frowning silence. Then he shrugged and turned toward the last empty bar-platform where the audience waited the beginning of the show. O'Byrne was dangerously overworked, he told himself. After this was over he must go to a sanatorium for a long rest. His mind was cracking . . .

Misty radiance closed down about him, veiling the 150 from his vision. There was a moment of murmurous wonder, punctuated by small, half-frightened screams from a few of the women as each spectator was shut off into a little world of silence and solitude.

Into the silvery mist that familiar rich voice rolled smoothly. For the third time Silvers saw the broad gray glades of Faeryland, hedged with immemorial forest, opening magically up about him. For the third time Titania trailed her streaming wings into the moonlight. Oberon strode with a jingle of mail from among the trees, and they met in fury halfway down the glade, their feet pressing the bending grass with elfin lightness. But there was no lightness in their anger. That ancient quarrel flared up in violence between them, and the breezes shivered with their wrath.

Again Hermia and Lysander came half laughing, half fearful into the woods. Again Helena sobbed Demetrius' name among the unanswering trees. Puck flitted in goblin glee about his business of enchantment and Titania lay down to sleep on the spangled grass among the wild thyme.

THIS TIME no telephone bell broke into the magic of the dream.

And again these were living people who moved so tangibly before the audience, the wind of their passing brushing them, the sound of their breathing in their ears when they stood near, going about their magic-haunted ways as obliviously as if the spectators were the phantoms, not they. Their loves and hates and heartbreak were vividly real under that incredibly real moon.

Once or twice Silvers thought vaguely that here and there in the action things happened not exactly as he remembered them. Had Titania actually slapped Oberon's dark, angry face before she swept out of the glade? Had Hermia and Lysander kissed quite so lingeringly under that deep-shadowed oak? But as the play went on Silvers lost all thought of times that had gone before, and sank fathoms deep in the reality of the scene before him.

Puck lured the spell-bewildered lovers into the vastness of the forest. They were stumbling through the fog, quarreling, blinded by mist and magic and their own troubled hearts. Swords flashed in the moonlight. Lysander and Demetrius were fighting among the veiled trees. Puck laughed, shrill and high and inhuman, and swept his brown arm down. And from Lysander came a choked gasp, the clatter of a fallen sword.

Demetrius bent fiercely above him. Silvers watched the bright blood bubbling from his side, saw the blade drip darkly, smelled the acrid sharpness of that spreading stain. The illusion was marvelous. Lysander's death was a miracle of artistry from the first choked gasp of pain to the last bubbling of blood in his throat, the last twist of handsome silk-sheathed limbs. Lysander's death—

Something troubled Silvers' memory, but before he could capture it a woman's voice cried hysterically somewhere in the misty forest, "He's dead—he's dead!" and suddenly, blankly, the forest was gone from about them and he was staring into dazed, half-dreaming faces where an instant before Faeryland had stretched depth upon depth of moonlit dimness, where Lysander had lain dying on the moss. Somewhere in the crowd a woman was sobbing hysterically.

"He's dead, I tell you! Lysander's dead, and he doesn't really die in the play! Someone's killed him! That was real blood—I smelled it! Oh, get me out of this awful place!"

Silvers brushed the fog of dreamland from his eyes and was halfway across the floor to the projection machine before the scream had ended, for he remembered now that tug of memory as Lysander fell. Shakespeare's play was romance, not tragedy. Lysander should not have died.

O'Byrne clung to his high stool, his fingers white-knuckled as he stared into Silvers' eyes.

"You see?" he said in a strained monotone. "You see what mass hypnotism will do? They couldn't help it—poor things—they must be half alive—wandering the fog . . ."

"Blair!" Silvers' voice rang sharply. "Blair, snap out of it! What are you raving about? Are you mad?"

The staring eyes turned to his almost apathetically.

"I was afraid," said O'Byrne, in that whispering monotone as if he spoke in a dream. "I was afraid to run it before this many people—I should have guessed what would happen when Acton and Graves and—"

"Are you still harping on that coincidence?" demanded Silvers in a fierce undertone. "Can't you see how foolish it is, Blair? What earthly connection can there be between pictures on a screen and living people, some of them half the world away? I'll admit what happened tonight was—"

"Did you ever hear—" broke in Blair softly, as if he were following some private train of thought and had not heeded a word of Silvers' harangue—"of savages covering their faces when explorers bring out their cameras? They think a photograph will steal their souls. It's an idea so widespread that it can't have originated in mere local superstition. Tribes all over the world have it. African savages, Tibetan nomads, Chinese peasants, South American Indians. Even the ancient Egyptians, highly civilized as they were, deliberately made their drawings angular and unlifelike. All of them declared and believed that too good a likeness would draw the soul out into the picture."

"Well, yes—everybody's heard of such things—but you're not suggesting—"

"After the Templeton elopement—and Ann Acton's fainting-spells and Philip Graves' illness—yes after what happened tonight, how can you deny it, Abe? No, the Egyptians, the modern savages, were closer to the truth than we. Only before now no likeness has been perfect enough to absorb sufficient personality so that people could notice it. But these illusions of mine—they're real, living, breathing. While you watch you can't believe the actual men and women aren't standing in front of you.

"It had an effect on Acton and Graves when only you were watching—enough of their personality was drained out of them into the illusion by your own temporary conviction that they were there, so that they went into vague dreams of woodland and music. I don't know how the other actors were affected—I do know that several of them were sick and dizzy that day. I haven't checked—maybe I've been afraid to . . .

"When the 12 board-members were watching, the drain was stronger; so that Graves was really ill on shipboard and Acton couldn't be roused from her faint until the telephone call to you broke the illusion here. It affected Templeton and Bill Fredericks another way—hypnotized them into believing what the audience was believing, that they were really in love—"

RECOLLECTION flooded into Silvers' mind. He remembered what he had felt when he read the headlines of the elopement. He said:

"*Could* it happen that way, Blair? How greatly could a mass mind affect the reactions of the people it concentrates on? I thought of it before—if twelve individuals, each convinced for a time that he saw two people desperately in love, might really work a sort of persuasion on those two—No, that's crazy! It couldn't happen!"

"You saw it happen," murmured Blair quietly. "You saw what happened when 150 people joined in that fierce concentration—that utter conviction that they saw a man's sword poised, aimed, descending—mass hypnotism, it was! For a majority of them that sword really struck—their imagination outran the actual fact and they thought they saw Lysander spitted on Demetrius' blade. They thought they saw him die."

"Well, he didn't, did he? I mean, nothing happened this time or they'd have called me."

A thin smile twisted up O'Byrne's strained mouth. He reached behind him. Silvers heard a click and realized that the telephone had been lying out of its cradle on the desk ever since he reached Blair's side.

"I wanted you to understand before they broke the news to you," O'Byrne was explaining gently. "And I knew the telephone would interrupt me unless I—"

Shrill buzzing whirred from the desk. With a little spurt of terror for what he had yet to learn, Silvers snatched it up. A voice shouted thinly in his ear:

"Silvers? Is that you, chief? My God, I've been trying to get you all evening! Acton's been in a coma for over an hour—doctor can't rouse her. And a call just came in from London that Phil Graves is out too—can't be waked! And—what's that? *What?* Chief! Word's just come in that Templeton's passed out too, and Bill Fredericks has dropped dead! What's the matter with this town? It's like the end of the world—"

"Abe—" O'Byrne's voice behind him twisted Silvers around like a hand on his shoulder. The receiver shrilled unnoticed as their eyes met. O'Byrne's face was almost serene—knowledge of what the telephone was crying showed in his eyes. He said:

"Do you believe me now? Do you understand? Do you realize how much of life itself I've woven into this damnable thing I've made? You—it's like two-dimensional pictures that carry a shadow of the third—enough dark to give a feeling of depth. In my three-dimensional picture I've somehow got a shadow of the fourth—life, maybe, or something too near it. Maybe that's what the fourth dimension it—life itself. But it won't kill men again—not again!"

THE CRASH of glass shattered into the hysterical buzz of the crowd. Silence like death fell over the confusion of the murmurous throng among the bar-platforms as they turned white faces toward the corner. O'Byrne's frail arms swung his heavy stool with desperate strength, crunching and smashing and crashing among the delicate intricacies of his projector. Silvers clutched the still shrilling telephone and watched him, not moving.

Eye To The Future
by Ree Dragonette

First name actually Rita. I believe at one time she was married to sf author Charles "Prisoner in the Skull" Dye. She attended the First World Science Fiction Convention and made an indelible personal impression on me with an act of human kindness unforgotten to this day. A young woman ahead of her time, died many years ago, but lives on in this story from the pages of Campbell's prestigious *Astounding Science Fiction* (now *Analog*). I always loved her name.

—FJA

Interoffice communiqué from Time Research Central to Chronoscope Department, June 17, 2372.
SUBJECT: Cessation of transmission from Chronoscope E-4 (location, New York State, Twentieth Century) as of 1:03 p.m. local time, June 15, 1946.
1. Subject report acknowledged.
2. The Director instructs that a transcription be made of the recording of the twenty-four hours preceding cessation of operation of chronoscope in question.

Tim Jackson angrily closed the door of the walnut paneled office. He didn't like the boss at any time, and this morning he hated him heartily. That smug, smooth-shaven face above the cigars and chrome decanter incited a sleeping fury that had been gnawing at Tim. He strode down the corridor, muttering. So the boss was being pressured by the distributors, was he? This was an emergency order. Optical blanks were needed out of all proportion to present supplies, and much indignation was issuing from the New York office. It was up to Tim to expedite things, was it? Fine thing! While the boss sat in his comfortable office, complaining and passing the buck. It was he, Tim, who had the real responsibility. Well, he just didn't care too much. He'd had enough, and the boss could do all the worrying from now on!

The haranguing he'd received from the boss was the final straw to Tim's misery that day. He had slept little the night before, with his wife nagging until his head split. She had not only refused his explanation for staying out, but also the money and the trinket he had won from Bill in the poker game. He brought the thing home especially for her, and the way she flung it back at him was infuriating. Jane loved pretty things, and the glass statuette was lovely, with clear, modeled eyes gleaming in its wise, oval face. It was odd for Jane to have acted so perverse, and when she carried it so far as to force him to get his own breakfast—that was too much! He always burned something, the eggs or toast, and he was late getting started. In his haste, he spilled hot grease on his hand, and finally had to leave without finishing the food, charred and bitter as it tasted. Tim's thoughts whirled annoyingly, and fixed themselves with alternate emphasis on Jane, and the boss. His burned fingers smarted and tingled, and his anger mounted. By the time he reached the melting furnace he was quivering with fury. Notions of escape assailed him.

Ordinarily, Tim was a cheerful, efficient worker, in spite of personal feelings of the difficulties of his trade. In charge of the "firing" process, he had a certain creative affection for the swirling stuff that eventually was annealed, and cut into blanks to be ground into lenses. Right now, however, he took no pride in his job, felt no compunctions about wasting time, or failing everybody who, directly or indirectly, depended on him. He wanted to destroy the whole flowing mess in the pot, let chips of clay or something get into it, and somehow release his chained violence before he ran away.

Tim conquered the rash desire and went sullenly about his work. As the day grew hotter, so did his temper, until machinery, melt, and even his thoughts beat like body blows upon him. He breathed in fierce gasps, and wiped sweating hands on his trousers. His fingers felt a small object in his pocket. Taking it out, he examined it curiously. An idea snaked slowly through him. What a way to fix the boss! He would damage the melt, but he would do it so cleverly that it passed all inspections until the blanks were ground and ready for shipping. The figurine sparkled temptingly in his fingers. If Jane didn't want his amber offering, he would dispose of it, to his greater satisfaction. He studied it closely. It was a fine color, pale enough to affect the melt so slightly that it would go undetected until it was too late to blame him. Let the inspectors take the punishment. Eventually it would come back to the boss, but good.

Tim hesitated, smiled stiffly, and dropped the round body into the vat. Its luminous eyes held the light before it was sucked into fluid depths.

The wall clock said 1:03 p.m. Tim realized he was very hungry.

EYE TO THE FUTURE 293

Interoffice communiqué from Time Research to Chronoscope Department, June 18, 2372.
SUBJECT: Cessation of transmission from Chronoscope E-4.
1. Report and brief of transcription acknowledged.
2. In regard to the Department's question as to procedure with E-4's receiver, the Director instructs that no steps be taken to make it inoperable at present. An effort will be made to transmit a substitute Chronoscope to the temporal area which has been scanned by E-4. The receiver will therefore be left in operation until further notice, and daily checks made on it to determine whether the substitute Chronoscope has reached E-4's location in space and time.

The telephone order called for two semi-finished cylinders: O.S.—A 3.25—O.D.—A 3.50, to be sent by special messenger immediately. The stock clerk who filled the order did so from the supply that had just been stacked. The blanks were well on their way when a memo was delivered from the testing laboratory, to the effect that the new Corbal semi-finished were defective due to "seeds" and must not be used.

"But I've just sent out a pair," moaned the clerk. "Inspection's a little slow down there, isn't it?"

"Sorry, that's the order," retorted the messenger. "You'll have to let one pair pass."

Everybody but Tim was in an uproar. His only trouble was that Jane had asked for the figurine and he didn't know where he could find another one.

Dr. Felden measured the pupillary distance once more, and made a slight change in the curve of the temples. Then, fitting the glasses with quick accuracy, she surveyed her stocky patient approvingly.

"There you are, Mr. Horton." She clicked off the table light. "I'm glad we refracted again. It's been a year, and there's enough change in this prescription to increase your comfort considerably."

"They seem fine, doctor. Convenient just now too, since we're piled up with statements and reports and our staff is small. Bad enough having extra hours without those headaches I've been having."

"Well, you shouldn't have any trouble. However, I'll check again next week. Wear them as much as possible, and if they bother you at all, use your old ones until you come in to see me."

He thanked her and went out into late sunshine. The glasses brightened everything.

He had some dinner, then returned to the office. Garey Barnes, his angular, bronze-haired junior accountant, was pounding speedily on the calculator and didn't look up as Jeff called hello. Jeff gave a moment's attention to this unsociableness before proceeding with his work. After several hours of steady concentration they stopped, put things in order, and left together. They went down in the elevator and said brief goodnights when they emerged on the main floor.

The following week Jeff kept his appointment with Dr. Felden. The glasses checked perfectly on the complex testing instruments, and the oculist assured him that they were as nearly correct as possible.

"Try to keep them on, now," she admonished as she showed him to the door.

IT HAD BEEN a cloudless, iridescent day, and Jeff, feeling a Saturday relief from the week's tedium, wanted a walk. Stepping to the sidewalk, he glanced about questioningly. In amazement he peered into gathering darkness. There had been no indication of storm, and it was far too early for sundown. Nevertheless, lights broke the shadowy bulks of buildings and the air looked wind-stirred. Jeff shook his head, senses taut. Nothing altered in the sound, or the feel of things, only in appearances. Jeff's prosaic, literal mind worked calmly, but his insides twisted in icy turbulence. No rain fell, and he felt none of the breeze he saw rippling the thin branches overhead. Traffic blared cacophonously, yet the street appeared vacant. Jeff found himself running, and slowed down to catch his breath. A procession of terrors pursued him. He had never known psychic disturbances; now he feared insanity or some hideous delirium. He stood still, and looked up at the sky, right into a swarm of stars. Twitching with bewilderment, he walked over to a lighted doorway. Wrist raised awkwardly, he could not believe either his watch, his sight, or his brain. He struggled back to the oculist's, pushing helplessly at the door. A neon sign shone dully in the window and he stared at it dazedly. He must be mad—it couldn't be the middle of the night. Only a few moments ago it had been noon, and life was normal. Now, some calamitous, fantastic things had happened to the world.

In a narrow margin at the rims of his glasses, he was aware of daylight. Frantically, he pulled them off. The day wheeled back into place, the sun pouring from a flawless sky. Hysterically, Jeff tried Dr. Felden's door again. Even when he remembered that she had been about to close when he left there, he continued to push fumblingly, rattling the knob. The spectacles hung from his numbed hand, he watched them in searchful horror, and battered at the door. Unable to think rationally, he waited, then turned away, the glasses still dangling. He rolled his eyes in an agony of confusion. At last the day's radiant familiarity soaked in, and by the time he reached the subway, his black terror subsided like a spent nightmare. Regaining control, he put the glasses away, and sat quietly through the short train ride to his home.

Over the weekend he tried to rest, but his mind circled, impotently, about his unnatural experience. Jeff had never suffered nervous disorders, or developed weird complexes. In spite of his present mental turmoil, his innate tranquility returned. Curiosity overcame fear, a curiosity colored with an adventurous spark. Up until this bizarre occurrence, his life had been dully uneventful. This new pattern was one of absorbing interest. Although it seemed futile to try to solve a problem he couldn't understand, it was becoming fascinating to investigate.

Excited and wakeful, he rose from bed. Switching on lights, he picked up the blue leather case which he had placed on the dresser. His hands reluctant, he adjusted the glasses gingerly on his face and resolved to remain unperturbed, no matter what.

Going to the window, he looked out, expecting a dazzling panorama. There was wide grayness instead. Ragged strands of rain wound down from a swollen sky. With the sleeve of his robe, Jeff brushed the pane, and leaned on the sill, pondering. It had been a clear night, forecasting fair weather. He glanced at his watch, believing it this time. He moved from the window and slumped in an armchair. A margin of electric light contrasted with the afternoon grayness before him. When he took off the spectacles it was night again and the room's incandescence was torturing. His eyes winced, then widened, to take in first the numeral on his watch, then the oblong of world bordered by the window.

When the first stains of dawn spread, Jeff went back to bed.

He was not a garrulous person, especially during business hours. Although he was in continual proximity with his assistant, they seldom talked. Most people liked Jeff, but Garey Barnes didn't evidence emotion of any kind, about anyone. Congenial, Jeff liked to exchange pleasantries now and then, but with Garey he had to be guarded and formal. Today he didn't much wish to speak to anyone and his assistant's presence disconcerted him more than usual. Once or twice he had glanced up to find Garey's green eyes fixed intensely on him, as if they could enter regions closed to intrusion. Jeff went back to his mathematical computations, frowning. His attention kept wandering to his fabulous glasses. When he managed to dismiss them, his thoughts turned to Garey. Both were tormenting mysteries.

Jeff's head throbbed. He had to wear his old glasses for ordinary purposes. If he put the new ones on, everyone in the office disappeared and he saw the emptiness of an evening scene with wastebaskets piled up and the drab figure of a cleaning woman. It just wouldn't do, except if he wanted to amuse himself in an idle interval. Therefore, he managed painfully with his old spectacles, since he didn't wish to consult an ophthalmologist for fear of learning that some obscure disease was causing the aberration. He did not want to become the subject of medical experimentation. To go back to Dr. Felden was equally unthinkable since, in her very extensive tests, she had found the glasses optically correct. He could hardly explain that after the first week some process had taken place and, that not many minutes after his final examination, the world of his sight had changed unbelievably. Keratometers and refractors don't lie, at least he wasn't going to try to tell anyone they did.

Jeff's reverie was interrupted by Garey's handing him a sheaf of statements. For a while there was no time for further meditation. After lunch and a few helpful cups of black coffee he felt better. By the end of the day he had quite cheerfully decided to keep his queer secret and make the best of it. Even Garey's laconic coldness in response to some light chatter didn't disturb him.

OVER A period of several weeks Jeff grew used to his gift of special sight and took pleasure in it. He came to certain definite conclusions. Actually, there was nothing wrong with the glasses, except that when he looked through them it was tomorrow—or very much later today!

He recorded all information, planning to compile the results and submit them to someone more competent than he to investigate such matters. In the meantime, however, he avoided disclosure. On one occasion when he had slipped them on at the office, the treasurer startled him by inquiring:

"Have you gone in for glamour in those dark glasses, Horton?"

Jeff made a hasty, noncommittal reply, puzzled until he realized that of course, since it was afternoon, the glasses would appear dark on his face. When he put them down they winked and glimmered whitely against the polished mahogany.

If the genial treasurer had not noticed something strange about the glasses, less friendly eyes might—Garey's for instance.

One evening when he was certain that no one else would be there, Jeff took the glasses into the office. His observations were the sort he had come to regard as routine. Standing by the window, he noted the spiraling of chimney smoke toward the quilted clouds, and the winging streak of a plane or two along the sky.

A humorous notion to watch the arrival of co-workers made him turn and face the door. It opened and Garey came through to stand limned in the morning light. Superciliously, his glance swung in the direction of Jeff's desk and a surge of loathing and contempt darkened his face. The shadow of someone rising opposite him fell upon Garey and, stiffening, he walked into the room, his face once more an impenetrable seal.

Jeff felt his pulse racing in shock. He sat down. Before his lowered eyes, a glass tray of pencils and pens glinted prismatically. He changed to his old spectacles and tried to do some work. Distracted, he soon gave up and left.

He walked across the Battery toward the river and thought worriedly about Garey. He had never disliked him but he often wondered what it was that separated him so distinctly from other people and made him appear so broodingly self-sufficient. Jeff knew little about him except that, according to company records, he was in his late twenties, had one college degree, and was once a newspaper reporter. Rumor whispered that he had left his home and a brilliant career in journalism because of some enmity toward his father, a wealthy publisher. Beyond this, a first-hand history was impossible, as Garey did not talk about himself, when he talked at all. Whenever he tried to make friendly overtures toward his sullen, but efficient aide, Jeff failed, to his embarrassment and chagrin. After many attempts at cordiality, Jeff had learned to confine their relationship to business and tried, in all fairness, to take no advantage of his authority over the younger man.

In gloomy reflections, Jeff reached the river. He changed to his new glasses and stood on the walk near the river-boat docks, scanning his surroundings. Leaning against a bollard, he gazed out over the river. There was a heavy mist and rain wafted in the wind, but his eyes were in the sun. Coolness fingered his face but he looked through to tomorrow's hot stillness. His sober thoughts jolted back to the extraordinary lenses.

A mountainous steamship was gliding by with her escort of small boats. Faces of foam bobbed up, sparkling. Jeff traced the outline of the ship's name on the flare of the bow, too faint to decipher. His eyes sought the side of the pilot house—now he could make out some letters—an O and an AI. When the huge liner passed him, he craned forward and read *Saxonia* in white letters on the stern.

Several feet away, in the shadow of boardings around the excavations for the Battery-Brooklyn tunnel, Garey was idling. After a few bourbons in a noisy bar, he had drifted riverward, where he lingered, often in nocturnal solitude. He had barely noticed the figure of the other man until something made him turn, straining astonished eyes.

The man's face was glowing.

In riveted disbelief, Garey got a second shock. The man was Jeff Horton.

Garey looked dartingly about in search of glaring floodlights. There were none. Yet his face was glowing. Lithe and tense, Garey stepped forward to speak and saw the man go right past him, his spectacles flashing.

Baffled, Garey swerved back into the shadows. Jeff was gazing out over the river. Once, he stretched forward trying to get a better view of something and murmuring indistinctly. Then he consulted his watch and Garey bent down toward his own wrist. Now he saw Jeff take something from a pocket and, pushing his glasses up on his brow, scrawl briefly with his right hand. Returning notebook and pen to his pocket, he readjusted his glasses and continued his scrutiny of the river. Garey moved silently, trying to follow Jeff's range of vision. He saw nothing on the black water but the boats that were always tied up at night.

At last Jeff removed his glasses and the glow from his face, turned, and walked away. Garey let him saunter some distance before he lit a cigarette and started homeward.

Interoffice communiqué from Time Research Central to Chronoscope Department, August 3, 2372.
SUBJECT: Report on signals recorded on Receiver E-4.
1. Subject report acknowledged.
2. Synthesis of opinion of Board members indicates that the vague and flickering signals reported, and their intermittent nature, do not indicate success in placing a new Chronoscope in the area scanned by the receiver. Signals of this nature have been known to occur when particles of a chronolens, or dilutions of the lens material, temporite, are subject to certain complexes of the Rhine factor—psychic aura. It would seem, therefore, that the reported signals merely indicate that some part of the Chronoscope E-4 is in intermittent contact with some psychic to which it responds. Chronopsychic radiations vary greatly with the individual and with the concentration of temporite exposed.
3. The Director instructs that records be kept but that this work be carried out as theoretical rather than practical activity.

Jeff was signing correspondence when he heard the door close. A chill crawled along the back of his neck. He knew who would be standing in the door, just as he had glimpsed in preview, with a violence of loathing on his face. He knew, also, that when he rose from his chair and cast his eyes upward, that look would be gone. Shoving a batch of letters aside, Jeff got up, raising his head to Garey's expressionless face.

That afternoon the office boy brought in the early edition of the evening paper. Jeff called to him.

"Would you mind looking up a ship arrival for me, Joe?"
"Was it due today, Mr. Horton?"
"That's right. It's called the *Saxonia*."

Garey was on the phone. He clutched the receiver tightly, his narrowing eyes like green wires. Muscles tied, he didn't try to move until the voice in his ear compelled him to lower his head and speak gently into the mouthpiece. "What was that again? I'm sorry."

Garey was long practiced in self-control and deviousness, so he was able to observe Jeff without arousing suspicion. And he wished to observe him very closely. Last night he had witnessed some provocative things. Linked to other isolated facts, the river incident was highly significant. This much was incontestable. Jeff owned a pair of phenomenal lenses, lenses which gave him unique vision. And he obviously did not intend to share his knowledge or he would have revealed it before now, being by nature a straightforward character.

Joe, the office boy, had flung the paper aside, saying, "The *Saxonia* docked at 10:40 this morning, Mr. Horton. Pier 18." Garey put down his pencil and leaned forward on crossed arms, ostensibly to study some reference material. He pieced together some curious scraps of information.

At 12:04 midnight, Jeff had looked at his watch and made notations concerning something on the river. Now he was comparing those notes with the arrival time of the ship *Saxonia*. Garey picked up his pencil, returning woodenly to his work. None of this made sense unless—*Jeff had seen that ship hours before it passed.* Garey's fingertips froze on the pencil. Jeff's face had been glowing in the dark, almost as if his glasses reflected next day's sunlight! Also, Jeff had come nearly face to face with him without even seeing him. Later he stood gazing intently over the water as if he was following the path of something that moved invisibly. 12:04 midnight. 10:40 a.m. today. It took a ship roughly forty-five minutes to dock after leaving the bay. Garey calculated rapidly.

Jeff had seen the Saxonia *ten hours before she arrived.*

Grinning wickedly, Garey shuffled the ruled papers under his hand. Everything was piercingly clear!

IN THE evening, Jeff sat home alone, contemplative—with the radio for choppy company. He was tired, his mood dismal. Things were increasingly unpleasant. He didn't know what to do about his glasses, and had been unsuccessful in his efforts to find a suitable scientific society to whom he might send the collected data. In addition, relations with his assistant were becoming intolerable. The memory of that look of ugly disdain and Garey's progressively sneering attitude rankled. He could leave his job or demand Gary's dismissal, but neither course was practicable at present. He rubbed his brow in deepening dilemma.

Going to the dresser he unlocked a drawer. The buzzer growled. Jeff locked the drawer again and slipped the keys in his pocket. When he opened the door, Garey entered. Jeff whispered a polite greeting, and waited for his caller to speak. Garey smiled thinly at Jeff's undisguised perturbation and loosened himself into a chair. As always his arrogant face was unreadable.

"What do you want, Garey? I don't imagine this is a social call."

"Hardly. I'm not a sociable soul." He coiled long hands behind his head. "Ordinarily, I mind my own business. But I happen to be interested in something you have. Quite interested."

"What are you talking about? I had no idea we shared any hobbies." The words fluttered out meaninglessly.

"We share one hobby, if you wish to call it that. Those new eyeglasses of yours. Get rid of the silly, puzzled stare. You know what I'm talking about."

"You're being ridiculous. Why should my spectacles suddenly interest you?" Jeff's voice was on a tightrope. He shuffled nervously over to the liquor closet and busied himself clumsily with bottles and tumblers.

"I mean your new wonder glasses, Jeff. The ones that give you such amazing sight. I'm interested for various reasons."

Jeff spilled some whiskey. Handing Garey a glass, he said, "You might as well have a drink and go. It isn't like you to waste time on conversation."

"I'm not thirsty. Since you seem anxious, I'll tell you exactly why I'm here. Never mind how I know what I know. I just want those glasses, and I came to get them." He stretched up from the chair, lean and menacing.

The tumbler trembled and Jeff put it down on the table. Unreasoning dread gripped him. "You better go."

Garey's fists closed, rock-hard. He stalked quietly to Jeff, who waited, shriveling.

The blows hammered at Jeff's neck, spinning him to the floor. Garey unknotted his fists and bent to rifle the unconscious man's pockets.

When he found the keys, he unlocked the dresser drawer where he had guessed the glasses to be hidden. The leather case nestled between piles of socks. He lifted it, opening it to make sure it contained its tortoise-shell treasure, before he pocketed it. Scraping a dry tongue over his lips, he glanced contemptuously at the feebly stirring man and padded out.

A short distance from the house, he paused to put on the glasses, in the shelter of a dim doorway. They were large for his bony features, but they stayed on without slipping down.

At first his vision was blurred, and he grew dizzy. The outlines of houses tilted crazily and street and sky shifted in a swimming mist. He took out a handkerchief and wiped the glasses carefully. When he put them back on they were slightly clearer and, after a few minutes, he could see enough to walk. He squinted along anticipating some fantastic effect. Nothing happened except that as his eyes forced themselves to adjust to their strange props, his vision improved. Things were still filmy and out of proportion, however, and time did not take a great jump forward. A clock in a store window indicated that a half hour had passed between the time he rang Jeff's bell and now.

He stumbled along, hopefully determined. Perhaps the transformation would occur slowly. Maybe he should go to some optician and have the glasses fixed to suit his eyes. But that might cancel their power. He'd have to wear them as they were and be patient. He had gone to a lot of trouble to get them and sooner or later it had to bring the results he wanted.

Wonderful dreams of racetrack winnings and stock market success paraded through his mind. Confidently, he stepped off the cub, then paused to let a speeding cab go by.

But it didn't go by. Horn blasting, tires screeching in a skid, it bore down on him. He saw it looming massively above him.

IN HEAD-CRACKING pain, Jeff emerged from oblivion. Struggling up, he looked foggily around. In a flood of remembrance, he lurched across the room to the dresser and clawed through the drawer for his missing glasses.

Half sick, clothes awry, he ran unsteadily down to the street. As he neared the corner he saw a careening taxi heave like some maddened, unleashed monster up over the curb and across the sidewalk. In a paralysis of horror, he watched Garey leave the safety of the street to step back on the pavement in the path of—under—the oncoming cab.

Something curved glittering high in the air and fell to fragments incredibly at Jeff's feet. He stopped to gather the mottled, weightless frames. Straightening slowly, he stared at them and gradually the realization of the power he had lost outweighed his shock. His fingers slipped inside the frames, around the futile grooves which had held, for a while, an undreamed-of power.

There were so many things he had not tried yet!

Footsteps echoed in the wakening street. Sashes swished open and heads punctuated the regimented windows. People rushed past him to the wreck and the tattered body under it. A stout man in an undershirt jostled him.

"Oops! Sorry." He pointed to the empty frames Jeff held in his numb hands. "Did you break your glasses?"

The beginnings of the regret that would taunt him all his life were in Jeff's voice as he answered, hoarsely, "Yes, yes, they're broken."

Nyork,
Janevery, 2501

Dear Jo,

Here's a chance for you to reiterate your old claim that I am an incurable romanticist. But here's the story.

In going over the records of the Twenty-fours Century Time Researchers, I have run across many interesting things. Of course, as you would imagine, they did everything the hard way in those days. But with their primitive equipment, they did manage to unearth a surprising amount of information about the nature of time.

The thing that tickled me was a little case history I ran across in the old records. It seems that something happened to one of their Chronoscopes—those little devices they scattered back in the time stream which would radiate visually everything that happened within their range. Well, one of them was destroyed. Since they hadn't the technique of making an accurate replacement, they failed in their attempt to send another one back to precisely the same area in time. But they left the receiver on and got a series of faint flickerings and hazy impressions. These made no sense to them. When the signals ended, they left the receiver on for a few months and then consigned the whole matter to the files. But to me—I've been studying the records for days not—they are fascinating.

I won't bother you with the intensities and co-ordinates and what-not of all this data. You're a mere artist and wouldn't be interested, but this is what I gather from it. Try to imagine yourself in the position of one of those half-savage, aboriginal ancients of the Twentieth Century, in such a spot.

The Chronoscope, which was made in the form of a figurine aesthetically gratifying to the inhabitants of the period, so that it would be kept out in the open, was destroyed in some way which alloyed it—diluted it. Perhaps it was dropped into molten glass or some such thing. It was made of temporite which is a substance profoundly affected by psychic forces.

Now, imagine this. Suppose someone back in those dark times got hold of a piece of this alloyed temporite. Looking through it—granted, of course, that his psy pattern matched the temporal-spatial crystallization of the material—he would be able to see into the future! The beauty of this supposition is that the "distance" he could see would depend completely on his psychic pattern. For one savage it might be a year; for another, thirty hours.

It seems to me that the records of this old chrono receiver bear out such a tale. One man got hold of it—in what form is hard to say—and could see, we'll say, ten hours ahead. He probably gained something thereby—imagine yourself as the only man on earth who could see ahead! And then one of his fellows learned of his powers and stole the temporite from him. But within minutes, this second man, whose pattern shows up so vividly on the records, was killed and the temporite smashed forever. I can conclude only that the thief thought that he, too, would see ten hours into the future, but actually, could see only a few seconds. It is easy to picture him seeing death approach him, three seconds ahead, and perhaps reflexively leaping into its path. What magnificent justice!

Well, perhaps this little explanation of hazy and forgotten records will be of some use to you in the creation of one of your fantasies. I, for one, would give a good deal to know what actually happened.

Goodbye for now. I'll "simil" you again when I run across more useless, romantic information.

As ever,
Teev

Flood

by L. Major Reynolds

No relation to the serial novella of the same name by Ray Cummings. My memory of Louise is of a crusty old dame (I don't think she would have objected to the appellation) with a cigaret holder in her mouth. Louise was, as F&SF editor Tony Boucher told his readers, a member of the Los Angeles Science Fantasy Society back in 1952. I seem to recall the womanuscript being titled "The River" when I submitted it but it wound up in print as "Flood"; so be it. I would have preferred to republish her more typical work, "It Will Grow on You", but I can't find a copy nor can her daughter. Now that I think of it, it was kind of a later variant version of the gimmick in "Yvala". L. Major Reynolds always seemed to suggest to me a masculine byline and perhaps that's what she wanted, or maybe Major was just her middle name. I never thought to ask her and her daughter doesn't know so it's too late now. But not too late to remember a female sf writer of nearly 50 years ago.

—FJA

The raging flood tore at the side of the rain-sodden mountain just below the city. Imperceptibly the surface of the tortured slope quivered, slid for a few inches, and subsided. The high cliff on the opposite bank stood rock solid ignoring the tumult below.

The driving spring storm drove its waters into the widening crevice formed by many centuries of freezing winters, opening it still more. The last of the ice disappeared, and the warmer waters rushed to fill the opening. The weight was too much. With a groan almost human, the mountain side slid with a rush, damming the river from bank to bank.

The torrent flung itself against the barricade and rose swiftly, forming a lake that backed rapidly toward the unsuspecting city.

A watery moon peered from a break in the clouds and shone down on the scene.

The streaming sewer outlets were soon covered, and the water crept higher and higher along the great pipes.

Below the streets the sound of scrabbling claws increased as the rats raced to escape the certain death that rushed upon them.

The pressure in the deepest sewer became unbearable. At several points the concrete cracked. In one place an entire section broke away and crumbled into fragments. The water reached eager fingers into the opening and tore great slabs of earth free, mingling it with the racing flood. Deeper and deeper the openings grew as more and more of the pipe gave way to the water.

A long fault opened, and the water raced down the steep slope to collect in a deep cavern far below the surface.

It was quiet for a breath, then a tremendous upheaval came and the water foamed and boiled. Something fought a battle with the roaring flood, and the cavern became a maelstrom. The upsurge tore the fault open to the top, and something rushed from the dark space in an attempt at escape.

Above ground, and bracing the rain, a nondescript cat left the dubious shelter of a packing case and slunk through an alley to the street. Some inner sense took him to the nearest sewer entrance, and he crouched above it, waiting for something he dimly sensed. A pair of eyes blazed in the half light and a mangy tom slid from the shadows to help with the vigil. Across the street more padding forms appeared. There was no thought of battle. Each accepted the other, and all feuds were forgotten in the instinctive call that had brought them there. The rain poured down on the waiting animals.

Suddenly the line tensed. There was a scratching sound at the curb, and the nose and whiskers of a giant old rat slid cautiously into view. The cats waited with the inborn patience of the hunter until the prey pulled himself into the street.

There was no audible sound, but only two of the cats made the leap that brought them, one on each side of their victim.

A quick rip of sharp teeth and the instant sheen of claws left the rat dead on the pavement, and the cats returned to their vigil.

Time after time the scene was repeated. As the water flooded higher, the rats became more frantic in their efforts to escape. Often, when the struggle ended, it was a cat who lay quietly in the street while the rat tried desperately to find an opening in the circle of enemies which surrounded him. But there was always another foe to face no matter where he turned.

There was excitement in the city now. The sound of sirens, and the roar of trucks as the aroused populace rushed to the river.

Giant searchlights split the sky and focused on the landslide. Wires hummed with hurried messages for help.

And still the water rose, eating away the dam with tiny ineffectual nibbles that could never keep pace with the volume pouring down from the distant mountains, building up the force of the water, till the pressure was almost unbearable.

FLOOD

Something in the sewers was going mad.

Something that hated the touch of water. Something that wanted again the dry solitude of its deep cavern. The water beat at it, and it beat back in insane flailings which smashed sections of pipe as if they were made of paper.

The weight of the water continued to increase, and wide crack opened to the street.

Something screamed soundlessly as the watery moonlight shone into the crevice.

Across the river, a truck loaded with dynamite started toward the scene along the river road. A wall of water hit a bridge and swept it away to add its debris to the barricade. One flailing girder reached out, struck the truck, and the night blooming with the flash of the explosion.

Smaller slides started along the mountain and the waves slapped against the opposite bank and overran the street.

Two battles were raging now. Man against the elements, and the cats against their hereditary foes.

The rats were pouring from the sewer in a steady stream, and the cats, reinforced by the arrival of several dogs, fought grimly. There was a tangled mass in the street now, but it was uncannily quiet except for an occasional squeal of rage and frustration from a cornered victim.

The rain-washed pavement shone oddly red in the dim light.

Far down the street a roof blossomed in scarlet flame, and a fire engine howled past the unheeding animals. No man-made noise could stop them. They were grim on the business of extermination.

Under the street in the sewers, things that had long lived beyond the sight of man moved upward as the surge completely filled the pipes.

The rain was slackening over the city, but dark masses of clouds hung blackly over the distant mountains. And still the water rose higher. At the landslide, great steam shovels dug frantically at the mass of earth and rock that was spelling the doom of the city. Drills and jackhammers pounded at the base of the cliff, only to be stopped by a harried engineer and sent to the top to start from there.

The tempo of the drills stepped up even faster; and as more lights were added, the scene became almost as bright as day. Frantic scurrying figures seemed to chase each other up and down the cliff face, laying the ropes to hold the hard-rock men in the race against time.

And the water rose, merciless and deadly.

In the city, where there was no eye to see, strange things happened along the main sewer route. Great cracks appeared in the pavements, and car tracks twisted as if endowed with some inner life. Manhole covers shot into the air as if propelled by mighty guns. Geysers of solid water held them up like tangible pillars for the moment, then blew them airily aside to fall with a destructive crash.

And in the sewers the black something keened in suffering as it forced itself higher and higher seeking the dry security left behind.

On the outskirts of the city a number of shadowy forms padded along the soaked ground. They hesitated when they reached the pavement, but some inner force urged them on. Pointed ears cocked forward, they slunk toward the compelling scent that had reached for miles.

The rats were frantic. The sewer opening was a squirming mass that churned within itself. Outside, the cats and dogs waiting in a grim circle for any brave enough to show himself. Inside, a menace they knew was there, but could not comprehend.

There was a movement on the outer edge of the ring, and room was made for the newcomers. The wildcats moved in silently and waited.

Down the street the water rose, keeping pace with the sewers. A long lithe water snake came from the opening and the line parted to allow it to pass. Enemy of the rats, as the waiting warriors seemed to sense, the sinuous form cleared the circle, coiled itself for action, and waited.

The mass of rats gibbered and squealed, trying in vain to communicate to their antagonists the presence behind them of a greater unknown foe, an enemy of *all* life.

For a moment it was stalemate. The steep slope of the street held the rushing waters back long enough for the rats to mass for the final charge.

An earth-shaking blast announced the first explosion, but not an eye moved from the milling rats.

Down at the river, men battled madly to open a way for the waters. Half the cliff was gone now, but the barricade was still too high for the rising water to surmount.

From the distant mountains came flashes of lightning, and the deep rumble of thunder tried to copy the man-made blast of explosives.

All roads were part of the river now, and the beleaguered ones looked toward the west in a vain search for help. But in that direction lay only the vast expanse of ocean.

Five hundred miles away there was sudden activity around a group of planes. Shiny fat-bellied bombs were being loaded, and each of the flying monsters vibrated with eagerness to be gone. A reassuring message was sent, but the last wires were swept away before the news was received.

One by one the ships roared into the air, and help was on its way.

The cats were becoming bolder now. Several of them had made a lighting-fast dash and pulled some of the rats from their hold. That seemed to break the spell that had held them in the entrance.

The battle was no longer quiet. It was a roaring mêlée of cats, dogs, rats and wildcats. And on the outskirts of the throng, the sleek water snake patrolled, alert for any rodent that escaped the maddened crowd.

And still the water rose. Down the street, and creeping closer, came the steady march, keeping pace with the sewers. The entire end of the city was one with the mighty lake the river had become.

The river had a new sound now. It was a low growl, as if it realized with some uncanny instinct that this time it had the ruling hand. Man had tamed its waters and made it do his bidding for too long. But now the age-old scale had shifted.

Time raced by as the flood occupied the city.

The rain started again, and the waters draining from the upper street were dappled with red.

It was uncannily quiet now. The rain lasted for only a few moments; then the sky cleared as if by magic. There was the first hint of the false dawn in the east, and hopeful eyes waited the coming of the day. But still the raging flood raced down from the mountains to drive the level still higher.

The battle was to the death now. Giant rats, who had lived in darkness for years, were coming out of the sewer. Four of them swung from the throat of a dog, slicing away the flesh till they reached the jugular. But even as victory was attained, other defenders fell on them and life was a fleeting thing.

There was a moment's pause as the final victims searched frantically for one last foothold inside the sewer. The first glint of water slopped over the edge into the street, and suddenly every rat made a wild scramble for the dubious safety of the open air. But they came in sorry shape. Some of them were oddly crushed and bleeding.

The defenders moved forward as one, only to stop dead in their tracks. The soundless screaming came again, was perceptible to all now, and each animal reacted in its own way.

The hackles of the dogs lifted, and they crouched, belly down and low rumblings came from their throats.

Cats, in midstride with one lifted foot, arched their backs and low rumblings came from their throats.

And the rats turned and faced the opening, waiting in the same menacing line with their recent enemies.

Something alien was just within the entrance of the sewer. Something older than life itself. Side by side, the animals waited, hearing subconsciously the soundless scream.

The light was strengthening as the sunrise grew brighter.

Suddenly the quiet was broken as the sound of roaring motors cut across the sky, and the great bombers came into view, heading for the river.

A black mass filled the sewer entrance and crawled out on the pavement. Every animal faced it tensely.

At the landslide, the populace cheered at the sight of the planes, and scattered to points of safety. The ships made a trial run over the site, and swung to come in on the line.

One of the fat-bellied bombs came free from the leading craft and spun downward.

The black mass was out of the sewer, ringed by a circle of fangs. Great gobbets were torn from it, as the frenzied animals fought with the courage of desperation. Higher and higher the unheard screams became, until even the pilots of the planes shifted uneasily in their seats and shook their heads, trying to force it from their minds. The townspeople seemed frozen as the keening went on.

The first bomb hit squarely on top of the slide, and half of it vanished in an upsurge of rocks and rubble. The next plane made its run, and again the perfectly aimed blast shook the earth.

As the third craft set itself, the first ray of the sun shone down upon the streets of the city. They struck the opening of the sewer where the battle was being fought. The mass of blackness suddenly exploded in a cloud of greasy smoke. Where it had been was nothing.

There was a final blast, and a wild cheer as the landslide was blown away. The river raced once more through its bed, and the flooding waters lowered rapidly. The rats that were left turned slowly, and threading their way through the crowd of erstwhile enemies, went once again into the darkness of the sewer.

And not a claw was raised to stop them.

Extra-Curricular
by Garen Drussaï

> The one occasion upon which we regret our policy of no interior decoration is when we introduce some of our authors—especially a few of our discoveries. Physical beauty is not (we are devoutly thankful!) a necessity for a literary career; but it can undeniably brighten the lives of a couple of middle-aged editors. Garen Drussaï, whose first story we present here, is Hungarian and stunning; she is an impassioned and articulate debater on such topics as pacifism and Forteanism; and she has a refreshing ability to come up with new variant on science-fiction notions. Just which notion she chooses to play with here shall, for the moment, go unmentioned; its concealment is part of the fascination of this appealingly offtrail story.
> —Anthony Boucher (from the original introduction)

Little Maria lay snug; sleeping deep down in her rough hewn cradle. Her mother's toe kept it rocking smoothly to the rhythm of the whirling spinning wheel. A high wind drew steadily at the log fire. All was comfortable and serene inside the cabin.

Ellen took her eyes off her work occasionally to lavish a glance at her year-old daughter. The ball of yarn was almost finished when a fearful whimper from the cradle drew Ellen's attention again.

The bright blue eyes were wide open, looking intently at her mother. Ellen stopped spinning and smiled reassuringly.

"Ah, so you're awake, my little Maria! My little pink rosebud."

Maria grasped the edges of her cradle and sat up. "For goodness sake, Mother. Stop that gushy baby-talk!"

Ellen stared woodenly, her smile fixed on her face.

"What are you looking at me like that for, Mother?"

She wrenched her eyes away from the innocent babyishness. The fire burned as brightly as before. She glanced at the door; it remained closed, the wind sucking at its edges. The room hadn't changed; it was as warm and familiar as always.

"Mother, what's the matter with you? Is it so inconceivable that a person my age can communicate verbally with an adult? Is that wrong?"

Almost against her will Ellen found herself answering.

"Maria, stop this nonsense! Your father won't be home for another hour. He . . . well, you know, he would have liked to have been here when . . ." her voice dropped in a sigh of helplessness. Great sogging tears, which she'd managed to hold back till now, rushed out on her cheeks. "My baby, my dear, dear baby—you're only a year old. I must be going out of my mind!"

Maria shook her blonde head in compassion. "Oh dear, I guess I didn't realize your mental status was so unstable. I thought speech would make it possible for us to communicate on an intelligent level."

It was too much! Ellen raised her hands in front of her eyes uncomprehendingly, and slumped to the floor.

A short while later Maria's father kicked the mud off his boots, and opened the door.

She sat in her cradle, contentedly chewing on her blanket.

"Ah goo, da da!" she gurgled.

BUBBLES SMILED from the lights. Directly at him, this time.

Bob Lawrence grinned back and pushed the empty glass to the center of the table. He waved an eager waiter away and settled expansively in his chair.

The line of shapely chorus legs swung mechanically into the last bars of the number, while all three pieces of the nondescript orchestra bawled their lungs out. There was a mad flurry of posteriors among the feathery costumes. Each of the girls "fluffed" as provocatively as was possible after having run through five shows, and raced off the stage for the dressing room.

Bob's usually pedantic face wore its most "lady-welcoming" expression as, a few minutes later, Bubbles maneuvered her hips through the tables toward him. He pulled her chair up, and brought his over close, saying, "Bubbles, you look positively enchanting this evening!"

She smiled enigmatically. A worried expression, as if she were trying to make up a wise-crack, passed over her face.

"Order me a drink, willya Bobbie honey? I suddenly don't feel so pretty good."

Bob smiled ingratiatingly and signaled the waiter.

"You know, Bubbles, you not only look divine, but you look different tonight." He cocked his head to one side exaggeratedly. "Can't exactly put my finger on it . . . you actually seem to have a certain cerebral quality about you."

Bubbles giggled vacuously, just as though she understood what he was talking about. She always did.

She took a sip of her drink and laid her hand across his, squeezing his fingers. "Your perspicacity is really amazing, Robert. Do you mean that it's that apparent?"

Robert's jaw sagged open.

"Do you want me to elucidate?" she smiled.

He shook his head feebly.

"Well, Robert, I want to explain to you anyway. You see, I've been thinking . . ."

Robert managed a weak smile.

". . . my current status in this stratum of existence is primarily the consequence of planet-wide stupidity."

Bob's eyes almost crossed. "What in the hell has got into you?" he spluttered, unmindful of the fact that he was attracting a few amused glances.

"You know, as well as I do, Bob, that there's really no need for female entertainers like myself to remain in a state of vacuity all their lives. One can amalgamate sexual and intellectual attributes, and be the more enticing for the coalescence.

"Now, Robert, close your mouth. You look like an idiot!"

He stared wildly at her, but she smiled soothingly back at him without changing expression.

"By God, I want to know, and I want to know right now, just what do you think you've been putting over?" The pitch of his voice had risen till, by now, several people at the bar and surrounding tables had turned to see.

"Robert, sit down. Please! You're making an exhibition of yourself. Besides, I'm not through telling you everything."

"No, I won't shut up and I won't sit down," he screamed. "I get it all now. You're one of those sorority-bred females on a slumming spree, aren't you, Miss Smarty? Well, let me tell you a thing or two now . . ."

Bubbles rose to her full five foot two, knocking her chair over in her haste. "Listen to me, you pompous ass," she cried. "You're insufferable, coming in here like a knight on a white horse, giving poor little Miss Nobody a whirl."

She stamped her foot. "You just want everybody to know how democratic you are!"

"So! You've just been pretending to be my intellectual inferior," he snapped back at her, "thinking it makes you more desirable. You little demon, you!" he reached across the table before she could step back, and gave her a head-ringing slap.

There was a gagged silence. But before Bob could make another move the bouncers were upon him. One grabbed each arm as Bubbles burst into tears.

"Oh Bobbie," she wailed, "How couldja do a thing like that? I never did nothin' to ya. Oh, go way, I dowanna see you no more!"

The bouncers lifted Bob to his toes and dragged him silently away, his face dazed and vacant.

ON THIS particular evening the Hotel Allington's Universe Room was humming with a different kind of din than usual. For inside, tonight, were gathered men and women representing every branch of science in the inhabited solar system, from astronautics to photosynthesis. There were experts and authorities from every race, nation and planet, and they were enjoying themselves completely.

Katherine Hewitt Baxter, in whose honor this extraordinary session had been called, sat with her half empty dinner plate before her. Dr. Katherine Baxter! she mused. In a few more minutes, an Honorary Member of the Solar Federation of Scientists.

Some of the people out there were her friends; some of them she'd barely heard of before. But, all of them, strangers and friends alike, had come to acknowledge her scientific achievement.

Katherine finally pushed her plate away and turned to the man on her left. "It's really so gratifying and splendid a thing to have happen to me, Dr. Mitchell, that I'm afraid I'm quite numbed." She shook her grayed, closely cropped head in a gesture of self-amusement.

"Nonsense!" boomed the Chairman, sandwiching her in grandly between mouthfuls. "You're a great scientist. The Solar System is enormously indebted to you for your discovery of Flotnium!"

Katherine pursed her narrow lips, and looked down at her lean, capable hands. "I've made it my life's work," she said simply.

Gradually the clatter of plates was silenced, and the waiters pushed the last dish-laden carts from the room. After officially clearing his throat several times and consuming two glasses of water, Dr. Mitchell rose.

Chairs shifted so that all the dinner guests faced the speaker's table. He adjusted the microphone and started to speak.

"Dear friends . . ."

She listened with just part of her mind. Only disjointed snatches of what Dr. Mitchell was saying reached her ears.

". . . one of the great in the world of science . . . has given her life to . . ."

She concentrated harder, trying to think only of the speech she was about to make.

EXTRA-CURRICULAR

"... believe that Flotnium will revolutionize the science of metallurgy for centuries to come. No honor is too great ..."

Abruptly her thin taut face started to soften. Then she smiled slightly and easily, as though the lines had finally fallen into place. Her hand played idly on the table; her fingers making random and pointless tracings on the white cloth.

Dr. Mitchell finished and, with the grandest gesture he could summon, turned toward Katherine.

"Fellow scientists: it is seldom that I have the opportunity to introduce so distinguished an individual as our new Honorary Member. I give you ... Dr. Katherine ... Hewitt ... Baxter!"

Katherine rose and smiled, nodding at the long ovation. Dr. Mitchell rapped the table smartly for silence, and leaned back in his seat to light his after-dinner cigar.

"My dear friends," she began, as the noise subsided, "with the acme and equivocation in the new motto, it quite understandably to make 60 out of remembrance! And familiarity notwithstanding, achromatic potential counterclockwise by no man. So the tractive force not dissociated of grapple, categorically lingers in the non-existence of suddenly tinsel!"

She paused briefly and, assured of the impact of her words, added, "Not so anyone simulate by the merry way ponder!"

There was a complete deadening silence in the large room. Dr. Mitchell leaned over to her, his face an apoplectic red.

"Katherine! Dr. Baxter! Whatever are you talking about?"

"Please, Dr. Mitchell," she whispered, "I'm just achieving a major point. What till the question period, and we can correlate all the inquiries."

He sat back reluctant and confused. A vague murmur started to rise from the audience.

"And so," she continued speaking, "the thermo e.m.f. will presently kernel the flux of the ingress dogmatic .... It paradoxically be that I gathered to collision a transmissivity expansion, and it was wove."

Suddenly the eminent Dr. Baxter hiccupped. Loudly, the sound of it bounced over the tables like an errant ping-pong ball. She crimsoned slightly, but recovered quickly and finished.

"Therefore, when I came to experiment number 1276 I realized that theoretically the merger of these two elements was possible after all."

Dr. Mitchell sighed with deep bewildered relief and managed a weak smile from the audience. Katherine continued.

"From there I went on with renewed effort, and finally with my 2003rd experiment I compounded Flotnium, in the form in which it exists today."

Flustered by the oppressive silence, she turned hesitantly and extended her hand to the embarrassed Mitchell. He took it automatically, but his grasp was less hearty than it might have been.

Frankly puzzled, she turned back to her audience, glanced hurriedly at the stunned faces . . . and abruptly sat down.

And still there was no applause.

RESEARCH 3 LAY dappled in the late afternoon sunlight. The animated galactic displays, silenced for the day, dwarfed the study tables below them. Only a subdued hum emanating from one of the machines broke the airy quietness; for classes were over for the day, and the children had long since gone to the recreation areas.

Miss Trece, walking quickly down the corridor outside, looked up just in time to see a figure disappearing down an adjacent hallway.

"Oh, Barth! Just a moment," she cried.

Barth tucked his papers under his arm and waited for her.

"I know you must be in a hurry, Mr. Barth. But I wanted to ask if you'd seen little Maura Thalen."

"Why no, I haven't," he answered. "I've been correcting papers over in Research 7 until just a minute ago."

Barth gestured back over his shoulder. "That reminds me; I noticed the power panel outside Research 3 was on when I came by. Thought maybe you were still inside working."

"No, I'd checked the children out of there last period . . ." Eone Trece ran her hand worriedly through her hair. "You say the panel is on? Well, I'd better see what it is."

"Good lord!" Barth looked at his wrist watch. "I've got to run. But I'll look in on my way back."

Sure enough, the panel was on. She opened the door and went in.

Something was drawing current, but she was sure that she'd checked everything before leaving. Nevertheless, there was a hum permeating the room; and it seemed to come from the further corner, over by the window.

Then it was that she noticed the warning light on the large machine that sat beside her desk.

"Hmmm!"

The sound escaped her lips speculatively. She walked quickly over and checked the timer dial.

It had another 52 or 53 seconds to go.

There was nothing to do but wait. In fact, under the circumstances, it was the best thing to do. She settled herself on the edge of the desk.

"Hey!" Barth hollered form the door. "What did you find, if anything?"

"Come on in." She pointed to the panel. "Take a look!"

"Oh ho!" he chuckled. "I see. I suppose you do have a faint idea who's using it."

"Well, we'll soon find out for sure . . ." Eone was interrupted by the red light flashing off. She and Barth turned towards the machine.

The door slid back. Maura pushed a strand of hair back from over her eyes and stepped out. She turned to snap the current off, and saw the two instructors coolly appraising her.

"Oh, Miss Trece! You startled me . . .. Were you looking for me?"

"Well yes, I was, Maura," Eone answered, disarmingly casual. "But, frankly, I didn't expect to find you here!"

"But I was out walking for a while . . ."

Eone broke in, changing her manner suddenly. "The point is, Maura, that you've been caught time-hopping! You know that you've been forbidden to use this machine for anything but supervised field trips. What have you got to say for yourself?"

"Well, as I said . . . I was out walking, and," Maura tried to explain, "and . . . I just got to thinking about my . . . thesis, and I just felt that I had to go back and re-check my findings. I just wasn't satis . . ."

"Is something the matter, dear?" asked Eone, suddenly gentle.

Maura's eyes widened into an ingenuous stare. Uneasy, Barth turned to look over his shoulder. There was nothing there—nothing but the darkening windows as the sun sank lower and lower.

"Why, no! There's nothing wrong!" Maura answered abruptly, jerking his attention back by the inconceivably alien tone she'd adopted.

"There's nothing wrong except that I've just about violated every rule there is in the time-travel code." The words ran together and separated irrepressibly. "I wasn't out walking, any of the times before, when you wondered where I was. I was time-hopping every time; and on every trip I behaved abominably . . . I just about wrecked several lives. And I'm so ashamed of myself, especially because of the woman scientist . . ."

The animatedness fell off, and a puzzled expression worried her eyes.

"Did I, Miss Trece?" she demanded. "Did I just say that I was ashamed of myself? Did I say that, Miss Trece, or did I just imagine I heard myself saying it?" Her eyes were on the borderline of tears, but she was trying desperately to hold them back, not quite knowing why they were there.

Eone nudged Barth's shoe. His half-smile vanished.

"You were telling us, dear," she answered, "what a perfect little idiot you'd been making of yourself. Now, let's finish about the woman scientist you—uh—visited."

"Oh dear," Maura objected, "did I mention that, too?"

"Yes Maura, you did," Eone replied. "And you were quite voluble about it, too; even though it was by proxy. Maybe you can tell us now, just how it feels to be taken over by a playful time-traveler?"

A Leak in the Fountain of Youth
by Amelia Reynolds Long

I once met Ms. Long in her home town of Harrisburg, Pennsylvania in the mid 1960's. I recall that she was a 50ish librarian type, a kind of Andre Norton of an earlier era. She wrote both sci-fi and mysteries under a variety of pseudonyms and, as one of the earliest female sci-fi writers, she wrote extensively for the pulps in the 1930s and 40s. Famous sci-fi short stories include "The Thought-Monster" (filmed as FIEND WITHOUT A FACE, 1958), "The Box From the Stars", and "The Undead".

—FJA

This is not an attempt to seek vulgar publicity for the extraordinary experimental work in gland control carried on by my friend, Professor Aloysius O'Flannigan; neither is it an effort to exonerate him in the public mind of the supposed murder of Gustavus Adolphus Lindstrom. In the first place, any type of publicity whatsoever is highly distasteful to Aloysius; and, in the second, the living presence of Gustavus himself is exoneration enough. All I wish to do is to set down the truth, in order that the wild rumors accusing a reputable man of science of such preposterous—not to say scandalous—behavior, may be stilled.

Although Aloysius O'Flannigan is still a very young man, he has already accomplished some most remarkable things in the field of biochemistry. Not least among these is his growth-and-age-control serum, based upon a series of highly intricate experiments with the glandular system.

"It is really quite simple when you get down to it, Eric," he told me one day in his laboratory. "Science has known for a long time that the growth and aging of the body are governed by certain glands. There is, for example, the pituitary gland, controlling skeletal growth; the thymus, regulating physical development to adolescence; the thyroid, governing mental and nervous development; and all the rest of them.

"Science has even realized that the control of these glands and their hormones means practical control of the development of the individual. And that is what I plan to do, Eric."

Here he leaned forward and tapped me impressively on the knee, while his blue eyes shone excitedly behind his shell-rimmed spectacles. "I mean to control the entire glandular system, so that a man may become old or young, large or small, at will. It's entirely logical."

I shook my head. "It may sound entirely logical in theory," I told him, "but you'll find it's going to be something else in practice. I don't want to hurt your feelings, Aloysius, but if you think, for example, that you can turn an old man into a boy, you're—well, due for a keen disappointment. It can't be done."

"And why not?" he demanded.

"Why not!" I echoed. "Well, for one thing, there's skeletal growth. Be reasonable, Aloysius. It is perfectly comprehensible that you may be able to arrest bodily development through control of the glandular system; but to claim that you can reverse the process is sheer nonsense."

"You understand the process of coalition in the unicellular animals, don't you?" he asked. The light of battle was beginning to appear in his unusually mild eyes.

"Certainly," I answered, a little nettled that he should question my knowledge on such an elemental point of zoology. "It is the reverse of the process of subdivision. Instead of one amoeba or protozoan subdividing to form two new individuals, two amoebae coalesce to form one. But what has that got to do with—"

He interrupted me. "And you realize that the individual cell structure of the human body is similar to that of the unicellular animals, including cell division in the process of growth, don't you?" he persisted. "Well, then, why couldn't coalition take place in a similar manner, also?"

"But it doesn't," I protested. "You know very well that it doesn't."

"But it could through control of the glandular system. Don't you see it?"

All I could see was that we were arguing in a circle, so I gave it up.

IT WAS about three months after this that the bank robbery occurred. I read the account of it in the morning paper as I ate my breakfast; but at the time noticed nothing beyond the fact that our largest suburban bank had been relieved of one hundred thousand dollars by a masked man who had entered just a minute before closing time the day before, and held up the place single-handed. Just as he was leaving, his mask had slipped down; the paying teller had seen . . . Here the story was continued on an inside page, and I, being in something of a hurry, did not take the time to finish it.

A LEAK IN THE FOUNTAIN OF TIME

I had planned to drop around to see Aloysius that morning to ask his opinion on an article I had written on the unemployment situation in early Babylonia, but when I reached his home, all thoughts of the matter were driven from my mind. Our old college friend, Gustavus Adolphus Lindstrom, had just arrived ahead of me and he was in trouble.

Now, being in trouble is not precisely a new position for Gustavus Adolphus. In the first place he is a free-verse poet, and in the second— But the first will cover everything, so I will not trouble to elaborate.

Usually his escapades are of the picturesque but comparatively harmless variety, but this one was different. In fact, it was so different that it centered around the Suburban Bank robbery, with Gustavus Adolphus cast in the leading role.

It was one of those damning cases of circumstantial evidence and mistaken identification. The paying teller of the bank had been taken down to police headquarters to try to identify the holdup man in the rogues' gallery. When he had failed to find his man among the accepted celebrities, the police, in desperation, had brought out a collection of minor offenders; and from these the misguided bank clerk had picked out Gustavus Adolphus!

"But, Gussie," inquired Aloysius, "how in the world did your picture ever get in the rogues' gallery?"

Gustavus Adolphus looked somewhat embarrassed. "You see, it was this way," he began. "A few years ago, I headed a movement for the practical revival of classicism. One of our aims was to bring back the ancient Greek form of dress for both men and women, and I, as head of the movement, felt it my duty to put the theory into practice.

"But, when I walked down Broadway in the tunic and sandals of Sophocles' time, I was arrested at Forty-second Street and charged with both appearing in public improperly clad and attracting a crowd that obstructed traffic. I—I spent three months in jail," he finished lamely.

WHILE HE was explaining this to Aloysius, my mind was busy with the problem at hand. "Of course, it's a case of wrong identification based on coincidental resemblance," I said now. To assume that Gustavus Adolphus would have held up a bank, even if he had known how, was naturally ridiculous. "But the mistake can be cleared up readily enough. All you need to do is produce your alibi for yesterday afternoon and then—"

"But that's just the trouble," he interrupted piteously. "I haven't got an alibi."

"You—what?" Aloysius and I stared at him in blank amazement.

"What I mean is, I've got an alibi, but I can't prove it," he explained. He looked pathetically from one of us to the other.

"But where were you?" I demanded.

"In a Greek sarcophagus at the university museum," he answered meekly.

I began to lose patience. "This is no time for flippancy," I told him. "Stop trying to create a sensation, and tell us where you were."

"But I have told you," he protested. "I wanted to write a poem on the death of Socrates, so I went to the Greek wing of the museum and climbed into the stone sarcophagus—the one with the opening above the face and shoulder of the occupant—to put myself in the mood. I—I'm afraid no one saw me there."

"Didn't anyone come into the Greek wing?" Aloysius inquired.

"Oh, yes," Gustavus Adolphus said. "One of the university students came in with a young lady. He came quite close to where I was, and flicked cigarette ashes through the opening of the sarcophagus. But since the interior of one of those things is rather dark, he couldn't have seen me unless he had deliberately leaned over and peered in."

"But you must have been able to see him," I pointed out. "Couldn't you recognize him if you saw him again?"

"I'm afraid not," he admitted regretfully. "You see, the cigarette ashes landed in my eye and I wasn't able to see anything for quite some time. All I know about him is that the young lady addressed him as Lover Boy, and that is hardly sufficient for identification.

Aloysius and I agreed that it was not.

"This is beginning to be serious," Aloysius said gravely, as we appeared to be at a deadlock. "If you can't prove an alibi, you'll never be able to convince the police that a mistake has been made."

"I realize it," Gustavus said, "and I don't know what to do or where to go."

I was tempted to suggest back to into the sarcophagus, but, as I had warned him only a minute before, it was hardly the time for levity. Something had to be done, and done quickly.

I looked at Aloysius. "What are we going to do?" I queried.

"I thought," Gustavus Adolphus ventured timidly, "that perhaps Aloysius could do something to me with his science, so that the police couldn't recognize me."

Aloysius' nostrils quivered. "Be quiet, both of you," he commanded, "while I think."

He began to stride up and down the room, his chin sunk forward upon his breast, and his hands clasped loosely behind his back. Gustavus and I watched him anxiously. We both knew that if he was to think of something, it would have to be fast and it would have to be good.

Suddenly he stopped in the middle of his pacing, and smote his left palm with his right fist. His eyes were gleaming behind his thick-lensed spectacles.

"I've got it!" he cried. "My glandular control serum, of course!"

I sprang out of my chair at the words. "No, Aloysius, no!" I exclaimed aghast. "You wouldn't dare!"

He ignored me, and addressed Gustavus Adolphus. "It's a new formula that I completed less than a week ago," he explained. "By its use, I can change you temporarily to a boy of about sixteen. Shall I do it?"

"Don't you let him," I warned Gustavus. "It's liable to kill you."

Gustavus looked uncertainly from me to Aloysius. "Is it dangerous?" he inquired.

"Of course not," Aloysius declared impatiently. "Why, only yesterday I changed a battle-scarred tomcat to a mewing kitten, and today it's enjoying life to the full."

"Will it hurt?"

"You'll have to ask the tomcat. But it's practically certain to be painless, since you merely fall asleep, and, when you waken, years have dropped from your age."

"It sounds rather attractive," Gustavus confessed.

"It sounds too quick to be good," I commented.

"Eric, you be quiet," Aloysius snapped at me. Now that the chance to try out his pet theory upon a human being had been practically dropped in his lap, he wasn't going to have it snatched away by anybody. "Under ordinary circumstances, the treatment would cover a period of months, but we've got no time for that now. We've got to act fast."

A SUDDEN, businesslike ring at the front doorbell was like an exclamation point after his words!

"The police!" Gustavus gasped, and went limp.

Aloysius seized him by the scruff of the neck, and propelled him toward the laboratory. "Answer the door, Eric," he said. "If it's the police, hold them off until I get back."

I had the sensation that each board I trod upon was on springs and gave under me as I walked down the hall to the front door. When I opened it, the worst was realized as a burly policeman confronted me!

"Are you Professor O'Flannigan?" he bellowed. I realized afterward that he must have spoken in only an ordinary tone of voice, but it sounded differently to me then.

"No, officer," I replied, glad that my first words, at least, could be the truth. "I'm only his friend, Eric Dale. Did you want to see the professor?"

"An' what would I be doin' here if I didn't?" he answered.

This didn't seem to call for an answer, so I didn't attempt one. "If you'll excuse me a moment, I'll go and call him," I offered instead, and started back down the hall. To my horror, the policeman followed me!

For a moment I had the hideous vision of his forcing me to guide him straight to the laboratory where Aloysius was doing heaven alone knew what to Gustavus Adolphus, and, then, clapping irons on both of us for aiding and abetting a dangerous criminal; but the situation was saved by the entrance of Aloysius in person, alone and wholly self-possessed.

"Was someone at the door, Eric?" he inquired innocently. Then, pretending to see the policeman for the first time, "Oh, good morning, officer. Can I do something for you?"

The policeman touched his cap. "It's about a friend of yours I've come, professor," he explained. "A man named Gustavus Lindstrom. Have you seen him this mornin'?"

Aloysius registered just the right amount of annoyance and concern. "Don't tell me that Gussie's gone and got himself into trouble again!" he exclaimed protestingly.

The policeman explained that Gustavus was wanted for the robbery of the Suburban Bank. Aloysius was properly shocked.

"I simply can't believe it!" he declared. "Why, I saw him only day before yesterday, and he said nothing at all about intending to rob a bank."

"They seldom do," the policeman said. "But seein' as you're such a good friend of his, he may try to get in touch with you now that it's over and, if he does, will you let us know, professor?" If he's innocent, you'll be doin' him a favor by helpin' him prove it."

Aloysius intimated that he would—without, however, definitely committing himself, and the policeman departed.

"Now," I demanded, turning with the ferocity of overwrought nerves upon Aloysius, "what have you done with Gussie?"

He raised a calming hand. "Gussie's all right," he assured me. "I gave him a large dose of the glandular control serum, and he's sleeping quietly in my room. Would you like to see him?"

I replied that I most certainly would.

He conducted me to his bedroom adjoining the laboratory. There lay Gussie sleeping peacefully, and with an expression on his face that for sheer guilelessness would have done credit to a hydrocephalic idiot.

I bent over him and examined him. "Heavens!" I cried almost at once.

"He's young already!"

Aloysius laughed. "Your imagination, Eric," he said. "The serum won't begin to take effect for nearly an hour."

In spite of Aloysius' assurance that everything was now all right and that Gustavus would be safe until the real bank robber was discovered, I returned to my home with a feeling of strong misgiving. Suppose the serum should fail to take effect upon a human being; or suppose, having been given in one large portion instead of small quantities, it should kill or cripple Gustavus! But, as the day wore on and none of the papers brought out an extra featuring either his capture or his murder, I decided that I was giving myself needless worry. And so I banished the matter from my mind.

BUT IT WAS false security. At three o'clock the next morning my telephone rang. Aloysius was on the wire.

"Eric," he almost whispered, "come over at once! We're in the devil's own predicament!"

"Gussie—" I began incautiously, but he interrupted.

"Don't ask questions over the phone," he warned. "I'll explain when you get here." He rang off.

I dressed as quickly as possible and hurried around to where he lived. He was waiting for me at the door.

"What on earth's happened?" I demanded. "Have the police—"

He waived the police aside as if they had been of no consequence.

"It's nothing to do with the police," he said. "Eric, we've got a *real* problem on our hands now. Come into the study."

He seized me by the arm and almost propelled me into the room. "Look," he commanded, and pointed dramatically at a large, overstuffed armchair.

I looked. Something was lying upon the seat of the chair. At first I thought that it was merely a blanket roll. Then, I realized that it was alive. Bending closer, I discovered with a sense of shock that it was a very young baby!

"Merciful heaven!" I gasped, and took a step backward. "Where did that come from?"

"Don't you know?" Aloysius asked.

I raised my eyebrows. "Doorstep contribution?" I inquired.

He made an inpatient gesture. "Won't you understand, Eric?" he asked piteously. There was soul sickness in his eyes. "It's Gussie!"

"GUSSIE!" I sat down weakly upon the nearest chair and tried to keep my head from spinning while he explained. It seemed that either he had given Gustavus a slight overdose of the serum, or the stuff taken in quantity acted differently than when taken in small amounts. In any case, Gustavus had failed to stop rejuvenating when he had reached the physiological age of sixteen, but had continued to grow younger and younger until he had reached his present state.

"It was terrible!" Aloysius said, shuddering. "For a while I was afraid he was going to vanish entirely right there before my eyes. Eric, what are we going to do with him?"

I considered the situation. Once the shock of beholding Gustavus as an infant had abated, matters did not really look so bad. After all, what Aloysius had set out to do was to disguise Gustavus so that the police would not recognize him, and that was precisely what he had done. Why not, I argued, permit Gustavus to remain as he was until after the real criminal had been apprehended, when he could be restored to his normal state?

This suggestion relieved Aloysius enormously. He permitted me to go home and finish my night's sleep in peace.

The following noon I dropped around again to see how he was getting on. I found him preparing a bottle for Gustavus.

"Eric," he said through clenched teeth, "this can't go on. I've done nothing since five o'clock this morning but wait on Gussie."

"Five o'clock!" I echoed. "That's no hour to get a child up. Why didn't you let him sleep?"

He looked at me in disgust. "That shows how much you know about it," he retorted resentfully. "*He* got *me* up. At five o'clock sharp he started to yell like a banshee, and I had to walk the floor with him for two hours before he'd quiet down. Since then it's been one thing after another. I tell you, I can't stand it!"

It was on the tip of my tongue to remind him that I had warned him against the experiment in the first place, but I saw the dark circles under his eyes and refrained. After all, it would be unkind to twist the weapon in the wound just then.

"There's only one thing to do that I can think of," I told him. "You'll have to hire a nurse."

He hired a nurse, a grim-visaged professional named Miss Mabel McGillicuddy. She was a woman with an iron jaw and a physique like a horse, but she understood the care of infants. Aloysius gave her an apologetic-sounding story about Gustavus' being his orphaned nephew, and conducted her to the nursery. She appeared a trifle dashed when she discovered that her charge's entire wardrobe consisted of an old, cut-down polo shirt and a dozen and a half dinner napkins, but she said nothing and got to work.

TWO MONTHS passed, not entirely uneventful. The police, for some reason that we never entirely fathomed, were positive that Gustavus had come to Aloysius the day after the bank robbery, but they could prove nothing. Repeated questioning of Aloysius and even a search of the premises during his absence, got them nowhere. And, meanwhile, he for whom they searched rode out in his own perambulator under their very noses.

Of course, we knew that this state of things could not go on indefinitely; but when the next move came, it found us unprepared. It was, in fact, nothing more nor less than the arrest of the real bank robber, taken in the attempted holdup of a bank in the neighboring city. Upon being identified by the teller of the Suburban, he admitted the first robbery. So the good name of Gustavus Adolphus Lindstrom had been cleared.

It would now seem that all that remained for us to do was to administer the serum that would restore Gustavus to his normal physiological age. That was what we thought, too, but we soon learned that it was not so simple. The realization came to us when we approached the nursery door with a hypodermic of the serum and discovered that Gustavus was not alone. We had forgotten Miss McGillicuddy.

"What," I inquired, "are you going to tell the nurse?"

Aloysius looked blank. "I hadn't thought of that," he confessed. "You—you don't suppose she'd believe the truth?"

"I *know* she wouldn't," I answered with conviction. "You'll have to do better than that."

He sighed. "The only thing I can think of is to tell her that her services are no longer needed," he said, "and I'll have an awful slim chance of getting away with it."

"There's only one other way," I pointed out. "The woman must sleep some time out of the twenty-four hours. You'll have to watch for your chance and give Gussie the serum then."

But it was easier said than accomplished. All our visits to the nursery found Miss McGillicuddy wide awake and on the job. Finally, we divided the day into six-hour shifts during which we alternately kept watch in an effort to catch her napping, but this met with no success either.

Worse yet, Miss McGillicuddy now seemed to know that she was under secret surveillance, for she began to regard Aloysius and me with a suspicious eye, and kept the nursery door locked most of the time so that we had to knock to gain admittance.

It was at about this time that Aloysius discovered that we ourselves were being spied on. He mentioned it to me when I dropped around one morning.

"Eric," he began uneasily, "I don't know what can be the matter, now that the bank robber has been arrested and Gussie is no longer under suspicion, but a policeman's been watching this house for the past three days. He's taken a room across the street and he keeps looking over here with a pair of field glasses.

"Miss McGillicuddy—" I suggested.

He nodded. "I'm afraid so," he said. "That female never did like me from the beginning. And now our watching her has made her suspect Heaven alone knows what, and she's gone to the police about it."

"I'm afraid we'll have to do what we should have done in the beginning," I told him gloomily. "Definitely discharge the woman."

We each took a neat drink of Irish whisky to help our courage. Then we tackled the job. To our amazement, it was easier than we had anticipated. Miss McGillicuddy said nothing, but she gave us one long, unreadable look. Then she executed a military about-face and marched off to her room to pack her belongings. A half-hour later we heard the front door close firmly behind her.

WITH A combined sigh of relief that sounded like the open steam valve of a locomotive, Aloysius and I bounded upstairs to the nursery. He was ahead of me as we reached the nursery door, and so it was he who first bent over the bassinet. The next instant I saw him clap his hands to his head and stagger back.

"Good Lord!" he groaned. "She's taken Gussie along with her!"

For a minute or so we could only stare at each other in dumb stupefaction. Then my brain cleared a little.

"It's kidnaping!" I cried indignantly. "She can't do this! We'll go to the police ourselves, and enter a complaint."

But we were saved the trouble. At that very minute the doorbell rang.

On the step stood the policeman who had called on us two months before!

"Professor O'Flannigan," he pronounced severely when he had shouldered his way into the hall. "I want to know what it is you've done with Gustavus Lindstrom."

And then the awful facts came out. Gustavus had been known to come to Aloysius' house that day after the bank robbery, but had not been known to leave. It had been assumed by the police that Aloysius was protecting his friend from arrest for the bank robbery, but when the real criminal had been apprehended and Gustavus still failed to appear, it was felt that something serious must be the matter.

When a check-up with Gustavus' relatives revealed no clue to his where-

A LEAK IN THE FOUNTAIN OF TIME 329

abouts, the police had formulated a theory. It was that Gussie had been foully murdered by his mad scientist friend, professor Aloysius O'Flannigan!

"But that's preposterous!" Aloysius protested indignantly. "I haven't harmed Gussie!"

"Then what have you done with him?" the policeman asked, not unreasonably.

Aloysius opened his mouth to reply, but closed it again without uttering a word. If he told the truth now, he'd be locked up as a raving lunatic.

"Professor O'Flannigan is not quite himself this morning," I put in helpfully. "His little nephew has just been kidnaped by the nurse who was employed to look after him."

The policeman smiled sourly. "We know all about that," he told me. "That nurse told us how the professor here was actin', and it was what decided us in thinkin' that something was wrong up here." He turned back to Aloysius, "I guess you'd better come along with me to the station, professor," he said. "The sergeant'll be wantin' to talk to you."

Aloysius paled. "Very well, officer," he said weakly. "Excuse me while I get my hat and coat."

He started slowly down the hall toward the laboratory. At the door, however, he turned.

"Eric, remember Socrates," he called, and disappeared into the room.

We waited in stony silence. What the policeman's thoughts were, I have no idea, but I know that mine were in a turmoil. If Aloysius was locked up on suspicion of having murdered Gussie, how would he be able to bring Gussie back to normal? And unless Gussie was brought back to normal, how was Aloysius going to prove his innocence? It would do no good to tell the truth. There are some things that even the police refuse to believe.

SUDDENLY I began to realize that Aloysius had been gone a very long time. The policeman, too, realized it, for his face became ominous and he made for the laboratory door. I, beset by a hundred whirling fears, followed and was immediately behind him when he entered the room. It was empty, but an open window told the story. Aloysius had realized his predicament and had chosen liberty by way of the laboratory window and the back fence.

For the next five minutes that policeman's language was awful. But he finally calmed down and, after grilling me on Aloysius' habits and possible hide-out, left for police headquarters. I, much to my surprise, was permitted to go home.

I spent the next few hours listening to police descriptions of Aloysius over the radio and wondering what he was doing. I had not the faintest idea where he could have gone, but I knew that I would have to get in touch with him some way to arrange for the restoration of Gussie.

And then, like enlightenment from Heaven, came the memory of his parting words to me, "Eric, remember Socrates."

I jammed on my hat and made a dash for the university museum.

The Greek wing was empty when I entered it. Nevertheless, I approached the stone sarcophagus with caution. I was in the act of lighting a cigarette with elaborate nonchalance when a voice spoke from the sarcophagus' interior.

"Eric, if you drop ashes in here I'll come out and murder you."

"Aloysius!" I gasped in relief. "Thank Heaven you're here!"

"According to Gussie's experience, it seemed the one sure place where nobody would look," he replied. He squirmed to a sitting posture, so that his head protruded just above the opening in the sarcophagus. "You've got to help me get Gussie back in shape," he said. "Do you think you can carry out a few simple instructions?"

"I'll try," I promised. "What are they?"

"First," he went on, "go to my laboratory and get the hypodermic with the corrective serum. You know which one it is. Next, take another hypodermic and make it one quarter full from the bottle on the end of the second shelf in my closet. It's a sleeping formula of my own, and is pretty powerful, so don't take too much of it. Then drive back here after dark and pick me up."

"What are you going to do?" I asked apprehensively.

"Never mind," he answered. "You know enough for the present. Now get going."

I had less trouble than I anticipated getting into the laboratory. The policeman on guard accepted my story that I had come for medicine for a sick dog, and let me take what I wanted from the drug cupboard, as long as I made no effort to disturb anything else. I had a moment's uncertainly over preparing the second hypodermic, for Aloysius had not told me which end of the second shelf he meant. I finally decided upon the right end, and took down the bottle that stood there. Then I returned to the museum.

Aloysius was waiting for me behind a tree across the street. "I nearly got caught getting out," he said, climbing into the car. "The damned burglar alarm went off."

"Where to now?" I asked, releasing the brake.

He gave me an address. "It's Miss McGillicuddy's," he added.

WHILE I drove, he explained his plan. I was to get in to talk to Miss McGillicuddy on some pretext, while he remained hidden in the car. Then, when I had talked her off her guard, I was to plunge the second hypodermic into her arm. As soon as she had gone under, I was to snatch up Gussie and dash back to the car. Aloysius would do the rest.

It sounded easy enough until I found myself standing on the doorstep facing Miss McGillicuddy.

"Well, what do *you* want?" she demanded uncompromisingly. Her iron jaw, when it moved, was overpoweringly suggestive of a cement mixer.

"Miss McGillicuddy," I began weakly, "I've got to speak to you about—about little Gussie. It's very important. May I come in?"

She moved aside reluctantly for me to enter. But the entrance was narrow and she was a large woman. In that minute I saw my chance and with a swiftness that surprised me myself, I plunged the hypodermic home. Miss McGillicuddy gave one startled snort and wilted before my eyes.

Fighting down a feeling of panic, I darted on into the house in search of Gussie. I found him without difficulty and was back to the car and had handed him to Aloysius in the back seat in less than two minutes.

"Now," Aloysius cried triumphantly, "drive somewhere—anywhere—until this stuff takes effect! It acts quickly."

We dashed off at top speed, with Gussie yelling like an Indian on the back seat. We took the corner on two wheels and almost collided with another car that was coming toward us. I heard the driver bawl a command at me to stop but I paid no attention. There was no time to stand by ceremony just then.

But a moment later I heard an exclamation from Aloysius. "Divil an' all!" he gasped. "That was a police car, Eric, and they're following us!"

My only answer was to step on the gas.

I shall never forget that wild ride, although its details were, even at the time, a series of blurs to me. I remember vaguely crashing through two or three red lights, while the shrilling of police whistles all but deafened me. Gussie's yells made our progress as conspicuous as that of the fire chief, and to add to our confusion, shouts of "Kidnapers!" began to arise from all sides.

At Aloysius' suggestion, I made for the open country but when I passed the city limits there were already three police cars and a whole squad of motorcycle police on our tail.

"If we can only hold out for an hour or two," Aloysius said, "we'll be all—Ow! Devil fly away with you!"

"What's wrong?" I demanded, wondering fearfully whether one of the police cars had opened fire and Aloysius had been hit.

But his reply reassured me. "Gussie's cutting teeth," he answered. "The little fiend just bit me."

During the next hour Gussie's growth was phenomenal. By the time we crossed the State line, he had reached the obstreperous stage, and was trying to climb over the back of the seat to assist me at the wheel.

It had been a little past eight o'clock in the evening when Aloysius had injected the corrective serum. By six o'clock the next morning, it had completely taken effect and, to our unbounded relief, Gussie was quite himself again, and with only a hazy memory of what had transpired in the interval. But now two problems had arisen. The car was almost out of gas and Gussie—except for the car's best blanket—was embarrassingly out of raiment.

"We'll have to stop at the next gas station," I told Aloysius. "We can do it in safety, for the police haven't followed us across the State line."

BUT I had reckoned without my radio. The keeper of the gasoline station glanced at our license, deliberately raised the hood of our car and did something to our spark plugs. Then he walked calmly into his house and closed the door. Before we realized what was happening, two State troopers had appeared from nowhere and taken possession of us!

"It's all right," Aloysius reassured us as we were herded into a police car to be taken back whence we had come. "We can produce Gussie now, so that will squash the murder charge. As for the remarks about kidnaping, Gussie can prove that he was the baby by the mole on his left thigh. Miss McGillicuddy, the nurse, can identify it."

"Ye Gods," exclaimed Gussie, aghast. "Did I have a nurse and does she know about that?"

Returned to our home city, we told our story, individually and collectively, to a skeptical desk sergeant.

"A likely soundin' tale you be tellin' me," he said. "I'm after thinkin' it's not Mr. Lindstrom alone that's had a second childhood, but all three of you. And I've a mind to put you all in the jug until you grow up."

Aloysius drew himself up. He can be impressive as well as persuasive when he tries. "Sergeant," he said, "I am a man of science and what I tell you about the gland control serum is the truth. You must, at least, give us an opportunity to prove it by calling in the nurse, Miss McGillicuddy."

The sergeant was not unreasonable. He dispatched a man to summon our witness.

Fifteen minutes passed. Then the telephone rang frantically. The sergeant took the call.

"My man O'Reilly's at the nurse's house," he announced tersely, as he hung up. "He says something's happened to her and he needs help. I'm going over there, and I'm takin' you birds along."

My heart sank. Aloysius had said that the sleeping formula was pretty powerful. Suppose I had given her too much and—

Aloysius must have been thinking something of the same sort, for he whispered to me as we entered Miss McGillicuddy's residence, "Eric, tell me quick. From which bottle did you fill that hypodermic? Right or left end of the shelf?"

"Right," I answered and then, from his horrified expression, I knew the worst. The bottle I had used had contained poison and now Miss McGillicuddy was a stiffened corpse! What, I wondered, was the penalty in our State for manslaughter?

And then a voice from the next room on our left spoke protectingly. "Nix, lady, lay off!" it was saying. "I'm a married man with a family!"

We rushed after the sergeant into the room beyond. And there a startling spectacle confronted us. Seated stiffly upon the edge of a chair was Officer O'Reilly, while perched coyly upon his knee—and very much alive—was Miss McGillicuddy! But not the Miss McGillicuddy we had known. Instead of an equine forty-odd, she was now a coltish, twenty-one!

"O'Reilly, what's the meaning of this?" the sergeant roared, but I think he must have guessed even before he got the explanation.

Aloysius turned to me and there was a look of mingled reproach and relief in his eyes.

"Eric, you're a blundering idiot!" he exclaimed. "But you've proven our story. You gave a shot of the gland serum to Miss McGillicuddy!"

To Live and Die in the World of Sci-Fi
by Jana Wells

Jana Wells is a photographer and sculptor as well as a writer. She lives in Southern California with her actor husband Lee Harris and four birds.
—*PK*

He had based his life on science fiction. He had read every book he could find. Seen every movie. Dream of it. Breathed it. So it came as no surprise to him that he awoke one morning to find a 5-foot Godzilla standing over him. He closed his eyes for a moment, but when he opened them again, Godzilla was still there. He glanced around his room. Yep, it was his room, not a movie theater. The TV was off, not a tape. Looking back up, Godzilla was still there.

How many times had he wished that he could be the hero in one of those movies. Saving the world from the monster. Well, maybe this was his chance. All he had to do was get to the door and warn the city.

Getting to the door was harder than it sounded. It was at least 10 feet to the only door. For the first time he wondered if it was such a good idea, living in his mother's basement. No windows to escape from. The basement had seemed perfect. No rent, free meals, laundry service. What more could a kid want? When he had moved in his friends had been jealous. At 16 he had his own pad. That was almost 20 years ago and it still seemed perfect to him. All the money he saved on rent and food, he could spend on his collection.

Ah, his collection. That was what made life complete. Why spend money on girls? Besides, if he let them touch any of this it would no longer be pristine.

Rolling off the bed, he began to crawl. It would have been easier if he hadn't weighed 300 pounds. He had to be so careful, Godzilla was watching him. Plus, he didn't want to damage anything. He almost crawled over his *Famous Monsters #5*. Oh, if he could only get his hands on *#1*, that would be really great. Sidney had 2 of them but wouldn't trade for them. Wanted cash. Right, like he was going to give him cash. Well, next week he was going to take some junk—er, rare things—to Forset J Ackerman and see if he could trade for a number 1.

There, lying on the floor, was the Star Trek communicator that he had just got at auction. He had to part with some big bucks for it but it was worth it. His mother was still mad over it. He had outbid her for it. Well, he had more money to spend than she did. She was living on Social Security. She was a big Star Trek fan and her collection of Star Trek memorabilia was bigger than his, but he had been surprised at how upset she was. She hadn't talked to him since. Well, he could live without her chatter, but she also hadn't cooked for him and he was getting pretty tired of fast food.

The fast food containers made loud noises as he crawled over them and attracted Godzilla's attention. He was almost at the foot of the stairs when something shiny made him look just as a large hatchet was planted in his scalp. His last thought was that if this was a Star Trek episode he could just say, "Beam me up, Scotty!"

Later that morning his mother stood at the sink, trying to get the blood stains out of her Godzilla costume. She had wanted to wear it to the next convention. Damn, blood was so hard to get out. All the time she worked she kept glancing over the table. She finally had her communicator. Well, it was her son's own fault. She had told him that she would kill to own it.

Let There Be Silence

by June Koblick

This is the first story to be published by this author who lives in San Francisco.
—FJA

Now he was safe.

Now he was alone, now the muteness of infinity wrapped him warmly, now the deep womb of timelessness carried him in sanctuary.

He looked out at the stars, at the friendly, loving stars that sustained the black abyss of space. They waited for him now, as they had waited so long and with such illimitable patience. They didn't mind that he was late in arriving. They waited for his coming, and he rejoiced with them and held out his hands in avid response to their solemn welcome.

Sanctuary.

The doctor's face had been carefully blank. Edward Norris had watched him intently, trying to penetrate that cautious mask.

"My secretary will send the report to Control, Norris." The doctor's voice, smooth and uncommunicative.

"Yes, sir." Then, "Can't you tell me now?"

"Sorry." A deprecating politeness, a genuine sympathy, a smile stretched tautly beneath the eyes that stayed blank. "Against the rules. You know that, Norris."

"Yes, sir."

Edward Norris walked out of the doctor's office, out into the hard bright sunlight and the yellow desert warmth. He looked across at the Administration Building. No need to wait for Control to give him the word. No need to wait for some scurrying gopher in a civil servant's uniform to process and duplicate and distribute the doctor's report. He knew what that report would be.

The sound of thunder caught him, transfixed him for brief seconds. Only it wasn't thunder. He refused to look up, to watch the Mars freighter braking in to a landing. It was nothing to look at, he told himself. She was only a tub. Not worth a glance.

He mounted the steps of the Ad Building quickly. He hoped he gave an appearance of jauntiness. He hoped he didn't seem to be running like hell.

He stopped outside the grilled window of the Personnel Record Room, looked through the window at the desk in the far corner. The tenseness about his eyes relaxed while he watched Grace in the few moments before she looked up and saw him. She was little, with fine bones and soft flesh, and she was the only girl he'd ever seen who could still look soft-fleshed in the gray government uniform.

Then she looked up and tossed the coppery hair out of her eyes and saw him. She smiled, the way she'd always smiled, a little bit of a smile that glowed with happy welcome. She shoved papers across her desk and got up, pushing through the frequency barrier that was keyed to the touch of her hand. She was outside the Record Room, walking toward him, smiling that happy welcome.

"I've been grounded," he said.

She stood beside him, the smile fading, her brown eyes anxious.

"How do you know?" she asked. "The doctor didn't tell you?"

"He didn't have to. I know."

She slipped her hand in his, soft and warm and confident. "Then you don't really know, yet. Let's go have some coffee, and don't think about it."

She looked up at him, her eyes deep and earnest, her eyes saying the things he knew she would say later, when they were alone. *It's alright darling, it doesn't make any difference, nothing will ever make any difference.*

They walked down the long corridors toward the canteen.

They sat in the canteen, coffee cups sending little wisps of steam curling between them.

"She'll never get over it," he said.

"Yes she will," Grace spoke reassuringly. "It'll take time, that's all."

"Neither will I," he said flatly.

"Oh, darling. Please. Please stop this. You have to stop brooding. It wasn't your fault."

He sat there after she left. She had something to do, she had a job to keep her busy, the people who came in and out of the canteen all had jobs they had to hurry back to. The spaceport swarmed with busy people. Only Edward Norris had nothing to do. Only Edward Norris was a misfit.

Then he stood up to leave, and he hadn't realized that it was so late. A swift urgency pushed him toward the exit nearest the pilots' quarters. It would take him 10 minutes to walk across the field. He might make it. He might get home before dark.

He reached the exit and knew that he was already too late. He waited a moment, and felt the trembling start deep inside him. His mouth filled with acid. He tried to breath deeply, tried to push air against his churning stomach. He opened the door and went outside.

And the vastness arched over him, the spangled vastness of space, the velvet black horror that rocked him against the building while silent screams shook him.

After awhile, after a long while, he looked up again. They were still there, the stars were still there, he'd have to look at them again some time, it might as well be now. His back pushed stiffly against the wall of the building and slowly the trembling subsided. He gazed upward, toward the invisible highways that had trapped him now in a no-man's land.

"Psychologically unfit for further duty." He knew how the microfilmed report would read, he'd seen them before, he'd shaken hands in farewell and thought, "Poor devil, what can he do now?" Nobody had ever seemed to consider that these unfits might be psychologically unfit for Earth.

They were wrong, the doctor was wrong, administrative policy was wrong. All I need is one more flight, I'd be alright then, I'd show them how wrong they are.

He began walking rapidly, the exhilaration of sudden decision upon him. He walked past the brightly lighted commercial hangars, with their noise and busyness. Beyond lay the public rental hangars, dozing lazily in semi-darkness.

He paused to examine the Control bulletin that posted tomorrow's flights. Then he went on toward the rental hangars, walking with the firm confidence he'd thought had deserted him forever.

He stopped before #14, a dainty private yacht, and the guard reached him with commendable haste.

"Mr. Coleman asked me to check the ship before his takeoff tomorrow," Norris spoke amiably. "It won't take long."

The guard was unimpressed.

"Ship was checked this afternoon," he said. "Mr. Coleman was here himself. He'd have told me if he was sending anybody else."

"The second jet worried him," Norris explained patiently. "He asked me to take a look at it. Here, I have a note from him." Norris reached into his coat, the guard's eyes following the movement. Norris's other arm flashed up with a force and suddenness that spun the guard around before he fell to the floor of the hangar.

With a slight grin, Norris nursed his knuckles briefly as he stepped over the man and approached the space yacht. She was a beautiful creature, with all the trim loveliness of a rich man's darling. Norris eyed her appreciatively, his fingers brushing the well-groomed hull.

He boarded her quickly and found her in readiness for tomorrow's flight. It was as simple as that.

Free fall. Norris had cut the jets and the little ship surged on her way through space with a human eagerness. Norris unstrapped himself from the pilot's seat and moved toward the tiny passenger lounge, his nerves tingling. A little surprised at what he had done, but also proud of it. Not regretting it.

He'd met the challenge, alright. He'd proved they were all wrong. He could handle himself in space as well as he ever could.

Just to the Moon and back, that would be all. That would be enough to show them. Everything would be alright, then.

The lounge was muralled with ports, bringing eternity in close. It was a fancy little ship, designed to give a billionaire his money's worth. Maybe more. Maybe it wasn't so smart to have the passengers surrounded by the wideness of forever. Maybe some people wouldn't like it. Norris gazed out the ports on one side, turned after awhile and stood staring out the other side. His eyes flickered, moving quickly around the jeweled blackness that ringed him in. It was like being in a fragile bubble. A bubble . . .

He was conscious of sudden sweat on his forehead and wiped it away almost angrily. It was just that he wasn't used to ports, he was used to dials, instrument panels, radar screens.

So what did he have to do? For most of a week there would be nothing to keep him occupied, nothing to do until deceleration. He shifted uneasily. The lounge was very small, the ports were too big. Only a crazy man would have designed a lounge like this.

He went back to the control room. It was pretty fancy, too; a lot of gadgets to increase comfort, which meant the owner was probably his own pilot. The dials glowed and winked at him, fuel, temperature, radarscope, repair tender—

He looked away, quickly.

The pilot's seat was more comfortable than any he'd ever known. He wouldn't even mind sleeping here. He could keep a better watch on the dials then . . .

He jerked himself up. Stop it, stop being a fool, the hell with the dials, there's nothing to watch this trip, forget the dials, forget the whole damn thing, it wasn't your fault, it wasn't your fault.

LET THERE BE SILENCE

He got up, forced himself to inspect the entire ship. She was built for luxury cruises, for entertainment and perfumed ladies. The sleeping quarters were decked out with mirrors and dressing tables and cosmetic supplies. A large library of movie tapes. Norris examined everything, touched everything, forced his mind to concentrate on each thing he looked at and on nothing else.

He hadn't anticipated the loneliness. He hadn't thought what it would be like without the companionship of a crew. It was just the loneliness that was making him uneasy. Anyone would be uneasy, alone in space. Formidable words, staggering concept. He could use a good fast argument with his old radio tech, right now. Or a bull session with the rest of the crew.

Oh, God, no. A chill plunged to the pit of his stomach as he remembered. His fingertips tingled. Forgetting was worse than remembering. Because you always remembered again, after awhile. And that coiled the reprieve of forgetting back upon itself, like a snake swallowing its tail.

He turned blindly back to the control room.

He sat watching the panels, half dozing, half listening for voices that would prove he wasn't really alone. He felt almost as though he were waiting for something.

And then it came. The sudden *tick-tick*, a tiny warning sound that crashed the silence like drumfire. A steady *tick-tick-tick*, a whisper of danger, a *tick-tick-tick-tick* that screamed through the soundless void. He started wildly out of his seat, lunged at the control board in helpless fumbling.

Then he sank back, his heart racing heavily, his breath coming in harsh, dry gasps. He shook his head tiredly.

It was only his watch.

There was no red glow on the dial panel, no metronome-like warning from the mechanism. It was only his watch, ticking softly through the heavy silence of half-sleep.

He was still shaking, he couldn't stop shaking, even though he recognized the trick of a haunted memory. He buried his face in his hands, tried to stop the sobbing breaths. Slowly he grew calmer, slowly the shaking stopped. Slowly his mind focused again upon the sharp clear lines of reality.

And it came again with teasing persistence, a gleeful *tick-tick*, a mischievous *tick-tick-tick*, an impudent, malicious *tick-tick-tick-tick-tick-tick*. He hurled himself out of his seat, the veins in his neck standing like knotted blue cords. With peculiar malevolence the watch boomed its tiny *tick-tick*.

Norris sang. He sang in a loud, raw voice, a voice that forgot words and faltered away from melody. Cadet songs. Love songs. Comic opera. He filled the silence with raucous singing, and the watch, intimidated, withdrew soundlessly. Until he was hoarse, until his throat ached, until his mouth was dry. Until there were no more songs. Until the only sound he could make was a rasping sigh. The brooding stillness crept back.

Tick-tick.

He whirled and lurched desperately toward the control board. His hand leaped at the jet switch and a roar of thunder filled the compartment.

Acceleration flung him against the wall. He stayed there for a timeless while, his eyes closed, his nerves relaxing in the welcome relief of sound. And with relief came coherence.

Idiot. What a damn fool thing to do. How much fuel have I got left?

He jerked off the switch and set to work examining gauges and making calculations. He was glad to be busy, it was a welcome diversion. But an expensive diversion.

There wouldn't be enough fuel to make a landing.

He could radio the Lunar Base when he reached orbit and tell them he hadn't enough fuel to land. They would come and get him.

And hold him. The only way he'd get back to Earth would be in a police carrier. He'd stolen a private yacht and nobody at Lunar Base would care what his reasons were.

He wondered, now, if the reasons were so important, after all. He thought of Grace, fashioned a vision of her, traced that smile of happy welcome on her lips and the loyalty in her eyes. Grace loved him. Grace wouldn't care if he was psychoed out.

Or would she?

Grace insisted it wasn't his fault. That was what everybody else said, too.

And me? What do I think? *Was* it my fault? What difference does it make, now? Will that change anything?

He closed his eyes and saw the Skipper of the *Marraine* come storming into the passenger liner's control room. He felt the lumpy discomfort of the co-pilot's seat, saw the tiers of control panels that required some fancy observing in times of stress.

"Bubbles!" the Skipper snorted. "Bubbles, floating around in space!"

"Sir?" Norris looked up, startled.

"Lit-tle, tin-y, bub-bles!" The Skipper spoke with sarcastic emphasis. "The passengers think they're so cute!"

"Excuse me, sir, I don't understand—"

"Water, damn it! There's a leak in the water tank! Where's that damn engineer?"

Blackie scrambled up through the hatch from B deck, like a genie answering a summons.

"I just saw them, sir. Cute, aren't they. I'll need the repair tender, sir."

The Skipper glowered while Blackie described the bubbles to Norris with enthusiasm. "Little globules, following us in orbit. Darndest thing you ever saw. Like a kid blowing soap-bubbles."

"I'm surprised at the *Marraine*," Norris commented. "That's beneath her dignity."

"Oh, I'll set the old girl back on her dignity." Blackie disappeared again. Norris turned back to the control board.

He never did see the bubbles.

The *Marraine* was an old ship, one of the first of the really big liners. She carried 1200 passengers and a crew of 250, and that made the problem of supplies an important one. Water was precious. The new ships had self-sealing valves on their storage tanks and the tanks were buried deep within the ship, fed by hundreds of feet of pipe. They required longer loading but the supplies were protected. The *Marraine*'s tanks were sunk just within the shell, closed by manually operated valves and hull plates that may or may not have been carefully secured after loading. The only access to the valves was outside the ship.

Blackie went out in the repair tender, a one-man skiff that carried tools and supplied him with oxygen. The tender was attached to the ship by an umbilical cord, and the pulse of that cord was reflected in a dial on the control board. Norris stood watch at the panels.

He never noticed how much time passed, it just seemed that it was a long time. It shouldn't have taken so long. It was a little thing, it shouldn't take more than an hour at most. He was aware of tension growing within the ship, silent jitters that built up within himself and on the faces of the rest of the crew. It shouldn't have taken so long.

When somebody came into the control room and said the tender was gone, he didn't believe it. The dial was normal. It had never glowed red. It had never uttered a single *tick*.

When they found the tender, it was too late. Blackie's oxygen supply had never been meant to last that long.

Tick-tick.

He got up and went out into the little lounge again. If he couldn't see the dials, it would be alright. He wouldn't hear it, then.

Tick-tick-tick.

The stars peered in at the ports, watching him, waiting for him to do something crazy. He stared back at them in contempt. Let them wait. He'd show them. They were all wrong, the doctor and the stars and the *tick-tick-*

tick. They thought he was space-happy. Well, of course he was. He was happy in space. That was what he meant, all along. He was alright. He liked being in space.

It was jut a little lonely, that was all. If he could get out of here for just a few minutes, and see people again—

The stars had come closer. They were just outside the ports now. In a minute they would be inside. Nobody could blame him for not wanting that. Nobody could blame him for wanting to get away if the stars were coming in.

Tick-tick.

He opened a door quickly. It was a stateroom, a pretty little stateroom without ports. He closed the door and leaned against it. He knew he was breathing too fast and concentrated on breathing slowly, calmly.

It was a lady's stateroom. And then he saw Blackie's wife sitting at the dressing table and he wondered for a moment how she had gotten on the ship without his knowing it.

She saw him in the mirror.

She turned around.

"Go back to the control room," she ordered. "You're not watching the board."

"It's not necessary," he explained. "There's nothing to watch. We're on robot."

"You fool!" Her eyes flashed. "Go back and watch the tender!"

He could see it would be hard to make her understand.

"There's no reason to watch the tender," he said patiently. "There's no one in it."

"Blackie's outside," she said harshly. "Blackie's outside in the tender and you're not watching the board!"

He tried to reason with her. "There's no one outside."

Tick-tick.

"You see!" she screamed in vindictive triumph. "Something's wrong with the tender and you're not watching the board!"

He wavered.

Tick-tick-tick-tick.

Her face distorted as she came toward him. He turned and fled back to the control room.

Tick-tick-tick-tick-tick. The control room rocked with the sound.

"There's no one in the tender!" he cried again as he snatched a wrench from its clip and flung it at the dial. It missed and smashed into the radar screen.

He blinked, and stared at what he had done. He rubbed his face with his hands and looked again at the disabled screen.

LET THERE BE SILENCE

He sat down slowly, heavily. What's wrong with me, why do I do these things? He gazed in bewilderment about the compartment. Then he got up and opened the tool locker.

He set about methodically to repair the radar screen. Occasionally he stopped, staring at nothing in particular, his eyes perplexed. Once he went back into the lounge and looked out at the stars for a long time.

"Why?" he asked them. "Why does this happen to *me*?" They gazed back at him, unflickering, biding their time.

He returned to the control room and redoubled his efforts on the screen.

When it was finished he sat very still and waited. And, inevitably, it came again.

Tick-tick. Tick-tick-tick. Tick-tick-tick-tick-tick-tick-tick.

He forced himself to listen. If there was no escape from it, he would have to accept it. It was the only sound in the universe. Nothing existed anywhere except Edward Norris and the watch. The two of them were imprisoned together in a capsule of space. They would have to get used to each other, they would have to learn to get along together. There was no other way. Survival depended upon cooperation. All it required was understanding. And the desire to understand.

He listened carefully. Trying to determine the nature of the creature imprisoned with him. The personality pattern that manifested itself in an exuberant *tick-tick*. After a long time he became aware of a modulation sequence, a rhythmic homophony marked by a sudden metric shift. *Ticktick-ticktick, ticktick-ticktick*. He found the accent and pursued it with hypnotic absorption. *TICKtick-ticktick, TICKtick-ticktick*. His mind followed the cadence with satisfying exactness. It lulled him gently, it enchanted him with lyric repetition.

An insidious variation occurred so subtly that he failed to notice the transition. He was conscious simply of the new accent and for a moment the high cunning of the thing angered him. He stumbled and then caught it dexterously—*ticktick-TICKtick, ticktick-TICKtick*. His whole body strained with listening, not to be tricked by such duplicity a second time. When the next transition came he bridged it with smooth triumph, his nerves responding exultantly to the churlish *tickTICK-ticktick, tickTICK-ticktick*. He waited with utter confidence, knowing that next time the accent would fall on the final beat.

It didn't.

With diabolic treachery, the thing reverted. *TICKtick-ticktick, TICKticktick*. And as he listened it changed swiftly, with spiteful stratagem it varied the patterns, with invidious maneuvering it juxtaposed the meter without logic or coherence, with relentless tyranny it heightened, lengthened, multiplied the variations until they merged and distended and then discharged in an explosive timpani within the inflammation of his mind and he jerked the watch from his arm and hurled it across the room.

"Lunar Base calling PY-1306-L. Lunar Base calling PY-1306-L. Come in, please, 1306-L."

Norris looked without comprehension at the radio receiver. The sound of a human voice in the compartment was alien and meaningless.

"Lunar Base calling Peter Yoke 1306 Love," the voice insisted. "Come in, please, 1306-L. Come in please, come in please. Edward Norris, are you receiving me?"

Mechanically he reached out and snapped the transmitter switch. "PY-1306-L to Lunar Base. Come in."

"PY-1306-L, we have determined your vector direction from Lunar Base. Please blip your radar and give us exact distance. Lunar Base out and over."

He stared at the receiver. "No."

A brief silence. Tiny, bursting crackles of sound.

"Lunar Base to PY-1306-L, you are ordered to give us your exact distance and stand by for boarding party. Over."

"PY-1306-L to Lunar Base. Go to hell."

More silence. More crackles.

"Lunar Base to PY-1306-L, hey, son, take it easy." A different voice this time. "Are you alright? Over."

"I'm just dandy, and I won't go back in a cop ship."

"Lunar Base to PY-1306-L, stand by. Lunar Base out."

Silence sifted down again. Norris turned from the transmitter. So they expected him to stand by for arrest. How space-happy did they think he was, anyway?

He glanced at the fuel gauge. And if he escaped the boarding party, just how was he going to land?

He closed his eyes, trying to marshal the chaos of his thoughts into orderly patterns. There must be a way. He'd figure out a way to get home without arrest. If he could get back to Earth, they'd never find him. He thought of the smile of happy welcome on Grace's lips. There had to be a way.

TICKtick-ticktick, TICKtick-ticktick. He listened cautiously. *Ticktick-TICKtick, ticktick-TICKtick.* The emphasis veered with subtle craftiness.

He gazed about anxiously. Where was it? The sound seemed to come from everywhere. *TickTICK-ticktick, tickTICK-ticktick.* He began to tremble. He got down on the floor and searched carefully, systematically. The sound rose and fell perversely, as through the watch waited for his approach and retreated quickly when he was almost upon it.

"Lunar Base to PY-1306-L, do you receive me? Over." The radio crackled noisily at him again. He looked up, frowning at the sudden interruption. How was he to find the watch if he couldn't hear the ticking?

"Come in, PY-1306-L. Come in, please. Lunar Base to PY-1306-L, come in please. Norris, come in. This is Commander Peterson. Norris, do you receive me?"

He brushed the words away as though they were buzzing insects, listened intently for the watch in the brief space of silence. *TICK-tick—* His hand groped blindly, almost closed over it, and it jumped away with fiendish cleverness.

"Norris, listen to me. You are off course, I repeat, you are off course, headed for deep space."

The jeering chatter of the watch laughed teasingly at his impotent searching.

"Norris, if you are receiving me, please change course for intercept and stand by for rescue party. You will not be placed under arrest. I repeat, you will not be placed under arrest."

Where was it? A soft whimper choked him.

"The ship's owner will not press charges and you will not be held for violation of the Space Act. You have my guarantee, Norris, there will be no arrest."

He found it. It crouched in the shadow of the chart table and he snatched it up with a predatory swiftness that aborted any attempt at escape. He placed it carefully on the chart table.

"Lunar Base to Edward Norris, do you receive me? Stand by for arrival of rescue party. You will not be placed under arrest. This is Commander Peterson, calling Edward Norris. You have nothing to fear, son. We want to take you home. Safely. Norris, do you hear me?"

He took a hammer from the tool kit and struck at the watch, over and over, until the pieces scattered in mutilated defeat.

"Lunar Base to PY-1306-L, please come in, Norris, do you hear me?"

The persistent, inescapable noise. He looked at the hammer in his hand, and turned to the receiver and smashed the crackling life from it.

He breathed long and deeply in the blessed silence. Then he moved toward the lounge with its ports, to greet the stars.

Final Victory
by Jill Taggart

> In the early '30s, before Jill Taggart (née Vuerhard) was born in this world, I saw her father, Dutch film star Roland Varno, say to Madame Dietrich in the classic motion picture *The Blue Angel*, "I love you."
> When Jillian was 12 or 13, I met her for the first time and by the time I was attending her Graduation Ceremony, I was frequently saying "I love you".
> Jill is a big girl now and has had her own radio program in the Southern California area and she calls me Uncle Forry and I still love her ... which did not deter me, as an editor, from rejecting the first 2 stories she submitted to me, even tho I would love to have, for auld lang syne, bought her first submission.
> But Jill made it with #3, finally victorious, breaking into professional print with this one.
> —FJA

The day the world died, and just before it was laid to its final rest, the few surviving remnants of humanity's mightiest, and last, civilization huddled together in the skeletal remains of a park.

A woman, too stunned to speak, held her sobbing blinded child.

A once-wealthy man lay on the grass and cried, his tears sparkling like the diamonds that glittered on his fingers as in shocked horror he regarded his legs lying separated from the bloody stumps of his knees.

Another man, who had been a criminal, leaned against a flame-scarred tree-stump and sometimes muttered, "Why?"

There were seven of them. Seven left alive in a war-destroyed world and, when they died, all the hopes and dreams and history of Earth would die with them.

Then an eighth man came. He stumbled out of the brown and black wood and stood uneasily on the small patch of browning grass. And hope came to the doomed seven, for this man wore the tattered uniform of a Gen-

eral, and they all knew that this was *Authority*, that here was a *Leader*.

"It's all right!" the General cried jubilantly and smiled, and six of the seven rose up and prepared to follow him.

They watched the grass turning black under their blackened feet, and the General smiled again. "It's all right!" he reassured them. "It doesn't matter because, you see, WE WON!"

Other Science Fiction & Fantasy Oriented Female Works (Novels)

†Recommended by FJA   ‡Recommended by PK

20*th* Century Cinderella, W. Y. Winthrop
After the Strike of a Sex, George Noyes Miller
Alice for Short, William De Morgan
Allan's Wife, H. Rider Haggard
The Alleluia Files, Sharon Shinn
The Amphibian, S. Fowler Wright†‡
Amy Girl, Bari Wood
And Then There'll Be Fireworks, Suzette Haden Elgin
Angels and Woman, Mrs. J. G. Smith
Anna's World, Marie-Claire Blais
April's Fool, John Glyder
Atlantide, Pierre Benoit (filmed)
Ayesha, H. Rider Haggard
The Bachelor Girl, William Hosea Ballou
The Bacillus of Beauty, Harriet Stark
Billy and Betty, Twiggs Jameson
The Birthday Girl, Robert Rush
The Black Flame, Stanley G. Weinbaum†
Black Oxen, Gertrude Atherton (silent film)
The Black Swan, Mercedes Lackey
Breakthrough, Ken Grimwood
Bride of Darkness, Margery Lawrence
The Bridge of Distances, Ella Scrymsour
Carrie, Stephen King (filmed)‡
Children of the Morning, W. L. George
The Chosen Ones, Julie Richer
Clara, Luisa Valaenzuela
Clever Claudia—A Scientific Quest for a Mate, Hugo Faarederick Herfuth Jr.
Consort, Anthony Heckstall-Smith
The Continuous Catherine Mortenhoe, D. G. Compton (filmed)‡
Costumes by Eros, Conrad Aiken
The Crowds and the Veiled Woman, Marion Cox
Crystal Sage, Kara Dalkey
Cupidevil, Hubert Monteilhet
Daughter of Fu Manchu, Sax Rohmer
The Day of the Women, Pamella Kettle

Deliver Me from Eva, Paul Bailey† (optioned for filming)
The Demeter Flower, Rochelle Sayer
Dorothy from Kansas Meets the Wizard of X, Linda Alexander
The Double Life of Janet Ashby, C. H. Le Bosque
Dream's End, Thorne Smith†
The Earth Girl, Frank Wyatt & C. H. Ross
Elixir, Dolores Hedges
Elmira, Harriet Payes Davis
The Encyclopedia of the Amazons, Jessica Salamanda Salmonson†
Erinna, Betty Askwith
The Eternal Maiden, T. Everett Harre
Evelyn—Something More Than A Story, James Francis Dwyer
Eve's Second Apple, Barnaby Dogbolt
The Face in the Mirror, Dorothy Macardle
The Fair Woman, Hilda Vaughn
The Fear of God, R. A. Chepaitis
Feminapolis, Albert Kelm
Femmes au Futur, Marianne Leconte
The Flutter of an Eyelid, Myron Brinig
Four-Sided Triangle, William F. Temple† (filmed twice—not right yet, worth a third try—FJA)
The Ghost Girl, Edgar Saltus
The Girl and the Gods, Charlotte Mansfield
Girl Everlasting, G. DeS. Wentworth-James
The Girl Who Slipped through Time, Paula Hendrich
The Golden Amazon (series), John Russell Fearn†
Goldengirl, Peter Lear
Governor Janae, Frank M. Boyce Jr.
Grenadine's Spawn, Robert C. Ruark
Hermia Suuydam, Gertrude Atherton
His First Million Women, George Weston
The Horrible Man, Frances Forbes-Robertson

How the Old Lady Got Home, M. P. Shiel
I, Martha Adams, Pauline Glen Winslow
The Immortal Girl, Berta Ruck
The Impregnable Women, Eric Linklater
Jane Carroll, E. Temple Thurston
Jerlayne, Lynn Abbey
Jirel of Joiry, Catherine L. Moore†
Joanna, Lisa St. Albin de Teran
Jungle Girl, Edgar Rice Burroughs†
The Jungle Girl, Gordon Casserly
The Ladies Came Undressed, Gilbert Anstruther
Ladies from Hell, Keith Roberts
Ladies in Hades, Frederick Arnold Kummer
Lady Century, Mrs. A. G. Kintze
Lady Christ—A Modern Mystery, Duncan MacGregor
The Lady Like Blue White and Other Stories, Irwin W. Groh
Lady Lilith, Stephen McKenna
The Lady of the Barge, W. W. Jacobs
The Lady Who Came to Stay, R. E. Spencer
The Laird and the Lady, Joan Grant
Llana of Gathol, Edgar Rice Burroughs†
The League of Grey-Eyed Women, Julius Fast
Leonie of the Jungle, Joan Conquest
The Leopard Woman, Stewart Edward White
Loneliest Girl in the World, Kenneth Fearing
Lora of Atlantis, John Russell Fearn†
The Maid with Wings, E. B. Osborn
Marjorie Daw and Other Stories, T. Bailey Aldrich
Martha Brown M.P.—A Girl of Tomorrow, Victoria Cross
The Master Girl, Ashton Hilliers
Maza of the Moon, Otis Adflbert Kline†
The Mermaid of the Swimming Pool, Douglas Wallop
Metropolis, Thea von Harbou† (silent film classic)‡ (available from Sense of Wonder Press)
Miss Beck, Tilbury Holt
Miss Carter and the Ifrit, Susan Alice Kerby
Miss Fingal, Lucy Clifford
Miss Hargreaves, Frank Baker
Miss Lucifer, Ronald Fraser
Miss Ludington's Sister, Edward Ballamy
Miss Shumway Waves A Wand, James Hadley Chase (filmed)

Mistress of Spears, Laurence D'Orsay
The Moon Maid, Edgar Rice Burroughs†
Myriam and the Mystic Brotherhood, Maude Lesseur Howard
A Naked Girl, Niko Athanassiades
Nameless, Mary T. Longley
Nellie Bloom, Margery Latimer
One-Man Show, Tiffany Thayer† (should be filmed)
The One Woman, Thomas Dixon Jr.
The Otherwise Girl, Keith Clair
Out of the Void, Leslie Frances Stone
A Paradise Valley Girl, Susanna M. D. Fry
Peggy the Aeronaut, J. L. J. Carter
The Prince of Time, Glenna McReynolds
A Princess of Mars, Edgar Rice Burroughs†
The Rejuvenation of Mrs. Semaphore, Hal Godfrey
Rosamund the Second, Mary Mears
The Sea Lady, H. G. Wells†
Seal Woman, Ronald Lockley
The Sea Priestess, Dion Fortune†
Shades of Lil!, Anita Campbell
Shadowleague (series), Maggie Furey
She, H. Rider Haggard (filmed many times)
She and Allan, H. Rider Haggard
Sirius, W. Olaf Stapledon† (recommended for filming)
Speaking of Eileen, Albert Ross
Spicy Lady, Joseph A. Daley
Star-Anchored, Star-Angered, Suzette Haden Elgin
The Star Crossed Woman, M. B. Cormack
Star Girl, Henry Winterfeld
The Story of Mona Sheehy, Lord Dunsany
Strange Daughter, Louis De Wohl
The Strike of a Sex, George Noyes Miller
The Super Woman, A. Oliver Sutter
Thuvia, Maid of Mars, Edgar Rice Burroughs†
To Say Nothing of the Dogs, Connie Willis‡
To the Lightning. Catherine Ennis
To Walk the Night, William Sloane†
Twelve Fair Kingdoms, Suzette Haden Elgin
The Twelve Maidens, Stewart Farrar
Turnabout, Thorne Smith (filmed)‡
The Uninvited, Dorothy Macardle (filmed)‡
Vampirella, 5 pocketbook series

353

The Venus Girl, Leslie Beresford ("Pan")
The Virgin of the Sun, H. Rider Haggard
Virginia of the Air Lines, Herbert Quick
Visit of the Princess (A Romance of the 1960s), R. H. Mottram
The Watcher, Kay Nolte Smith
The Wench Was Wicked, Gilbert Anstruther
When Women Rule, anthology by Sam Moskowitz†
Who Needs Men?, Edmund Cooper
The Winged Girl of Knossos, Eric Berry
Wisdom's Daughter, H. Rider Haggard
The Witches of Eastwick, John Updike (filmed)‡
Woman Against the World, George Griffith
Woman Alive, Susan Ertz†
Woman Clothed with the Sun, F. L. Griffith ("The worst science fiction novel ever written"—Robert Heinlein)
A Woman for Mayor, Helen M. Winslow
The Woman in the Moon, Thea von Harbou (filmed)
A Woman of the Ice Age, L. P. Gratacap
The Woman of Orchids, Marvin Dana
The Woman on the Beast, Helen Simpson
A Woman—Or What?, Mrs. Normal Lee
The Woman Who Did, Grant Allen
The Woman Who Loved Reindeer, Meredith Ann Pierce
The Woman Who Stopped War, Cornwallis West
The Woman Who Was No More, Pierre Noileau & Thomas Narcejac
The Woman With A Heart, G. E. Burgin
The Woman with White Eyes, Mary Borden
Women of Wonder, anthology†
The World Above, Martha Foote Crowe
Wrapt in Crystal, Sharon Shinn
The Young Diana, Marie Corelli (lost silent film)

Note: There is no telling how many female writers may be, like C. L. Moore originally, anonymous behind initials.

READERS OF THE WORLDS, WRITE!

The anthologist of this volume is anxious to hear from YOU!

How did you enjoy the overall contents?

What few stories did you like the most?

What few stories did you like the least?

Would you like to see a collection of FJA's own approximately 50 stories? (Starting in 1929!)

Would you like to see an Ackermanthology of a selection of Mr. Science Fiction's favorite sci-fi stories of the past 75 years? Favorite Fantasy?

Any requests for the anthologist?

Forrest J Ackerman may be contacted directly at:

4511 Russell Avenue

Hollywood, CA 90027

FAX: 323-664-5612

Mr. Sci-Fi

Forrest J Ackerman,

a regular on the Sci-Fi channel, edited and published Ray Bradbury's first story in 1938, edited the seminal *Famous Monsters of Filmland* magazine for years, has appeared in over 50 sci-fi and horror films, and has helped to inspire countless professional careers and his fans' lifelong admiration, including such notables as George Lucas and Stephen King. A writer, editor, filmmaker and collector of science fiction material for over 70 of his 86 years, he is the author of dozens of stories and editor of six previous complete anthologies.

He coined the term "sci-fi," received the first Hugo award (and has won 6 in total), contributed to the first fanzine, started an sf club in 1929, has attended 57 of 60 World Science Fiction Conventions . . . The Academy of Science Fiction, Fantasy and Horror has twice honored him with Golden Saturns.

We could go on. His love of the genre and his pioneering efforts are truly irreplaceable: He opens his home/museum to the public most weekends, and he can be contacted via the information on the facing page.

Sense of Wonder Press presents
FAMOUS FORRY FOTOS
FORREST J ACKERMAN from birth to 2001! Over 70 years of history from Forry, the Ackermansion, the Acker-family and Ackerfriends! Mr. Sci-Fi and Dr. Acula share the Kodackerman Memories of a lifetime! Includes Forry, Family & Friends; Forry Fandom; Monsters & Aliens; Movies & Television; and The Ackermansion. 117 pages, 6x9, illus., **Paperback**, $14.95
ISBN: 0-918736-32-3
Hardback, $24.95
ISBN: 0-918736-56-0

Back after more than 6 lustrums, ***FORREST J ACKERMAN AND FRIENDS PLUS***, with 31 offerings from FJA and friends, including 7 new collaborations. Some of Forry's solo efforts abide alongside collabs with the likes of A. E. van Vogt, Robert A. W. Lowndes, Charles Nuetzel, Catherine L. Moore, Big Name Female In Hiding, Donald A. Wollheim, and Theodore Sturgeon. Golden Friends from a golden age.

Sense of Wonder Press, 205 pages, 6x9
Paperback, ISBN: 0-918736-26-9, $14.95
Hardback, ISBN: 0-918736-58-7, $26.95

75th Anniversary Edition

Lavishly Illustrated, Oversized Edition of Fritz Lang's Science Fiction Classic Film

Thea von Harbou wrote the screenplay for Fritz Lang's film from her novel, revising both as the filming progressed. Out-of-print for too long, this classic is brought to life with over 50 illustrations and photos from the film, behind the scenes photos, and promotional graphics and art for both the book and the film. Lavishly "stillustrated" with photos, graphics, and art from Fritz Lang's film and Forrest J Ackerman's 75 years of *METROPOLIS* memorabilia.

FJA says, "You will have an experince in reading that will last you all the rest of your life."

PAPERBACK EDITION
8x11 paperback, illustrated
ISBN: 0-918736-35-8
$18.95
TRADE HARDCOVER
ISBN: 0-918736-54-4
$34.95
HARDCOVER LIMITED EDITION
500 hand-numbered copies signed by FJA
8x11, illustrated, ISBN: 0-918736-34-X
$60.00, *Available directly from the publisher only.*

SENSE OF WONDER PRESS

Expanded Science Fiction Worlds of
FORREST J ACKERMAN & FRIENDS PLUS

Back after more than 6 lustrums! With 31 offerings including 7 new collaborations. Authors include C. L. Moore, Theodore Sturgeon, Donald A. Wollheim, A. E. van Vogt, Charles Nuetzel and more! 6x9, 217 pages, *Available Now*

Paperback, $14.95, ISBN: 0-918736-26-9, Hardback, $26.95, ISBN: 0-918736-56-0

Metropolis: 75th Anniversary Edition

Includes the English translation of Thea von Harbou's original novel which is lavishly "Stillustrated" with fotos from Fritz Lang's film and Forrest J Ackerman's 75 years of Metropolis memorabilia. Hardcover limited to 500 copies, signed & numbered. 8½x11, 242 pages, Illustrated, *Available Now*

Limited Ed., $60.00, ISBN: 0-918736-34-X, *(direct from publisher only)*
Trade Hardback, $34.95, ISBN: 0-918736-54-4
Paperback, $18.95, ISBN: 0-918736-35-8

Rainbow Fantasia, 35 Spectrumatic Tales of Wonder

A huge and colorful Ackermanthology of classic tales (many from sci-fi's pulp tradition) including stories by Mary Elizabeth Counselman, Ray Cummings, Donald Wandrei, Gustav Meyrink, A. E. van Vogt, Frank Gruber, Nat Schachner, Eli Coulter, Nictzin Dyalhis, Robert W. Chambers and Brad Linaweaver. 6x9, 576 pages, Illustrated, *Available Now*

Paper, $23.95, ISBN: 0-918736-36-6, Hardback, $39.95, ISBN: 0-918736-59-5

Ackermanthology: Millennium Edition

From Dennis Palumbo's three page tale of truly diabolical revenge to Jill Taggart's one page epiphany on leadership and victory, the original *Ackermanthology* will arouse your sense of wonder! Stories by Ray Bradbury, Isaac Asimov, and H. G. Wells are nestled comfortably among lesser known authors such as Oliver Saari, David A. Kyle, Anne Orhelein and others. Foreword by John Landis. 6x9, 306 pages, *Available Now*

Paper, $14.95, ISBN 0-918736-25-0, Hardback, $26.95, ISBN: 0-918736-59-5

CLAIMED by Francis Stevens

H.P. Lovecraft called this *"One of the strangest and most compelling science fantasy novels you will ever read."* An eerie classic, chosen by FJA. Gertrude Barrows Bennett, the mysterious woman who wrote under the pen name "Francis Stevens" has been hailed as the greatest female fantasy writer between Mary Shelly and C.L. Moore! 6x9, 192 pages, *Available Now*

Paper, $14.95, ISBN: 0-918736-37-4, Hardback, $26.95, ISBN: 0-918736-57-9

Famous Forry Fotos

Kodakerman Memories! Famous Forry Fotos, from birth to 2000—over 70 years of photos from Forry at the Ackermansion, and before: photos of science fiction, fantasy and horror writers, film greats and more, with Mr. Sci-Fi as your guide! Friends, family, monsters, some great "Con" memories and much more! 8½x11, 117pages, Illustrated, *Available Now*

Paper, $14.95, ISBN: 0-918736-32-3, Hardback, $24.95, ISBN: 0-918736-56-0

Martianthology

Barsoom! Deimos! Phobos! This Ackermanthology includes stories by A. E. Van Vogt, Robert A. W. Loundes, Ross Rocklynne, Harl Vincent and many others! 6x9, apx. 250 pages, Illustrated, *Summer 2003*

Paper, $14.95, ISBN: 0-918736-45-5, Hardback, $26.95, ISBN: 0-918736-46-3

Lon Of 1000 Faces

Forrest J Ackerman's long out-of-print classic on silent film great Lon Chaney, Sr. Over 1100 illustrations from photos, as well as many tributes, biographical sketches and appreciations by Robert Bloch, Ray Bradbury, Vincent Price, Lon Chaney, Jr. and many others. 8½x11, 296 pages, Illustrated, *Summer 2003*

Paper, ISBN 0-918736-39-0, $21.95, Hardback, $38.95, ISBN: 0-918736-53-6

Dr. Acula's Thrilling Tales of the Uncanny

"Brush your hair with epoxy resin before reading this creepy collection, otherwise you're liable to lose it when your hair stands on end."—Dr. Acula. With a preface by Pamela Keesey. 6x9, apx. 250 pages, Illustrated, *Fall 2003*

Paper, $14.95, ISBN 0-918736-30-7, Hardback, $26.95, ISBN: 0-918736-xxx

Please check our website or write us for more titles, updates and complete listings of stories/authors in our anthologies.

SENSE OF WONDER PRESS BOOKS ARE DISTRIBUTED IN THE U.S. BY INGRAM DISTRIBUTORS

Sense of Wonder Press

BROWSE, ORDER, RESERVE, HANGOUT
http:\\www.senseofwonderpress.com
Find a complete listing of stories for all our "Ackermanthologies," updates on title availability and payment information. Or write to us at:

Sense of Wonder Press
9710 Traville Gateway Drive, Box 305
Rockville, Maryland 20850

email: info@senseofwonderpress.com

Printed in the United States
1231900002B/1-24